THE UNEXPECTED GUEST

Hania Allen

CONSTABLE

First published in Great Britain in 2023 by Constable

1 3 5 7 9 10 8 6 4 2

All characters and events in this publication, other than those clearly in the public domain, are fictitious and any resemblance to real persons, living or dead, is purely coincidental.

A CIP catalogue record for this book is available from the British Library.

ISBN: 978-1-40871-784-4

Typeset in Bembo by Photoprint, Torquay
Printed and bound in Great Britain by Clays Ltd, Elcograf S.p.A.

Papers used by Constable are from well-managed forests and other responsible sources.

Constable
An imprint of
Little, Brown Book Group
Carmelite House
50 Victoria Embankment
London EC4Y 0DZ

An Hachette UK Company
www.hachette.co.uk

www.littlebrown.co.uk

PROLOGUE

WARSAW – DECEMBER

It had been a quiet day for the funeral. Which made it all the more surprising when the bomb went off.

Dania and Marek had arrived an hour earlier, and had been directed by the stoop-shouldered custodian in the moth-eaten fur coat to the part of the cemetery still in use. The woman had given them clear instructions; without them, they'd never have found the location among the crowded headstones, which listed alarmingly, like crooked teeth. What had made things worse was that, the previous day, a mist had descended and now lay like a pall over the city. Without the woman's insistence they follow the path, regardless of how it meandered, Dania doubted they'd have made the service on time. The word 'path' was a misnomer, as it had a tendency to disappear, and their route would suddenly be blocked by a weathered headstone or ivy-covered tree, leaving them not knowing which way to turn. Fortunately, other guests had arrived minutes earlier and, provided Dania and her brother kept the blurred, shimmering shapes within sight, they wouldn't go far wrong, although it didn't stop them losing their footing in the matted undergrowth.

Dania had visited the cemetery once before. At school, she'd studied Warsaw's wartime history and learnt that Adam Czerniaków, the head of the ghetto's Jewish council, was buried there. Even in bright sunshine, it had taken her a while to find the grave, which she knew was not far from that of Ludwik Zamenhof, the creator of Esperanto. That was the trouble with ancient cemeteries: no neat rows of identical headstones, no well-kept straight paths. This necropolis was more of a design by committee, which, given the changes in Jewish customs over the past two hundred years, was unsurprising. And yet, despite the difficulty in navigation, she'd found the place fascinating and haunting. She'd spent so much time examining the carved symbols on the headstones that she'd lost her way and arrived home late.

But this second visit to Okopowa Street had been unplanned. She'd been in Warsaw for three days when she'd received the notification about the funeral. There was no question but that she'd attend. Marek, who'd been in the city for nearly a week, had also been invited. She stood at the open grave, listening to the rabbi's muffled voice reading in Hebrew, pausing to translate the text into Polish. Although he was standing a short distance away, he appeared as a dark stain in the fog. Most of the guests huddled round the grave had their heads covered, and their faces were indistinct, so it was hard to distinguish the men from the women.

A gold-tasselled red cloth embroidered with Hebrew lettering lay over the simple wooden coffin, which had been lowered into the ground before the service began. As there were no family members, each guest had taken a shovelful of soil and sprinkled it into the grave. The rabbi was speaking in Hebrew again, and Dania sensed the ceremony was coming to its end. She was listening to the language, wondering how easy it would be for a non-native speaker, when she felt a movement behind her. There was a sudden rush of cold air. Something had been thrown upwards. In the stunned silence, she saw a wreath of lilies disappear into the foggy whiteness. It reappeared and landed with a thud on the coffin.

There was a growing murmur of disapproval – flowers at a Jewish funeral were typically prohibited. And throwing them? The rabbi had paused, then continued with his speech. Dania glanced at Marek. He was staring after the figure with a frown of disapproval. As he turned his attention to the service, he caught her eye and shook his head in distaste.

The rabbi finished with a few words of Hebrew. The guests stood in silence, their heads bowed, as he switched to Polish and thanked everyone for attending. He left quietly, his dark shape dissolving into the mist. He was followed by the mourners, who were still muttering to each other about the wreath. The diggers, who hadn't yet arrived, would have to decide what to do with it.

Dania took Marek's arm and they followed the guests, trying to avoid colliding with the headstones. It was easy to lose one's way and, unfortunately, that was what they did. After several minutes of frantic to-ing and fro-ing, they stumbled upon the custodian's booth. Dania paused at the iron gate to use the hand-washing cup since the water pump no longer worked, then waited as Marek did the same.

It was as they were closing the gate behind them that they heard the blast in the distance. It came from within the cemetery.

Dania pushed against the gate and rushed inside. The custodian had left the booth, and was standing clutching the collar of her coat, her arthritic fingers buried in the fur. She looked around in bewilderment, her gaze finally resting on Dania. Her eyes grew wide with fear.

For an instant, Dania thought she wanted to ask her something, but she turned and stared into the dense fog shrouding the cemetery.

'*Boże mój*,' she whispered, crossing herself.

CHAPTER 1

DUNDEE – TWO WEEKS EARLIER

'How many of those glasses of champagne are you going to guzzle?' Dania said, in Polish.

Marek smiled. 'As many as possible. I'm celebrating, don't forget.' He took a sip and closed his eyes, an expression of bliss on his face. 'I can't remember when I've tasted bubbly as good as this.'

'I suppose you expect me to carry you home afterwards.'

He opened his eyes. 'Isn't that what sisters are for?'

'It's certainly what *this* sister is for.'

They were in the spacious, white-columned reception area on the ground floor of DC Thomson's Meadowside building. On display in the glass cases were the previously unknown letters between Chopin and his Scottish friend and pupil, Jane Stirling, which Marek had discovered. His research had taken him the best part of a year, necessitating several trips to Warsaw and Paris. Dania remembered this period as one of frenetic activity on the part of her brother, who was single-minded in his pursuit of the letters to the point of ignoring everything – and everyone – else. As a detective, she knew how this felt.

It had come as a surprise to many readers of the *Courier* that Chopin had visited Scotland not long before his death, and more of a surprise that he'd had a Scottish pupil. The two had met during one of Jane's trips to Paris, and it wasn't long before she started piano lessons, tutoring being something for which Chopin was in high demand. In the fullness of time, Jane became his patron, agent and business manager, arranging his concerts and supporting him financially. She was a wealthy woman, having inherited from her parents.

After a brief trip to London, Chopin and Jane travelled to Scotland. But by now, the composer's illness was taking its toll, although it didn't prevent him from giving concerts. Eventually, he grew so weak he had to be carried on and off the stage, so he returned to Paris where, a year later, he died. Jane remained in close contact with his elder sister, Ludwika, helping to manage Chopin's estate and manuscripts, including the posthumous publication of some of his works.

In the few years in which Jane and Chopin had known each other, they had regularly exchanged letters. Some were displayed in museums or were in private hands. But the ones Marek had spent so much time pursuing were the subject of an anonymous tip-off from a Polish contact. This person referred to letters written in 1845, when Chopin was in Paris and Jane in Scotland. They had been in Jane's possession when she was with him in Paris during the final period of his life. But what had happened to them afterwards was a mystery. They might be in Paris, but the contact was convinced Ludwika had had them with her when she returned to Warsaw.

However, it was not the letters *per se* that had fuelled Marek's enthusiasm but what the contact claimed was in them. One letter allegedly referred to an unknown work – a third piano concerto.

Could it point to the location of the manuscript? The thought of finding these letters was too much for Marek, who, having convinced his boss of the kudos for the *Courier* if he were successful, devoted himself to the quest.

After months of searching, he had traced the letters to a location in Warsaw. On his return to Dundee, he'd arranged for an expert to verify their authenticity. Jane Stirling was fluent in French, and had communicated with Chopin, who knew no English, in that language. An academic from the university's French department, who was able to read the cursive script, had painstakingly translated the letters into English. DC Thomson had agreed to put the six letters and their translations on public display after a private viewing the day before. As Marek's sister, Dania was one of the lucky few to receive an invitation. The Polish consul general and other dignitaries had arrived from Edinburgh and, above the tinkle of champagne glasses, the main language that could be heard was Polish.

Although the display area was bright and spacious, the lights had been switched on, as November afternoons in Scotland darkened quickly. Dania squinted at the letter in the nearby case. 'And you have no idea where this manuscript is?' she said, glancing at Marek.

He shook his head in frustration. 'If it was in the possession of either Jane or Ludwika, I'm convinced the concerto would have been published posthumously.' He gestured with his chin. 'Have you read what Chopin says?'

'He makes it clear he wishes to have it performed.' Dania straightened. 'Interesting he doesn't say he wants to perform it himself. He might have felt too ill to play a piece as lengthy as a concerto, especially in public.'

'When do you think he wrote it?'

'I forget the dates, but his first two concertos were written when he was about twenty. He left Warsaw shortly after. Before the November Uprising.'

'My history never was as good as yours. Remind me when this particular Uprising took place?'

'It began in 1830.'

'You think he wrote this third one around the same time?'

'I'm inclined to think it was after he'd settled in Paris.' Dania studied her brother. He throbbed with nervous excitement. 'You're going to look for it, aren't you?' she said.

'Wouldn't you?' He smiled. 'Of course you would. I can tell from your face.'

'So, where will you start? Paris again?'

'Warsaw. My contact is convinced it's there.'

'When are you going?'

'At the end of the week. I'll be staying in our parents' apartment.'

'What does your boss have to say? You've spent nearly a year tracking down the letters. The manuscript is likely to take longer. Assuming it still exists. Remember how Warsaw was obliterated at the end of the war.'

'And yet those letters were still there. My contact was right about that.'

Dania sipped her champagne. 'You haven't told anyone where you found them.'

'That's going to be the subject of a longer article.' He ran his index finger across his lips. 'Until then, I'm keeping it zipped.'

'And there was no sign of the manuscript?'

'I searched the place thoroughly.'

Shortly after Marek's feature had appeared in the *Courier*, DC Thomson had been inundated with requests from the international press. And once the letters and their translations had been published, interest had sky-rocketed. And it was interest in the missing manuscript. Consequently, Marek was now a celebrity in Poland as well as in Scotland.

He raised an eyebrow. 'Did I tell you I've been contacted privately, and offered a huge sum if I find the concerto and hand it over?'

'And would you?'

'Of course not. I intend to give it to the Fryderyk Chopin Museum. I've discussed this with my contact, who is warmly enthusiastic about the idea.' He lowered his voice. 'And I've received an offer of marriage.'

'Good heavens,' Dania exclaimed. 'From whom?'

'An American. She saw my photo online and said I was Chopin incarnate.'

'She's obviously never seen that famous photograph of him. He had dark hair. Yours is the colour of wheat.'

'Maybe she recognised the romantic in me.'

'Ah, but maybe she thought you'd find the manuscript, sell it and become filthy rich.'

Marek tried to look shocked. 'When did you become so cynical, Danka?'

'When I became a police officer.'

'Talking of which, how are things down at West Bell Street? Are you close to catching your Polish drug lord?'

'An interesting way of describing him.'

'Well, didn't you say he heads a huge syndicate?'

'I don't know how huge. That's the problem.'

'What did you say his name was?'

Dania glanced round the room to check they weren't being

overheard. 'I know him only as Merkury,' she said, pronouncing it in the Polish way with the accent on the letter *u*.

'The Roman god? And do you know how he's bringing in the stuff?'

'In transported goods, or within hidden compartments in vehicles. I've had a breakthrough.'

'Someone on the inside?'

'An informant who's infiltrated the syndicate. She's Polish. Told me to call her Magda. I doubt that's her real name.'

'She's taking a huge risk.'

'She has good reason. Her man died of an overdose.'

'Of drugs he bought from one of Merkury's men?'

'I'm sure of it. Merkury's close to cornering the market.'

Marek said nothing. If Magda's role as an informant were to be discovered, she'd end up floating in the river Tay. They'd pulled two bodies out that month. Merkury's signature was the throat cut from ear to ear. As murder fell within Dania's remit, she was liaising with the Drugs Squad to bring him to justice.

'So, do you think Magda can discover Merkury's identity?' Marek was saying.

'He takes no chances. No one uses real names. And they never meet in the same place twice. Phones are handed in at the door so nobody can take photos or record anything, and everyone is searched thoroughly in case they're wearing wires.' Dania lowered her voice further. 'But I've got a physical description – wavy mid-brown hair, and pale eyes – although that could describe any of the Poles in Dundee. Magda added that he's good-looking.' Dania paused. 'But there's one thing that might help us. She happened to walk into the room when he was changing his jumper. She saw something round his neck. A chain with the Syrenka Warszawska.'

The Syrenka, or mermaid, was a symbol of Warsaw, and her

statue could be found in several locations in the city. According to legend, a rich merchant imprisoned her, but a young fisherman heard her cries and came to her rescue. Full of gratitude, she promised to provide all fishermen with protection. And, armed with a sword and shield, she extended this protection to the city and its residents.

'You think he's from Warsaw?' Marek said.

'And known to the police there. Magda told me there have been long periods when he's vanished. It's possible he goes back and forth.'

'Are you thinking of a trip?'

'I'm hoping that won't be necessary. She's come up with a plan.'

'To uncover his identity?'

'To catch him red-handed. He's taking in a shipment. I'm meeting her later to get the details.'

Marek was silent for a moment. 'Be careful, Danka. People like Merkury don't play nice.' There was anxiety in his voice. 'Look, can you not leave this to the Drugs Squad?'

'He's wanted for murder. I intend to arrest him.' Dania set down her glass. 'There's another reason I need to be there. If we can sneak in when he's picking up the shipment, we might hear something to our advantage.'

Marek made a gesture to indicate she was talking nonsense. 'Why not let the Drugs Squad do that?'

'None of the Drugs Squad speaks Polish.'

'And his people are Poles?'

'Most are, according to Magda.' Dania glanced at her watch. 'I'd better go. I don't want to be late.'

Marek gripped her arm, then released it reluctantly.

'It's all right, Marek. Nothing will happen to me.' She felt her lips twitch. 'Anyway, if it does, I've been to Confession, so I'm covered.'

It was the wrong thing to say. He stared at her with a stricken expression.

'I'll just say goodbye to the consul general,' she murmured.

It was nearly 6 p.m. before Dania reached Kingsway West retail park. She'd arrived early but Magda had arrived earlier. Neither woman wanted to miss the other as a no-show would signal something was seriously wrong, leaving open the possibility the other would disappear. So, each had developed the habit of reaching the agreed meeting place earlier and earlier until it bordered on becoming ridiculous.

Dania let her informants choose the time and place. It was less that it made them feel trusted, and more that she'd given up trying to find suitable venues. Magda had come up with a range of locations, all large stores. They'd developed a technique where they wouldn't speak directly, or look at one another. Their attention was on what was on the shelves, and their conversation was in snippets as they passed. They spoke in English, as Polish would have attracted attention. Magda never wavered from this protocol. And, in all the time Dania had known her, she had never used a mobile. She mistrusted technology. Whenever she wished to get in touch, she left a particular item in the window of the Dundee Contemporary Arts gift shop, where she worked part time. The item would specify the location, and the meeting was to be the same day at 6.30 p.m. The system wasn't foolproof – on one occasion, when Magda was on a break, another assistant had sold the item, with the result that Dania missed the appointment. Today, however, the green whale indicated they'd be meeting at Tesco.

Dania spotted Magda as soon as she was through the door. That tousle of red hair, which looked impossible to comb, was unmistakable, as were the patterned jeans. She couldn't see Magda's face but knew the skin was heavily lined, the mark of a five-pack-a-day smoker. The woman was at the newspaper rack, flicking through a magazine and ignoring the leaflets dropping onto the floor. As Dania wheeled her trolley, she brushed against her, then murmured a rapid apology. Remembering Magda's Tesco-based instructions, she headed towards the fruit and veg. A short while later, Magda approached and paused to inspect the satsumas. As she reached across, her face not far from Dania's, she murmured something, her gaze not wavering from the fruit, which she picked up and scrutinised. She counted six into a paper bag, and shoved it into the trolley.

Dania selected a bag of apples, then made her way to the tinned food, passing Magda who was heading in the opposite direction. Dania picked up a tin of plum tomatoes before wheeling her trolley to the alcohol section, stopping en route for more items. As she stood gazing at the bottles of vodka, Magda passed, clanging her trolley against Dania's. She extricated it with an embarrassed apology, then murmured the rest of her instructions. She took two bottles of Wyborowa, and disappeared down the aisle.

Dania finished shopping, paid for her groceries, and left. Her heart was pounding. She now had the information she needed to nail Merkury.

'Are you sure you don't want to leave it to us, ma'am?' the sergeant was saying. 'I don't need to tell you things might get rough.'

'I understand,' Dania said, 'but my informant is likely to be present, and I promised her I'd be there.'

The man looked doubtful. He had a solid, muscular build, as did his companions. They were dressed in riot gear and one was carrying a heavy-duty battering ram.

'And you'll need someone who can speak Polish,' she added, sensing she wasn't making a strong enough case.

The officer ran a hand over his stubble. 'I don't expect there'll be much in the way of conversation when we go in, eh,' he said, with a crooked smile. 'But it's your call.'

'Thanks. I know how important this raid is to you.'

'Aye, well, we've been waiting a long time to catch this particular gang. And catching them in the act of taking in a shipment gives us a good chance of getting intel on those higher up.'

'I promise I won't get in your way.'

'Best to stay behind us,' he said. He jerked his head at his companions. They filed out and clambered into the two waiting vans. Dania joined the sergeant in the front vehicle.

It didn't take them long to reach Hawkhill, a district where people had once hunted with hawks. The buildings gave way to trees, their leaves long since fallen and swept away. They passed the Whitehall Theatre and were soon driving through the sprawl of industrial outlets. The road led westward, and would eventually become Perth Road. But well before then, the driver signalled right and turned on to Peddie Street.

'You know this area, ma'am?' the sergeant said.

'I attend Mass at St Joseph's on Wilkie's Lane.'

'You think this Polish gang leader attends, too?'

'I doubt it, somehow.'

'You can ask him when we get the cuffs on.'

'I've got more important questions,' she said wryly.

The officer grinned, causing the wrinkles crosshatching the corners of his eyes to deepen. He had an open, friendly expression, which confused those he was questioning. Dania had seen him in action in the interrogation room. He never lost it, and therefore got his man every time.

They passed the purple-painted Hawkhill Tavern, and the NHS Day Hospital. On the left was a four-storey stone building that bristled with satellite dishes, indicating it had been converted into flats. In contrast, the single-storey brick structure opposite was part of the industrial estate.

The commercial unit they were after was roughly halfway along. The van behind stopped, and the men piled out and took up position facing the main entrance. But, according to Magda, the sale would take place at the back, where the service entrances were located, and that was where the sergeant's van was headed.

At this time of the afternoon, the gates to the estate were open. They drove through, and turned left.

'Something's wrong,' Dania murmured.

The sergeant looked hard at her. 'Why do you say that?'

'The shutters to these units are down. And the doors are padlocked.'

'That's normal,' the driver chipped in, over his shoulder. 'They're only open when deliveries are made, ken.'

But Dania couldn't shake the feeling they were sailing into disaster. The sergeant was studying her, wondering perhaps whether she'd be a liability when the moment came.

'This is it,' the driver said, pulling up outside a red door. The padlock was hanging open.

The sergeant glanced at his watch. 'We're bang on time. They should still be inside.'

He repeated his instructions quickly. And then everything happened with lightning speed. The men jumped out of the van, sprinted towards the back door, and positioned themselves on either side. At a nod from the sergeant, the officer with the battering ram slammed it into the door. It flew open and, with shouts of 'Police!' they rushed inside.

The large, dimly lit storage room smelt of sawdust and old wool. Sample carpet rolls in every colour were stacked against one wall in such a way that the slightest touch would bring them tumbling. Against the opposite wall were several large boxes, one of which was split at the side, spilling grey-green carpet tiles onto the floor. The only other items in the room were a desk and chairs. Behind the desk was a door, which presumably led to the visitors' area.

'He's flown the coop,' the sergeant muttered. He slammed his hand against the wall. 'How the *hell* did they know we were coming?'

Dania ran her hands through her hair. 'Maybe he changed the arrangement and didn't tell my informant.'

'What's her role in the organisation?'

'Merkury gives her packets to sell. She pours the powder down the toilet and gives him the money I leave for her in a dead drop. She's been doing that for about six months.'

The sergeant's eyes narrowed. 'When did you last meet with her?'

'Four days ago, in Tesco.'

'Could your conversation have been overheard?'

Dania shook her head firmly.

'Could she have been followed?'

Tesco had been crowded. It was possible Merkury had put a tail on Magda. But why would he suspect her?

'Sarge!' one of the men shouted. He was standing at the door to the visitors' room. 'You need to see this.' He glanced at Dania, then dropped his gaze.

She made to push past the sergeant, but he grasped her arm. 'Wait here,' he said. 'It may not be safe.' He disappeared into the room. A few moments later, he came to the door and beckoned to her.

The men were standing staring at a thick roll of beige carpet. Blood had seeped through the fabric onto the floor, where it had pooled in a wide circle.

The sergeant nodded at the men. A broad-shouldered giant stepped forward and, gripping the edge of the carpet, unrolled it. The metallic stench of blood grew stronger.

'God Almighty,' someone murmured.

Dania had seen Merkury's handiwork before, although by the time the bodies were pulled out of the Tay, they were bloated beyond recognition. That was not the case here. And the red hair and patterned jeans, still identifiable despite being soaked through with blood, told her immediately who this was. She was familiar with victims who'd had their throats cut, and had even seen it done. The gash quickly filled with a line of blood, but was rarely deeper than necessary, especially when administered by an expert. This incision, however, was so vicious that Magda's head was almost severed. But it was the look of terror on the woman's face that sent a shiver racing down Dania's spine.

'Is that your informant?' the sergeant said.

'You're right. She must have been followed.'

'And that means Merkury will know we're close to collaring him, right enough.'

'He'll be wondering how much she's told us.' Dania glanced at the bruises on Magda's face. 'Unless, of course, he managed to beat it out of her.'

'And what do you think his reaction would have been? Apart from cutting her throat.'

'It must have rattled him. He can't be sure we've not uncovered his identity.'

'Maybe he'll move on and start up somewhere else, eh.'

'Or go back to Poland. And take his people with him.'

Dania pulled on her gloves and, ignoring the blood on the floor, knelt beside Magda. 'I remember Milo Slaughter saying the larger muscles are the last to be affected by rigor mortis.'

'Is that the Slaughterman?' someone said.

Professor Milo Slaughter's surname had landed him with this unfortunate nickname. He was either unaware of it, or it didn't bother him. Knowing the man, Dania would have put a wager on the latter.

She felt Magda's thigh muscles. 'Her leg's completely rigid. I'm not an expert but I think it means she's been dead for several hours. The blood congealing suggests it, too.' She got to her feet. 'He usually throws his victims' bodies into the river. We were intended to find her.'

'He's laughing at us,' the sergeant said, gritting his teeth. 'The wee shite.'

'I'll call it in.'

'You're not thinking you've let her down, are you?' he asked, in a soft voice.

'I know I have.'

'If she was tailed to your meeting place, they already suspected her, eh. She must have slipped up, somehow.'

'That doesn't make me feel better.' Dania ripped off her gloves. She pulled out her phone and called Milo first, then West Bell Street.

'We'll have to search the place for drugs,' the sergeant said, 'although my guess is business was conducted elsewhere. Or is being conducted as we speak.'

But Dania doubted it. Something told her that Merkury, suspecting the police were closing in, had wrapped up everything and left Dundee for good. So, where had he gone? And then she remembered her conversation with Magda, and how the woman had spotted the Syrenka Warszawska round his neck. The Syrenka Warszawska – the mermaid of *Warsaw*.

Dania rang West Bell Street again, and instructed her staff to check recent flights from Edinburgh to Warsaw. She had her answer a quarter of an hour later. Although there were always Poles travelling to Warsaw, a block booking for eight people had been made the previous day. The flight had left Edinburgh more than five hours earlier. Direct flights took about two and a half hours. Merkury and his crew would have landed by now. And there was no point in wasting time on names. Magda had confirmed the Poles had false passports from many European countries, and several for Poland.

'So, what will you do now, ma'am?' the sergeant said.

'I'm going home to pack a suitcase.'

CHAPTER 2

WARSAW – DECEMBER

Inspector Maksymilian Robak was slouched in the chair, his arms crossed, his head tilted to the side. His expression was not unfriendly but he was studying Dania closely, having dropped her passport onto the table. They were in an interview room in Warsaw's police headquarters at Mostowski Palace. The palace had once been the seat of the Tsarist authorities, then the Polish army, and then the civic militia, but Dania knew it as one of the places where Chopin had given concerts. After the Second World War, all that survived of the eighteenth-century baroque building was the façade, with its signature arches and columns. Like much of Warsaw, it had been rebuilt, although the interior with its multitude of modern offices was unlikely to be true to the original. She'd had little difficulty in finding Mostowski as her parents' apartment was situated in the nearby Muranów district.

The grey-walled room Dania had been escorted to was gloomy and smelt of floor polish. Apart from her passport, the only other item on the table was a rusty desk lamp, which in Communist times would have been used to shine light into the eyes of the hapless person being interrogated. Dania wondered why it hadn't been removed, especially since the bulb was missing. Perhaps it was a reminder of how interrogation techniques had improved. The room had no radiator – also a throwback to earlier times – and the chill in the air made her glad she was wearing her thick tartan coat. The officer, on the other hand, was in jeans, a blue-and-purple waistcoat and an open-necked white shirt with the sleeves rolled up. His firearm was still in his shoulder holster, making her suspect he was so used to carrying it he'd forgotten it was there. On the wall behind him was the blue-and-silver emblem of the Polish police.

The inspector had apologised for having to conduct the interview in this room, but the others were occupied. He'd introduced himself as a member of the Policja Kryminalna, the division of the state police involved in the investigation and prevention of serious and violent crime. Unlike most Polish men, who wore their hair short, his light-brown hair was shoulder length. He wore it brushed back off his forehead, which served to enhance his high cheekbones and blue-grey eyes. He was above average height, and what Dania could see of his toned body suggested he spent a fair part of his free time in the police gym.

'And you have no idea who this unexpected guest was?' he was saying. He had a deep voice and spoke briskly, using the polite form of address.

'I didn't see his face,' Dania said. 'I felt a movement behind me, and the next thing I saw was a huge wreath of white flowers being thrown into the air. I heard it land on the coffin.'

'Could it have been a woman throwing it?'

'It could. I saw only a shape disappearing into the fog.'

'Why were you attending Jakub Frydman's funeral? What was your interest?'

'He was my piano teacher.'

The expression on the officer's face changed to one of respect. He straightened. 'When did you take lessons from him?' he said reverentially.

'When I was a child.'

'You lived in Warsaw?'

'Until 2002. I was fourteen when we left for Scotland.'

She could see he wanted to quiz her about the circumstances behind the move, but he kept his questions relevant.

'How did you come to meet Jakub Frydman?' he said.

'My grandparents hid him during the Occupation. After the war, he lived with them. His own parents had died in the Ghetto Uprising.'

Robak said nothing. For Jews of Jakub Frydman's age, it was a common enough story.

'He became a piano teacher,' Dania went on. 'But because my family had sheltered him, he gave me free piano lessons.' She looked directly at Robak. 'I doubt they'd have been able to afford them otherwise.'

'What sort of person was he?'

She smiled sadly. 'I remember him as a kindly man. He'd have been in his sixties when I was a child. He used to have a picture of the Warsaw Conservatory as it looked before the war. I'm sure you know it's now the Chopin University of Music.'

'Ah, yes. There have been a few name changes for that institution.'

'Although he retired from the Chopin University, he continued giving private lessons. Whenever I visited Warsaw, I'd go to his apartment and play. And he'd advise me on how to improve.'

'So, in a way, the lessons continued?'

'He wanted me to become a concert pianist. But I'm afraid I disappointed him.'

Robak riffled through his folder. 'He outlived his wife, according to our records. And there were no children.' He glanced up. 'Do you know of any relatives?'

'He told me he was the last of his line. His relatives didn't survive the war. Or so he assumed. It's possible some are living, and perhaps don't know they're Jewish.'

'That happened to a colleague. His parents hid their identity under the Communists. He only recently discovered he was Jewish.'

'And how did he react?'

'The first thing he did was to throw this away,' Robak said, lifting the chain round his neck and displaying the crucifix. 'He replaced it with a Star of David. Then he had his grandfather's prisoner number tattooed on his forearm as an act of respect.'

'And where is he now?'

'He emigrated to Israel.' After a pause, Robak said, 'Why do you think someone would throw a wreath packed with explosives into Jakub Frydman's grave?'

Dania shook her head. 'I've no idea.'

'When the news of the explosion reached us, I thought it was wartime ordnance. An unexploded German mortar was unearthed last year during renovation of the oldest part of Okopowa. Fortunately, our bomb squad removed it safely.'

'A mortar? From the 'forty-four Uprising?'

'That area was on the front line.'

'I'd forgotten what a dangerous place Warsaw can still be.'

'Forensics have been working at Okopowa since yesterday's explosion.' Robak gazed at her without blinking. 'Not only was there nothing left of the coffin and its contents, many nearby graves were destroyed.' He must have seen the shock on her face because he changed tack. 'Are you in Warsaw visiting relatives?'

Dania ran a hand over her eyes. 'Actually, I'm here on business.'

'May I ask the nature of this business?'

'I'm a police detective. I work in Scotland.'

If he was surprised, his expression didn't show it. 'Then it must feel strange to be on the other side of the table in an interview room,' he said, smiling for the first time. His eyes glowed with warmth. The effect was stunning.

'Yes, it does.'

'And you have police business in Warsaw?'

'I'm here to meet with your drugs people. But I've had no success so far.'

'Oh?'

'They don't return my calls. And I've been unable to make an appointment. I'm trying to track down a drug dealer who I believe has come to Warsaw.'

'So, you work in the Anti-drugs Squad in Scotland?'

'I'm in the Murder Squad. This man butchered one of my informants.'

Something shifted in Robak's expression. 'Leave it with me. I'll make certain our people meet with you.'

'I'm sure they're overwhelmed with their own problems.'

'The way drugs are spreading, I think that's true everywhere. To get back to Pan Frydman, we're struggling to find a motive for why his grave should have been desecrated. Do you know anything of his activities under the Communists?' When she said nothing, he added, 'You look surprised. Did you ever discuss politics with him?'

'We discussed Chopin, and how I should successfully tackle Chopin's Ballade Number 4.'

Robak's lips twitched. 'And did you? Tackle it successfully, I mean?'

She shook her head. 'So, do you think Pan Frydman was involved with the Communist authorities?'

'There are many who collaborated with the secret police. And there are those who are now taking the law into their own hands and trying to right perceived wrongs.'

'But surely they'd have targeted someone while he was still living. What is the point of desecrating a grave?'

'I'm inclined to agree. But we have to keep all avenues open. We can check the archives at the Institute of National Remembrance.'

The institute had been created to deal with, among other things, the country's Communist past – its secret police and its secret collaborators – and when citizens who'd lived through that era were targeted, the police would search the institute's archives as part of their investigation.

'I don't suppose you caught this unexpected guest – to use your phrase – on camera,' she said.

Robak clasped his hands and placed them on the table. 'Now you're behaving like a detective,' he said, smiling.

'I hope you don't think I'm being disrespectful.'

'Not at all. I welcome your input.' He rolled down his sleeves and buttoned them at the wrist, as though only then appreciating it was cold in the room. 'We have many cameras, including an automatic number-plate recognition system similar to yours. But with this thick fog, camera systems are useless.'

'There's a tram stop opposite the main cemetery gate. Is there a camera there?'

'We thought of that. But, as I said, no camera can record anything in this fog.'

'Weather like this is unusual.'

'The fog comes and goes. Today it has partly lifted. But I agree this is exceptional. It's snow we tend to have in the run-up to

Christmas.' He closed the folder, adding in a businesslike voice, 'How long are you planning on staying in Warsaw?'

'It depends on whether I find my drug dealer.' She smiled. 'It would be wonderful to stay, but what will the lights in the Royal Garden at Wilanów be like in the fog?'

'Blurred, I should imagine, like everything else. It will be something of an experience to see Wilanów through the mist.'

'My brother, Marek, was always sneaking off there.'

'Marek Górski?' he said, frowning. 'He's your brother? I saw the name on our list and assumed you were husband and wife.' He glanced at her right hand. 'I see now that you're not wearing a wedding ring,' he added sheepishly. 'So much for my powers of observation.'

Dania didn't need to look at Robak's right hand to establish he was single. She'd done it as soon as she'd been introduced. The detective in her had a habit of weighing people up the instant she met them.

'Your brother has been in the news lately,' Robak was saying. 'At least, I'm assuming he's the same Marek Górski who's searching for the missing Chopin manuscript.'

Interesting he mentioned the manuscript and not the Jane Stirling letters, Dania thought. But, then, the local daily, *Życie Warszawy*, made mention only of the manuscript. It carried an article on the front page, complete with a photo of Marek. The whole of Warsaw would know by now who he was and what he was doing there.

'He is indeed my brother. He's an investigative journalist.'

Robak opened the folder and leafed through the papers. 'He's also living in Dundee.' He tilted his head. 'Do you work together?'

'Not intentionally. But our cases sometimes cross.'

'He's coming in this afternoon. I see he's staying at the same address as yours. Are you renting the apartment?'

'It belongs to our parents. They're in the States.'

Robak sat back, studying her. 'In the various conversations you've had over the years with Pan Frydman, can you think of anything he said that suggested he had enemies?'

It was the question she, as a detective, would have asked. And the question she'd been asking herself since she'd learnt the explosion had occurred at Jakub Frydman's grave.

'The only thing I can think of . . .'

'Yes?' Robak prompted, when the pause had gone on too long.

'. . . but I'm not sure how relevant it would be . . .'

He said nothing. She looked into his thoughtful eyes, almost forgetting what she was doing there. 'He was involved in the Solidarity movement,' she said finally.

'He talked about this?'

She hesitated. 'My parents told me.'

'And they said Pan Frydman was an activist?'

'It came up in conversation once, but I can't remember the details.'

They gazed at one another, each seeing on the other's face the thoughts going through their own minds. She and Robak had been born after the rise of Solidarity, a movement that had been followed by the instigation of martial law and years of political repression. Poles of their generation had learnt what life was like under the Communists from their parents, just as they'd learnt what life was like during the Occupation from their grandparents.

Robak played with his pen. 'If Pan Frydman was active in Solidarity, it's hard to see why that would lead to someone destroying his grave. But we can check our archives, assuming there's anything there.' From the tone of his voice, it was clear the interview had come to an end. His leather jacket was hanging over the back of his chair. He pulled a card from the pocket. 'If anything comes to mind that you think might be relevant, please call me. It doesn't matter what time of day or night.'

She took the card, feeling a sudden dull ache in her chest. She drew in her breath sharply.

'Are you all right?' Robak said. 'Would you like a glass of water?'

'I'm fine. It's taken this long for it to sink in that someone wanted to do such a thing to Pan Frydman.'

Robak leant forward. 'You should console yourself that Pan Frydman would have known nothing about it,' he said gently.

Dania felt the tears welling. She wiped her eyes with her fingers.

Robak got to his feet and shuffled the papers in his file, clearly intent on not embarrassing her.

He returned the passport, and walked her to the door. Halfway there, he stopped and held out his hand. Dania smiled to herself. He was one of those Poles who didn't like to say goodbye in a doorway or over a threshold. Her parents were the same, riddled with superstition. A particular saying she remembered was that someone had to be buried before the Sunday after they died, or another family member would die the same year. Neither she nor Marek had paid much attention to what her brother referred to as childish mumbo-jumbo.

Dania put her hand into Robak's, hoping he'd kiss it, but he shook it firmly.

'I'll speak to the Anti-drugs people,' he said, releasing her. 'You should expect to hear from them today.'

'Thank you,' she said gratefully.

He opened the door, and exchanged a word with the

uniformed officer. The man indicated politely to Dania that she should follow him.

She turned to smile at Robak, but the door had closed.

Maksymilian Robak returned to the chair and sat for several minutes, thinking about Danuta Górska. He picked up the pen and made notes for the file. So far, he'd interviewed four of the guests from Jakub Frydman's funeral. His staff were questioning the others. They should be finished by the end of the day, but he doubted they'd learn anything. None of those he'd interviewed had said they'd be able to recognise the unexpected guest who'd thrown the wreath. Even if they tracked him down, they'd have a hard time pinning the crime on him. Forensics might come up with something, as handling explosives left a trace. But time wasn't on their side. Their best bet was to establish the motive. The incident had understandably left its impression on the mourners, who had been affected to a greater or lesser degree, but whether it was shock at the act of desecration or the knowledge they'd narrowly missed certain death was unclear. In Danuta's case, however, Maks was sure it was the former. He couldn't dispel the image of her face and the tears simmering in her hazel eyes. He gathered up his papers and left the room.

He took the steps to the top floor two at a time, and found the corridor leading to the rooms used by Anti-drugs. He knocked at the door to the main office and, without waiting for an invitation, stepped inside.

Maks coveted this room as it gave the occupant a view of Krasiński Garden. In winter, when the trees were like splintered bones, it was possible to glimpse Krasiński Palace. Each time he saw it, he remembered how he'd taken the oath of office in the front square. His own room, on the other side of the building, looked out onto modern apartment blocks.

The person sitting hunched over peering into his computer screen was exactly the person Maks was looking for. Oskar Dolniak had blank blue eyes and, like many Polish officers, his head was completely shaved. The almost permanent frown on his face had etched deep lines into his forehead.

Maks took the chair opposite. Oskar looked up as though only then realising someone else was in the room. He dredged up a smile. 'Hello, Maks. I take it this isn't a social visit.'

'I've been speaking with one of the guests from the Okopowa cemetery service.'

'And did he shed light on what had happened there?'

'She didn't.'

'A lady? Was she beautiful?'

'Oh, yes.'

'Lucky for you, my friend. I deal only with men, and ugly ones at that.' His gaze sharpened. 'That was a bad business, though, a crime in a Jewish cemetery. The newspapers are loving it. But I expect you're not here to talk about that.' He had a sing-song eastern accent. Maks had often wondered if it lulled his suspects to sleep when he interviewed them.

'This lady is a detective from Scotland,' he said. 'She's chasing a drug dealer who, she believes, has come to Warsaw.'

'Ah.'

'Yes, so you'll have guessed why I'm here.'

The man spread his hands. 'Look, Maks, I'm snowed under with my own problems. I can't take on hers as well.'

'Except her problems may soon become yours if this drug dealer has indeed come to our fair city. It's greatly in your interest to work with her.'

The officer sighed in the way people do when they appreciate the force of an argument but find themselves powerless to do anything about it. Maks knew he'd have to find a way to persuade him. He had an inexplicable urge to help the detective from Scotland. 'She's from Dundee,' he said, examining his nails. He looked up. 'Did she tell you?'

'I can't remember the details of her message.'

'So, you know what that means.'

Oskar's Anti-drugs unit had liaised with its counterpart in Dundee before now and, the way things were going, would be doing so again. The days when all the Warsaw unit had to worry about were illicit cigarettes and alcohol were over.

'I promised this detective you'd contact her today and arrange a meeting,' Maks said, keeping his tone friendly. 'After all, if you can find this dealer, think what it will do for Scottish-Polish relations. To say nothing of what it will do for your career,' he added meaningfully.

Oskar rubbed his eyes. 'My people are in Praga on a raid.' He gestured to his screen. 'I have reports to write. I practically live in this office. My wife is threatening to leave me if I don't come home once in a while.' He tried a grin. 'Mind you, that would be no bad thing.'

Maks nodded in a way he hoped wasn't condescending. Mention of Praga had given him an idea. 'I'm wondering what I could offer to make this decision easier for you,' he said delicately. 'Perhaps my ticket for the final of the national speedway competition?'

Like many Poles, the two men lived for speedway. Tickets for the final were like gold dust but Maks, as a former contestant, had secured one for the competition the following year. It was to take place in the National Stadium in Praga South.

Oskar's eyes widened. 'You'll give me your ticket?' he said, in a whisper.

Maks leant across and picked up the handset. He held it out to his colleague. 'With everything you've got on your plate, you might forget to call this detective,' he said, with a smile. 'So, why not do it now, Oskar? Mm?'

CHAPTER 3

Dania left Mostowski Palace, deep in thought. It was past midday and she considered returning to her parents' apartment, but decided against it. Marek was unlikely to be in. And, anyway, the fog was lifting, but for how long? She'd find somewhere to eat that had a great view of Warsaw.

She was about to cross the multi-lane road named for General Anders when she remembered that jaywalking in most circumstances was an offence. The steps leading to the pedestrian underpass were a short distance away. She emerged on the other side and, minutes later, boarded the old Communist-era tram, validating her ticket in the yellow box. The fog had driven the cars from the roads, and the three coaches were almost full. Everyone was playing with a mobile. As she was taking her seat at the back, her phone rang. It was the head of the Anti-drugs unit, inviting her to Mostowski Palace. Would the following day suit? It would, she said eagerly. They arranged a time, and he rang off. So, Robak had been as good as his word. She'd have to find an opportunity to thank him.

Dania sat gazing through the window until the road became the Marszałkowska. On a whim, she disembarked and strolled through the Saski Garden. The park stretched eastwards towards

Marshal Piłsudski Square, and beyond was the university area, which had an excellent selection of eating houses.

Winter had taken the colour from the landscape and, although the haze was thinning, it softened the outlines of the bare-limbed trees. The park was deserted except for the statues looming out of the mist. As Dania sauntered along the path, she asked herself what had prompted her to lie to Maksymilian Robak. To her knowledge, Jakub Frydman had never worked for Solidarity, although like many he might have been a quiet supporter. It was her parents who had been activists, which had led to their arrest and imprisonment. Was it because Robak's suggestion of collaboration had raised her suspicions, and she wanted to throw him off the scent by alluding to Jakub's anti-Communist sympathies? It was a stupid thing to do, she realised. If Jakub had indeed worked for the Communist government, the evidence would be on file. And Robak would find it. But the thought slipped into her mind that perhaps Robak knew the appalling truth and wanted her to confirm it.

Her mind drifted to the last time she'd met with her piano teacher. It was on one of her recent visits to Warsaw. He'd welcomed her into his Muranów apartment, offering her tea and cake. The place was more of a tip than Dania remembered. Parts of it were tidy enough, but his housekeeper had been forbidden to enter the huge study. The walls were lined with sagging bookshelves, and every inch of floor was covered with piles of notes and manuscripts. Although in his nineties, Jakub walked upright without a cane, his deportment making it clear he'd reject an offer of help. His movements were slower than she'd remembered, but he carried the tray to the kitchen table without mishap. It was when he pushed the jar of mustard towards her, instead of the jam, that she understood his sight was failing. But it made little difference to his piano-playing. He entertained Dania with the mournful first movement of Beethoven's Moonlight Sonata. But then he smiled at her, and a glint of mischief appeared in his dark, soulful eyes. Without pausing, he launched into Beethoven's Rondo a Capriccioso in G major, Opus 129, known as 'Rage over the Lost Penny'. At five and a half minutes long, it started off furious and manic, growing more furious and manic before finishing with two angry chords. It was a vindication of what he'd told her: playing difficult pieces requires not so much good eyesight as an excellent memory. Which he evidently had, even in old age.

Yet although she had known him all these years, they had never spoken of life in Communist Poland. She and Marek had been born the year before the Round Table Agreement, signed in April 1989, had started Poland on the road to a free democracy. In the years following, they'd been too young to appreciate the turmoil engulfing a country emerging from four decades of what was in effect Soviet rule. Decades Jakub had lived through and they hadn't. But now, her mind was suddenly assailed by doubts. It was barely credible. Could he have collaborated with the Communists?

Dania passed the stone fountain, which was spurting so energetically the droplets thickened the mist, making it look like smoke, and arrived at the fragment of colonnade marking the Tomb of the Unknown Soldier. The arches were all that was left of the huge palace, which, like the park, had been built in the eighteenth century. The building had been destroyed in the war, and this fragment of the palace kept as a memorial. But Poles knew the Saski Palace in another connection. In the 1930s, it had been the home of the Polish Cipher Bureau. Weeks before the war began, Polish mathematicians who had broken the German Enigma military code years earlier had passed its secrets, including the procedures of code-breaking, along with a reconstructed Enigma machine, to the British and French code-breakers.

Dania had reached the main road, and was crossing at the zebra when she became aware that someone was watching her. The feeble sun had thinned the mist to the extent that she had little difficulty making out the short, stout figure. She didn't need to see the bow tie and blue-patterned waistcoat to recognise Adam Mazur, a retired professor at the Chopin University of Music. He was standing motionless next to the statue of Józef Piłsudski, a statue himself. The last time she'd spoken to him was at the funeral.

She lifted her arm in greeting, and he responded with a hesitant wave. After what could only be described as a furtive glance around, he hurried towards her, clutching his briefcase under his arm.

'Pani Górska,' he said, greeting her formally. He gave a slight bow, causing his shock of fine white hair to fall over his forehead. 'I hadn't expected to see you here,' he said, in his husky voice.

'I'm looking for somewhere to have lunch.'

He smiled. 'I know a place. Shall I give you directions?'

'Actually, would you be free to join me?'

'Of course. It would be my privilege.' He bowed again. 'It's this way.'

He set off at a brisk pace, as though aware of the time and fearing the best of the food would be gone. Dania was grateful she could see several metres in front or she'd have collided with the pedestrians.

They arrived at Krakowskie, often referred to as Warsaw's spine. It was part of the Royal Route travelled by the kings of Poland from their main residence in the royal castle to their summer home in Wilanów Palace. Adam turned left, smiling over his shoulder to check Dania was keeping up.

Before they reached the statue of Copernicus, he paused and indicated they needed to cross. Fortunately, there was a pedestrian walkway so they didn't have to resort to jaywalking. Just as well, Dania thought. Although the mist was thick enough to blur their faces on camera, whether it would blur the lines of her tartan jacket was another matter.

Adam paused at the glass case displaying the replica of the Canaletto painting. 'Where we are going is straight ahead, Pani Górska. Do you know the area?'

'Yes, I've been there many times.'

Dania and Marek had frequented the lively student district with their parents, who loved the cafés and particularly the bookshops. Marek usually had to be dragged away from the second-hand volumes, some written in Russian, dating from the Communist era. He'd started to learn the language at school but hadn't got far due to their move to Scotland. Before they'd left, their parents had quietly returned the Russian books to the bookshops.

Minutes later, Adam stopped at the edge of a park. On the ground floor of the apartment block beyond was a café. The door was open, releasing the smell of strong coffee and sweet pastry.

'Do you know this place?' he said.

'Kawiarnia Kafka? I've never been here.' It struck Dania that the English translation – Café Kafka – sounded better.

'In summer, the proprietors put out deckchairs on the grass. Pan Frydman was a frequent guest. As soon as someone recognised him, word would spread and he'd find himself surrounded. Pity there's no piano in this café.' Adam frowned. 'Perhaps it's just as well. They'd never have let him leave. That happened once in a restaurant, I believe. They had a grand piano. He didn't get to finish his dessert,' he added, scandalised.

The interior was light and airy, thanks to the floor-to-ceiling windows giving onto the park. Wooden tables and chairs stood on the black-and-white chequered floor, which morphed into red-and-white as they approached the counter. Dania chose pancakes with cottage cheese and lemon, and Adam settled for a mozzarella sandwich. They took the food and coffees to a table by the window.

He must have seen her gaze travel to the shelves on the walls. 'This place is great for students,' he said. 'They can buy or exchange books. They're priced by the kilogram, and not expensive.'

'Marek would love it. I'll have to tell him.'

'So, have you been interviewed by the police?' Adam said, cutting his sandwich in half.

'I've just come from there. And you?'

'I was questioned first thing this morning.'

'By Inspector Robak?'

'It was a lady. She bombarded me with questions about the funeral. But what could I tell her?' He shook his head sadly. 'I saw nothing except that wretched wreath flying through the air.'

'I suspect there are questions the police have to ask. But I doubt anyone saw anything in that fog. Marek might be able to give them a description. He was best placed to see that man.' She squeezed the lemon over the cheese. 'Why do you think someone would do that? Blow up a coffin at a funeral?'

Adam set down the sandwich, and wiped his fingers on his napkin. 'I think it was an anti-Semitic attack.'

'Surely not. Pan Frydman was dead.'

'Not Pan Frydman. Rabin Steinberg.'

'The rabbi?'

'He was the only other Jewish person there.'

Dania stared at him. 'You think the explosion was intended to kill the *rabbi*?'

'It was lucky for him the bomb failed to detonate immediately.'

'But the explosion would have killed everyone there, not just him.'

She could see this hadn't occurred to Adam. The colour left his face. 'Did you discuss this theory with the police?' she added.

'I confess I didn't. It only occurred to me after I'd left Mostowski Palace.' He seemed agitated. 'Do you think I should call them?'

'I'm sure they have a number of theories to explore,' Dania said kindly. 'Anti-Semitism will be one of them.'

He nodded, but he didn't look convinced. 'This police officer – her name was Pola Lorenc – asked me how long I'd known Pan Frydman. Of course I'd known him all my professional life. I was his student at the Chopin University of Music and, after I graduated, he encouraged me to apply for a position there. But for some reason, Pani Lorenc was more interested in whether I'd had dealings with the Communist authorities.'

'Whether *you*'d had dealings?'

'And whether I knew Pan Frydman had,' he said, his voice tailing away. 'Her question came as something of a shock. I thought that piece of history was well buried.'

'What do you mean?' Dania said, pausing in the act of lifting her fork. 'Pan Frydman collaborated with the Communists?'

'Well, it was only a rumour.' Adam must have seen the expression on her face because he added quickly, 'Many people did it. Life was impossible otherwise. Unless you had hard currency, there were certain things you couldn't buy. Everything was in short supply, and you had to resort to the black market. The authorities knew this. They approached us, not the other way round . . . If you were educated, the secret police kept a file on you.'

Dania was unable to believe her piano teacher had worked with the authorities. But the way Adam gabbled made her suspect he was speaking not about Jakub Frydman but about himself. Yet what he was saying was what many Poles said about those times, wanting to dissociate themselves, as if living in the Communist era had left them tainted.

'And what form did this alleged collaboration take?' she said, setting down her fork.

It was several moments before Adam replied. 'There were staff at the university who were active members of Solidarity. They lost their jobs. And also their pensions,' he added.

Dania gazed at him in disbelief.

It was obvious he wanted to change the subject. 'So, tell me about Marek,' he said, smiling suddenly. 'We've been terribly excited about these Jane Stirling letters. Did you get a chance to see the originals?'

'They've been on display in Dundee.'

'Did he tell you where he found them?'

'He's keeping that to himself. I think he intends to publish everything in due course.'

'I'd have thought a documentary would be more appropriate. I'm sure there are filmmakers here in Warsaw who'd love the chance to work with him. I could introduce him,' he added hopefully. 'Let me give you my contact details.' He rummaged in his waistcoat pocket and handed her a card. 'And what about this missing manuscript?' he said, in a slightly tremulous voice. 'Is he close to finding it?'

'He's cagier about that.'

'He must have a contact. Unless he's been working from documents.'

'I understand there's a gentleman here in Warsaw who's been helping him. Communication is done electronically. He knows him only by a pseudonym.'

Adam smiled. 'Ah, yes, Warsaw's famous pseudonyms.' He played with his sandwich. 'Is that why you're here, too, Pani Górska? As a detective, you have skills that would help him.'

'I haven't the time. I'm here in another connection.'

'Police work?'

'I'm afraid so.' She attacked the pancakes. 'Marek is on his own with this manuscript.'

'I wish him luck.'

'And how are you getting on with Pan Frydman's estate? I believe you're his executor.'

A look of anxiety crossed Adam's face. 'You've seen his apartment, Pani Górska. It will take me months to clear. There's a long list of beneficiaries – students and colleagues – who will stand to gain to a greater or lesser extent.'

'I understand he died of heart failure.'

'His housekeeper found him sitting in his armchair. She thought he was taking a nap, until she moved closer. He had a book in his lap.'

'Not a bad way to go.'

'It's how we'd all like to go, I suspect.'

They finished their lunch in silence. Dania studied Adam surreptitiously, wondering what had prompted him to share his suspicions about Jakub. It could only be because he'd wanted to divert attention away from himself and his activities. What a murky world the men had lived in.

'I'm afraid I must be going,' Adam said. 'I'm giving a lesson this afternoon.' He lifted his briefcase and stood up. 'Academics rarely retire. Musicians never do.'

'It was the same with Pan Frydman,' Dania said, getting to her feet.

'I take it you and Marek are staying at your parents' apartment on Dzielna Street,' Adam said, when they were on the pavement. 'I heard they're abroad.'

'A Polish-American genealogy convention in Florida.'

He pulled on his gloves. 'Do say hello to Marek for me. And the two of you should drop in. I'm at home most evenings. How long are you staying?'

'I have a flight booked next Friday.'

'So, you're not here for Christmas?'

'I'm afraid not.'

'Ah, that's a pity. I'll bid you goodbye, then.' With a slight bow he walked briskly away.

Dania watched him go. With his bow tie and long camel coat, he was the epitome of the bachelor professor. Some might even call him absent-minded. Except he was anything but. An intellectual who had survived – even thrived – under the Communists must have had his wits about him. And, like everyone in Warsaw, he wanted Marek to find the missing manuscript. As a Chopinist himself, he'd be wondering about the composition, whether this third concerto was like the other two, was it written before or after, why had it been hidden and not performed? But then Dania's thoughts slipped back to his comments about Jakub Frydman, and the man's possible collaboration with the Communist authorities. That had left her shaken. She'd be visiting Mostowski Palace the following day. Perhaps, once her meeting with the Anti-drugs head was over, she'd drop in on Maksymilian Robak.

There was a knock at the door, and Maks poked his head round. 'Pola, can you do something for me?'

Pola Lorenc glanced up from her computer screen. 'What do you need?' she said, peering over her round glasses.

'I've had a call from Ujazdów Avenue.'

'Forensics?'

'They want me over there.'

She sprang to her feet, and kicked off her huge slippers. 'I'll fetch my coat.'

'Actually, I'm due to interview Marek Górski in fifteen minutes. I'd like you to do it.'

Pola fought down her disappointment. As Maks's number two, she had no choice but to take his orders, although he always made them sound like a request.

'Of course,' she said, forcing a smile.

'He's the last on the list. If I'm back in time, we can regroup and go through what we know. Otherwise, it will be tomorrow morning.' He was shutting the door, but then opened it again. 'By the way, did you get anywhere with the florists?'

It had been Pola's idea to see if she could trace the wreath. She went through what she'd uncovered. Most of the guests had thought the flowers were lilies but, to be sure, she'd instructed the team to make enquiries about all wreaths ordered recently. Surprisingly, there had been several, but they'd narrowed it down to two possibles: one lily wreath had been bought by the Convent of the Franciscan Sisters for the funeral of one of their order. The other, much larger, had been ordered and collected in person.

And paid for in cash. Which was unusual, and was why the florist had remembered it. However, the lady was unable to give a good description of the purchaser. He'd worn his cap low, and his scarf muffled the lower half of his face. As for the name on the order, Pola said, it was likely to be a fake as so far it hadn't turned up in their records. They were still searching, she added.

'How big was this wreath?'

'At least a metre in diameter. And several centimetres thick, according to the florist. The purchaser was specific about the frame. As soon as the lady described it, I saw immediately that it would have been straightforward to remove the lilies, pack the frame with explosive, and replace the flowers.'

'Anything on the cameras around the shop?' Maks said. 'Forget it. I can tell from your face. So, when was the wreath ordered?'

'Monday morning, not long after she opened, which was ten o'clock. It was picked up in the late afternoon.'

'Monday morning? This was the day after Jakub Frydman died.'

Pola spoke in the businesslike voice she used when she was sure of the facts. 'Jakub's body was found by his housekeeper in his apartment early on Sunday. She contacted Adam Mazur immediately. The death notices went up the following morning, and there was also an announcement on the news.'

'So, our guest had Monday evening and all of Tuesday to charge the wreath with explosives, ready for the funeral on Wednesday.'

Pola gazed at Maks. Having worked with him for so long, she knew what was going through his mind. The same question was going through hers: why blow up a coffin with a dead man inside? That was their challenge, to find the motive that would lead them to snare this 'unexpected guest'. She had to smile at Maks's choice of phrase, a reference to the evening meal on Christmas Eve – Wigilia – when it was customary to lay an extra place for the unexpected guest. But, then, Maks was such a romantic she could have predicted he'd come up with that. But it was less his personality and more his brilliance as a detective that had made her struggle up the ranks, and apply to work in his team as soon as a position fell vacant.

She remembered the day he'd chosen her from the crowd of applicants. She'd made it through the selection process to the final six, and Maks had then set them a task, the final one in a series. But this exercise was to be conducted as a team, with each candidate given one piece of information on a sheet of paper. They'd sat looking at one another until Pola had taken the reins, gathered the sheets and arranged them on the table. Then, after studying the information, she'd put forward her theory, challenging the others to come up with theirs. Eventually – and it was like pulling teeth – she'd got them to communicate. The problem was, as she'd told Maks afterwards, the others were either afraid of showing their ignorance, or were trying to work out the puzzle on their own and claim the credit. But Pola knew that wasn't how detectives worked. They had to present their theories, however far-fetched, and working as a team was essential. In fact, the problem couldn't be solved, as a key piece of information was missing. But that was intentional. Maks had wanted to see how they'd react. He'd sat by the door, arms crossed, watching Pola with a look of mild amusement. Half an hour later, he'd offered her the job.

'I'd better get going,' Maks said.

'Has Górski arrived?'

'He's waiting downstairs. The interview rooms are all occupied. I had to use that god-awful room without a radiator when I interviewed his sister.'

'I could take him to the Sala Biała.'

'That'll make an impression.' With a smile, Maks left the room.

The White Room, so called for its white-painted walls and ceiling, was used for large meetings, and the conferring of awards. Pola slid her feet into her slippers, picked up her notebook and pen and, straightening her skirt, made for the corridor.

Marek Górski was staring at the notices on the wall, under the watchful eye of a uniformed police officer.

'Pan Górski?'

He wheeled round. A tall woman, her brown hair in plaits, was studying him, an expression of intense curiosity in her pale-blue eyes.

'Yes, I'm Marek Górski.' He held out his hand.

She put hers into his and he bent to kiss it. As he was releasing her, he caught sight of her legs. They were long and muscular, and he'd have spent more time admiring them but his gaze had travelled to her grey slippers. They had huge eyes and small elephant trunks, the kind a child would wear, except they were adult size.

He lifted his head. She continued to study him, and he wondered whether he should make a comment, but decided anything he said would sound either flippant or offensive.

'I'm Pola Lorenc. I've been wondering what you look like,' she said suddenly. 'The photos in the papers don't do you justice.'

Marek raised an eyebrow.

'You look much younger in the flesh,' she said, as if feeling the need to clarify her remark.

'Well, those photos were taken when I was older.'

She laughed, showing small, perfect teeth. 'I'm afraid you're with the B-team today, Pan Górski. My boss is away this afternoon, so

I'll be conducting the interview. It's this way.' She headed for the stairs.

He followed her to the floor above, trying to keep his eyes on her back. Had it not been for the elephant slippers, she'd have looked stylish in the long blouse and short, black skirt. She must have known he'd spotted the slippers. That it didn't bother her was what he found intriguing.

The corridors had been painted in light shades of blue, the colour of the Polish police, and were wide enough to accommodate display cases. Some had windows, which Marek suspected gave onto the inner courtyard, but the sun was close to setting and he could see little. Pola hurried down a long passageway, then through a door on the right. She threw a switch, and stood back for him to enter. If he hadn't known this was a police station, he'd have said he was in an eighteenth-century salon.

The long room was exquisitely proportioned, and divided into three sections by pairs of white columns. The central area was filled with rows of chairs, which faced a table and a large screen, suggesting presentations were held there. At one end, several dummies stood on a plinth, each wearing a different police uniform. Given the number of women Marek had seen, he couldn't help wondering why all the dummies were of men. At the opposite end, behind a corded barrier, stood a black grand piano, its lid open.

Marek moved further into the room. The immaculate parquet floor, its slight sheen and scent of lilac suggesting it was polished daily, reflected the light from the chandeliers. As he lifted his head and peered at the ceiling roses and walls stuccoed with decorative plaster, he imagined himself in the eighteenth century, wearing waistcoat and breeches, and a powdered wig. And then his gaze dropped to Pola's slippers, and reality dragged him to the present.

'Please take a seat, Pan Górski.' She must have seen him hesitate because she added, 'Anywhere you like.'

He took a chair roughly halfway along the nearest row. She sat beside him, turning to face him, then put on her glasses and opened her notebook.

'How well did you know Jakub Frydman?' she began, without preamble.

'Well enough. He taught my sister the piano. My parents invited him and his wife over for dinner on occasion.'

'Did you learn the piano, too?'

'I must confess I didn't. I had no aptitude for it.'

Pola rested her gaze on his. 'Why do you think someone would throw a wreath packed with explosives into a grave?'

'Unless it was a sick anti-Semitic statement, the only conclusion I can come to is that the intention was to kill one of the guests.'

He saw the interest flicker on her face. 'And who do you think the intended victim was?'

'I've no idea. I didn't know the other guests, except Pan Mazur.'

'With this fog around, I don't suppose you caught a glimpse of the person throwing the wreath,' Pola said, writing.

'As a matter of fact, I did.'

Her head jerked up. She was so close Marek could see the flecks in her irises.

'He was behind me when he threw it,' Marek went on. 'I turned round and saw his face. He was as close to me as you are now.'

The remark prompted her to lean back, which hadn't been his intention.

'What did he look like?' she said, scribbling again.

'I couldn't see his hair because he was wearing a cap. But he had blue eyes, and a wide mouth. The skin was slightly pock-marked around the nose.'

'Your powers of observation are excellent.'

'I'm an investigative journalist. I've been trained to memorise facial features. But what will help you find him is that he had burn scars here.' He ran a finger across his left cheek.

Pola stopped writing. Her gaze sharpened. 'Would you work with an artist to recreate this man's face?'

'Of course. I've done it before with the Dundee police. They use something called E-FIT. It stands for Electronic Facial Identification Technique.'

'We use it, too. Please come with me,' she said, getting to her feet. She hurried out of the room, Marek following.

On the top floor, she opened the door into a well-lit open-plan area. The hum of activity reached Marek's ears, reminding him of West Bell Street. Some officers were speaking into their phones, others tapping at their keyboards. Pola looked round the room until she found the person she was looking for. 'Stefan,' she called across.

The officer at the window glanced up. He had startling blue eyes, and a shaven head with a thin plait at the nape of the neck. Seeing Marek, he got to his feet.

'Can you get the E-FIT started?' Pola said, using the familiar form of the word 'you'.

He straightened. 'Sure.'

She made the introductions. 'Pan Górski will be working with us,' she added.

The men shook hands, and Stefan pulled out a couple of chairs.

'Is it a man or a woman, Pan Górski?' he said, switching on a large tablet.

'A man.'

Stefan worked quickly and accurately, following Marek's instructions and suggestions. Marek had seen the process many times but was always astounded at how an image was created. Stefan began with the basics such as the head shape, the eyes and nose. The skin tone came next, including the pockmarks. The burn scars presented more of a challenge but Stefan worked tirelessly until Marek was satisfied.

He held out the device. 'Tell me what you think. Take your time.'

'Can you make him a little older?'

'No problem.'

'I didn't see his hair because he was wearing a cap.'

Pola nodded at the tablet. 'He'll take it off when he sees this, but it will be too late by then.'

Marek gave Stefan a description of the type of cap the man had been wearing. It was a common enough piece of headwear.

'Yes, that's him,' Marek said finally. 'No question.'

The officers looked at him appreciatively. 'You've done us a great service, Pan Górski,' Pola said.

'Only too happy to help.'

'I'll see if I can get this into the *Express Wieczorny*.'

'The evening paper?' Marek said. He was about to add 'good luck with that' when it occurred to him that maybe it could be done faster in Poland.

Stefan was looking at him curiously. 'Haven't I read about you in the papers? You're the journalist from Scotland who's looking for this missing Chopin manuscript.'

'That's right.'

Pola smiled. She kicked off a slipper, and massaged her big toe. 'We'll have to invite you back to give us a talk. Everyone here would be interested in how you picked up the trail.'

'I need to find the manuscript first. And I must confess I didn't get this far single-handed. Someone in Warsaw pointed me in the right direction.'

He could tell they were intrigued. But, then, wouldn't detectives be? Wasn't it that desire to solve a puzzle that made them join up in the first place? And had made him become an investigative journalist?

Pola handed him her card. 'If you think of anything else that might be relevant, please call me.' She tugged on the slipper and stood up. 'I'll take you down to the entrance.'

They passed several officers on the flights of steps, but no one gave her footwear a second glance.

At the main door, she thanked him once more, addressing him as Pan Górski. He very much wanted her to call him by his first name, but etiquette required she make the first move and suggest it. And she hadn't.

CHAPTER 4

'You're sure it's Amatol?' Maks said.

The elderly scientist threw him a look of contempt, probably wondering why the young upstart had had the temerity to question his judgement. 'There's no doubt,' he said, his voice level. 'It's not as if this is the first time we've come across it.'

Maks nodded, not wanting to provoke the man. When it came to explosives, there was no better expert at the police's Central Forensic Laboratory.

'Given the relative percentages of TNT and ammonium nitrate, it's highly likely to be from war-era unexploded ordnance,' the man went on, 'which, as I'm sure you know, is regularly unearthed by construction workers. Along with human remains from the 'forty-four Uprising.'

Unearthed, and sold on the black market. Maks had seen such cases before. At least he now knew where to concentrate his resources.

The scientist was studying him, a shrewd expression in his eyes. 'Given the dimensions of that Amatol-packed wreath, the kill radius would have been of the order of fifty metres.'

'*Jezus Maria*,' Maks muttered. 'It's a miracle those guests survived. What about the fuse? There must have been a time delay.'

'I suggest you call in on Roman. He's expecting you. I'll send over my report before I leave today.'

Maks thanked the man formally, then left the laboratory and negotiated the corridors to the other side of the building. He found the door, and knocked loudly.

'Come in, Maks,' said a man's voice.

Maks pushed open the door. 'How did you know it was me?' he said, with a grin.

The officer was an old pal. They'd met at a speedway course and become firm friends, even though Maks had persevered with the course, and Roman hadn't. Losing control of the motorcycle and skidding into the boundary wall had dampened his enthusiasm to the extent that he'd vowed never again to ride a motorcycle without brakes.

'How did I know it was you?' Roman said, swivelling his chair to face Maks. 'It's the way you advertise yourself. Most people give three knocks, but for some reason you give four.'

'I hadn't noticed.'

'You wouldn't. You always have something else on your mind.' He ran a hand through his blonde hair. 'You've been working out, my friend. I can tell you've put on muscle.'

The remark caused the red-haired assistant at the window to glance up and smile. She continued her work, bending over the microscope, adjusting the controls with one hand and writing with the other. Maks admired how the opposite sex could multitask with such ease, especially when it involved a degree of manual dexterity. Pola was the same. He'd discussed it with her once, complaining God had not treated the male sex – and him in particular – fairly in this respect. Pola had thrown him an old-fashioned look, and told him he'd never have become a speedway champion unless he'd been able to control the vehicle, keep himself on it, make sure he didn't crash into the other competitors, and all at the same time. Wasn't that multi-tasking?

'So, what have you got?' Maks said, addressing Roman.

'I've laid everything out for you.'

On the table was an assortment of charred, twisted metal fragments.

'It was easier to scan them than try to fit them together by hand,' he added. 'The software is much better at that. And this is what it gave us.' He played with the controls on the tablet. 'Have a look.'

Maks slipped into the seat beside him. He recognised the image immediately. 'It's a detonator.'

'Go to the top of the class. But, then, you've seen this type before.'

'Set off by a signal from a mobile phone.'

'Correct. You can find instructions on how to build it on that wonderful invention called the internet.' Roman's gaze sharpened. 'You think it's the usual suspects? Our friends in construction?'

'War-era Amatol? It's our friends, no question. The problem is there are so many it's difficult to know where to start.'

'These air-dropped bombs are the most dangerous.' Roman shook his head. 'I've never understood why construction workers don't find another line of work. The irony of being killed by a German bomb, seventy-five years after the event, because your shovel has scraped the metal shell or the fuse attachment.'

'The workers must think it's worth the risk. Selling Amatol to the bad guys is highly lucrative.'

Roman threw him a sympathetic look. 'You're going to have your work cut out, my friend. I don't envy you. So, where are you going to start? The construction industry? Or the bad guys?'

Maks scratched his chin. 'Both, I think.'

'Excellent idea. A two-pronged attack.' He winked. 'Go for it.'

It was dark by the time Maks returned to Mostowski Palace. He called the team together and went through what he'd learnt at Forensics. No one looked surprised to hear the explosive was Amatol.

'So, we need to start questioning our construction workers,' Maks finished.

'There are several companies operating in Warsaw,' someone ventured. 'We'll have to prioritise them.'

'I suggest we concentrate on those in the centre. Forget the Praga district, at least until we've covered the rest of the city.'

Praga, on the east bank of the river Vistula, had remained relatively untouched by the war. It had suffered bombardment in 1939, but escaped the destruction of the rest of the city, specifically the many Luftwaffe bombings during the Uprising. Consequently, fewer unexploded bombs were unearthed there. The Amatol used in recent crimes had been sold on the sly by construction workers employed in the city centre.

'What about criminal gangs?' Pola said.

'Most of their crimes are finance-related. When they kill, they use knives or guns. I can't see them behind this incident with the wreath. No, I think we're looking for an individual who targeted one of the guests at the funeral.'

'And killing all the mourners would make it difficult for us to establish which one.'

'Exactly. But the problem is the perpetrator had little time to come up with a plan. Jakub Frydman's death notices go up on Monday morning. The perpetrator hears the news on the radio, and immediately orders the wreath. He'd have to know his intended victim would be at the funeral.'

Pola opened her file. 'I've gone through the interviews. With the exception of Marek Górski, all the other mourners had been Frydman's pupils.' She looked up. 'And, apart from the Górskis, they're all residents of Warsaw. If our unexpected guest knew of the connection between his victim and Jakub Frydman, he'd have assumed – no, he'd have known – the victim would attend his funeral.'

'We need background checks on the guests,' Maks said. 'Start at the Institute of National Remembrance. See if they hold their records from the Communist era. And check if the archives have anything on Jakub Frydman. Danuta Górska said he was a member of Solidarity.'

'What about Rabin Steinberg?' someone said.

'He'd been a pupil of Frydman's, too,' Pola replied. 'So, the perpetrator would have expected him there, either as a mourner or as the rabbi conducting the service. Maybe he was the intended victim.' She paused. 'An anti-Semitic attack?'

'We'll keep all avenues open,' Maks said. 'What about the custodian at the cemetery? Who interviewed her?'

'I did,' Pola said.

'Did she see the unexpected guest?'

'She said she saw no one carrying a wreath.'

'I find that hard to believe. You have to walk past her booth to get to the graves.'

'She's lived under the Communists, don't forget. Her generation's used to seeing and hearing nothing.' Pola shrugged. 'Anyway, it would have been too foggy for her to see him clearly.'

'Except he'd have asked for directions,' Maks pressed. 'Unless, of course, he entered the cemetery by another route.'

'There's an easy way in on Młynarska Street,' someone chipped in. 'Part of the wall is missing. He'd have had time to scout the place.'

'Actually,' Pola said, 'none of this is relevant. We've had an excellent description of the unexpected guest.'

They stared at her.

'We have an E-FIT, courtesy of Marek Górski. He saw the man's face because he turned to look at him. The image will be in this evening's *Express Wieczorny*.'

'Thanks to your contact there, I'm guessing,' Maks said, enjoying the look of mild embarrassment on her face. Everyone knew the editor, a widower nearing retirement, had completely lost his head over her. He was too much of a gentleman to make a move, thinking it would spoil their excellent working relationship.

'So, let's see this image,' Maks added.

Pola handed out prints of the E-FIT. 'The main thing to note are his burn scars. Someone must recognise those.'

'And hopefully be prepared to give him up,' Maks said, studying the image. 'Okay, you know what to do.'

They left the office.

'Pola,' Maks said, calling her back.

'Yes?'

'What did you tell the editor of the *Express Wieczorny*?'

'This is the man we want to question in connection with the explosion at Okopowa. I was careful not to say how we came by the image.' She must have seen the frown on his face. 'Did I do something wrong?'

'No, you did right. We need to find this man. I was just thinking if Marek Górski was close enough to get a good look at his face . . .'

Pola said it for him. '. . . then *he* would have been close enough to get a good look at Marek Górski's.'

'And he's likely to know who Marek Górski is because his photo has been in all the papers.'

Pola left Maks's office, the thoughts whirring round in her mind. It bothered her she might have put Marek Górski's life in danger by getting that E-FIT image into the evening paper. Yet what else could she have done? They needed to find the scarred man, and getting his picture out there might give them their only lead. But she was being too judgemental. The perpetrator might not assume it was Marek who'd given the police a physical description. It could have been the custodian. She hadn't been prepared to tell the police much, and the more Pola had pressed her, the more she'd clammed up. Although the woman had denied seeing the unexpected guest, Pola knew she was lying.

She made her way to her office, and powered down the computer. Tomorrow she'd arrive early and arrange the quotas. They had a huge task ahead of them: background checks and interviewing. And that was for starters. But tonight, she was off shift. And there was somewhere she intended to be. She kicked off the slippers and pulled on the fur-lined boots. As she zipped them up, she remembered she'd eaten nothing that day. It would have to be the soup she'd made in bulk and kept in the freezer. She grabbed the thick woollen coat off the door peg and hurried out.

An hour later, she'd finished her bowl of *żurek*, the sour rye soup served with hard-boiled egg she'd fallen in love with as a child. She showered, then put on her make-up, which she never bothered with normally. Her outfit – short black skirt, long jacket and an ice-white blouse with a starched butterfly collar – was hanging ready. The finishing touch was the signature red bow tie. She piled her hair on top of her head, knotting it tightly. Then, taking care not to disturb the knots, she slipped on the long, red wig with the thick fringe she'd had made especially, tugging it firmly into place. Each time she wore it, she thought of her grandmother who, like all elderly women who'd wanted to colour their hair, had had to dye it this shade of red, as it was the only colour available in Communist Poland. Pola studied her reflection. She was unrecognisable.

She slipped into the black stilettos, and left the building. Her apartment was in a dreary, graffiti-covered block not far from the Palace of Culture and Science. The general neglect by the landlord ensured the rent was cheap. Everything from the plaster walls to the threadbare carpets was in either Communist brown or beige, the kitchen was tiny, and the heavy wooden furniture dated from an even earlier period. Pola couldn't decide whether the pieces were antiques, and worth good money, but it made no difference as the furniture wasn't hers. The heating worked, although the loud hum and rattle when it started would put off many apartment-hunters, which was why she'd got the place relatively easily. And it suited her well enough. The public transport links were excellent, since the building was near the main railway station and the tram stop was only a short walk away. Which was just as well: trekking down the two flights of stairs from her apartment was enough to make her squashed toes squeal in pain.

The fog had cleared completely and, had it not been for the tall buildings with their illuminated windows, she'd have glimpsed the spatter of glowing stars. But this part of the city was famous for its skyscrapers with their award-winning designs, and it was only in the small hours that it was dark enough to see the night sky.

She rode the tram south towards the Old Mokotów district, a wooded residential area, although the trees had long since shed their leaves. After leaving the tram, she walked for several minutes, then turned into a narrow road. She counted off the doors, and pressed the buzzer on the intercom. When she heard a voice, she stated who she was, and waited for the click that would admit her. The door, which led into an entrance hall, swung open.

With one hand on the rail, she took the stairs to the basement, hearing the snatches of conversation grow louder. As she entered the room, the smell of stale cigarette smoke told her her audience had been waiting. The basement was well lit, with state-of-the-art strip lighting running the length of the ceiling. The plaster walls had been finished in moon grey, and at the side a long table served as a makeshift bar.

Groups of well-dressed men were standing around chatting. As they caught sight of her, the conversation stopped. A man in a cream suit and dark shirt approached, smiling. After greeting her with a bow, he removed a small silver case from his jacket pocket. It contained her favourite brand of cigarillo. She thanked him and picked one out, waiting as he snapped open a lighter. He lit the cigarillo, his gaze never leaving her face. She smiled, then made her way to the bar, where a small glass of *wiśniówka* was waiting for her. Cherry vodka was her drink of choice, and this place served the best in Warsaw. As the sweet, searing liquid slipped down her throat, she was glad she'd had a couple of slices of bread with her soup. *Wiśniówka* had a habit of fogging the brain, and she needed her wits about her tonight. The barman lifted the bottle questioningly, but she shook her head.

She turned and surveyed the room. The men were watching her expectantly. One was seated at a small table. He had prematurely greying hair and alert blue eyes, and his expression was one of invitation.

She took a quick breath, and addressed the room. 'Gentlemen,' she said, making her voice husky, 'shall we begin?'

CHAPTER 5

Dania handed her passport to the policeman at the checkpoint. 'I have a meeting with Inspector Dolniak,' she said.

'One moment, please.' The man studied his roster. 'Pani Górska. Eleven thirty. You're early, I see.'

She looked up at Mostowski Palace's creamy-yellow façade. 'I wasn't sure which part of the building the inspector's room is in. And I hate being late.'

'Me, too,' he said, smiling conspiratorially. 'I'll phone through and tell the inspector you've arrived.'

A few minutes later, a uniformed policeman appeared. He gave a slight bow and asked Dania to accompany him. She followed him through a large courtyard into the building, where they took the stairs to the top floor. He led her along several wide, blue-walled corridors, and it was only by glancing through the windows on to the courtyard that she was able to orient herself.

The officer stopped abruptly, and knocked at a door. Without waiting for a reply, he opened it, and stood back to let Dania pass.

The long room had a desk at one end and a table at the other. It was painted in shades of the same quiet blue-grey as the walls in the corridor. The only other colour in the room was from the red shield mounted on the wall. Its white eagle, the national symbol of Poland for more than a thousand years, had lost its crown when the Communists took control. The crown was restored only in 1989, when Poland regained its sovereignty. Dania was old enough to have seen examples of white eagles that a decade later were still waiting for their stolen crowns.

The man at the desk glanced up, then sprang to his feet. 'Ah, Pani Górska? We haven't met. I'm Oskar Dolniak.' He hurried round to where she was standing, took her hand and kissed it lightly. 'Please, do take a seat,' he said, pulling out a chair.

'Thank you.'

When they were settled, he leant forward, his hands clasped. 'I'm sorry I haven't been able to see you before now.'

'I understand. Anti-drugs units are busy.'

'And getting busier,' he said, with feeling. He removed a sheet from his folder. 'So, before you can work with the Polish police, you'll need to sign this.' He rolled his eyes. 'The usual formalities. Perhaps you could read through it, and then, if you're happy, please date and sign it.'

Dania cast her eyes over the text, then added the date and her signature. 'Excellent,' he said, inserting it at the back of the folder. He removed another sheet. 'Now, according to your communication, you suspect members of one of your drugs syndicates have come to Warsaw.' He scanned the page. 'You sent us a list of names, and the flight they were on.' He looked squarely at her. 'Why do you think these are the men you are after?'

'It was a block booking made the day before one of my people was murdered. I think they knew we were on to them. I'd hoped to take the next flight out, but my presence was required in court the following week.' She could still remember the heated discussion she'd had with DCI Jackie Ireland. The woman had understood, but there was no question about it: Dania would attend the hearing. It wasn't often she and the DCI crossed swords. She'd left the office feeling bruised.

'I've had my people check the names,' Oskar said. 'These Poles did indeed arrive on that flight to Warsaw's Chopin airport.' He ran a hand over his scalp. 'But, after that, there's no record of them.'

'Magda – my informant – told me they have a number of false passports.' Dania recognised the hunted look on Oskar's face: he was close to giving up. Before he could tell her there was nothing further he could do, she added, 'The leader of the group wears a chain round his neck. The Syrenka.'

Oskar nodded respectfully. He loosened his tie, then unbuttoned his shirt and pulled out something that flashed silver. 'Many Varsovians wear the Syrenka,' he said.

'He's known as Merkury,' she persisted.

Now she had his interest. 'A pseudonym?' he said. 'Bad guys love pseudonyms. Some even use ones from the Uprising. I've come across a few who had them tattooed on their arms or shoulders. Is it the same in Scotland?'

'Not in the way it is here.'

'My grandfather was in the Home Army. His pseudonym was Mamut.'

'Mammoth? That's a good one. My grandmother's was Sacharyna. Saccharine.'

'The younger officers here have started to adopt pseudonyms.' He straightened his tie. 'But this isn't helping you.'

'There's one other thing I should tell you. When Merkury disposes of his enemies he does it in a particular way. He cuts their throats so deeply the head is almost severed.'

Oskar looked at her for a long moment. Then he turned to the computer screen. 'I remember a similar case. A jogger found a body washed up at the side of the river. It had been in the water too long, and was badly swollen. The throat was cut in the way you describe.'

'When was this?'

He tapped at the keyboard. 'Almost exactly a year ago. It was Maks's case. He never found the perpetrator.' Oskar glanced up. 'How long has this Merkury been operating in Dundee?'

'About nine months. We were lucky to have someone infiltrate the group. She managed to get some useful intel.'

'But not Merkury's real name.'

'She knew better than to ask.'

'What kind of drugs did Merkury peddle?'

'Only heroin.' Dania leant forward, 'Look, Inspector, if Merkury did indeed fly out on November the nineteenth, and it's now December the third, he's been back in Warsaw for two weeks. Have you seen renewed activity in the past fortnight? A new gang starting up, perhaps?'

'It's the run-down part of Praga that's the hotspot for drug dealing. There are many abandoned buildings. I'd need to check my reports, but the heroin trade is pretty constant.'

'Do you have people on the inside? Merkury could have thrown in with an established syndicate.'

'I have a few. We've caught some of the middle men that way. But it's the one at the top we want. And can't identify,' he added, with a thin smile. 'Let me show you what we've got.' He produced a pack of playing cards from the desk drawer, and laid them out, face up. They were aces, kings, queens and jacks. But instead of the customary images, there were men's faces. Except the Ace of Spades, which had a large question mark.

'These are what you might call the usual suspects,' Oskar said. 'Some we have evidence against, but they've disappeared, possibly left Warsaw. Others are mere suspects and we can't arrest them, although we have them under surveillance. But this one,' he said, tapping the Ace of Spades, 'is the man we're after. We believe he's at the head of the heroin import into, and distribution within, Warsaw.'

'And no one's been able to come up with a name?'

'The people lower down don't know his identity.'

'He sounds like our Merkury. My informant told me he disappears occasionally.'

Oskar frowned, deepening the lines in his forehead. 'Do you have a description?'

Dania was conscious she was starting to sound desperate. 'Magda said he was handsome, with mid-brown hair and pale eyes. But that could describe any of the Poles in Dundee.'

'And are things as bad in Dundee as when I was there?'

'When was this?' she said, in surprise.

'About three years ago. I worked with your Drugs Squad trying to establish supply chains. We thought the drugs coming into Warsaw were sourced from Dundee. I must say I was impressed with the set-up. And with the city. I was asked to give a talk to the students at the university.'

'Which one? We have two.'

'Ah, yes, it was the University of Dundee. I was asked to emphasise how drugs can ruin a person's life. I brought along a couple of case studies. The students listened politely, but their questions were more about what life is like in Poland now the Communists have been booted out. And will Brexit make it harder to get work there. They were a friendly bunch.' He grinned. 'They offered to take me round the Dundee bars afterwards.'

'And did you go?'

Oskar looked scandalised. 'It would have been rude to refuse.

We ended up in a hotel. I remember it was called the Hampton. We more or less took over the bar.'

'How did you get on with the Dundee accent?'

'Impossible to understand. But there was a Polish student who acted as translator.'

Dania laughed. 'How did the evening end?'

'I left them sleeping on the sofas.' A look of puzzlement crossed his face. 'It was strange. A few glasses of Polish vodka and they fell asleep.'

Dania had had a similar experience at the Metropolitan Police in London. She'd sourced a bottle of Sobieski rye vodka and invited colleagues over for drinks. A short while later, she was helping her tottering guests into taxis.

'How long will you be in Warsaw, Pani Górska?'

'I'm flying home next Friday.'

'If there's been an increase in activity, it will be in the reports. I'll be in touch as soon as I've checked.' Oskar tapped the desk with his pen. 'But I'd talk to Inspector Robak about the body in the river. He may have more information. He's in the building today, as far as I'm aware. I'll ask one of my men to accompany you to his office.'

Marek had finished lunch and was in the kitchen, gazing into his laptop. He'd received a communication from his contact, whom he knew only by the pseudonym Baletnica, or Ballerina. It was an interesting choice of pseudonym, given that, in a language as highly inflected as Polish, the forms of some words immediately established Baletnica's gender as male.

He'd been incredibly lucky to find this source. Except Baletnica had been the one to find him. Marek had made his acquaintance online a couple of years earlier when an email had landed in his mailbox tipping him off about a forthcoming visit to Scotland by one of Poland's ministers. It transpired this man was making secret deals with the Russians to undermine the Polish government. The proof obtained by Baletnica and passed on to Marek seemed irrefutable, and he knew people in Poland who could check it. Baletnica had made clear he wasn't in a position to take this further himself, and Marek totally understood his reasons. It was the elemental fear Poles have of Russians. So, he'd agreed to take it on. During the subsequent email exchanges, Baletnica had suggested they adopt the familiar form of the word 'you' along with its associations. It wasn't long before Marek began to imagine himself as a Cold War spy communicating with his handler.

His article – written under his preferred *nom de plume* of Franek Filarski – had been rejected by DC Thomson as too explosive. His editor, however, intrigued by the content, had urged Marek to put it out online, but in such a way it couldn't be traced either to himself or to DC Thomson. In a matter of hours, the article had been copied many thousands of times, resulting in the disgrace and ultimate resignation of the minister.

Baletnica had been effusive in his thanks. And that was the last Marek had heard. Until another email had landed in his inbox asking whether he'd be interested in tracking down some unknown letters of Chopin's. Again, Baletnica had been cagey about how he'd come by the information but, as he'd delivered the goods before, Marek had decided it would be worth the time to pursue this. His editor had agreed. So, for the next few months, Marek had communicated regularly with Baletnica, who provided him with the results of his ongoing research. Not everything moved the investigation forward, however, making Marek wonder how his contact was coming by the information.

He was on the point of giving up when he received an urgent email from Baletnica. It led him to what had been the private library of a Warsaw collector of rare books. Some collections had survived the war, thanks to the dedication of the city's library directors, who rescued books from houses destroyed in the first wave of bombing and brought them to the libraries for safekeeping. The Germans, on occupying Warsaw, had seized these books along with the collections in the university and the National Library, among others. After the Uprising, and up to the end of the Occupation, they continued their destruction of the city, including burning the contents of libraries.

But not everything was destroyed, and Baletnica had it on good authority that in the Wola district Marek would find Chopin's letters. In further emails, he was able to narrow down the location to one of three possible apartment blocks. The letters were among a collection of books most likely hidden in the basement of one of the buildings. Marek had flown out on the next plane, and had wasted no time in finding the first street on Baletnica's list. The high brick building stood derelict between two modern apartment blocks, its balconies intact and the ground-floor windows boarded up. As with many buildings in Wola, the bullet holes in the walls were a testament to the executions of civilians.

The crumbling archway led into a wide courtyard. The wind had piled litter against the walls, although even in Poland it wasn't strong enough to shift the broken bottles. The lower windows weren't covered but were protected with bars, whose paint was peeling off. The walls were defaced with graffiti, but the artist had been careful to avoid spraying near the *kotwica*, the famous anchor-like emblem of the Polish Underground. The *kotwica*, formed from the superimposed letters P and W, came to represent the phrase '*Polska Walcząca*', or 'fighting Poland'. As a child, Marek had seen it on the few buildings that had survived, and on the growing number of plaques recognising Resistance activity. He'd been sufficiently intrigued to make it the subject of a school project, and had discovered it was the winning design in a contest run by the Home Army. The winner, a Girl Scout, whose pseudonym was Hania, was later arrested.

In the corner of the courtyard was a wooden door. Marek fingered the padlock, which was rusted through, then gave it a sharp tug. It came away in his hands. He paused to listen, but the only sound was from the passing traffic. He pulled the handle. The door opened partway, then refused to budge, but with some effort he pushed his way inside, leaving the door open. The short hallway ended in a flight of steps, which curved upwards. But to the left, hanging off one hinge, was a door. Beyond, stone steps disappeared down into darkness.

Surprised he'd found the basement so easily, Marek switched on his torch. He pulled at the door, which fell off the hinge with a clatter. His heart thudding, he waited for the sound of running boots, but once the echoes of the crash had died away silence returned.

There was no banister so, with one hand against the wall, he descended slowly, hearing something crunching beneath his feet. The light from the torch bobbed on the steps, illuminating broken glass and bits of debris. He reached the basement and swung the torch round. The large room had brick walls and a low ceiling, and was about thirty metres square. What made his heart sink was that it was crammed with junk. There was probably a light switch, but he had a feeling the electricity to the building had long since been disconnected. He fished inside his rucksack for the head torch.

He positioned it, and switched it on, adjusting it so the beam was straight. It was one of the best on the market, and surprisingly powerful. As he turned his head, the light illuminated discarded furniture, planks, rolled-up carpets. Even a rusty bicycle frame, missing its wheels. He'd leave nothing to chance. The upholstery would have to be prodded and cut open, the furniture examined for secret panels, and the carpets unrolled. There was an acrid, dusty smell, but the place didn't have a damp feel about it, which could work for him, as damp paper had a habit of falling apart.

Marek worked systematically for the best part of two hours. One item he came across was a yellowing copy of *Biuletyn Informacyjny*, the Polish Underground's weekly. It was dated March 1943, and was taped under one of the drawers in an oak sideboard. The tape was starting to perish, and the wood beetles were making a good fist of shredding the paper.

He was wondering if it was time to abandon the search, and try one of the other buildings on Baletnica's list, when his gaze fell upon something in the corner. He'd have missed it had he not been on his knees, as it was hidden behind coarse planking. He moved the wood aside. Behind was a large packing crate covered with coarse sacking. After several attempts at prising off the lid, he levered up a corner and yanked it back sharply. It splintered with a painful crack. He pulled away the shards of wood, seeing inside a piece of red felt, faded and musty-smelling.

Under the felt were books, books and more books. This had to be where the Chopin letters were hidden. His heart beating wildly, he lifted out a leather-bound volume. It was *Heart of Darkness* by Polish author Joseph Conrad. He'd written it in English, and this was a Polish translation.

Next came the complete works of Henryk Sienkiewicz, one of Poland's Nobel laureates. A glance through the pages told Marek these were first editions signed by the author. What they were worth he had no idea. He'd never read Sienkiewicz, although he'd seen the Hollywood film of *Quo Vadis*. Carefully, so as not to damage them, he flicked through the pages of each volume looking for Chopin's letters. Next was *The Promised Land* by another Polish Nobel laureate, Władysław Reymont, and a book Marek *had* read. Set in the textile city of Łódź, it told the story of three men, a Pole, a German and a Jew, who go into business together. Again, a search through the pages revealed nothing.

He worked his way through the remaining volumes until he reached the bottom of the crate. There, sandwiched between two pieces of red felt, was a wooden puzzle box. These boxes, which he remembered from his childhood, were hand decorated and stained or painted. This one, however, was adorned with exquisite brass inlays. Through the centuries, the boxes had been gifted to the royal families of Europe, who hid their treasures inside. But to open them, you had to know the trick, which could involve sliding, unlocking, rotating, et cetera. If the Chopin letters were in this crate, they had to be inside this box. Marek felt his heart jump at the thought. But rather than waste time trying to open it here, he'd take it to his parents' apartment. If he was proved wrong, well, there were two more apartments he could search the following day.

He put the box into his rucksack, replaced the books and piled the planks around the crate. He'd look suspicious leaving the courtyard wearing a head torch, so that followed the box into the rucksack. He was about to switch on the hand torch when he became aware of the stealthy sound of footsteps. They came from the floor above. He froze. Instinct made him crouch behind a chest of drawers. The footsteps grew louder, then stopped. A shape blotted out the light trickling in from the hallway.

Marek felt a pricking on the back of his hands. Whoever it was appeared undecided about braving the dark cellar without a torch.

After what seemed an eternity, the light from the hallway reappeared. The footsteps receded, finally fading altogether.

Marek waited several minutes before emerging from his hiding place. He slipped the torch into his pocket, and made his way across the room by feeling the outlines of the objects. His heart beating wildly, he climbed the steps, placing his feet carefully and trying not to make a sound. In the hallway, he looked back towards the front door, which he remembered having left open. It was closed. Whoever he'd heard had either come in or gone out that way. Or both.

Marek hurried out of the building. The courtyard was deserted, as was the street beyond. Dusk was stealing over the city, and he was tempted to race back to his parents' apartment. But something made him linger. There were no cars or trams. No cyclists. He peered up and down the street but could see no one. Yet the hairs on the back of his neck told him he was being watched. It was time to leave. On the main road, he took the metro to the Muranów district and walked the short distance to the apartment.

He spent the next hour trying to open the box. Part of him was tempted to take a hammer to the thing, but he'd heard of boxes that had Indiana Jones-type booby traps designed to destroy the contents. It was only after his parents had returned from shopping and his father had played with it for a while that his patience was rewarded. His mother brought in glasses of tea. She took one look at the box, and opened it by rotating three of the feet one way and the fourth the other. They stared at her. She shrugged, saying it was obvious.

Marek lifted the lid. The box was lined with bronze-coloured satin. Inside, lying on red felt, a bundle of letters was tied with a fraying red ribbon. With trembling fingers, he worked at the knot. There were six letters, three with an address in Scotland, and three in Paris. He squinted at the first envelope, studying the address: 9 place d'Orléans. One of Chopin's Paris apartments! Slowly, he teased out the letter. It was dated 9 April 1845, and was written in French. He was conscious of his parents' gaze as they sipped the tea. But, Marek, weren't these just letters? They'd seen others in the Chopin Museum, and anyway there was a film on television they wanted to watch. He decided it would be best to study them elsewhere.

He carried everything to his bedroom and read the letters slowly, although he was accustomed to cursive script. It was Chopin's last letter that caused the blood to rush to his ears. The composer had written: *How I wish that my third piano concerto could be performed here in Paris. But I fear I will never hear it played.*

He powered up the laptop and sent a message to Baletnica, notifying him the mission had been a resounding success. It was disappointing there were no clues in the letters as to the location of the missing concerto, but Baletnica promised to continue his researches and would be in touch when he had something concrete. Marek added that in a crate in the corner of the basement there was a collection of books, many of which were first editions, some signed by the author. Baletnica promised to deal with them, which Marek took to mean have them donated to one of Warsaw's libraries. Given the mass executions in the Wola district, it was unlikely there were living descendants to claim them.

But his euphoria at finding the letters soon evaporated. Who was the figure he'd seen silhouetted at the top of the basement steps? Was it a passer-by who'd spotted him clandestinely entering the building, and decided to check up on him? Unlikely. Marek had been there for two hours. Why wait so long before peering into the basement? As he mulled over the possibilities, the thought drifted into his head that someone else was after the letters. And what they contained. But could Baletnica be sharing his information with another investigator? Perhaps hedging his bets in the hope that, if Marek didn't find the letters and the concerto, this other person would? Of course it was possible, yet after thinking through his interactions with Baletnica, he rejected the hypothesis. And that meant only one thing – the path Baletnica was following in his researches was being followed by someone else. Marek toyed with the idea of sharing this conclusion with his contact but decided against it. It might silence the man completely. And that was the last thing he wanted. But the more he thought about it, the more he began to suspect there was a much simpler explanation. Even an uninhabited building had a caretaker, whose job it was to check on the state of the place, and report back to the authorities if, for example, the ceilings were falling in and it was becoming unsafe. Marek had left the door to the courtyard open. It would have attracted attention from someone doing the rounds. Yes, that would be it.

Now, months later, back in his parents' apartment, Marek sat staring at the latest message from Baletnica, asking him to be patient. It was clear from the tone of the email that, although the man was trying to firm up on where in Warsaw the manuscript was located, he was getting nowhere.

Marek puffed out his cheeks and read the message again. He needed the type of intel that had led him to the Chopin letters. He emailed Baletnica, asking when he'd have the information.

But Baletnica had disconnected.

CHAPTER 6

Dania left Mostowski Palace, uncertain how to proceed. Maksymilian Robak hadn't been in his office, and his associates had no idea when he'd return. She'd tried his number, but her call went to voicemail. There was nothing more she could do except wait for Oskar Dolniak to get back to her.

She strolled along the street named for Ludwik Zamenhof, then turned on to Dzielna. There were fewer cars parked on the road because, now the fog had lifted, Varsovians were willing to risk driving. She felt out of sorts. Her reason for coming to Warsaw was to hunt down Merkury, but it was looking increasingly unlikely that that would happen. She had less than a week before she returned to Dundee and, although Oskar Dolniak had offered his help, he had little to go on. And now there was this dreadful business at Okopowa Street.

She reached her parents' apartment block, and rode the lift to the top floor.

'Is that you, Danka?' Marek called from the kitchen.

'Reporting for duty.'

He glanced up as she entered.

'Have you eaten?' she said.

'I had something light. I thought we could go out this evening.'

'What did you have in mind?' she said, opening the fridge.

'We could find a restaurant near Wilanów, and then go and see the Christmas lights.'

'Good idea,' she said listlessly. She rummaged around at the back of the fridge and found the cheese and smoked sausage.

'You don't sound too enthusiastic.' Marek got to his feet. 'Here, I'll cut the bread.'

'I'm getting nowhere,' she said, watching him slice the dark rye loaf he bought when in Warsaw.

'Be kind to yourself. You've only been here a week.'

'And I'm flying back to Dundee in a week's time. I was naïve to think the police would know who Merkury is.'

'Did you learn *anything* from the Anti-drugs unit?'

'Warsaw has a drugs kingpin of its own, and the police don't know his identity. That's a lot of bread you're buttering, by the way.'

Marek grinned. 'I've decided to have a second lunch. You know what I'm like. I smell rye bread and Polish sausage, and I'm ravenous.'

She smiled. 'And what have you been up to?'

'I've had a communication from my contact. Oh, and have you seen yesterday's *Express Wieczorny?*' he said, arranging slices of sausage on the bread, and topping them with pieces of gherkin. 'The lady in the flat opposite gave me her copy. She knew we'd been to Jakub Frydman's funeral and thought we'd be interested.' He gestured to the dresser. 'It's on the top.'

'What am I looking for?'

'Try page three.'

Dania flattened out the newspaper and turned the page. The face of a man in a peaked cap stared out at her. It was the scars on his left cheek that held her attention. She scanned the article.

The police were looking for this man in connection with Wednesday's explosion at Okopowa Street cemetery.

'They were quick off the mark,' Marek was saying. 'I worked with their E-FIT guy only yesterday afternoon.'

'So, this is the man with the wreath. You must have been close to have seen those scars.'

'I was lucky there. I expect someone's already phoned in with an ID.'

'Maybe that's why I was unable to get hold of Inspector Robak. He may be dealing with this. Perhaps he's arrested him.'

'Perhaps. So, why were you hoping to talk to the inspector?'

'Oskar Dolniak told me that a year ago a body was washed up on the bank of the Vistula. The throat was cut in the way Merkury does it.'

'The head hanging off, you mean?'

'That's one way of putting it.' She bit into her sandwich. 'I'll try him again tomorrow.'

'Assuming he's on duty.'

'He told me to phone him at any time. I say the same to people I'm interviewing. Police don't really go off duty, do they?' she added, with a crooked smile.

'Neither do journalists. Where's the mileage in making yourself unavailable?'

'So, now you're having your second lunch, can you tell me where you found the Jane Stirling letters?'

'It was Wola.'

'But where exactly?'

'In the basement of an abandoned pre-war building. You know that puzzle box in the living room? The letters were inside.' He hesitated. 'Something strange happened while I was in that basement, Danka.'

So, he'd decided to confide in her. 'Tell me while I make the coffee,' she said.

As Dania busied herself, she listened to Marek's account of how he'd searched the basement, finding the puzzle box at the bottom of a crate. When he came to the figure at the top of the basement steps, she paused in what she was doing. Marek wasn't someone who embroidered his accounts. If anything, he toned them down. But it was clear that this incident was preying on his mind, and had been preying on it since it had occurred.

'How did you get home?' she said.

'Here, you mean? I took the metro, then walked.'

'Did you see anyone follow you? Did anyone get off at the same stop?'

'A few people did. It's a busy stop.'

'What about when you turned into Dzielna?'

'It was dark by then. There were people on the street, in front of me, behind me. On the opposite pavement.'

'Anyone acting suspiciously?'

'It's hard to define acting suspiciously when you can't see much in the dark.'

Dania brought the mugs to the table. 'What about the following day?'

'The following day, I flew back to Scotland with the letters.'

'This Baletnica, have you any idea how he sources his information?'

'I haven't asked. It's one of those unwritten rules with contacts. I'm sure it's the same with you. Anyway, I'm hoping that when I've found the manuscript he'll tell me.'

'Why wouldn't he tell you now? It's obvious he wants the manuscript found. If he told you how he gets his intel, you'd be able to hurry the process along. Two heads are better than one.'

Marek turned the mug in his hands. 'I doubt I'd be able to help. The intel comes in piecemeal. And it doesn't always lead anywhere. It's as if Baletnica is hearing bits of conversation. I imagine a student working in a library, desperately trying to listen to a group of professors whispering in a corner, and catching the odd word or phrase.'

'Have you tried to locate him? DC Thomson's tech department must be at least as good as ours.'

'He uses a VPN – a virtual private network. It's not difficult to set up things nowadays so you can't be traced. And when I happen to be online at the same time, he's rarely on for long.'

'To get back to this person you saw in the basement, what's your theory as to who it was?'

'At the time, I thought it was the caretaker. I'd left the main door open.'

'And now?'

He ran a hand through his hair. 'It's possible someone else is on the same trail. Maybe Baletnica isn't the only student who's overhearing what the professors are saying, to use my example.'

'You were in that basement for a good two hours. Do you think this person was already in the building when you showed up?'

'I heard nothing the whole time I was searching the place. He must have arrived minutes before I saw him.'

'Perhaps he *was* there all along. You were fixated on finding the letters, remember, so you may not have noticed the odd bump from upstairs.' Dania took a sip of coffee. 'There's another possibility. He could have followed you to the building.'

'So, why wait around for two hours?' Marek said doubtfully.

'Think about it, Marek. He has little idea where the letters are, but somehow he knows you're also on the trail. And that suits him fine. After all, why go to the trouble of searching a dingy basement in an abandoned building when someone can do it for you? So, he follows you and waits patiently – and silently – assuming you'll be there an hour, tops. But as time ticks by, he grows anxious and pokes his head through to see what you're up to.'

'I didn't have the torch on then. It would have been pitch black.'

'And he thinks he's mistimed it, and you're long gone, so he leaves. All right, so he's missed an opportunity to get his hands on the letters.' Dania leant forward. 'But it's not the letters he's after. He wants you to find the manuscript. That's why he's checking you're following your contact's instructions.'

The more she thought about it, the more plausible it seemed. Someone was getting the same intel as Marek and was tailing him, and waiting until he found the letters and manuscript before making a move. But what form would that move take? Simple theft? Or something more sinister?

Marek shook his head. 'There's a problem with that. He'd have had to know I'd be in Wola on that particular day, and on that particular afternoon. And searching that particular basement. And no one knew that.'

'You told no one of your plans? Nothing posted online?'

'Only Baletnica knew. As soon as he sent me the address, I replied that I'd be on the next plane out of Edinburgh.'

'And Baletnica could easily have established which flight that was. And seen you arrive at the airport and followed you here. And then followed you to the apartment in Wola.' She set down her mug. 'So, either it was the caretaker. Or,' she added, drawing out the word.

'Or what?'

'The mystery man you saw in the basement?' Dania laughed softly. 'He's none other than Baletnica himself.'

Maksymilian Robak strolled into the dimly lit casino nightclub and made his way to the bar. This end of the large room was where the drinking was done, evidenced by the long counter with its obscene array of bottles. Although it was only four in the afternoon, there were several guests – mostly men – sitting on the stools or at the low tables. Gamblers entered the casino through an archway at the other end, but the red-waistcoated croupiers had yet to arrive as the card tables wouldn't be in use for another two hours.

Directly opposite the bar there was a raised platform deep enough to accommodate a band. Today, however, two women were dancing the tango to piped concertina music, and gazing into each other's eyes with fierce concentration. They were wearing low-cut halter-neck dresses, one in black, the other in red, their hair scraped back into tight buns fastened with elasticated ribbons. Maks watched them for a while, wondering why he was suddenly thinking of Danuta Górska. Neither dancer looked remotely like her. It must be the height. Danuta was tall for a woman.

'The usual, sir?'

Maks turned to the barman. 'Yes, please.'

The man took a bottle from the freezer and poured a glass of vodka. He placed it in front of Maks, leaving the bottle on the counter. Maks watched the frost collect on the bottle, then reached for the pepper pot and sprinkled a generous measure of the pungent black powder into the glass. He took a breath and drank the vodka. As he breathed out, he felt the searing liquid reach his stomach. The vodka was the highest quality because the owner of this riverbank club was the wealthiest man in Warsaw. The dress code at four in the afternoon was strictly suit and tie, which was why Maks had stopped at his apartment to put on his light-blue suit and dark-blue tie. A detective rarely wanted to attract attention.

'Another, sir?'

'One more.'

Maks let it sit, in no hurry to leave an empty glass on the counter. A man with a Stalin moustache sauntered in. He glanced round the room, and his face softened into an expression of recognition. He walked briskly towards someone at the other end of the bar. The two men gripped hands and hugged fiercely. Maks watched the dancers for a while, then let his gaze drift round the room. Two women wearing identical peach-coloured dresses in shot silk were sitting at the end of the counter, sipping exotic-looking cocktails and speaking to each other in low tones, all the while devouring him with their eyes. As his gaze met theirs, they smiled invitingly. They had pale oval faces, made paler with moist red lipstick, and their sandy hair was cut shoulder-length, with the ends curled out.

'Is Mr Zelenski in today?' Maks said to the barman.

The man nodded towards the entrance. 'He's arriving now, sir.'

Two men had entered. The one in front was wearing a cream suit, a coffee-coloured shirt and a black tie. His greying hair was expertly cut, drawing attention away from his unremarkable face. As he walked, his limbs appeared loosely jointed, as though not properly attached. His slight frame couldn't have been more different from that of the stocky giant behind him. Maks wondered why Zygmunt Zelenski would choose such an obvious shaven-headed muscle man for a bodyguard. And one with an earring in each ear, no less. But, then, there was no accounting for taste. Interesting there was only the one guard. When he visited this nightclub, Zelenski usually arrived with three hardmen, all dancing attendance.

The giant took a table that gave him an uninterrupted view of his boss, and sat down, crossing his legs. His suit bulged across his abdomen but not enough to reveal the weapon Maks knew he was carrying. But, then, the muscle man couldn't see Maks's pistol either.

'Inspector Robak,' Zelenski said. He extended a hand, unfazed that a police officer was sitting drinking in his club.

Maks saw no reason not to reciprocate. Ignoring the outstretched hand would be impolite. And where Zelenski was concerned, politeness was the order of the day. Maks shook the hand firmly. Preliminaries over, Zelenski stepped across to Maks's other side, a shrewd move as it gave his bodyguard an uninterrupted view of the officer.

'I'll have a Scotch,' Zelenski said to the barman. 'A double Glenfiddich. No ice.'

He spoke carelessly, the way successful men do when they no longer have to worry about what others think. And Zelenski was nothing if not successful. This casino nightclub was the most famous – and most expensive – in Warsaw. As someone who had grown up under Communism, he had wasted no time in flexing his capitalist muscles when the régime fell.

He eyed Maks, his expression not unfriendly. 'So, Inspector, are you here for business or pleasure?' he said politely.

'A bit of both,' Maks said, sipping the vodka.

Zelenski gestured towards the twins, who were smiling dreamily at Maks. 'I think the ladies are showing an interest,' he said. 'You get two for the price of one, I believe.'

'When I want sex, I get it. I don't pay for it.'

He knew the remark would rankle. It was an open secret Zelenski's wife rarely left her rooms, and her husband arranged for a stream of high-class escorts to visit the house.

'Shall we get down to business?' Zelenski said, taking a gulp of Scotch. 'What do you wish to see me about?'

'I don't wish to see you about anything. It's your son I've come to speak to.'

'My son and I are business partners. Anything you have to say to him you can say to me.'

'Come, now. We both know he has . . . How shall I put it? Little business ventures of his own.'

Zelenski smiled. 'Anything my son is involved in, I know about, Inspector.'

Maks was inclined to snap back that that was so ridiculous as to be an affront to his intelligence, but he'd learnt from experience that losing one's temper was counterproductive. And in his dealings with Zelenski, the man had never lost his.

'Very well,' Maks said. 'I wish to speak to him about Salomon Steinberg.'

'The rabbi? But why? That unpleasant business was several weeks ago. It's finished.'

'Is it?' Maks said, turning the glass in his hand. 'Rabin Steinberg calls out your son's dealings in the property business, leading to a sharp loss in revenue, and you say it's finished?'

It had been a stroke of luck that one of his team had come across the newspaper article in the archives. He'd wasted no time in copying it to Maks. On reading the text, Maks had immediately recalled the case. The rabbi, not a man to mince his words, had openly accused Zelenski's son of operating a property scam that, given its nature, was immoral to say the least, and possibly illegal. Not many were rash enough to criticise a member of the Zelenski family so publicly, but Steinberg was evidently prepared to take the risk. He had disappeared briefly, leading to speculation that Zygmunt had had the man murdered, but it transpired the rabbi had been on a trip to Jerusalem, and was alive and well. Maks had concluded Zelenski's son would have waited for an appropriate opportunity to take his revenge on the rabbi. And what better occasion than a funeral, with so many guests blown to pieces that the police were unlikely to establish the identity of the intended victim?

Zelenski's smile was becoming forced. 'And what is your interest in Rabin Steinberg, Inspector?'

'I'm not prepared to say.'

'Then I'll say it for you. Although the press hasn't reported the identities of the guests at Jakub Frydman's funeral, I believe Rabin Steinberg would have been present.' He inclined his head respectfully. 'I may be wrong, of course, as Steinberg isn't the only rabbi who could conduct such a service, but given Jakub Frydman's reputation, he may have attended as a guest.'

Maks finished the vodka. 'Where is your son, Pan Zelenski?'

'He's out of the city at the moment. On business.'

'And when will he return? As someone who claims to know everything his son is involved in, I'm sure you're aware of his movements.'

'I'm certainly aware of his movements, but I've no idea when he'll be back.' Zelenski downed the rest of the whisky. 'It depends on how quickly he conducts his business. That isn't always within his control.'

Maks reached into his inside pocket, conscious the muscle man was straightening and lifting his right arm. Seeing the officer remove his wallet, he relaxed visibly.

'No need, Inspector,' Zelenski said, holding his hand up, palm out, to indicate Maks wasn't to pay. 'It's on the house.'

Maks left a couple of notes on the counter, and strolled out of the building.

Zygmunt Zelenski watched as the inspector pushed through the revolving doors. The slow tango music had changed to something more frenetic, and the dancers were whirling each other around, locking and unlocking their legs. The barman was chatting to the twins, who looked disappointed the officer had left. Seeing Zygmunt glance in his direction, he hurried over.

'Another Scotch,' Zygmunt said.

'Of course, Pan Zelenski.'

Zygmunt was tempted to message his son, but decided against it. He needed to think through his encounter with Robak. The explosion he'd read about had taken place in a Jewish cemetery, and it was obvious the police would be questioning everyone who had links to the guests, however tenuous. But it was interesting Robak had neither confirmed nor denied the presence of Rabin Steinberg. That in itself suggested the rabbi had been in attendance. Yet was that what the officer had wanted to speak to his son about? Or was it nothing to do with the funeral, and everything to do with the rabbi's crusade against the Zelenskis' property dealings? Although the word 'crusade' was hardly the appropriate one to use for a rabbi, it described his campaign perfectly.

As Zygmunt swirled the whisky, he let his thoughts wander back to his long journey to prosperity. He'd been a teenager when mass opposition to Communist rule had started in Poland, whose Solidarity movement had set the example followed by Hungary, East Germany and Czechoslovakia. During the upheaval that follows revolutions, he'd taken advantage of the expansion of private enterprise to start building an empire. His father, a staunch anti-Communist, had always believed the régime would fall. He was fond of quoting Stalin, who had famously said that introducing Communism to the Poles was like putting a saddle on a cow. It was a matter of time, he'd said, urging Zygmunt not to join the rising political movement and risk arrest as he himself was doing, but remain patient, lay his plans and strike when the moment came. So, in the early 1990s, unlike the entrepreneurs who'd bought state-controlled enterprises, Zygmunt had started an entirely new private construction company.

Business had been good; marriage and fatherhood had followed. His son had eventually joined the company, although he was constantly champing at the bit and wanting to branch out on his own. But he was headstrong, and hadn't yet learnt how to compromise, and also how to lose an argument in order to win it later. That came with experience. So, although he loved his son with the desperate love one has for an only child, Zygmunt would have to continue to rein him in. The lad was in Gdańsk, and returning late that evening. It would give them time to come up with a suitable narrative in case the police came calling again. Which Zygmunt knew they would.

CHAPTER 7

In the event, neither Marek nor Dania made the outing to Wilanów. Marek announced he was coming down with something, and wasn't up to a long trip. When Dania suggested they visit Castle Square, which was nearer, that didn't appeal. But he urged her to go, saying he didn't want to spoil her evening. He was going to have an early night and see if he could shake off this bug. She offered to cook but he shook his head. His appetite had vanished. Why didn't she try one of the eating places near the castle? She concluded he needed to sleep, so she made him tea with lemon and paracetamol, and left him hugging the hot-water bottle.

Dania phoned one of the restaurants in the Old Town Market Square and booked a table. There were no direct buses, but the fog was staying away, so she should see something of the Christmas lights if she went on foot. She set off briskly, skirting Krasiński Garden, and approached Castle Square from the west. The sun had long since retired for the night, and the closer she came to the square, the more the twinkling lights grew in strength.

In front of the pink-stone castle was a Christmas tree almost as tall as the building itself. At least, Dania assumed it was a Christmas tree, as nothing could be seen of the foliage: every inch of the conical structure was covered with glittering amber stars. The choir was singing *kolendy*, or Polish Christmas songs. She stopped and listened, feeling the tug of nostalgia for a childhood long gone. The singers were holding fat custard-yellow candles, and the heavy-scented, perfumed wax caught in her throat. Surprisingly, it didn't affect the choristers.

Around the square, where during the day the café owners set out tables and chairs, a Christmas market was in full flow. Dania wandered among the stalls seeing the type of ware on offer at all Christmas markets. In addition to the ornaments and local handicrafts, there was more than the usual number of *szopki*. It was hard to find a simple definition for these structures. They were a fusion of nativity scenes with local culture, and were sought after by tourists and locals alike. In Warsaw, the backdrop to many of the cribs was the royal castle. Multicoloured and glittering, the sizes of the *szopki* ranged from ones that could fit in your hand to those that were metres tall. Dania was tempted to buy one but (a) she'd have to carry it to the restaurant and (b) her parents already had a large number, which Marek had dusted off and arranged around the apartment.

As she followed the narrow cobbled passages spiralling up towards Market Square, her mind slipped back to Marek's account of how he'd found the Chopin letters. If her theory was correct, the man in the basement was indeed this Baletnica, who was feeding him intel, and checking he was following it up. It was a strange thing to do: have someone else find the letters and manuscript when the means to do it were within one's own hands. Baletnica seemed to know Marek's movements intimately. The thought that her brother was being shadowed for a reason as innocent as finding a lost manuscript left Dania with a distinct feeling of unease.

She reached Market Square with its pastel buildings, and saw that, unsurprisingly, there was another glowing Christmas tree and another Christmas market. The sweet, burnt smell of gingerbread and hot wine followed her as she moved from one stall to the next. The last time she'd been here in December, there was an ice rink round the statue of the Syrenka. As one thought inevitably follows another, her mind harked back to Merkury, and the reason she was in Warsaw. Perhaps he was here, in this crowded square, at this very moment. With only a week left in Warsaw, her hope of finding him was fading. And with it, her hope of bringing to justice the man who'd murdered her informant. Yet each time she thought of Magda, whom she'd failed to protect, it only served to strengthen her resolve.

Dania made another circuit of the square, resisting the temptation to buy trinkets she neither needed nor wanted, then forced her way through the growing crowd towards the restaurant.

She'd been lucky to get a table, as this was the best-known eating house in Warsaw. The décor was not to Marek's taste. He preferred the trendy international restaurants in the Nowy Świat area. But she loved it, which was why she'd decided to take advantage of his absence to eat there.

Not much had changed since her last visit, except that winter plants had replaced the summer blooms bordering the stone steps, and the lantern candles had been lit, their warm glow an invitation to passers-by. The reception area, with its sophisticated, old-style furnishings, was as she remembered it. To the right there were the padlocked display cases full of every type of glassware, bottles of vintage wine on the lower shelves. On the wall opposite hung ancient rugs, their rust-gold and honey-yellow colours bleeding into each other.

Dania gave her name to the smiling receptionist, who summoned a waiter. The man bowed politely and led her through the curtains into the main dining room, where the air was thick with the blended odours of flame-grilled meat and caramelised onion. This was a new experience for Dania. The last time she'd visited, it had been summer, and she'd eaten on the patio. The waiter took her coat and showed her to a table. He was about to pull out a chair, when she indicated she'd prefer to sit against the wall as it would give her a better view of the room. He smiled charmingly, shook out the napkin and dropped it onto her lap.

The woman next to Dania nodded in a friendly manner. Her dark hair was wound round her head and secured with an amber clip. With her burgundy lace dress and matching amber brooch, she looked like a pre-war countess. All of the women were smartly dressed and wearing evening make-up. After going through her mother's wardrobe, Dania had settled on a plain but elegant navy suit, but she was starting to wonder whether she should have worn one of her mother's more flamboyant cocktail dresses.

The waiter returned with a jug of water. She ordered chanterelles with dill and sour cream, followed by lamb chops crusted with walnuts and basil. She'd already decided on the dessert, since she'd scanned that section first. It would be the traditional 'Cheesecake from Vienna'.

As Dania was gazing at the gilt-framed paintings crowding each other, she became aware of raised voices at the doorway. A man in a dark grey suit was remonstrating with the maître d'. He was speaking politely, but definitely remonstrating. She was too far away to hear what they were saying, but it involved her because the maître d' was throwing glances in her direction.

A waiter was standing nearby. She beckoned him over.

'Do you know what the problem is?' she said, in a low voice.

The man looked embarrassed. 'That gentleman takes this table every Friday evening. The staff are told to keep it free, but it appears someone made a mistake and allocated it to you.'

'Isn't there another free table? In the other dining room, perhaps?'

'We are fully booked.'

'Has the gentleman come alone?'

'He always comes alone.'

'Then ask him if he'd like to join me.'

The waiter gaped at her, scandalised, making her wonder if she'd made a faux pas. The restaurant was frequented by celebrities. She studied the sharp suit and immaculately cut hair. He looked like a film director.

'He can only say no,' Dania added serenely.

For a second, she thought the waiter was going to request she give up the table. Which would have meant leaving to find another restaurant. She wondered what would happen if she refused. Then he straightened his shoulders and strode across to the door. He spoke in low tones to the guest and the maître d', nodding towards Dania.

The guest threw a glance in her direction, and smiled. He said something to the maître d', who looked so relieved that Dania could almost hear his sigh. The guest marched across, still smiling. As he was older than she was, Dania got to her feet and shook his outstretched hand.

'I'm Dania Górska.'

'Delighted to meet you,' he said, pausing for her to sit down before pulling out his chair. He didn't wait for anyone to shake out his napkin, but did it himself. 'This is an unexpected pleasure. I usually eat alone.'

She wondered why, given the wedding ring on his right hand. Perhaps he was a widower, who had decided not to move it to his left hand as was the custom. Or perhaps he'd escaped from his wife for the evening, which was why he hadn't given Dania his name.

The waiter hurried over.

'I'll have the usual,' the guest said. He had blue-grey eyes and a flattish nose. And a fine-boned but otherwise unremarkable face. 'Please call me Salamandra,' he said to Dania. 'It's how my friends address me.'

Salamander. 'A pseudonym? I hear them whenever I visit Warsaw.'

'You're not from here?'

'I was born in Warsaw but I live in Scotland now.'

He looked at her with interest. 'What made you move to Scotland?'

'We went as a family, nearly twenty years ago. My parents eventually returned, but my brother and I decided to stay.'

Something passed across his face. Then his expression cleared. 'Your brother must be Marek Górski. Am I right?'

How quickly Marek had become a household name. 'He is indeed my brother,' she said.

Salamandra smiled. 'I can see something of the family resemblance, now I know.'

The waiter brought a bottle of wine and two glasses.

The first courses arrived. Salamandra's order was sautéed foie gras with apple sauce.

'And are you helping your brother in his quest for the Chopin manuscript?' he asked, his voice businesslike.

Something made her say, 'I am, as a matter of fact.' It wasn't a complete lie. Since hearing Marek's account of how he'd found the letters, she was in no doubt he'd be sharing his intel with her. And she'd be doing her best to help him make sense of it.

She was unprepared for the change in Salamandra's demeanour. He lowered his fork, his gaze sweeping over her face as though searching for something only she could give. She felt a pricking on the back of her neck.

He smiled suddenly. 'And how is he coming by his information?'

'I'm afraid he doesn't share that with me.'

Salamandra drew his brows together. 'But he's your brother.'

Dania was beginning to regret admitting to helping Marek. 'What I know is that he has a contact. I don't know who the contact is, or how he gets his intelligence.'

'And is this contact in Warsaw?'

'I'm not sure.'

'Shall I tell you what I think?' he said, in a provocative tone. 'Your brother's found the manuscript, and is keeping everyone guessing.'

'If he'd found it,' she said testily, 'he'd have publicised the fact. He doesn't intend to keep it for himself, if that's what you're suggesting.'

'Not at all.' He seemed surprised at her tone. 'I'm sorry, Pani Górska. I didn't mean to offend you. It's that brothers sometimes keep things from sisters.'

Except Marek wasn't like that. Although it took a while, he confided in her eventually.

She inclined her head, conceding the point. 'The way things are going, it's looking increasingly unlikely he'll find the manuscript. None of the information he's received recently has helped him.'

Salamandra looked as though he didn't believe her. 'Yet he found the letters,' he said. 'Surely he isn't giving up.'

She thought back to Marek's account of how he'd spent the best part of an afternoon in a dingy cellar. 'I have to admit that once he gets his teeth into something he never lets go.'

'And are you the same?'

'Unlike my brother, I know when I'm beaten.'

They ate in silence. No sooner had their plates been removed than a waiter arrived with the next course. Salamandra's usual order was the beef sirloin in a wild-mushroom sauce.

'So, what do you do in Scotland, Pani Górska?'

'I teach English to the Poles.' Again, it wasn't a complete lie. But she didn't intend him to know she was a detective.

'Ah? There's an English school where you live?'

'I work freelance.'

'Does it pay well?'

'Well enough.' She wasn't about to add that she worked for free, as the lessons she gave were in the pub, and were little more than nudging her compatriots, whose English was excellent, towards a less textbook form. In other words, towards Dundonian.

'Freelance work isn't a bad way to make a living,' Salamandra said. 'You can set your own hours.'

'And what do you do?' she asked, wanting to move the conversation on.

'Me?' He lifted his wine glass. 'I'm a humble businessman.'

'Is there such a thing?'

He laughed then, a throaty sound, as though he'd swallowed gravel.

'What sort of business are you in?' she said.

'This and that,' he replied, in a tone that suggested he wasn't prepared to elaborate. 'Although, as a businessman, I'm always on the lookout for new opportunities.'

And, as a businessman, Dania thought, he was keeping his cards close to his chest. There was no point in pursuing it. But she'd concluded that, whatever he was, he wasn't a film director.

After a while, she said, 'You must have read about the explosion in the cemetery.'

'The whole of Warsaw is talking about it.' He looked thoughtful. 'There are various theories doing the rounds. The fact that it was a Jewish cemetery . . .' He left the sentence unfinished.

'Are there many burials in Okopowa?'

'I'm not sure. But Poland's Jewish community is growing.'

'I understand the man being interred was a great pianist.'

'I heard Jakub Frydman play many times. It was his Chopin concerts I made a point of attending.' There was a strange light in Salamandra's eyes. 'I've often wondered what this missing concerto must sound like, and particularly what Pan Frydman's interpretation of it would have been.' He paused. 'But we'll never know, will we?' He finished the sirloin. 'Did you ever hear Jakub Frydman play?'

'I did. He had a light touch on the keyboard.'

'Rivalled only perhaps by Rubinstein.' A wistful look crossed Salamandra's face. 'I heard Rubinstein play once. In Łódź, in 1975. I was nine years old. He walked onto the stage and everyone got to their feet. They gave him a standing ovation. And he hadn't played a note.'

'What was on the programme?' Dania said eagerly. 'Can you remember?'

'How could I forget? He played Chopin's second concerto. Then, after the intermission, he played Beethoven's Emperor. At the end, people threw red and white flowers onto the stage. I still have the programme somewhere.'

'Did he play an encore?'

'He had to. The audience was roaring. They wouldn't let him go.'

'Which piece was it?' she said impatiently.

'Can you guess?' he said, his eyes twinkling.

'The Grande Polonaise Brillante?'

'Bravo. The orchestra must have been notified in advance, because they accompanied him.'

Dania gazed at Salamandra, not bothering to hide her envy. She had been born after Rubinstein died so had never heard him play. It was a constant source of regret.

'Did you ever hear Rena Adler?' she said.

'Several times. She was often referred to as the next Rubinstein. But I believe she's retired.'

The waiter arrived to take the dessert order.

'I'll have the cheesecake,' Dania said promptly.

'Same for me,' Salamandra said, closing the menu. 'And will you be staying in Warsaw for Christmas?'

'I'm afraid I'm returning to Dundee next Friday.'

'And your brother?' he said, trying not to appear too interested.

'He'll be staying on. For how long, I don't know.'

Salamandra straightened his tie. 'If your brother feels the need of a helping hand, I'd be honoured to assist him in his quest.' He removed a card from his jacket pocket and laid it on the table.

She was surprised by the suggestion, and wondered what Salamandra's interest was in the manuscript. Would he hire an orchestra and have it played by the top Chopinist in the land before donating it to the Chopin University? Or, as a businessman looking for new opportunities, would he sell it to the highest bidder?

'Thank you,' she said. 'I'll pass that on to him. Ah, here's the cheesecake,' she added, relieved they could talk about something else.

They chatted about Warsaw, Christmas, Polish politics. The cheesecake and coffee finished, the conversation tailed off.

'If you are ready to leave, Pani Górska, I'll be happy to escort you home.'

'That's kind of you,' she said quickly, 'but we live on Dzielna, which isn't far. And I'd like to look round the market.'

'Then I'm afraid I must leave you. Thank you for your company. It's been a great pleasure.' He smiled, glancing at the card on the table as though wanting to ensure she didn't forget it. 'Will you excuse me?' he said.

'Of course.'

He got to his feet and bowed slightly. As he was leaving the room, he spoke to the maître d'.

Dania called for another coffee, realising then that Salamandra had left without paying. She gulped her coffee, and beckoned to the waiter.

'May I have the bill, please?'

'There is nothing to pay. The gentleman you had dinner with has settled everything.' He said it as though it was obvious: didn't Dania understand this is Poland, and anyway, do gentlemen ever let ladies pay?

She picked up the card. 'Zygmunt Zelenski.' She glanced up. 'Who is he?'

'You mean he didn't enlighten you?'

'He didn't.'

'He's a property developer. This building work around Warsaw is down to him.'

'And that's a good thing?'

'He's building new apartment blocks.'

She looked at the waiter with interest. 'And the apartments are affordable?'

'Most are. But not only that, he's involved in charitable work. He tries to keep that quiet, but the newspapers have a habit of finding out.'

'What sort of charitable work?'

The man blew out his cheeks. 'Well, for example, last month he made a huge donation to the Franciscan Sisters of the Family of Mary. Do you know them?'

'Remind me.'

'They run shelters for the homeless, and work in orphanages. That sort of thing.'

'I see.'

'Would you like another coffee?'

'No, thank you. I need to be going.'

'Shall I call you a taxi?'

'I'll walk. It's not far.'

'Perhaps next time you come, you can bring your brother. I'm guessing he's Marek Górski.' He smiled shyly. 'I saw your name on the booking and assumed you're related.'

Dania got to her feet. 'I'll let him know you're inviting him.'

The waiter made to say something, but Dania lifted her hand. 'No, I'm sorry, but he hasn't found the Chopin manuscript.'

CHAPTER 8

'And how are you today?' Dania said, hearing Marek stumbling into the kitchen. She glanced up from the newspaper, then stared, trying not to show her alarm. He was still in his pyjamas, his cheeks were flushed and there was a glazed look in his eyes.

'I'm not feeling brilliant, Danka.' He collapsed onto a chair.

She laid a hand against his forehead. 'You're burning up. Right, I'll make you tea with honey, then it's back to bed.'

'What if Baletnica emails me?'

'You'll have something to look forward to when you're better.' A smile crept onto her lips. 'Don't worry, I won't peek at your correspondence.'

'I think you should. You know my password. You can wake me if there's anything important.'

'Nothing is so important it can't wait a day.' She filled the kettle, then cut a lemon in half and squeezed the juice into a glass. 'Do you want a hot-water bottle?'

'Please.'

She made the tea with lemon and honey, and stirred in a couple of crushed paracetamol. He sipped slowly, watching her fill the hot-water bottle, squeezing it against her chest to let the air out before tightening the plug. 'I should have asked,' he said. 'How was your evening?'

'I met a gentleman at the restaurant.'

She had Marek's interest. 'Was he your type?' he said, trying a smile.

'He wasn't. But he was pleasant enough. He's offering to help you find the manuscript.'

Marek frowned. 'Did you tell him you're my sister?'

'He guessed from the name.'

'So, who is he?'

'Zygmunt Zelenski. He's a property developer. According to the waiter, he's building apartments all over Warsaw.' She handed Marek the hot-water bottle.

'And what are your plans for today?' he said, staggering to his feet.

'I have to ring in at West Bell Street.' She'd already decided to stay at home with Marek. 'I've reports to finish,' she added.

'What about Wilanów?' he said, leaning heavily against the door frame. 'Don't you want to see the lights?'

'There'll be time. I'm here till Friday, remember.'

His eyes were closing. She helped him to his room. After she'd tucked him in, she went searching for another blanket. Unable to find where her parents kept them, she took the one from her bed.

When she returned, the rhythmic breathing told her he was asleep.

In the kitchen, she connected to West Bell Street's VPN and worked on the reports she'd left half finished. Some were overdue. It was midday before she'd submitted the final one. She decided she'd earned herself a coffee. While it was brewing, she tiptoed along the corridor into Marek's room. He'd thrown off the covers, and was lying on his back, his arms outstretched. She listened to the soft purr of his breathing, then leant over and laid a hand against his forehead. He still had a temperature. She replaced the covers, tucking them in at the sides, and returned to the kitchen.

She gazed out at the apartment block opposite. A man was holding a baby on his shoulder, rubbing its back as he walked round the room. The coffee made, she called West Bell Street.

DS Honor Randall replied. 'Hi, boss, how are things?'

'Oh, you know. Soldiering on.'

'Are you still set for coming back on Friday?'

'That's the plan.'

'I overheard the DCI telling someone she needs you here now.'

'But we agreed Friday.'

'That murder in the Caird Hall? The stabbing? There's been no progress. We're short on DIs, boss. Which is why the DCI is grumbling. Anyway, dare I ask how things are going where you are?'

'Warsaw has the same heroin problem as Dundee.'

'About that, I checked with the Drugs Squad. The heroin trade on the streets has dipped sharply since you found Magda's body. Merkury must have been on that flight from Edinburgh. And it looks as though he hasn't returned.'

'The head of the Warsaw drugs unit is looking through their records to see if there's been enhanced activity during the same period. I'm hoping he'll get back to me before I leave.'

They discussed the progress, or otherwise, of their ongoing cases, and Dania issued instructions, which Honor would relay to the teams. Then she rang off.

She was thinking about making herself a sandwich when she spotted Marek's laptop. Her brother had been keen for her to check his mail, so she powered up and logged in. There was little of interest in his inbox, other than a message from his editor asking how he was getting on because DC Thomson had been contacted by an American film-maker who wanted to make a documentary about the search for this manuscript, and was Marek close to finding it? And it would be helpful if he could drop the editor a line from time to time, instead of leaving the man to guess what Marek was up to, ken.

Curiosity made her open the folder marked 'Baletnica'. Marek, being highly organised, kept a record of his replies. Dania settled down to read the correspondence, which began with a message from a Hotmail address. The username was a jumble of letters and numbers. The email was simple, and consisted of a couple of lines: the sender had proof a Polish minister was conspiring with the Russian Federation to bring down the Polish government. Would Marek be interested in this story, especially as this minister was coming to Scotland? It was signed, Baletnica.

Dania was familiar with the case, so she skimmed the subsequent messages until she came to the email asking whether Marek would be interested in recovering some unknown letters of Chopin's. She smiled as she read his effusive reply. Baletnica went on to say that the Jane Stirling letters had come into Ludwika's possession, so he would be concentrating his research on what had become of the personal effects of Chopin's sister. Further emails followed but they were less informative. Names were mentioned, and addresses in Warsaw. Then follow-up emails telling Marek to ignore the previous messages as the information was suspect, and Baletnica would dig around and get back to him. The emails eventually firmed up on the buildings in Wola.

But it wasn't the content of the emails that interested Dania so much as their style. She was used to emails that were more like text messages, hurriedly put together by busy people who didn't bother to correct their typos. But these messages, although often brief, were perfectly constructed without extraneous words. They made her wonder what Baletnica's day job was. If she had to hazard a guess, she'd have said he was an academic, a history professor perhaps.

She was about to power down the machine when there was a ping, and an email landed in the inbox. She considered leaving it for Marek until she saw who'd sent it. Her heart went cold as she read the message:

Marek, you are not the only person looking for the manuscript. Be aware that you may be in danger. You must constantly be on your guard.

This was the first time Baletnica had delivered a warning. Dania chewed her thumb. Her mind went immediately to Marek's account of the incident in Wola. Perhaps the mystery person silhouetted in the basement doorway hadn't been Baletnica, as she had concluded. Maybe someone else was aware of Marek's movements, and knew where he'd be. And where he was right this minute.

She felt a deepening sense of anxiety. Marek would shrug his shoulders and say it was the price investigative journalists paid and, anyway, wasn't he always careful? She was tempted to delete the email, but what would that achieve? No, when he was well enough, they'd discuss it. And also discuss the best way of responding. Her instinct was to tell him to return to Dundee. But it struck her he wouldn't be safe even there. Because another possibility presented itself. Could it be that, unknown to Baletnica, the manuscript had already been found? And whoever had it wanted to keep it? And that meant making sure that Marek, who had a proven record in uncovering Chopin's letters, would no longer continue his search. Not now. Not ever.

CHAPTER 9

Dania bowed her head, trying to ignore the sharp chill in the church. She should have been listening to the priest's sermon, but her mind was elsewhere. Part of her felt guilty at leaving Marek in bed, and the rest of her was studying the back view of the man seated three rows in front.

She'd been late for the service, having spent more time than she should impressing upon Marek he must open the door to no one. And that included the neighbours. If he heard the bell, he was to look through the spyhole so he could give her a description of the caller. And, after she'd gone, he needed to get out of bed and throw the bolts on the front door. And he was to keep his phone within reach. Marek, who was sitting up drinking tea and looking remarkably better, had studied her in the way he did when he thought she was demented but was too polite to say. He was convinced the mystery man in Wola had been the caretaker, checking because he'd found the main door open. As for other people looking for the manuscript, that was to be expected. Baletnica was mistaken, he wasn't in danger. Dania had given up and, not wanting to miss Sunday Mass completely, had left for St Augustine's Church. Fortunately, Nowolipki Street was less than five minutes away if you were walking. And three minutes if you were running.

Most of the rows in the long church were full. Dania slid into a near-empty pew at the back. She wasn't the last to arrive. A tall, well-built man with shoulder-length hair strode in and took a seat three rows in front. He was dressed smartly in a navy-blue woollen coat that fitted so well it could have been tailor-made. So, Maksymilian Robak worshipped at St Augustine's Church. She wondered if he was on shift and had sneaked out to attend the service. It was the same distance to the church from Mostowski Palace as from her parents' apartment.

As Mass progressed, with Dania making the automatic responses, she toyed with the idea of collaring the inspector afterwards. She'd not tried him since her phone call on Friday, and time was slipping away. But she concluded it would be inappropriate to do this straight after the service. She'd ring him on Monday.

Before she knew it, they'd reached the Lord's Prayer and Communion. She was one of the first up. The sweet, cloying smell of incense grew stronger as she walked along the nave. She took the Host, and was returning to the pew when she nearly bumped into Robak. His gaze of recognition swept over her face, then he nodded solemnly and stood back to let her pass. Seated in her pew, she watched him stride firmly along the black-and-white chequered floor until he disappeared into the crowd at the altar. Everyone seemed to be queuing for Communion, and it would be a while before the priest's blessing and dismissal.

Dania allowed her gaze to wander over the white columns and vaulted arches. She'd seen an aerial photo of St Augustine's taken after the war. The surrounding district, part of the former ghetto, was rubble to the horizon. The only buildings standing were the church and tower, a red-brick Romanesque-style structure, which was then, and was still, the highest in the area. She never did find out why they'd escaped the planned destruction of the city. After the '44 Uprising Hitler had given the order to demolish Warsaw, so someone in the SS had screwed up. The district had since undergone something of a transformation, with its skyscrapers and modern apartments. But Dania's grandmother, who had helped the priests from St Augustine's to smuggle Jews to what was known as the 'Aryan side', would tell her that, long after the war, as she walked through the streets of Muranów, although she never saw their faces, she'd still hear the ghostly voices of the dead.

Mass had come to an end, and the worshippers were shuffling out. Dania felt behind her for her handbag, but it had vanished. She glanced along the pew, seeing a little girl, who couldn't have been more than five, brushing her hair with Dania's brush. The child had taken the bag, probably when Dania went up for Communion, and was playing with the contents. Dania slid along the bench, took the hairbrush gently from her hand and replaced the scattered items, telling her it wasn't something she should do again. The parents were too busy speaking to people in the row in front to notice. Dania edged out into the nave, genuflected and made her way to the exit. She pulled on her gloves, and tugged her red woollen hat over her ears. Maksymilian Robak had already left with most of the congregation.

In front of the church was a statue of the Virgin Mary surrounded by low bushes and tall cypresses, with a metal railing preventing churchgoers from getting too close. They were gathered in clusters, in no hurry to go home, having what Dundonians would refer to as a 'wee blether'.

Dania peered into the hazy blue sky, wondering if the fog was about to descend. She needed it to stay off until the end of the week, when she was due to return to Scotland. Although there was no wind, the cold sliced into her bones, reminding her of what a Polish December is like.

'Pani Górska.'

Maksymilian Robak was leaning against the wall, arms crossed. His coat was unbuttoned, revealing black trousers and a light-blue shirt. No sweater. He was without scarf, gloves or hat. In other words, one of those Poles who hardly felt the cold. Where that was concerned, there were different categories of Pole, she'd decided. Compared to the Scots, she outranked them on the coldness front. But if you added in the Poles, she was on the lower rungs. Living so long in the UK had done it.

'I had no idea you worship at this church,' Robak said, smiling warmly.

She returned the smile. 'My parents' apartment is only a few minutes away.'

'As is mine. It's on Karmelicka.'

'Are you working this morning?'

'My shift starts at noon,' he said, straightening. 'Would you take a walk with me?'

She hesitated, thinking of Marek. But he'd reassured her he'd follow her instructions to the letter. For once, she was inclined to believe him. And she had questions for the inspector. 'Where shall we go?' she said brightly.

'The nearest green space is Krasiński Garden.'

'It'll be a pleasant change to see it in sunlight.'

'That fog we had recently was weird,' he said, as they reached the pavement. 'It came from the east.'

She thought of the haar in Scotland that crept in off the North Sea. 'Not from the north?'

'Not according to the weather boys. They said it was a present from the Russkis.' Robak threw her an amused glance. 'We sometimes have face-to-face meetings with our Russian counterparts when there are issues of mutual interest. They try to arrange conferences on the seventeenth of September.'

'Ah, yes, the date they invaded. They like to rub our noses in it, don't they?'

'And they can't resist reminding us of their "fraternal assistance" after the war. Anyway, the worst thing they send over now is bad weather.'

They reached the main road named for Pope John Paul II, and crossed at the zebra. Nowolipki Street was an orderly row of apartment buildings, with shops on the ground floor. They were shut, which seemed strange to Dania, having lived in the UK longer than she'd lived here.

'Inspector, may I ask how you're getting on with the Jakub Frydman case? I know there are things you can't tell me.'

He paused before speaking. 'We've identified the explosive as war-era Amatol.'

'From an unexploded bomb?'

'Around ten per cent of bombs didn't detonate. We find them regularly in Poland.'

'And how does someone get hold of Amatol?'

'The usual way is to bribe a construction worker. They're the ones who dig up the ordnance. That's where we're concentrating our resources.'

'So, who'd buy Amatol? I mean, what would they use it for? Other than blowing up a grave.'

'Blowing up the door to a bank. That happened earlier this year. And then there was an incident where the bad guys shattered a section of road to hijack a prison van transporting one of their group.' Suddenly he put an arm round her shoulders and pulled her out of the way of a speeding electric scooter. She could see he wanted to run after the boy, but he shook his head, muttering under his breath. 'Those things are a menace to pedestrians,' he said. 'Anyway, yes, Amatol. With that explosive, it's not difficult to put together a simple fuse, which you trigger from a mobile phone.'

'So, either the man with the scar purchased the explosive, or someone else did and paid him to throw the wreath. Although he got his timing badly wrong.' When Robak said nothing, she added, 'I'm sorry. I can't help thinking like a detective.'

He laughed. 'It's good to get another detective's perspective. But we've failed to establish the identity of the man who ordered the wreath. The name he gave to the florist was a fake.'

'What about the intended victim? I can't believe this unexpected guest wanted to kill all the mourners. Have you any theories as to who it was?'

'One or two,' he said cagily.

'I did wonder if it was a guest who couldn't make the funeral.'

Robak looked hard at her. 'We were given a list by Pan Mazur. He arranged everything, I understand.'

'But was it a list of those he invited? Or only those who made it to the service?'

'It was a list of those who attended. We assumed everyone invited had attended since Pan Mazur told us nothing to the contrary.' Robak looked at her appreciatively. 'But perhaps it didn't occur to him that a discrepancy would be significant. We'll follow it up.'

Dania looked straight ahead. 'I ran into Pan Mazur on Thursday.'

Robak must have picked up on her reluctance to continue because he said softly, 'Is there something you'd like to tell me, Pani Górska?'

'When you interviewed me, you suggested Jakub Frydman might have collaborated with the Communists. And that you'd check the archives.'

'We're still doing that. Although the secret police held a huge number of records, seemingly on everyone, not all have been digitised. We have some way to go.'

'The reason I've brought this up,' she said, choosing her words, 'is that it's possible one of the *other* guests collaborated with the Communists.'

'Which is why we're checking records on all the guests. But you mentioned running into Pan Mazur. Did he say anything to you about his own collaboration, by any chance?'

'Why? What have you found?'

'Nothing. So far.' He threw her a sidelong glance. 'What was it that made you suspect him?'

'It was the way he spoke about those times. He was very nervous.'

'Ah, yes, everyone was then. Although it's amazing how Poles managed to keep their sense of humour. I remember reading jokes from that era.' There was an amused expression in his eyes. 'How does a Pole start a joke, Pani Górska?'

'Tell me.'

'By looking over his shoulder.' When she said nothing, he went on, 'We'll find out eventually what, if anything, Pan Mazur was up to.'

They'd reached Krasiński Garden. In summer, it would be impossible to see the palace because the thick-leaved trees obscured it, but in winter, the naked branches gave teasing glimpses of the building. They strolled through the park, skirting the lake and playground, and found a free bench facing the palace.

Robak removed a paper bag from his coat pocket. 'I've brought *ptasie mleczko* from Wedel's. Would you like some?'

This chocolate-covered confection had a soft, milky centre, and was a favourite of Dania's. 'Do you always bring something sinfully sweet to eat after Mass?' she said, in a playful tone.

'Well, taking Communion means my sins have been forgiven. So, I may as well start over by eating these.'

He sounded so serious that, at first, Dania didn't think he was joking. But then he looked sideways at her, and a smile touched his lips. He held out the bag. She took off her gloves and picked out one of the chocolates.

'Take a few,' he said.

They sat eating in silence, gazing at the fountain, until they'd emptied the bag. He crunched up the paper and put it into his pocket.

'I had hoped to take you to lunch but everything's closed today,' he said, licking his fingers. 'Is it the same in Scotland?'

'It's not a Catholic country, so restaurants are open. And shops.'

'There's the canteen at Mostowski Palace, of course, but what's on offer is hardly edible.'

'The *ptasie* were an excellent substitute, Inspector.'

He looked at her as though trying to make up his mind about something. 'You asked earlier who I thought the intended victim was,' he said finally. 'There's a strong possibility it was Rabin Steinberg.'

'An anti-Semitic attack?'

'Not anti-Semitic.' He played with his hands. 'What do you know about property ownership after the war, Pani Górska?'

'There wasn't any.'

'Yes, our Communist president issued a decree to nationalise all property. But, since the fall of Communism, the descendants of former owners have been trying to reclaim what belonged to their ancestors. And which now belongs to them as sole heirs.'

'I remember my parents making an application.'

He looked at her with interest. 'Were they successful?'

'They didn't have the documents to substantiate their claim.'

'That was the case for a large number of applicants, I'm afraid.'

'I'd have thought there'd be few descendants, given entire families perished during the war. So, are claims still being made?'

'For restitution of property, and plots of land. Surprisingly, claims are being upheld despite the main stumbling block being – as your parents discovered – uncertainty over ownership due to lack of land-registry documents.'

Dania sneered. 'I'm guessing the process is ripe for fraud. I bet there are more than a few successful applications that aren't legitimate.'

Robak tried to look shocked. 'When did you become so cynical, Pani Górska?'

It was the question Marek had asked. She gave the same reply. 'When I became a police officer.'

The smile failed to reach his eyes, telling her it was the same with him. 'What has been happening recently,' he said, 'is that empty properties, many of which are dilapidated, are being sold by the successful claimants to developers, who bulldoze them and build expensive new apartments in their place.'

'So, what does this have to do with Rabin Steinberg?'

'Many of the properties belonging to Jews have remained unoccupied since the war. Not in Muranów, which was destroyed, but east of the river, in Praga. As I'm sure you know, before they were forced into the ghetto, many Jews lived there.'

'Including the rabbi's ancestors?'

'I've no idea. But where Rabin Steinberg comes in is that he believes one particular developer is operating a racket and buying these properties illegally. The rabbi isn't good with details, just with rhetoric. What got his blood up was that one of the buildings bought and then demolished was a former synagogue.'

'But I thought the only synagogue in Praga was the Great Synagogue. And wasn't that damaged, and then pulled down?'

'It turns out there was a much smaller synagogue, which survived because pains were taken to disguise it. Even the window God looks into was bricked up. I believe the building was used for storage after the war. But the rabbi, who's something of a scholar, knew of its existence. He'd been campaigning for the council to restore it. So, you can imagine how he felt when he'd heard it had been demolished.'

'What did he do?'

'He posted a scathing article online, and had it printed in one of the newspapers, accusing the property developer of operating fraudulently since no documents existed to show that any individual owned that building.'

'When was this?'

'About a month ago. There was an uproar, which is putting it mildly, and the developer's business tailed off. Although it's picked up again, the loss of revenue would have been considerable.'

Dania gazed at him. 'Considerable enough to want to take revenge on the rabbi?' she said, with a question in her voice.

'And do it in such a way it wouldn't be obvious who was the target.'

'He'd have had to know the rabbi would be at Pan Frydman's funeral.'

Robak considered this. 'That's true. But it would be worth a try, don't you think? You buy a wreath and pack it with Amatol, you arrive at the cemetery, you scan the guests – you know what the rabbi looks like because his photo has been in the media – and if he's not present, you walk away.'

'And come up with another plan. But, if it was this developer, do you think he'll try again?'

'If he does, it's unlikely to be for a while. He'll let the dust settle first. This is speculation, of course. There may have been another funeral guest someone wanted to make disappear.' He glanced at his watch. 'I'm afraid I need to be going, Pani Górska. My shift is about to start.' He got to his feet.

'Could I meet with you before I leave Warsaw?' she said, standing up. 'Pan Dolniak told me of a case of yours that might be of relevance to mine.'

'Of course. Why not come along now? I have no meetings scheduled.'

She hesitated. 'I need to get back to Marek. I want to make sure he eats something. He's not been well.'

Robak frowned. 'Nothing serious, I hope?'

'Just a bug. He's improving slowly.' She was about to add, 'You know what men are,' but decided against it. She had the impression Maksymilian Robak wasn't the type to let a bug keep him from anything.

'And how are you feeling?' he said, looking intently into her eyes.

'I'm fine. I rarely come down with colds and flu.'

'I meant about Pan Frydman,' he said gently. 'You're still grieving, I think,' he added, inclining his head. 'I can see it in your eyes.'

'Grief is something that has to run its course, Inspector.'

His expression softened. 'I'm sure you know the old Jewish saying: God is closest to those with broken hearts.'

Dania smiled. 'My grandmother was fond of that one.'

After a pause, he said, 'I'm with the state prosecutor all day tomorrow. What about Tuesday morning in my office?'

'Fine.'

'And what time would suit? Ten o'clock?'

'Ten o'clock.'

Robak held out his hand. She put hers into his, and he shook it firmly. As he turned away, he said, over his shoulder, 'Tell your brother to take plenty of liquids. And I don't mean vodka.'

'I will.'

She watched him stride back into the park, heading in the direction of the main road. Minutes later, he'd arrive at Mostowski Palace.

She sank onto the bench. Robak's account of Rabin Steinberg's article had intrigued her. Could the rabbi have been the intended victim? But, as the inspector had indicated, it was only a theory. His words drifted into her head: *There may have been another funeral guest someone wanted to make disappear.* The most likely candidate – assuming she was right about his collaboration with the Communist authorities – was Adam Mazur. She remembered his agitation on telling her how some people had betrayed their countrymen. As a detective who'd conducted many interviews over the course of her professional career, she knew when someone was trying to withhold information.

She sat staring at the baroque façade of Krasiński Palace, wondering idly how it differed from the façade of the seventeenth century, until she remembered that the outer shell of the building had survived. It was the interior that had been set on fire. The palace was now part of the National Library, storing manuscripts in its special collections.

The thought of manuscripts caused her mind to slip back to Marek. She needed to get lunch sorted. She retraced her steps, pausing at the lake to watch children throwing bread at the ducks. Then, without knowing why, Baletnica's warning flew into her head:

Marek, you are not the only person looking for the manuscript. Be aware that you may be in danger. You must constantly be on your guard.

Dania felt a sudden pounding in her temples. What if neither Rabin Steinberg nor Adam Mazur was the intended victim of the unexpected guest? What if it was Marek? Could her theory about the manuscript be correct, that someone had found it? And wanted to ensure Marek never would? With trembling hands, she pulled her mobile out of her pocket.

CHAPTER 10

'Enter,' Maksymilian Robak said, hearing a knock at the door. He looked up from his desk.

'You sent for me?' Pola said, opening her notebook.

He indicated the seat opposite. 'I wanted to check how the search at the Institute of National Remembrance is going.'

'There's a huge amount of cross-referencing.'

'I ran into Danuta Górska this morning. She told me she suspected Adam Mazur has an interesting past.'

'Interesting in what way?'

'He worked with the Communist authorities.'

Pola twirled one of her plaits. 'Any evidence to back that up?'

'It was a hunch. But if you've not yet pulled his records, I'd like you to make him a priority.'

'Right. On the subject of the archives, we did find something. The Górskis' parents were Solidarity activists. They were arrested in April 1983.'

'Under martial law? What was the charge?'

'There wasn't one. Martial law was lifted later the same year, but they weren't released.' She checked her notes. 'It was 1986 before they were set free under the amnesty.'

Maks turned to the computer screen and brought up his records. 'Danuta and Marek Górski weren't born until 1988. Just as well it was after all that,' he added grimly.

'And here's another interesting fact. Jakub Frydman was *also* a Solidarity activist. According to the records of their interrogations, they'd continued their Solidarity-related activities, which had been banned under martial law. The three of them had set up a clandestine network of print shops with Frydman in charge of distribution.' Pola peered at Maks over her glasses. 'There was no trace of Jakub Frydman cooperating with the Communists. If collaboration was the motive, we can rule him out.'

'Agreed. And Danuta and Marek Górski?'

'I can't think of a reason why they'd have been targeted . . . although I believe Marek could be in danger now.'

'From the unexpected guest, who might have seen his face?'

'Don't you think we should warn him?'

'I'm not sure what that would achieve,' Maks said, thinking that if Marek was unwell, the last thing he needed was the added stress of believing he was the target of an assassin. Seeing the anxiety on Pola's face, he added, 'Before you ask, we can't offer him protection, assuming he'd accept it. I can't spare anyone.' He felt his mouth form into a smile. 'From that wistful look in your eyes, am I right in guessing you have growing feelings for Pan Górski?'

A soft blush transfused her cheeks. It made her look like a teenager, Maks thought. In fact, with her elephant slippers and black dungarees, she couldn't have looked less like a police detective. Yet she was his best officer.

'I'll get started on those records,' she said, getting to her feet. With a brief smile, she left the room.

It was after three, and the man Maks wanted to talk to would likely be at home. He could phone ahead but that might prove counterproductive. Anyway, it was only a couple of tram stops to the apartment on Królewska.

He pulled on his coat and left the building.

'Pan Mazur?' Maks said, as the door opened a crack. He knew the director would have studied him through the spyhole, so he'd made it easy by facing the door. He held up his warrant. 'I'm Inspector Maksymilian Robak. May I have a word?'

Mazur froze, his eyes widening. It was a reaction Maks had seen before when Poles of that generation were confronted by the police, although the SB – the Communist secret police – had tended to make their arrests in the small hours. But Maks hadn't come to quiz him about the past. Pola would uncover what they needed to know, assuming there was anything to uncover.

'May I come in?' Maks said, smiling in a reassuring manner. 'I have a couple of questions.'

Mazur seemed uncertain, but at least he no longer looked like a rabbit in headlights. He opened the door wide and stood back to let Maks enter.

He found himself in an elegant living room. The décor, which was straight out of the nineteenth century, was of the highest quality. One wall was hung floor to ceiling with gold-framed oil paintings, an arrangement he'd seen only in art galleries. A number of decorated wooden boxes stood on a walnut sideboard. But Maks's eye was drawn to the black, lacquered grand piano, leaving him in no doubt as to the profession of the owner. His first thought was that no one strolling on the pavement would guess this dreary grey Communist apartment block held such treasures. His second was: how could a former director of an institute afford this?

Mazur was watching him. 'Please take a seat, Inspector.'

'Thank you.' Maks gathered up the papers on the sofa, and looked around for somewhere to put them.

'Let me take those,' Mazur said. 'It's work I'm doing for a book.'

'Oh? You write as well?'

He smiled faintly. 'I've been researching Julian Fontana. Do you know anything about his life?'

'I'm sure I'll learn about it when your book comes out.'

'He was Chopin's musical executor. After the composer's death, he brought out a collection of the man's previously unpublished manuscripts. Fontana had an interesting life, at least what we know of it. It's been a mammoth task piecing it together from publications, letters and so on. But highly rewarding.'

'Are you close to finishing it?'

'Alas, no. But forgive my manners,' he added, gesturing to the sofa.

Maks sat down, sinking further than he'd expected.

'You've caught me at a bad time,' Mazur said, glancing at his clothes. He was wearing worn brown corduroy trousers and a blue sweater showing its age. 'I've come from Pan Frydman's apartment, you see. I've made a start on working through his effects. There's a large number of bequests to deal with.'

Maks tilted his head enquiringly.

'They're mainly books, and a few trinkets,' Mazur said, taking the nearest armchair. He lifted a hand and let it drop wearily, as though even that gesture couldn't convey the enormity of the task. 'You should see Pan Frydman's apartment, Inspector. Piles of books, and papers in boxes. And not just in the office. And I thought *my* study was untidy.' He must have realised he was gabbling. He put his hands on his knees. 'So, what can I help you with?' he said, with affected eagerness.

'I'm investigating the explosion in Okopowa.'

'I believe I told your associate everything I know,' Mazur said slowly.

'I understand, but something has since come to my attention. My question concerns the names of the guests for the funeral.'

'But I handed a list to your colleague,' he said, in a tone bordering on exasperation. 'I was asked to bring it.'

'That was a list of those who *attended*. But is it the same as the list of those you *invited*? Was there anyone who didn't show up?'

Mazur stared vacantly. 'Now you mention it, there might have been one or two. The fog made travel difficult.' He got to his feet. 'The list should be in the study. If you'll excuse me?'

'Of course.'

Maks waited, hearing the rustle of papers. Then more rustling. He stood up with difficulty and wandered around, scrutinising the objects. A number of framed black-and-white photographs stood on the mantelpiece next to the French ormolu clock. They were of a young ballerina in a variety of poses. He picked up the nearest photo. The dancer gazed dreamily into the camera as though this was what she'd been born for. Maks wondered who she was. Mazur's daughter, perhaps? Although he'd have expected the photos to be in colour.

'That's my mother.'

Maks hadn't heard Mazur come in. 'She's beautiful,' he said, meaning it.

'She was twenty-four when those were taken. Her career had just started. And then the war broke out.'

'Did she take it up again afterwards?'

'Briefly.' He spread out his hands. 'I'm afraid I can't find the list of invitees, Inspector. I have a feeling it will be in my office at the university. In fact, the more I think about it, the more certain I am. I remember Rabin Steinberg and I sat at my desk and compiled the list. I then sent out the notifications.'

'When was this?'

'Monday morning. The day after Pan Frydman died.'

'And the list you gave to my colleague, Pani Lorenc? You're certain those people actually attended?'

'I compiled *that* list the following day.'

'From memory?'

'As soon as the police contacted me.'

Maks kept his voice conversational. 'With that fog, how were you able to recognise the guests?'

'The rabbi and I greeted everyone as they arrived. We were close enough to see their faces.'

It was possible they'd missed someone, Maks thought. It would be easy enough to check once he had the list from Mazur's office. He threw the man a quick smile. 'Are you going in to work next week, Pan Mazur?'

'I am, yes.'

'Perhaps you could drop the list off at Mostowski Palace?'

Mazur looked greatly relieved. 'Of course. It will be no trouble.'

'Then I'll be going.' Maks nodded. 'Thank you for your time.'

'That's all you wanted to see me about?'

'That's all.'

He was making his way to the door when his glance fell on the wooden boxes on the sideboard. 'I see you're something of a collector, Pan Mazur. Or perhaps you do woodwork as a hobby?'

'Good heavens, I could never make anything as intricate as that. Those are puzzle boxes.' He picked up one shaped like a book, and embossed with a gold floral design. 'This is from the Tatra mountain region.'

'May I see?'

'Of course.' His eyes were gleaming. 'Can you open it?'

Maks tried lifting back the wooden panel as though it were a book cover, but it wouldn't budge. He tested the bottom panel, then ran a finger along the edge, feeling for a button or some indication of how it would open. He was on the point of handing it back when it came to him that the spine was slightly wobbly. Gripping it, he pulled it upwards, then tried pulling it down. There was a click, and the upper panel lifted slightly. He pulled it back, seeing green-felt lining. The box was empty.

'Bravo, Inspector,' Mazur said, beaming. 'Not everyone manages it, or at least not so quickly. You have the gift, I think.'

Maks studied the other boxes. No two were the same. 'Do you know how to open these?'

'It took me a long time to work it out.'

'And were they empty?'

'Unfortunately, yes. Sometimes you're lucky and there's jewellery inside. But, alas, not with these.'

'How did you come by them?'

'You can find them online. Or sometimes at village fairs.'

Maks handed back the box. 'I'll have to look out for them.'

'Try this one, Inspector. It foxes most people.'

'Now, that's a challenge I can't resist,' he said, smiling.

This box was larger, and made of different types of wood. After playing with it for a couple of minutes under Mazur's watchful eye, Maks finally found the key. It involved sliding one side out but only partway, then sliding the opposite side in the other direction. When both sides were out the same distance, he heard a click, which allowed him to lift the lid.

'I'm impressed,' Mazur said, shaking his head. 'As I said, you truly have the gift.'

Maks gave a slight bow, acknowledging the compliment. He replaced the box on the sideboard. 'I think I've kept you long enough, Pan Mazur. I'll let myself out.'

CHAPTER 11

'You're looking better today,' Dania said.

'I'm back to my usual rude health. It was a twenty-four-hour thing.' Marek grinned. 'Or a forty-eight-hour thing.'

'How about coming out for a walk?'

He finished his coffee. 'I think I'll pass. Something tells me Baletnica's going to email this morning. I want to be here when he does so I can get my questions in. But you go. The weather's set to change, so you should take the opportunity.'

'Set to change how?' She lowered her mug. 'What have you heard?'

'Snow is forecast.'

'Heavy or light?' she said, thinking of the disruption to flights.

He looked at her as if to say, Light snow in Poland? Are you serious?

She lifted her hands in resignation. 'All right, I'm going.'

As she pulled on her coat, she resisted the urge to remind him to lock the door. Yesterday's sense of panic had dwindled, leaving her feeling slightly embarrassed. Her theory that Marek had been the intended victim of the unexpected guest now seemed far-fetched. The only people who'd known he'd be at the funeral had been present themselves. They'd hardly endanger their lives to throw the police off the scent. No, if Baletnica's warning was to be taken seriously – and it's possible he was just trying to keep Marek on his toes – then the threat, if it materialised, would come from a surprising direction.

'Will you be here for lunch?' Marek said, glancing up from the laptop. 'You don't have to be if you find a nice eating place. I can easily make myself something.'

The idea of having lunch at one of Warsaw's gourmet coffee shops was growing on her. 'What about this evening? Are you up to going out?'

She could see he didn't want to commit. Finding the manuscript had taken over, thrusting everything else to the bottom of the pile. 'Well, we don't have to decide now,' she said.

But he'd stopped listening.

Outside the building, she paused to consider her options. She could head to one of Warsaw's parks, or return to the Old Town Square and the Christmas market. In the end, she decided on a stroll by the river. That morning, she'd opened her curtains filling the windows with blue sky. The Vistula would be the same colour. She set off, walking briskly on account of the cold.

The route skirted Krasiński Garden, guiding her along the narrow cobbled streets past the Barbakan. She studied the sky. There wasn't a sliver of cloud. What was Marek talking about? Snow? Really?

After reaching the main road, she took the underpass that brought her onto one of the riverside paths. These tracks were a haven for joggers, although there were fewer around at this time of year. In summer, however, it was impossible to enjoy a peaceful stroll without having to step out of the way of the runners, cyclists and skateboarders. As she ambled along, she wondered what the following day would bring, and whether Robak could tell her anything that would help her snare Merkury. Because when she wasn't thinking about Jakub Frydman, his shredded body scattered across Okopowa cemetery, she was thinking about her informant, Magda, with her head almost severed.

Dania was nearing one of the many cafés on the riverside boulevard when she saw a jogger making straight for her. He was wearing a grey sweatshirt with the hood pulled over his face, and staring at the ground as though afraid he'd miss his footing. She stepped smartly out of the way but, at the last minute, he raised his head and she gazed into a pair of mad, burning eyes. Without warning, he lifted his fist and struck her on the side of the head. As she toppled to the ground, he snatched her shoulder bag and ran off the way he'd come. A wave of agony travelled from her chin to her cheekbone, and tears of pain stung her eyes.

'Hey! You! Stop!' The voice came from behind.

Someone rushed past. The jogger slowed, and glanced over his shoulder. Which was a mistake as it enabled the figure to catch up with him. He leapt like an athlete, landing on the jogger and bringing him crashing to the ground. The men wrestled and rolled about, throwing punches, or trying to. Moments later, the jogger struggled to his feet and stamped viciously on the other man's stomach. Then, not bothering with the bag, he raced off.

The man on the ground curled into a ball, groaning. Slowly, he rolled onto his hands and knees, and hauled himself to his feet. He picked up the bag and limped over to where Dania was lying. She started to get up, but a wave of dizziness overcame her.

'Don't move,' he said, in a hoarse voice. 'Here, let me.'

He crouched and put an arm round her shoulders, then helped her gently to her feet. Her head was throbbing, but at least she didn't feel too light-headed to walk.

'Thank you,' she gasped.

'I think you need some water,' he said, looking around. 'There's that place over there. Come on, I'll help you.' He had on a black sheepskin, which came down to his knees, and a striking, somewhat ridiculous grey fur hat with earflaps. He kept his arm round her shoulders, and didn't hurry her, for which she was grateful.

The building was a Bar Mleczny. Although milk bars had served mostly dairy food when meat was rationed in the Polish People's Republic, this was no longer the case, and they now offered a wider range of home cooking. They were still partly state-subsidised, which meant prices were kept low. The décor was such that milk bars rarely advertised themselves.

They shuffled up the steps, and pushed through the door into a wide room with functional furniture. Dania had the impression the place had just opened for the day: there were no guests, and a girl was chalking the menu on the blackboard. The heating hadn't been on long, and it was too cold to take coats off.

The man helped her to a window table with a view over the river. She noticed there were kayaks on the water, their occupants making the best of it before the snow came. Yet the sky was a roof of pure blue.

'Are you all right to wait here?' he said.

'I think so.'

He smiled and made for the counter.

She noticed he was still limping, although only slightly. He returned with two glasses of pinkish liquid.

'Cherry *kompot*,' he said. 'I think the sugar should help with shock.'

'Wonderful. Thank you.'

He took the seat opposite, and pulled off his hat. Now she had a chance to see him properly, she was surprised at how young he looked. He reminded her of a teenager who should have been at school but had done a bunk. He had blue eyes, and hair cut short at the sides. What was left on top and over the back of his neck was streaked blonde.

He gestured to her face. 'I'm afraid you'll have a bruise tomorrow. Is it painful?'

She laid a hand against her cheek. 'Nothing's broken. It could have been worse. That bastard could have knocked my teeth out. What about you?' She glanced at his stomach. 'I saw what he did.'

'It's nothing,' he said dismissively. 'I work out, so my abs are strong.'

'My name's Danuta Górska, by the way.' She stared into the glass. 'Given you've had your arm round my shoulders, to say nothing of getting my handbag back, I think we can dispense with the formalities, don't you?' She lifted her head. 'So, please call me Dania.'

'And I'm Tomek,' he said, evidently delighted she was using the familiar forms of the language. 'Tomek Hodak.'

The girl was hurrying over. 'I believe this is yours, sir. You must have dropped it when you took out your wallet.'

Dania recognised an officer's warrant card. The blue-and-silver logo with the word *Policja* was similar to Inspector Robak's. The girl had opened it out, presumably to check the name, giving Dania a glimpse of Tomek's photo.

'Thank you,' Tomek said, smiling disarmingly.

The girl nodded and left.

'You're a detective,' Dania said.

'Obviously a careless one.' He shoved the warrant into his coat pocket.

'Do you work at Mostowski Palace?'

'In Kraków. I'm on furlough for a few days. Visiting friends in Żoliborz. I arrived yesterday.'

She sipped the *kompot*. 'I'm a detective too, as it happens.'

He looked surprised. 'What a coincidence. Two detectives. Both attacked.'

She laughed lightly. It was a mistake. Stretching the muscles of her face had caused the pain to flare. Her hand flew to her cheek.

'It'll hurt for a while, I think. So, where do you work, Dania? Here in Warsaw?'

'I live in Scotland now. In Dundee.'

He shook his head to indicate he'd not heard of it.

'It's on the south-east coast.' She looked past him at the apartment blocks on the far bank of the Vistula. 'It's also on a river, but the view is slightly different. What you see is mainly farmland.'

'What's the city like?'

'Where to begin? It has a vibrant arts culture. There's a V and A museum of design. It stands for Victoria and Albert,' she added, seeing his puzzled look. 'It puts on fabulous exhibitions. There's also the street art, which you can't miss. Oh, and the ship that took Scott and Shackleton to Antarctica, the RRS *Discovery*, is on display in the harbour. It was built in Dundee.'

'And Brexit hasn't made you want to return to Poland?' he asked, watching her.

'The Scots voted to stay in. They're very welcoming to the Poles.' She looked at Tomek with curiosity. 'So, which line of work are you in?'

'Anti-drugs.' He glanced around, but the place was empty and they were out of earshot of the girl at the counter. 'There's a growing problem in Kraków,' he added.

'There's a growing problem everywhere.'

'Are you also in Anti-drugs?' he said, lifting his glass.

'I'm on the Murder Squad. My informant was murdered and I think the perpetrator has come to Warsaw.'

'Is that why you're here?'

'I'm trying to track him down.'

'Then Inspector Robak's your man. There's no finer detective.' He threw her a crooked smile. 'I've not met him, but his reputation has made it as far as Kraków. My boss is constantly trying to head-hunt him. It never works.'

'Our paths have crossed. I don't know if you've heard about this explosion in Okopowa cemetery.'

Tomek shook his head, frowning.

'I was attending a funeral last Wednesday,' Dania said. 'Someone threw a wreath packed with explosives into the grave.'

He stared at her. 'Into a *grave*?'

'No one was hurt. In fact, we'd all left before it detonated. But Inspector Robak is the investigating officer. He questioned me afterwards.'

Tomek set down his glass. 'Has he tracked down the man responsible? I'm assuming it's a man.'

'I think he's still trying to establish the motive.'

'And is he helping you with your own investigation? Into this person who murdered your informant?'

'Actually, it's the Anti-drugs head I've been working with.'

'Oskar Dolniak?'

'That's right. Of course, you'll know him.'

'And how's that going?'

'It's early days.'

Tomek nodded sympathetically. As an officer in an anti-drugs unit, he'd appreciate the difficulty in gathering the evidence needed to apprehend a drugs kingpin.

'Are you staying in Warsaw long?' he said.

'I'm flying back to Dundee on Friday.'

'Whether you've found your man or not?'

'You know what it's like. I have other cases. But if I get nowhere, I'll be returning to Warsaw.' She felt her anger rising. 'Because I intend to find this man and bring him to justice.'

Tomek looked at her appreciatively. 'You know, with an attitude like that, you should come and work in our team in Kraków.'

A thought struck her. 'Maybe this man is no longer in Warsaw. He could have travelled to Kraków and established himself there. Does the name Merkury mean anything to you? It's his pseudonym.'

Tomek shook his head. 'I could check our records. If I find anything, I'll get in touch. Have you seen this guy? Could you recognise him?' he said, pulling out his phone. The shiny case was like the Polish flag, red and white.

'Unfortunately not. It was my informant who worked in his gang.'

'Okay, let me have your number.'

They exchanged contact details.

The room was starting to fill. 'I think people are arriving for lunch,' Dania said, in a tone that suggested she wasn't hungry. The ache in her temple had chased away the thought of food.

Tomek laid a hand against his abdomen. 'Looks as if my abs are softer than I thought. I'd offer to buy you lunch, but I don't think I could keep anything down.'

'Me neither.' She smiled, ignoring the pain. 'I think I'd better go home and rest.'

'Do you live near here? Let me walk with you.'

'I'm going to take a taxi.'

'I'll call one.' He pulled out his phone again.

Outside, they took the steps up to the pavement. Tomek waited with Dania until the taxi arrived.

'Thanks again,' she said, extending her hand.

He kissed it lightly.

She climbed into the car. As it sped away, she glanced back.

Tomek was standing watching, pulling the black sheepskin round himself. He must have seen the movement, because he raised his arm.

At least he hadn't asked how Marek was getting on with finding the manuscript, Dania thought. But, then, the man had just arrived in Warsaw.

Dania paid the driver and made her way to her parents' apartment, her thoughts swirling. Her comment to Tomek that Merkury could have left Warsaw and set up his drugs business elsewhere had been playing on a loop at the back of her mind. She imagined Merkury and his team arriving at Chopin airport, making straight for the main railway station and buying tickets for Kraków. Or maybe Merkury had instructed the team to continue business in the capital, while he set up a new network. And perhaps not in Kraków. He could have gone anywhere. Needles in haystacks sprang to mind.

Dania took the lift to the top floor, making a mental note to run this past Oskar Dolniak. He'd be well connected with the Anti-drugs heads in the main cities, and it should be straightforward to check if they'd heard the name Merkury. She felt suddenly marginally cheered.

At the end of the corridor, she turned right. The door to her parents' apartment was standing wide open. Marek wasn't the type to forget to lock it on the way out and, anyway, hadn't he said he'd be at home waiting for a communication from Baletnica? She felt her neck muscles tense. Part of her wanted to run inside but her detective's training kicked in, and she paused to work through the most likely scenarios. She listened, but heard nothing. Slowly, she stepped into the hall, trying not to make a sound. Marek's coat and woollen hat were hanging on the rack. If he'd left the building, he wouldn't have done so without outdoor clothes. With growing fear, she peered into the kitchen. The laptop was on the table. On the floor beside Marek's upturned chair a mug was lying in a pool of coffee. Several sheets of paper were scattered about, those nearest the mug soaked through.

Like a woman in a dream, Dania walked through one empty room after another. Her strength suddenly left her. She staggered back to the hall and collapsed onto the chair. Opposite was the large mirror her mother used when adjusting her hat. Dania stared at her reflection, seeing nothing. With ruthless logic, she went through the dwindling number of possibilities. But the only viable one was that Marek had inadvertently let in his attacker, there'd been a struggle and he'd been abducted. She pulled out her phone and rang his number, hearing the familiar buzzing from the kitchen. He'd left his mobile on the table.

Unable to sit upright, she keeled over and slumped onto the floor. The desire to sleep was overwhelming. She'd have to make a plan, perhaps call Robak. She closed her eyes, intending to rest for only a few seconds, but the darkness behind her eyelids grew heavy.

'Danka!'

Her eyes flew open. Marek was kneeling on the floor, leaning over her, his face so close she could feel his breath.

'What the hell happened?' he said, his voice shaking. 'That mark on your face. Did you see who did this? Are you all right? I need to call the police.'

The situation she now found herself in, with Marek firing questions at her, restored her self-possession.

'There's no need to call the police,' she said mildly. She struggled to sit up.

'What were you doing on the floor?'

'I fell off the chair.'

'Falling off a chair wouldn't give you a bruise like that.'

'The bruise dates from earlier. I was mugged.'

He stared at her. Then his face contorted with anger.

She held up her hand. 'Before you say it, no, I didn't call the police. The attacker had his hoodie over his face, and he ran off, and there were no cameras. Anyway,' she added wearily, 'someone came to my rescue. And also rescued my bag. So, no harm was done.'

'No harm was done?' Marek said, disbelief in his voice. 'I still think you should call the police.'

'Believe me, it's a waste of time. Now, help me up.'

When she was on her feet, she remembered why she'd been on the floor. The temptation to yell at him evaporated before it went anywhere. 'I saw the front door was open,' she said. 'And there's a mess in the kitchen. It looked as though there'd been a struggle.'

He ran a hand over his face. 'I was working at the laptop when I heard a scream from the flat next door.'

'The woman with the toddler?'

'That's right. The scream was like nothing I've ever heard. I must have dropped the mug. I ran out and banged on her door. She let me in, and I saw immediately what had caused her to scream.'

'What was it? A spider?'

Marek rolled his eyes as if to suggest she wasn't taking him seriously. 'Her two-year-old had climbed onto a chair – how do two-year-olds learn that so quickly? – and he was at the window, which was open. Come to think of it, the woman had a duster in her hand. Anyway, the boy was balanced on the sill. I'm surprised his mother's scream didn't tip him over. It was clear she was incapable of rational thought so I had to come up with a way of distracting him. His toys were on the floor, and I knelt down and started to play with the train. That was enough to get him to climb down. We'd have had a great time together, actually, had his mother not started to yell at him.'

Marek had a soft spot for children. His eyes lit up whenever he talked about them. 'Looks as if you did the right thing,' Dania said.

'She asked how she could repay me. I noticed the plate of *chrust* on the table. She must have seen me staring because she told me to eat it all, and then she said she'd make another batch and bring it over.'

Dania started to laugh, then stopped, grimacing with pain. 'I need to lie down for a bit, Marek.'

'Shall I heat up some soup first?' he said. He raised an eyebrow. 'Or will it be something stronger?'

CHAPTER 12

Tuesday morning saw Dania up early. Her short nap of the previous day had developed into a deep sleep, and she'd wakened at five. Afternoon snoozing wasn't her thing, but she'd put it down to the blow to her head, and her fright at thinking something had happened to her brother. Marek had been sitting in the kitchen frowning into his laptop. He'd heard nothing from Baletnica, and had decided to do some sleuthing of his own. Which was leading nowhere. On the table was a large pyramid of *chrust*. The pastry was dusted with vanilla-flavoured icing sugar, and the sweet smell permeated the room. Dania had wondered how he could resist demolishing the lot until she remembered he'd eaten the same amount earlier. They'd had supper and watched television, as neither felt up to going out.

Now, Dania was getting ready for her meeting with Inspector Robak. Tomek had been right about the bruise. So far, it was yellow and orange. The deeper colours would develop later. In her parents' bedroom, she searched for the heavy foundation her mother used, hoping she kept a jar in her bedside cabinet. She did. Dania patted it over the bruise, managing to disguise the worst of it. It wasn't ideal, but she hoped Inspector Robak wouldn't notice or, if he did, that he'd make no comment.

Through the window, she glimpsed the thin mist hanging over Warsaw. Not something to worry about, she thought, twirling a lock of hair round her finger, but it would be wise to wrap up. She rejected the tartan jacket in favour of her mother's long sheepskin and matching hat, pulled on a pair of thick gloves and called goodbye to Marek.

She'd been right to take the sheepskin. It was so cold outside that the air seemed to stretch around her. Everyone was dressed for the weather, heads covered, chins tucked into collars. Fortunately, it was a short walk to Mostowski Palace.

The same policeman was at the checkpoint. His smile and the fact he merely glanced at her passport suggested he'd recognised her. 'Pani Górska?' he said. 'Inspector Robak is expecting you. I'll phone and let him know you've arrived.'

Dania waited, resisting the urge to stamp her feet. Although she'd brought industrial-strength gloves, she'd not paid the same attention to her choice of boots.

'The inspector is on his way,' the policeman said. He must have seen Dania shuffling, because he added, 'I'll take you inside.'

'Thank you,' she breathed, feeling warmer already.

Inside the building, he instructed a colleague to take her to Robak, then left with a smile.

They followed the passageway, and climbed the stairs to the first floor. Partway along the corridor, they passed an officer who, on seeing the policeman, called after him. From the shoulder insignia, it was evident this man was of higher rank. The policeman glanced anxiously at Dania and said, 'Will you excuse me a moment, Pani Górska?'

The men huddled against the window, speaking in low tones. It was clear the policeman was being reprimanded in a friendly but firm way for a minor misdemeanour.

Dania moved away, not wanting them to think she was listening, and pretended to examine the stand displaying three large flags: Poland's, Warsaw's and the flag of the European Union. Opposite, a white door had been left ajar. She peered into the room, seeing white columns, an exquisite parquet floor and rows of chairs. Her heart was racing. This must be the famous Sala Biała, or White Room, where Chopin had given his concerts. She imagined the furniture a salon like this would have had. Then she spotted the grand piano at the far end. The lid was open.

She paused to listen to the conversation from the corridor. Although she couldn't make out all the words, whatever the men were talking about was unlikely to be resolved soon. She crept over to the piano, and slipped behind the low, corded barrier. After pulling off her gloves and unbuttoning her sheepskin, she sat down and adjusted the seat. She stared at the keys, wondering what to play. In the end, it was obvious. Chopin's Opus 33, a series of four mazurkas, was dedicated to his pupil, Countess Róża Mostowska, the youngest child of Tadeusz Mostowski, who had owned this building.

Dania closed her eyes, filling her mind with the music, and brought her hands down on the keys. The first mazurka was in a minor key, slow and tinged with melancholy. It was little more than one and a half minutes long, enough to tell her the piano was slightly out of tune although not to the extent many would notice. She moved on to the second mazurka, lively and dance-like, and written in a major key. The third piece was slow and romantic. The final was the most challenging. It began slowly with the sort of haunting melody for which Chopin was famous, but then the pace quickened before returning to the original lyrical theme. She finished with a flourish, remembering then that as a child she'd played these mazurkas for a music exam Jakub

Frydman had coached her for. She'd been nervous – who isn't at that age? – but thanks to his kindness and perception, her confidence had grown and she'd passed the exam with distinction. Simply passing it would have satisfied her, but she'd wanted to do more than that. For him.

Dania closed the lid, and stood up, only then aware of the crowd that had tiptoed in. They were standing staring. Except for Inspector Robak, who was leaning against the wall, arms crossed, an amused smile on his face. He was in jeans and an open-necked white shirt, and was wearing his shoulder holster over a blue-grey checked waistcoat.

'It's not often we're treated to a concert, Pani Górska,' he said, straightening. He addressed the officers. 'I think we should show our appreciation, don't you?'

The burst of applause filled the room. The officers nodded respectfully. Reluctantly, with glances over their shoulders as if not wanting to miss an encore, they filed out. Dania gathered up her gloves.

Robak's smile faded as she approached. His eyes narrowed. He gripped her chin gently but firmly, and turned her head so he could see her cheek. 'Who did that to you?' he demanded.

She was tempted to say she'd walked into a door, but that would insult his intelligence. 'I was attacked by the river,' she said calmly. 'It was a man out jogging. He was after my bag.'

Robak released her. 'And did he succeed?'

'Someone came to my rescue. He managed to get it back.'

'I take it you've reported this.'

'Inspector, we both know how difficult – and time-consuming – cases like this are to resolve. The attacker's face was partly concealed, and he ran off before anyone could do anything. And there were no cameras.'

'There'll be cameras further along.'

'By which time, he'll have taken off his hooded jacket, and put on a hat and sunglasses. He'll be unrecognisable.'

Robak's expression suggested he appreciated the force of the argument.

'But if I see him again, I'll rearrange his face.'

'Pani Górska!' he said, trying to look shocked. A smile danced in his eyes. 'I hope you know that sort of behaviour is prohibited in the Republic of Poland.'

'I do.'

The smile had reached his lips. 'Then you will consider yourself duly warned.'

'I will.'

'And can I be there when you do?'

'Do what?'

'Rearrange his face.'

She started to laugh, then stopped, wincing with pain.

'I'm afraid you'll have to stop laughing for a while,' he said.

'Then try not to say anything funny.'

He smiled apologetically. 'So, shall we go to my office?' He stood back. As she passed him, her gaze was drawn to the firearm in its holster. The faint, acrid smell of gunpowder reached her.

He must have seen her looking because he said, 'I had a shift on the firing range this morning. I'm afraid the smell lingers. It's this way,' he added, indicating she should turn right. 'I'm at the end of the corridor.'

Robak's office had a desk at one end and a table at the other. A large whiteboard was fixed to the wall below the same Polish coat of arms Dania had seen in Oskar Dolniak's office. Above the window behind the desk was a crucifix.

Robak pulled out a chair. 'Please take a seat, Pani Górska.' He sat next to her. 'You said you wanted to discuss something with me.'

'It's about the body found washed up on the riverbank a year ago. Inspector Dolniak mentioned it. The throat was cut so deeply the head was almost severed.'

He frowned. 'I remember it well.'

'The man I'm chasing kills his victims in the same way.'

'Including your informant, you said?'

'Including her. We found his other victims in the river Tay.'

'Perhaps we'd better sit at my desk and look through what we have.'

Moments later, they were gazing into the computer screen, working through the crime-scene images.

'The body was decomposing, which didn't help,' Robak said. 'We could hardly put out a photograph. No one would recognise a face as swollen as that, with the skin missing. The pathologist said he'd been submerged for at least three months.'

'I'm guessing there was no ID.'

'No ID. No characteristic markings. We ran his DNA through our database. Again, nothing.'

'And the forensics report? Were there traces of drugs?'

Robak tapped at the keyboard. 'Not in the bloodstream.' He scrolled down. 'None on his clothes, but that's not surprising given how long he'd been in the water. But we found several packets sewn into the lining of his jacket. They contained heroin.'

'Why wasn't he washed into the Baltic?'

'He was weighted down. The ropes eventually perished, and he rose to the surface.'

'I understand you didn't find the perpetrator.'

'For a while, we didn't know the identity of the victim. We looked back through the missing-person reports.' Robak pulled up a record. 'A woman had claimed her son was missing. She gave a good description of what he'd been wearing. The red-and-blue-checked shirt made us sit up and take notice.' He pressed a key. 'These are the clothes he had on when we found him. They're in the condition you'd expect after so long in the water, but the checked shirt is unmistakable.'

Dania's attention was on the boots. Robak must have seen her fixed stare, because he said, 'Yes, heavy-duty footwear.'

'The kind a soldier would use?'

'Or a construction worker. Which is what the man turned out to be. His mother gave us a sample of her DNA and that was it. We had him. This is the photo the woman sent us.' He pressed another key and an image appeared of a man with blonde hair, and arresting dark-blue eyes.

'So, throat cut and concealed packets of heroin. It sounds like he fell foul of Merkury.'

Robak looked at her sharply. 'Did you say Merkury? Is that the name of your man?'

'It's his pseudonym.'

He muttered under his breath and picked up the phone. 'Oskar? Get yourself to my office. Now.' A pause. 'I don't care if you're busy.' He disconnected before the other man could reply.

'While we're waiting, Pani Górska, could I get you a coffee? There's a machine in the corridor.'

'I thought that was a photocopier.'

'It's round the corner from that.'

'I'd love one, thank you. Milk, no sugar.'

'I won't be long.'

As he closed the door, her gaze was drawn to the oil painting next to it. The man's moustache and his Winged Hussars told her it was Jan III Sobieski, the king who'd saved Europe. The cold determination on the riders' faces told her better than words that they were more than ready to fight for Christendom at the Battle of Vienna. She wondered if Sobieski was a hero of the inspector's. He was a hero of hers.

Robak reappeared a short while later with Oskar Dolniak.

'Ah, Pani Górska,' Dolniak said, hurrying over. He took her hand and lifted it to his lips. If he'd noticed the bruise, he said nothing. 'It's a pleasure to see you again.' He glanced nervously at Robak, who was setting the tray of plastic cups on the desk. 'I've been meaning to get in touch,' he added quickly.

'Pull up a chair, Oskar,' Robak said, handing Dania a cup. 'And start at the beginning and tell Pani Górska what you told me yesterday.'

Dolniak licked his lips. 'Right. So, we received a report yesterday morning about increased activity in Praga. There's always activity, of course, but this is an escalation.'

'Within the last few days?' Dania said.

'My man tells me things began to accelerate towards the end of November.' He picked up a cup. 'That's when you thought your drugs kingpin had returned to Warsaw.'

'And what is this group peddling?' she said, trying to contain her excitement.

'Only heroin. Pure-grade.'

'What's your man's role in the organisation?'

'He's low down. He's given packets of stuff to sell.'

Dania sipped her coffee. 'So, how did he come by this information?'

'He took an enormous risk. The guys higher up meet in an abandoned warehouse. He'd learnt there was to be a meeting, so he got there early and hid in the rafters. Two guys arrived to discuss the next shipment. It's coming in on Thursday. That's the day after tomorrow,' he added meaningfully.

'And do we know where?' Robak said, crossing his arms.

'They didn't say. But he did hear something else. The name Merkury. He's taking over the operations in Praga.'

They stared at one another.

Robak broke the silence. 'Your man, Pani Górska.'

'And he's going to supervise the taking in of this shipment,' Oskar said. 'Personally.'

'We need to find where it's arriving, Oskar.'

'Easy for you to say. My informant doesn't know.'

'Who *does* know?' Dania said impatiently.

'The men at the meeting. Remember my pack of cards? Well, they're two of the kings. Clubs and Diamonds.'

'Can we pick them up?' Robak said. 'Put pressure on them?'

'It'll expose my informant. And if Merkury gets wind of it, he'll call the whole thing off.'

'Could we put a tail on one of them? Or both?' Dania said. 'It's unlikely Merkury will be taking in this shipment on his own.' She could sense Oskar's hesitation. 'You have the chance to catch the three of them in the act. *And* confiscate the drugs haul into the bargain.' When he continued to say nothing, she slammed her hand on the desk and said, 'Give me their addresses, goddamn it, and I'll do it myself.'

Dolniak stared, open-mouthed. Robak looked at her as if seeing her properly for the first time. 'I think Pani Górska has made an admirable suggestion, Oskar,' he said slowly. 'We should indeed have them followed.'

'I can't spare anyone,' he said, with a catch in his voice.

'But *I* can. I have an excellent team, who've been especially trained in surveillance.'

Dania's anger evaporated. It was the word 'team' that gave her confidence. If the modus operandi was like that at West Bell Street, there'd be a shift system so officers would be rotated in and out, ensuring the mark wouldn't see the same face twice. The one who tailed kept in touch with the others via a hands-free radio and, depending on the circumstances, they'd swap roles. As a junior officer at the Met, Dania had been trained in surveillance: don't get too close, avoid getting in the mark's line of sight, watch out for shop windows or mirrors, if possible change your clothes, hair, the way you walk, and if the mark enters a building, find somewhere like a café or bus stop to wait it out, but don't hang around in public view for no reason. And – most importantly – if in doubt, walk away.

She looked pleadingly at Robak. 'Can I work with you on this?'

'If you're asking whether you can be part of the surveillance team, then I'm afraid the answer is no. But we can keep you appraised, minute by minute if you prefer, of how things are developing.'

'Can I at least be there when you pull in Merkury?' she said to Dolniak, trying to keep the desperation out of her voice.

'We'll be armed, Pani Górska, and you won't.' He smiled sadly. 'There'll be no one to protect you.'

'Oh, but there will,' Robak said. He uncrossed his arms so they could see the gun in its holster. 'Pani Górska has come all the way from Scotland to find this man. I think we owe her that at least, don't you, Oskar?'

CHAPTER 13

Zygmunt Zelenski was perched on the edge of the white-leather sofa, studying the chessboard on the black-glass coffee table. His son, Konrad, lounging in the armchair opposite, was studying his father.

'And you'll be able to amuse yourself while I'm out, will you?' Zygmunt said, without looking up.

Konrad gulped his cocktail. 'Don't I always?'

He smiled, and glanced at his son. 'If you take my table at the restaurant, you might meet a lady as charming as Dania Górska.'

Konrad snorted. 'I've other plans. I'll be at the villa tonight, so you won't see me at breakfast.'

Zygmunt moved a chess piece, then moved it back. When his son slept at the villa, he didn't sleep alone.

'So, what else did Dania Górska tell you?' Konrad said.

'She teaches English to the Poles in Scotland. You know, when I saw her sitting at my table, I thought Maksymilian Robak had planted her there.'

'What? To quiz you about your business dealings?'

'To quiz me about Rabin Steinberg.'

'And did she?'

'She didn't. She did bring up the explosion, but the name she mentioned was Jakub Frydman's.'

'She couldn't have been a plant. Robak's too smart to put his people in our way so clumsily.'

'You think?'

Konrad finished his drink. 'Why don't you give up chess, Dad? It takes so much of your time and energy. And the few occasions I've seen you play, you've never won.'

'There's always a first time.' He moved a black piece, then a white one.

'Hadn't you better be getting along to wherever you're going? You don't want to be late.'

Zygmunt looked fondly at his son, then got to his feet. 'By the way, talking of Robak, have you heard from him yet?'

'I haven't. I'll be ready for him when he calls.'

'You should have checked what that building was before you bulldozed it.'

'Look, there was no way of knowing it had been a synagogue.'

'The rabbi knew.'

Konrad shrugged. 'Anyway, Robak's got nothing on me. Why would I want to kill Steinberg? Because he wrote that article? The inspector's delusional.'

Zygmunt said nothing. He left the lounge and took the corridor to his bedroom. As he changed into a navy suit, he thought not of his son and his business dealings, but of the evening ahead. It was a close friend and erstwhile business partner who'd introduced him to the event in the Old Mokotów district. At first, he'd been sceptical, but his curiosity had been piqued, especially when he'd discovered the event was to take place in an old smoke-filled basement. He'd known many of the men, and had thought this was nothing more than a networking opportunity, although the venue left much to be desired. But then the door opened. The woman was exquisitely dressed in a short black skirt, long jacket, white blouse and stilettos that showed her legs to best advantage. It was the starched butterfly collar, or perhaps the red bow tie, that must have made her choose the pseudonym Motylek, or Butterfly. The most noticeable thing about her was her long hair, which was the same shade of red as her tie. But it was her eyes that drew him. None of the men knew who she was, and were content to leave it that way. But Zygmunt was dazzled. And he decided he'd move heaven and earth to establish her identity. Which would lead to getting to know her better.

He left the house and took the steps to where his chauffeur was standing waiting. The man didn't need to be told where they were headed. He started the engine, and cruised through the landscaped garden. As he approached the wrought-iron gate, he pressed a button on the dashboard and the gate opened smoothly.

'The weather seems to be on the turn, sir,' he said.

'It's only mist. The sun will burn it off tomorrow.' Zygmunt took a silver case from his jacket pocket. It contained Motylek's favourite brand of cigarillo. He lit one, wanting his clothes to smell of it, hoping it would excite her in the way it excited the whores he brought to his house.

The car accelerated, and they left the Wawer district and reached the highway that crossed the bridge. They continued in silence until they arrived at Old Mokotów.

The driver pulled up outside the building. 'Here we are, sir. The usual drill?'

'The usual drill.'

Which meant Zygmunt would phone him when he was ready to leave. What the man did with himself and the car didn't interest him.

On the pavement, Zygmunt pressed the buzzer on the intercom, announcing himself. There was a click, and he was in.

Motylek had already arrived. She turned as he entered, and the corners of her mouth lifted. She was smoking, which gave him a pang of regret: he enjoyed Motylek leaning into him as he lit her cigarillo, her eyes on his. No matter. He'd laid his plans. This was one butterfly he intended to capture.

She stubbed out her cigarillo on the ashtray, then surveyed the room. 'Gentlemen,' she said, 'shall we begin?'

There was a murmur of approval, and the men exchanged glances of anticipation. Motylek took her seat at the chess table. Tonight, she was to play Zygmunt, as his name had been drawn in the ballot. He picked up two pawns, one black and one white, put his hands behind his back, then brought them to the front. It hardly mattered which she chose as, black or white, he'd never seen her lose. When Zygmunt had started attending, he'd been stunned at her proficiency. A guest had murmured that, yes, there'd been a time months earlier when Motylek had lost matches, but those instances had grown fewer with time. He put it down to the fact that she now knew the strengths and weaknesses of her opponents and used them to her advantage. To begin with, the guests would bet on the winner, but then it became pointless. So, now they bet on how long the match would last. That was trickier because, although Motylek had played everyone several times, her opponents were skilled enough to try different opening moves, and new tactics, so the game could take minutes, or hours. But, whoever won the bet, Motylek came away with a healthy slice of the winnings.

She tilted her head and pretended to be making up her mind, teasing Zygmunt and the other guests. Then she laid her fingers on his left hand. He felt a thrill course through his body at the warm touch of her skin. He opened the hand to reveal a black pawn.

Motylek gazed at him for a long moment. Then she laughed.

Pola Lorenc left the building, her bag stuffed with a wad of 100-złoty banknotes. It was later than she'd intended, and the following morning she was on the early shift. But Pan Zelenski had insisted he buy her a glass of *wiśniówka* before she left. One glass had become two, and then three. After that, he was happy to let her go. But she hadn't picked up anything of interest to Maks, which was one of the reasons she continued with these matches.

It had been the year before last when Maks had learnt from the barman, a speedway competitor friend, of this event, and discovered who was attending. And how they gossiped freely among themselves, knowing – or believing – there was no danger of being overheard. Given the level of corruption among businessmen, he saw an excellent opportunity. He called Pola into his office and referred to her CV, where she'd stated she'd been runner-up in the Individual Polish Chess Championship. After a brief conversation, they'd come up with a plan, known only to the two of them: Pola would play chess, but keep her ears open for anything of interest to the police. Whenever there was information Maks could use, he'd be careful to muddy the waters as to how he'd come by it.

Their main challenge was to insert Pola into the group. Having discussed various possible ways, she'd made a suggestion: she'd arrive heavily disguised, and ask if she could play, she'd heard rumours about these matches and, being a chess player herself, had wondered if they'd let her in. Rather than try to draw attention away from the fact that she was a woman, she'd dress in such a way as to do the opposite. It would work, or it wouldn't, she'd told Maks. And it had worked spectacularly. The men, all middle-aged, had decided to try her out. She'd played so convincingly, losing by a narrow margin, that they'd asked her back. Not every guest played, but those who did used techniques that were transparent. The trick was not to win too easily, but to give her opponent a run for his money. Or, rather, a run for *her* money. Because the winner received a percentage of the takings. After a while, the men grew accustomed enough to her presence to speak freely, especially when they saw her gossiping with the barman. Or appearing to. And Maks's gamble soon paid off as she started to deliver the kind of intelligence that assisted the police.

The men had tried to probe her background. But she was so good at deflecting questions, she could have been a politician. When she did provide answers, they were sufficiently vague as to be worthless. One or two slipped their business cards into her pocket, and one guest went so far as to proposition her blatantly. And they all wore wedding rings. Tut, tut.

But, recently, she'd noticed that Zygmunt Zelenski was paying her more attention than usual. He was one of Maks's people of interest, so she'd gone along with it, even encouraged it. And, as he'd been her opponent that evening, she'd prolonged the game as far as possible, putting herself in a precariously losing situation before regaining the advantage. She was well aware he studied her more than he studied the game, which wasn't wise, but would have made no difference as he was a middle-ranking player. He lost gracefully, as they all did, congratulating her and kissing her hand. She wondered how far she was prepared to go with him to get her intel.

At the street corner, Pola stopped to switch her phone back on – it was a house rule that mobiles had to be turned off during a game – and the footsteps stopped also. Rather than continue to the tram station, she headed eastwards, following the grid of roads to Łazienki Park. She pretended her phone had rung, and lifted it to her ear, pausing to lean against a wall. It gave her the opportunity to look around slowly, as people do when speaking into a mobile. The shadows were deepening, their edges softened in the evening mist, but she spotted the figure ducking behind a tree. If this man had intended her harm or wanted to rob her, he'd had plenty of opportunity, since the streets were deserted at this hour. There was only one conclusion: he was following her because he wanted to know where she lived. What she needed to do was outfox him in such a way he wouldn't know he'd been rumbled.

As she approached Belwederska, she heard chanting. It grew louder, and she made out, 'God, Honour, Fatherland.' A huge crowd carrying flares and waving Polish flags was milling outside the iron gates of Belweder Palace. Pola couldn't think what was behind this demonstration until she remembered the Russian prime minister had arrived on an official visit, and was staying at the palace. It couldn't have been better. She inserted herself into the crowd, which consisted mainly of men, and joined in the chanting. The demonstrators shifted restlessly, allowing her to pick her way through the mêlée and slip out the other side. She crossed Belwederska and, taking street turnings at random, stumbled upon a tram stop. Her luck was in, as one was about to leave. She climbed on, and sat where she could see the doors. No one boarded after her. A few stops later, she left the tram, walked a short way and found one that would take her home.

Half an hour later, she was in her living room, rubbing her toes. She pulled off the wig and removed the clips, shaking out her hair. The following morning, she'd visit the convent of the

Franciscan Sisters of the Family of Mary, a five-minute walk from her apartment, and present them with her winnings. The nuns had created the so-called 'Window of Life', a baby box in the convent wall, accessible from the street. It was there for women who couldn't care for their newborns. Since learning from Oskar Dolniak that Maks had been left outside the convent as an infant, with a note saying his name was Maksymilian, she'd decided the Window of Life would be a suitable place to deposit the winnings. What she'd never told her boss, however, was that she'd overheard someone at the chess club remark that Zygmunt Zelenski regularly made donations to the Sisters, adding sneeringly it was to avoid paying tax on the money. She didn't want Maks to learn that Zelenski was funding the very orphanage in which he'd been raised.

Pola pulled her laptop onto her knees and logged in. She had emails to deal with and reports to write, although most could wait until the following day. Another time, she'd have connected to the city's cameras to see if she could identify the person following her, but there was no point. The mist and the dark would make identification impossible.

She thought through the events of the evening. She'd not considered herself in danger from the men at the chess club, but one member had either engaged someone to follow her, or more likely had followed her himself. She'd concluded the man tailing her had wanted to discover where she lived. But she might have been wrong. Perhaps he'd intended to murder her away from the building, so as not to risk suspicion falling on a guest. He might even have planned to murder her in her apartment. She ran her fingers through her hair, then started to plait it. The next time she attended a match, she'd take a more roundabout route home. And before she left work, she'd sign out a firearm.

CHAPTER 14

Maks was perched on the edge of the desk, surveying his team. He'd long since concluded early-morning briefings were the worst, as most of his officers were half asleep. But today was different. They were alert, and chatting away, even the glum ones exchanging smiles. He put it down to Legia Warsaw's having won their match the day before.

He and Oskar had already been at work for an hour. They'd instructed the surveillance teams to start following the two kings, Clubs and Diamonds, with everyone reporting in as soon as they were swapped out. Although the shipment of heroin wasn't due until the following day, Maks had a hunch the kings would relocate to a safe house in Praga, and he was determined not to lose them. Fortunately for the teams, yesterday's mist had all but evaporated. Otherwise they'd find themselves following the wrong people. Information had begun to filter through not long after they'd set to work, and the software on his and Oskar's computers was plotting the routes the marks were taking. So far, the kings had boarded a number 24 tram from the city centre.

Maks had messaged Danuta Górska, inviting her over, but had received no reply. Right now, however, he needed to catch up on the Okopowa cemetery case.

'So, how did it go with the construction workers?' he asked, looking round the room. 'Any luck with the Amatol?'

'You know how it is, boss,' an officer at the front said. 'We've asked that question so many times, they just roll their eyes. But we tried something different. We said we'd check their bank accounts for unusually large deposits.'

Maks grinned. 'I bet that went down well.'

'We didn't tell them how long it would take to get the required permission. But it had the desired effect.' He glanced at his companion, a tough-looking woman with messy red curls. 'One or two looked distinctly uneasy.'

The woman returned the glance. 'They were guys we've investigated before for selling Amatol.'

'And?' Maks said.

'We got nowhere. Either last time or this time. They told us to do our worst.'

'Who owns the construction company they work for?' he said, knowing the answer.

'Zygmunt Zelenski.' She lifted her head defiantly. 'But that doesn't mean the Zelenskis had anything to do with the explosion.'

Maks had to concede the point. The Amatol could have been unearthed and sold on the quiet without the foreman's knowledge. Or the foreman could have been in on it and not reported it. 'And what about our unexpected guest? Did you show them the E-FIT?'

'We got the same response,' someone said. 'They shrugged, and said they didn't know him. We checked the company's employment records going back a year or two. There was no one who looked like him, scars or no scars.'

'What about the other construction companies?'

'Their reactions were the same,' the red-haired woman replied. 'They looked as though they genuinely didn't know him. It was the burn scars. They said they'd remember those. I mean, who wouldn't?'

'And the public haven't been in touch? The E-FIT image went into the *Express Wieczorny* last Thursday. It's Wednesday today.'

Their blank looks gave him the answer.

'I can't believe no one knows our unexpected guest,' the red-head said.

'Oh, they know him,' Maks said. 'But they don't want to come forward. Either for fear of the consequences, or because their silence has been bought. All right, let's move on to the guests at the funeral. I know we've not finished, but did the background investigations throw up anything?'

'We ran checks on the guests and their families, and even some acquaintances,' Pola said. 'There's nothing remotely interesting about them. They're fine, boring, law-abiding citizens. And none of their names appears in the archives at the Institute of National Remembrance. The only one there's still a question mark over is Adam Mazur. I've not finished searching the records on him.'

'There's also Rabin Steinberg,' Maks said. 'I haven't had time to meet with Konrad Zelenski, and it doesn't look as though it'll be this week.'

'I can do that,' Pola said. 'He's always at his father's casino nightclub.'

'You want a flutter at the tables,' someone said, raising a laugh.

Maks looked at her for a moment, then nodded. He reached behind him. 'Right, so here's my contribution.' He held up a sheet. 'This was handed in yesterday evening. It's from Adam Mazur. It's a list of names of those he invited to Jakub Frydman's funeral.'

'I thought we had that,' someone said.

'That was a list of those who *attended*. There might have been someone *invited* who was unable to attend. And, as it happens, there was.' Maks paused for effect. 'Lidia Lipska.'

They gaped at one another.

'*The* Lidia Lipska?' someone gasped.

'How many Lidia Lipskas do you know?' the redhead said, with a sneer.

Lidia Lipska, a renowned pianist and teacher, had recently left her musical career to stand for public office. As a member of the Civic Platform Party, her campaign had centred on bringing the ruling Law and Justice Party to account. She'd been elected with a huge majority.

'She's been interviewed often enough about her career as a musician,' Maks said. 'If someone had wanted to kill her, he'd have known she'd been a pupil of Jakub Frydman's. And therefore invited to his funeral. The problem is she's made so many enemies in government that we'll be spoilt for choice.'

'Do we know why she didn't make the funeral?' Pola said. 'If everyone knew she was out of the country, for example, then she can't have been the intended victim.'

'These are issues we need answers to.' He looked round the room. 'Questions?'

They shook their heads. Maks lifted a hand to indicate the meeting was over. They made for the door, all speaking at once.

As the room emptied, he returned to his chair. He glanced up from the screen to see that Pola had hung back. 'Second thoughts about visiting the Zelenski nightclub?' he said, smiling.

'No, it's not that.'

He detected hesitation in her voice. 'Have a seat,' he said.

She took the chair opposite. She was wearing black tights and a short skirt, which she pulled down as far as it would go. 'I went to the chess club last night,' she began.

'And do you have something to report?'

'Nothing of relevance to our enquiries. But after I left I was followed.'

Maks frowned. 'A man from the club?'

'I'm certain of it.'

'What happened?'

'Nothing. I lost him.'

'Were there places where he could have attacked you? Deserted streets?'

'There were several. So, my guess is he wanted to know where I was going.'

'Who do you think it was?'

'It could have been any of them.'

'Is this the first time it's happened?'

'Yes.'

Maks studied her. She wasn't remotely disturbed by the experience. It was as though she was giving him a routine report. 'My guess is either someone at the club wants to have sex with you,' he said, 'or they've seen through your disguise, and suspect you're working undercover.'

Pola shifted in her seat. 'Zygmunt Zelenski was more interested in me than usual.' She shrugged. 'But that could be because I played him at chess.'

'And did he take it well when he lost?'

A smile touched her lips. 'They all do.'

Maks's immediate reaction was to put an end to her chess sessions. But the intelligence she was delivering had proved invaluable. And, given that whoever was tailing her hadn't made a move, she didn't appear to be in immediate danger. Although that could change. That she'd spotted the tail and thrown him off was down to her training. But he had to weigh up the value of the intel against the threat to her life.

'How do you want to proceed, Pola?'

'I want to continue.'

'I can have someone wait outside the club.'

'And put a tail on the tail?'

'We've done it before.'

'It's too risky. If he's spotted, the game will be up.'

'It could be a she.'

'Even so.'

'When's your next match?'

'A week today. It'll be the last before Christmas.'

He was of two minds. He could order her not to go and, as a subordinate, she'd have no choice but to obey. But she was an experienced officer, and he'd sent her into dangerous situations before. He gazed at her steadily. She gazed back without flinching. He wondered what her reaction would be if he ordered her off the case. Would she react as Danuta Górksa had, showing her anger by slamming her hand on the desk? Although Pola had had plenty of cause to be angry, he'd never seen her show it. In fact, he knew no one who had such supreme control of her emotions.

'From now on, you carry a firearm,' he said.

She nodded, her face expressionless.

As he watched her leave, he wondered what playing Zygmunt Zelenski would have been like. And what losing to a woman would have been like for Zygmunt Zelenski. The man had told him good losers don't make good winners. And he didn't like to lose. It irked Maks that the businessman made regular donations to the Franciscan Sisters of the Family of Mary. He'd thrown it in

Maks's face, knowing full well that that was where Maks had been raised.

A sudden sound from the computer dragged him from his thoughts. It was a member of the surveillance team checking in. The two kings were now at the King Cross mall in Praga South on a shopping spree. So far, they'd bought trainers and clothes. Maks tilted back in his chair. Interesting they'd crossed the river when there were many excellent shopping malls in the city centre. Could it be they had a rendezvous? With Merkury, perhaps? The surveillance team had been warned to be extra vigilant when it came to meetings. Maks checked his messages. Still nothing from Danuta, although it was only ten o'clock. But perhaps she'd decided to wait until the following day, when the shipment was arriving. And once her man was in custody, she'd be flying back to Scotland. He found himself thinking not about Merkury, and their plan for apprehending him, but about Danuta, how she'd brought her hand down on the desk. And as he recalled the fire in those hazel eyes, he felt a sudden tightness in his chest, like a breath that had been held for too long.

CHAPTER 15

'So, I heard from Baletnica last night,' Marek was saying.

'Mm?'

'You're not listening to me, Danka.'

'I'm sorry. I've got a lot on my mind. What were you saying?'

Marek studied his sister. She'd hardly touched her breakfast. Worse still, she was fidgety, rearranging her mug, running her fork through the remains of the pancakes. Marek was familiar with the symptoms and knew that if she continued like this she'd wear herself out. The only thing he could do was distract her. He tried again. 'I was talking about the letters I found in Wola. Remember I said the puzzle box was at the bottom of a crate of books? Well, I'd told Baletnica many were first editions, and he replied to say he'd take care of it.'

'And did he?' Danka said, scraping the last of the jam from the bottom of the jar.

'I presume so. But I got to thinking the books had belonged to Chopin's sister, Ludwika. Until I remembered most were written after she'd died. *Quo Vadis*, for example.'

'Perhaps it was only the puzzle box that had been hers. And the person who owned those books had acquired it not knowing what was inside.'

'Exactly. Which is why I've decided to research the books' owner, in case he acquired other possessions of hers. The manuscript, for example. I emailed Baletnica asking if he knows who the books belonged to. Turned out it was a collector of rare editions. Books *and* papers. And I've got his name.'

'How will this help you find the manuscript? This man might have sold it. It could have changed hands many times since.'

'I'm going to start by assuming it didn't, that this collector had it and kept it. What I need to establish is what happened to his other books and papers. The manuscript might be among them, hidden by accident and forgotten.' Marek ran a hand through his hair, messing it. 'Okay, I see doubt on your face. Yes, it may be a false assumption, but I have to start somewhere.'

'Let's go back to the letters. Why would Ludwika have put them inside a puzzle box?'

'I've no idea.'

'To hide them?'

He took a gulp of coffee. 'Does it matter?'

'Maybe the box wasn't hers. Maybe this collector stored the letters there. He couldn't put the manuscript into a small box like that, though. With the orchestral as well as the piano score, you're talking between fifty and a hundred pages.' Danka licked the jam off the spoon. 'What became of Chopin's other unpublished works?'

'Ludwika, with her mother and sister, Izabella, authorised Chopin's friend, Julian Fontana, to publish them.'

'But if Ludwika had the concerto, why didn't Fontana publish it?'

'It can only be because he didn't receive it.'

'Wouldn't Ludwika have done something about that?'

Marek played with the mug. 'She might not have had the

opportunity. Regrettably, she died of the plague a couple of years later.'

'How do you intend to conduct the research? Online?'

'That'll get me only so far. No, I'm going to start at the National Library and see what they have on this collector. They may know what became of his other books and papers.'

'Is that why you've put on a jacket and tie?'

'How perceptive of you, Danka.'

'Does Baletnica know you're doing this?'

'I've run it past him. He thinks it's definitely worth a shot. I suspect he's hit a wall.' His expression brightened. 'He said he'd try the National Library himself if he has time. Who knows? I might run into him. Okay, I'd better get going. I've reserved a slot in the reading room, and I don't know what happens if you're not on time.'

'Do you want me to walk you to the tram stop?'

'Look, Danka, nothing's going to happen to me. I'll be surrounded by people. You must stop worrying. And, anyway, aren't you meeting with Inspector Robak? You might want to put on something to cover that bruise. It's more colourful today.'

'It's tomorrow that things will happen.' Her spirits lifted. 'If all goes according to plan, we'll have Merkury, and I'll be flying home on Friday.'

'In that case, we need to plan a visit to Wilanów and see the lights. How about tonight?'

'Maybe.'

Marek downed the rest of the coffee. 'Shall I come back for lunch?'

'Not on my account. I'll be holed up all day.' She gestured to the window. 'The sun's out. I'd make the most of it.' She smiled for the first time that morning. 'So, what happened to the snow we were going to get?'

Pola Lorenc pushed through the door of the Golden Sunrise, pausing to let her eyes become accustomed to the gloom. Opposite the bar, on a low platform, an elderly couple was dancing the tango less energetically than the small band was playing the music. She watched the movements, remembering her first visit to this casino nightclub. An officer in Oskar's unit had asked her out, suggesting this place because he'd heard about the tango music. Unfortunately, he'd then asked her to dance. As neither had any idea how to tango, they'd made fools of themselves. She'd taken lessons in the hope that she could entice him back to the nightclub, but he'd moved on to someone else by the time her classes had ended.

Aware of the nightclub's dress code, Pola had put on a dove-grey suit and white blouse. As it was midday, a cocktail dress would have been inappropriate. And, anyway, she was there on business. The barman was trying to catch her eye, but she ignored him and made for the door next to the archway.

In the dim corridor, she looked around, unsure of her bearings.

'Can I help you?'

A man was standing in the doorway of what she assumed was the office, since she could see a desk in the room. His face was in shadow.

'Pan Zelenski?' she said, holding up her warrant.

He hardly glanced at it. 'That's right.'

'I'm Sergeant Pola Lorenc.'

'I know who you are.'

For a moment, she couldn't think how since they'd never met, until she remembered people like the Zelenskis made it their business to learn the names of police officers, just as police officers made it their business to learn the names of corrupt businessmen. She wondered how Konrad Zelenski would react if she told him that.

'I'd like to ask you some questions,' she said.

'Then we'd better make ourselves comfortable.' He stepped back, extending an arm to indicate she should enter.

There was little in the way of furniture: a desk and chairs, and two large filing cabinets. One cabinet would hold papers and correspondence for the nightclub and for the Zelenskis' construction business. The other would hold the 'official' documents they'd send to the National Revenue Administration. But she wasn't there to talk about the Zelenskis' tax affairs.

Without waiting to be asked, she pulled out a chair. Konrad took a seat behind the desk. He leant back, clasping his hands behind his neck, waiting for her to speak. The light from the window fell onto his face, giving her a good view of his features. The resemblance to his father was uncanny. His hair wasn't grey, as he was still in his late twenties, but the facial features were remarkably similar: the pale eyes, the shape of the nose, the cheekbones.

He'd be waiting for her to bring up the explosion at Okopowa, Pola thought, so she intended to surprise him.

'I'm here about the building on the corner of Strzelecka,' she said, adjusting her reading glasses. She studied him as she opened her notebook.

A frown crossed his face. He lowered his arms slowly.

'The synagogue,' she added, when no response was forthcoming.

He'd recovered his composure. 'The warehouse, you mean.'

'It was a synagogue disguised as a warehouse. I understand one of the Zelenski companies bought the building.' She kept her gaze steady. 'Why was that?'

It was a question that could have had several responses, but Konrad fell into the trap. 'We bought it to redevelop it.'

'You bought a synagogue to redevelop it as a synagogue. Is that what you're saying?'

'I'm not saying that, no. We're building an apartment block in place of the synagogue. In place of the warehouse, I mean.'

'Yet you knew it was a synagogue.'

'Of course we didn't. How were we supposed to know?'

'Didn't you check the land registry?' Pola knew she was on shaky ground, as she'd not checked whether the synagogue was listed there. But she guessed the Zelenskis wouldn't have checked either. Before Konrad could answer, she added, 'Don't you pay attention to due diligence when you acquire properties, Pan Zelenski?'

His anger was rising. 'Of course we do,' he said, through clenched teeth.

'Then you'll have the relevant documents.'

'This is about Rabin Steinberg,' he said, glaring at her defiantly.

'What does Rabin Steinberg have to do with this?'

'He wrote an article accusing me of fraudulently buying the synagogue. Which was totally untrue.'

Pola tried to look mystified. 'Did he? I don't recall. But if he did, and the accusation was untrue, why didn't you take legal action?'

'You're here because of the explosion in Okopowa,' Konrad said, suddenly triumphant. 'You're trying to find a motive. The rabbi was present, and you're looking for people with a grudge against him.'

'How do you know he was present, Pan Zelenski? The list of guests hasn't been published.'

She wished she had a camera to record the hunted look on his face. Before she could press home her advantage, she heard a voice behind her.

'I think this interview is over, Sergeant.'

Zygmunt Zelenski was standing in the doorway.

'My son and I have business to attend to,' he said smoothly. 'So, you'll understand why I'm asking you to leave.'

Pola turned to Konrad. 'Thank you for your time, Pan Zelenski.' She stood up, smoothing her skirt. Remembering how Zygmunt had looked into her eyes at the chess club, she kept her spectacles on and her gaze averted as she left the room.

'Ah, Pani Górska,' Inspector Robak said, getting to his feet. He nodded to the uniformed policeman, who left promptly.

'Is this a good time?' Dania said.

'Of course.' Robak shook her hand. 'Oskar will be joining us shortly.' He indicated the large screen on the table. It displayed a map of Warsaw. 'Let me show you where we are.'

They sat side by side, close enough that Dania could smell his cologne. It was the same spice-and-sandalwood brand Marek wore. Robak picked up the mouse. 'So, this shows the route our two kings, Clubs and Diamonds, took after they left their respective apartments this morning.' He enlarged the map. Two red lines appeared, then converged to a single thicker line. 'That's the tram route they took to the King Cross shopping mall in Praga South.'

'So, they live in the city centre?' Dania asked, leaning forward.

'Not far from each other.' He played with the controls, and a series of still images appeared. 'And here they are in the shopping centre. Some of these were taken with the surveillance team's bodycams, others on their phones.'

The photos showed two thickset men wearing heavy quilted jackets. One wore a knitted beanie, the other a Russian hat with the earflaps down. They were leaving a shop that sold sportswear, each carrying several bags.

'I see they're wearing rucksacks,' Dania said.

'Given Merkury is operating in Praga, it's likely that's where he'll take in the consignment. These guys might be intending to stay in the district overnight in case there's a problem with transport.' Robak threw her a sidelong glance. 'I hear snow is forecast.'

'And do you think Merkury will stay in Praga, too?'

'It depends how seriously they take this forecast. Or, if they take it seriously, how bad they think the snow will be.'

'What do *you* think about the forecast?'

Robak sat back, crossing his arms. 'The mist has cleared. The sun's been out all day.'

'But it could change overnight.'

He angled his head. 'It could. But I've been studying the weather sites. Only one of them mentions snow in Warsaw. It's a site in western Russia. The Polish TV stations have latched onto it.' He smiled. 'Because Poles like to see snow at this time of year. It's just over two weeks to Wigilia.' His gaze lingered on her face. 'Have you decided to stay in Warsaw for Christmas?' he added softly.

'I'm flying back to Scotland the day after tomorrow. I have cases that require my attention.' She thought she detected disappointment in his eyes. 'Marek wants to see the Royal Garden of Lights at Wilanów. We've run out of time, so it'll have to be this evening.'

'Ah, Wilanów. I hope you enjoy it.' Robak turned to the screen, and pressed a key. 'Okay, this is where the two kings are currently. Having a long lunch at McDonald's.' The stills showed the men queuing, then seated. They'd taken off their hats, but left their jackets on. One man sported a frizzy reddish mop, and the other had dark hair cropped close to his head. She recognised them from Oskar Dolniak's playing cards.

'Once they're outside,' Robak said, 'one of my Romeo pairs should be able to get close enough to record what they're saying.'

'Romeo pairs?'

'I'm sure your surveillance teams have them. Basically, it's a man and a woman, who are all over each other, and constantly taking selfies. Except they're not taking selfies, they're taking photographs. Because they're likely to be ignored by the marks, they can get closer than most. We have no shortage of volunteers.' His lips curved into a smile, making Dania wonder if he'd taken such an assignment himself as a junior officer.

'My Romeo pairs have state-of-the-art voice-recording equipment,' he went on. 'We may hear something once the kings leave.' He glanced at the screen. 'It looks as though they're still at McDonald's.'

'It wouldn't be my first choice of eating place. I'm sure there are better cafés in the area.'

He looked at her with interest. 'Do you know Praga?'

'Not well. I visited the zoo as a child.'

'That's now on the tourist route, I understand.'

'Tourists visit Praga North?'

'Films set during the war are shot there. Since Polański's *The Pianist*, people have wanted to see the area.'

There was a sudden sharp knock at the door.

'Enter,' Robak called.

Oskar Dolniak put his head round. 'Ah, excellent. You're here too, Pani Górska. I'm about to get food sent up. Unless you've eaten?'

'We haven't,' Robak said.

Dolniak spoke to someone in the corridor, then breezed in. He took the seat on Dania's other side, lifting her hand to kiss it. 'So, where are we?' he said to Robak. 'I've come from a meeting, so I've not been following developments.'

Robak gestured with his chin. 'The kings have spent two hours at McDonald's, and now they're on the move.'

The red line had reached the Ibis hotel, south of the shopping mall.

Dania squinted at the map. 'Maybe that's where they intend to stay over.'

There was a loud buzz, and a light came on. Robak tapped the screen. 'It's one of my Romeo pairs.'

The recording was crackly, but they had no trouble making out the words. The kings were talking about the two prostitutes they'd be meeting at the Ibis, and arguing about which man would take which, and whether there'd be time to swap and do it again. It was clear this wasn't the first time they'd met the women, whom they referred to by their first names.

'Sex on a full stomach?' Oskar said, in a scandalised voice. 'They've been two hours at McDonald's!'

Dania caught Robak's amused look. She turned away so Dolniak couldn't see her smile.

'So, while we're waiting for them to finish pleasuring themselves,' Robak said, 'let's talk about Merkury. Do we have a description, Pani Górska?'

'My informant said only that he has wavy mid-brown hair and pale eyes,' Dania said.

'And he's good-looking,' Dolniak chipped in. 'But so are most Polish men. Wouldn't you agree, Maks?'

'Well, that's a question for Pani Górska,' Robak said, a smile playing about his lips.

Before Dania could reply, there was a knock at the door. It opened and a man entered, wheeling a trolley loaded with food.

'Thanks,' Robak said. 'Leave everything on the end of the table.'

The man offloaded three large serving plates, and made to leave. 'Can you give us one more?' Dolniak said. 'We're expecting someone.'

The man threw him a look, but set down a fourth plate.

'And what about cakes?'

He sighed and lifted something from the bottom of the trolley. It was a plate of *makowiec*. Dania's mouth started to water as she gazed at the poppy seeds.

'Are we expecting someone else, Oskar?' Robak said, after the door had closed.

'No, but three plates of *kanapki* is nowhere near enough. Pani Górska is going to think we don't look after our visitors.'

She was about to add there was more food here than she usually ate in a week when Dolniak lifted a plate and held it out. 'Take a few,' he said, dropping a paper napkin onto her lap. The open sandwiches were exactly as she liked them: Polish sausage and gherkins on dark rye bread. She wondered if they'd be as good as Marek's.

'So, how does Merkury take in his shipments?' Robak asked.

'We've never been able to track down the source,' Dania said, 'but my informant confirmed they come in with freight. Packets are hidden inside children's toys, for example. Occasionally, they're inside the vehicle's chassis, or the upholstery. Magda was too low down in the hierarchy to get this information in advance, so we could never catch him in the act. She heard about it afterwards.'

'Do the lorries come over the border from England? Or by sea, directly to Scotland?'

'Our Drugs Squad were never able to establish that.'

Robak took a sandwich. 'It's more than likely Merkury is still sourcing his heroin from the same place. In Poland, it either crosses the land border, or comes in via the Baltic.'

'We can ask him when we arrest him,' Dolniak said, reaching for another plate of *kanapki*.

'How many men will you have tomorrow, Oskar?'

'Enough.'

He looked supremely confident, Dania thought, munching her sandwich. Too confident. But, then, he'd not seen Merkury's handiwork close up.

'How does it operate in Dundee, Pani Górska?' Robak said, breaking into her thoughts. 'How does the heroin get onto the streets?'

'There's an army of street sellers. They have a good eye for those looking for drugs. And they have their "regulars", addicts whom they know well and who can be found easily.'

'And do the police know who these addicts are? Do they have them watched?'

'It's a case of manpower. There aren't enough officers in the Drugs Squad. They close down one ring, and two more spring up. One of the men told me it's like trying to sweep up leaves on a windy day.'

'What about street cameras?'

'We have plenty of those. But Dundee's an ancient city. It has narrow streets and alleyways with no cameras.' She shrugged. 'And the sellers and buyers are pros. They know how to conduct business without making it obvious.'

'It's the same here, Maks,' Dolniak said, offering the plate of *makowiec* to Dania. 'There's no point in going for the street men. We need to cut off the monster's head. Right, I'll get the coffees,' he added. He left the room.

'How's your brother?' Robak said. 'He was unwell when we spoke on Sunday.'

'Greatly improved. It was a twenty-four-hour thing.'

'And is he back to looking for the manuscript?'

'He's at the National Library today, researching a collector of rare books.'

'What would you do if he found the manuscript?' He picked up a slice of *makowiec* and examined it. 'Perhaps I should say what *will* you do *when* he finds it?'

'I'll try playing it.'

'You can play Chopin's concertos?'

'I've never played them with an orchestra, of course. But Pan Frydman gave me instruction. He played them beautifully.' Thinking about her piano teacher made her ask, 'Is there any progress with the Okopowa case?'

'No one has come forward to identify our unexpected guest.'

'But someone must know who he is. He may live alone, but there'll be neighbours, surely. Those burns scars are pretty distinctive.'

'I think there are people who know, but have their reasons for keeping quiet.' Robak bit into the *makowiec*. 'We're concentrating our resources on possible motives.'

'And will you keep in touch after I've returned to Dundee? To let me know how the case is going?'

'Of course,' he said, smiling. She remembered that warm glow in his eyes from the first time they'd met.

'I've never been to Dundee,' he added. 'Oskar has fond memories of his visit.'

As if on cue, the door opened and Dolniak appeared with a tray of coffees. He set it down on the table, stacking the empty plates and pushing them away.

Before he could hand round the mugs, the screen light came on with a loud buzz. 'It's my Romeo pair,' Robak murmured, tapping the screen. They heard a woman's voice.

'Inspector, you need to listen to this. They've left the Ibis. And there's a third man with them.' The urgency in her voice made Robak stiffen.

There was crackling, and a man's voice said, 'Then it's agreed. Tomorrow at ten.'

Images flashed on the screen. Three men, having left the Ibis, were strolling past a garage in the direction of the shopping mall. Between the kings was a man dressed in jeans and a black leather jacket. He was wearing sunglasses, and a red baseball cap with the white Polish eagle. He wore it low over his forehead, hiding his hair. The little that could be seen at the nape of his neck was light brown.

'And the beach will be deserted?' a voice asked.

'Are you serious? It'll be dark.'

'We sometimes get boats on the river at night. People bring lights and have a barbecue.'

'At this time of year?'

'Okay, maybe not.'

'Anyway, there's supposed to be snow tomorrow. Although I doubt it myself.' A sneer. 'I don't believe anything the Russkis say about the weather.'

'Shall we meet there or in the city centre?'

'On the beach. And don't be late. The quickest way is the path across the road from the zoo. I'll be parking my vehicle on Ratuszowa, in front of the gates.'

There was a pause. The woman's voice again. 'Inspector. They've split up. The man in the leather jacket is leaving. Should we follow him?'

'No, he'll be suspicious if he sees you again. Pass the details on.'

'And the other two?'

Robak glanced at Dolniak, who nodded. 'Have them followed,' Robak said. He disconnected.

He looked at Dania, then at the image of the three men. 'I think we've had our first glimpse of Merkury, Pani Górska.'

Dolniak's eyes were gleaming. 'Better than that, Maks, we know at which beach the drop is being made. "The quickest way there is the path across the road from the zoo."'

'And where is it?' Dania asked impatiently.

'La Playa beach,' the men said, in unison.

Dolniak laughed. 'So, do we bring our swimming gear?'

CHAPTER 16

Marek was sitting at a window in the National Library's main reading room, gazing into a computer screen. He was poring over a list of the books and manuscripts saved during the war, and catalogued in the years following. His aim was to ascertain whether any of the items listed had belonged to the owner of the puzzle box. So far, he'd hit a wall. He had, however, established that the collector had lived at the address in Wola where the crate of books was hidden. He'd also discovered the man hadn't survived the war. His role in the Underground had been discovered, resulting in his being sent to a concentration camp from which he hadn't returned.

What Marek had established by talking to one of the librarians was that, thanks to an anonymous tip-off, they'd recently acquired a number of rare books, including first editions, belonging to this collector. So, Baletnica had been as good as his word. However, none of this was helping. For the first time, Marek began to doubt that he'd find Chopin's third concerto. It was learning about the scale of the loss caused by the war that had made his spirits slump. So much had been destroyed that the odds of the concerto surviving were small. And yet he'd found the letters. Could it be that somewhere in another Warsaw basement the manuscript lay hidden in a crate, perhaps bundled in with other papers? And forgotten? Maybe this collector owned more than one property. What Marek needed to do was research the man and his life.

He leant back, stretching his arms above his head. The action caused a few readers to look up. Perhaps one of those gazing at him was Baletnica. He smiled self-consciously. No one smiled back. They returned to their work. Except for a man at a nearby table, who was watching him with calculation in his eyes. Suddenly he got to his feet and hurried over.

'Pan Górski,' he said, in a fierce whisper, his face breaking into a smile.

Marek stood up. He kept his voice low. 'Pan Mazur. How nice to see you.' He glanced over the man's shoulder. 'What brings you here?'

'I'm writing a book about Julian Fontana. When I've a spare moment, that is.' Before Marek could reply, he added, 'I'm glad I've run into you. I have something for your sister. I believe she's leaving Warsaw the day after tomorrow?'

'That's right.'

'Is she at home now?'

'She's out. And likely to be out all day. And possibly all day tomorrow.'

An anxious expression crossed Adam's face. 'In that case, I'll give you this now.' He hurried to his table and returned clutching his briefcase. He drew out a large, sealed envelope and handed it to Marek. Danka's name was scrawled on it.

'What's this?' Marek said.

'I'm dealing with Pan Frydman's estate. This is his bequest to your sister.'

'Do you know what's inside?' Marek said, his curiosity rising.

'I've no idea. Knowing Pan Frydman, it will be something musical. Although I could be wrong.'

'I'll make sure she gets it.'

'That's one less thing to worry about.' Adam reached into his pocket and drew out a red-patterned handkerchief. He mopped his brow. 'I've many such bequests to deal with. You have no idea how time-consuming it is. And I've only just started. Part of the problem is tracking people down. Many are no longer in Warsaw.'

'And you'll have his apartment to sell too, I expect.'

'That will be the final thing. Another headache.' He closed his eyes briefly. 'It was so much simpler under the Communists. No one owned anything.' He stopped abruptly as though he'd said too much. 'So, are you also doing some research, Pan Górski?'

Marek glanced round the room. One or two people were showing him more than usual interest, but in a friendly way, suggesting they recognised him. 'I'm on the trail of someone who might have owned Chopin's concerto,' he said, lowering his voice further.

Adam's eyes widened. He licked his lips nervously. 'And have you discovered anything useful?' he said, closing the briefcase.

Marek was reluctant to mention his conversation with the librarian. As a journalist, he kept to himself details of assignments and articles he intended to write. But Adam was waiting for a response.

'He was in the Underground. I need to find out more, but there's nothing here.'

'If he was in the Underground, there are various online databases that will have information.'

'That's a good idea,' Marek said, smiling his acknowledgement. He'd come to the same conclusion.

'I can help, if you like,' Adam said eagerly.

'I wouldn't want to take up your time, Pan Mazur. Not with

everything you have to do for the estate.' He glanced at the man's papers scattered across the table. 'And there's your research.'

'Well, I wish you luck. Please do give my regards to your sister.'

'Of course.' Marek held up the envelope. 'And thank you.'

With a brief smile, Adam returned to his table.

It was four by the time Dania reached the apartment. She strolled into the kitchen to find Marek at his usual seat, gazing into the laptop. He glanced up and, seeing her, his face broke into a smile.

'Productive day?' she said.

'Yes and no. You know what it's like. Two steps forward. One step back. It could be worse. It could be the other way round. What about you?'

She was tempted to tell him about the plan for the following evening, but thought better of it. If Marek knew she was going to be present when they apprehended Merkury, he'd try to talk her out of it. Throughout her career, she'd been careful to leave out of the conversation any mention of the danger she frequently found herself in. Consequently, he had little idea of what her day-to-day life was like. Perhaps that had been a mistake.

He must have seen her hesitate, because he said, 'I ran into Adam Mazur at the library.'

'Not Baletnica?'

'If he was there, he didn't make himself known.'

'So, how is Adam?'

'He's up to his ears dealing with Jakub Frydman's estate. Talking of which, I've got something for you.' He pushed across the envelope. 'This is Jakub's bequest.'

She gazed at the familiar scrawl. 'What is it?'

'I've no idea. As you can see, it's sealed,' he said wryly.

She took a knife from the drawer and slit open the envelope. Inside there was a bundle of papers. She drew them out slowly.

'There's a note from Jakub,' she said, her hands trembling.

Marek got to his feet, and came over. 'What does it say?'

'It says: "Dania, this is a manuscript given to me by Artur Rubinstein. It is Chopin's Ballade Number 4 Opus 52, with Rubinstein's own annotations. Learn to play it the way this great master did."'

'Oh, Danka,' Marek murmured. 'What a wonderful legacy.'

She sank into a chair. Setting the note aside, she picked up the manuscript. And, as she leafed through the pages, seeing Rubinstein's interpretations – sometimes overriding what Chopin had written – she felt as though the clock had been turned back, and she could hear Jakub's voice encouraging her to let the music wash through her, to become one with it, and think of nothing else. The notes became blurred and she realised her eyes were filling with tears. Not wanting them to drop onto the manuscript, she pushed it away and leant back.

Marek gathered the papers and replaced them in the envelope. He put an arm round her shoulders and squeezed. 'I'll make tea,' he murmured.

She continued to stare straight ahead as he bustled about the kitchen, boiling the water and bringing the glasses and the jar of cherry jam to the table. Her mind was only half on these familiar sounds. She was thinking about Rubinstein's manuscript, imagining Jakub poring over his list, deciding upon the various bequests. So, what had made him leave the manuscript to her and not, for example, to Lidia Lipska, his most famous pupil, who had made a career as a concert pianist? Or to Rena Adler, another famous Warsaw pianist? Then, as the tears streamed down Dania's cheeks, she was transported to that morning in Okopowa cemetery – was it only a week ago? – when she'd had her last sight of the wooden coffin with its gold-tasselled red cloth. The image, as clear now as it had been then, overwhelmed her, and she covered her face with her hands and wept silently.

'So, are we going to Wilanów later?' Marek said, clearing away the plates.

He was trying not to sound too eager, Dania thought, in case she said no. 'Of course we are.'

He stopped and looked at her in surprise.

'There might not be an opportunity tomorrow,' she said. 'I have to go to Mostowski Palace.'

There was suspicion in his voice. 'At night?'

'Tomorrow's my last day, and I want to keep the evening free. So, let's go to Wilanów. Now,' she added, with affected eagerness.

He stared at her. 'Fine, let's go.'

Wilanów Palace and gardens were at the end of the Royal Route, and much too far to walk. There were several ways to get there but, after checking, they decided on the bus, although they'd have to change.

'Maybe we can get tickets online,' Marek said. 'The last time there was a huge queue at the ticket office.' He tapped away. 'Oh, I don't believe it,' he murmured.

'What it is?' She peered over his shoulder. 'I see. It's closed this week.' She could almost taste his disappointment. 'But it'll be open next week,' she said. 'You'll be able to go then.'

'It won't be the same without you, Danka.'

He was thinking of his childhood, and how they'd gone to Wilanów every Christmas. What was it about Polish men that they were such romantics? He sounded so low that she said, 'Well, let's go out tonight, anyway. We can take a walk, and see the Christmas lights in the streets. Or go to Castle Square.' When this produced no response, she added, 'Or we can try that new vodka bar, the one that's opened somewhere near the Barbakan.'

He lifted his head slowly, and raised an eyebrow.

Maksymilian Robak locked the door to his apartment, and climbed the steps at the end of the corridor. They led to a trap-door that gave access to the roof. Living on the top floor of a ten-storey building meant he had an enviable view of Warsaw, one of the selling points that had made him rent the small dark studio flat. In summer, he'd bring his supper here, and watch as the sun began its decline, and the blue of the sky deepened and, one by one, lights flicked on in the windows of Warsaw's buildings. To the west lay the burial grounds – Okopowa, Powązki, and the smaller cemeteries. To the east, across the river, was Praga, specifically the area of Praga he and Oskar would be staking out the following night.

Maks had brought a bottle of Wyborowa and a couple of lemon quarters. Two shots was all he'd allow himself, as it was too easy to slip into the habit of pouring and drinking, and he needed his mind clear for what was to take place the following day.

After Danuta Górska had left, the reports had filtered in. The two kings, Clubs and Diamonds, had been tailed continuously, and the team could confirm the men were bedded in at their respective apartments. From now on, they'd be watched night and day, and followed to Praga where – if all went according to plan – they'd be apprehended. As for the man they thought was Merkury, he'd taken a tram into the city centre and had managed to elude his shadows. He'd given no indication he knew he was being followed, and the officers had concluded it was simply bad luck. Although it would have been a huge bonus to discover where he was living, Maks knew they'd have to catch him red-handed to bring him in. And it was now down to Oskar. The man was well practised in conducting drugs raids, and although Maks had offered his own people, Oskar was confident he could manage with his squad.

The two men had briefed Danuta on how things were likely to go. From what she'd told them, she was no stranger to raids. Maks was confident she'd pose no problem. Oskar was less sure. She'd be without a firearm, he'd told Maks afterwards and, if things went down, Maks might not be in a position to help her.

A sound from the building opposite lifted him from his thoughts. The blonde violinist who lived on that side had climbed onto the roof and was tuning her instrument. This wasn't the first time Maks had had the privilege of hearing her play. Although she was of concert standard, when she gave roof performances she played only Neapolitan songs. She glanced across, tucking the violin under her chin. He raised his glass, and nodded his acknowledgement.

He gazed out over the distant lights of Praga, listening to the sobbing of the violin. The previous evening, he'd seen the moon standing high, its light peachy-yellow through the mist. And tonight the sky should have been clear. But clouds were massing from the east, and the moon, which should have been a bright white ball, was no more than a faint smear. Maks watched the clouds thicken, growing darker, creeping over the river towards the city centre. Seconds later, the first flakes tumbled from the sky, disappearing as they landed. He stood watching the snow falling lazily onto the roof. The forecast had been correct. Bloody Russians, he thought, as he downed the vodka.

CHAPTER 17

Dania was sitting at the kitchen table, having finished a call to West Bell Street. After listening to Honor's progress report, she'd relayed her instructions. It was a strange way of working, and she found herself missing the buzz of activity in the incident room. She'd have been telling herself that the following day she'd be back in Dundee, but that had been called into question as soon as she'd drawn back her bedroom curtains. The roof of the building opposite and the street below were heavily powdered with snow. And the low grey sky suggested more was on the way. That in itself wouldn't pose a problem. Poland was used to snow, and the streets – and airport runways – were cleared promptly. But to reassure herself, she'd put in a call to Mostowski Palace and had been told by Robak's secretary that, as far as she knew, nothing in the inspector's timetable had changed, so Pani Górska was to assume whatever they'd arranged would be going ahead. If she was still worried, she should phone again later in the day.

Marek was none the worse for wear after consuming a large number of vodkas in the bar near the Barbakan. They'd strolled through Krasiński Garden, but the lights in the trees were nothing compared to what was on offer at Wilanów, and Marek had hardly lifted his head. But an evening out had raised his spirits, and he now had the fire in his belly that signalled he was on to something. He was searching through databases and making notes. She left him to it.

In the living room, she lifted back the lid of the ancient upright piano her parents had bought when she'd taken up the instrument. After breakfast, she'd studied Rubinstein's manuscript, and now felt able to put his recommendations into practice. She knew this ballade reasonably well, although some sections needed attention. She spent the rest of the morning striving to become finger perfect, and committing the ballade to memory, despite the piano being so out of tune.

Marek wandered in as she was getting to her feet.

'Lunch?' he said. 'I'd suggest going out, but I don't think you've brought your snow boots.'

'I can wear Mother's. I tried them earlier and they fit. Everything she has fits me. But let's stay in. You can tell me how your research is going.'

Over mushroom *pierogi*, he recounted what he'd learnt about the rare-books collector who'd owned the puzzle box. He'd died in a camp, but his wife and son had survived the war. Neither was alive now, but there was a grandson. Marek had found the man's birth record from 1965.

'And is he living in Warsaw?'

'That I've still to establish.' He smiled. 'Okay, I recognise that look on your face.'

'I don't want you to be disappointed when you find him and discover he knows nothing about the letters or the manuscript.'

'It's the only lead I've got, Danka.'

'Let me know if there's anything I can do to help.'

Her phone rang.

'Dania? It's Tomek. I hope I'm not disturbing. How are you?'

'Hi, Tomek. Yes, I'm fine.'

'And the bruise?'

'It's changed colour a few times. But it's starting to fade.'

'That's good to hear. Now, the reason I'm calling is that I've been in touch with my group in Kraków. Remember you said this Merkury might have set up a network there? I asked my people to check our files, and there's no record of anyone with that pseudonym, or that name. Either in our current records, or in the archives.'

'It was good of you to go to all that trouble.'

'No trouble at all, Dania. We detectives have to help each other.' A pause. 'It looks as though this Merkury may still be in Warsaw, then.'

It was on the tip of her tongue to tell Tomek they were hoping to arrest him that night, especially in view of the trouble he'd gone to on her behalf, but she stopped herself. Chatting with a detective was one thing, but revealing details of an operation was another. Particularly since the operation was Oskar Dolniak's.

'I'll have to keep looking,' she said.

'And you're still planning on leaving tomorrow?'

'If this snow doesn't affect my flight.'

'Have you checked with the airport?'

'I'll wait until later in the day.'

'So, the other thing I wanted to ask was whether you'd like to have dinner with me this evening. I'm returning to Kraków tomorrow morning.'

'I'm afraid I can't, Tomek. My brother and I have made plans. It's my last night.'

'Of course. I understand. Well, if you're ever in Kraków, look me up.'

'I will.'

'Have a safe journey home.' He disconnected.

'Who was that?' Marek said.

'The man who saved me when I was mugged. He's a detective from Kraków.'

Marek was frowning. 'And what's this about you and I having made plans tonight?'

There was no point in pretending. 'I'm joining the detectives from Mostowski Palace on an operation.'

'What operation? Can you tell me?'

'I can't.'

'Is it to do with Merkury?'

'I can't talk about it, Marek.'

He had the good sense not to press her. 'What time will you be leaving?'

'I need to check with Inspector Robak.'

'I take it you'll be returning?' The surprise must have shown in her face because he added, 'Sometimes these things go on into the small hours. Didn't you once tell me it was easier to sleep in a police cell than trudge home?'

'I'm sure I'll be back. But I don't know when. So, do remember to leave the chain off the hook.'

He busied himself making coffee.

Dania rang Mostowski Palace. This time the secretary put her through to Robak.

'Pani Górska.' There was warmth in his voice. 'I was about to ring you. Oskar's putting the finishing touches to the battle plan. We'll pick you up at nine.'

'I can come to Mostowski Palace if it's easier.'

'There's no need. We'll arrive in an unmarked vehicle. And I'd wear something warm. Have you got boots for this weather?'

'I have. So, can you fill me in on what will happen?'

'There'll be time to go over everything in the car.'

'I'll see you this evening, then.' She ended the call.

She turned to Marek. He had his back to her, saying nothing.

CHAPTER 18

Dania was pulling on snowboots when the doorbell rang.

'I'll get it,' Marek called from the kitchen.

She heard footsteps, then the sound of the door being opened. And voices, although she couldn't make out the words.

She buttoned up her mother's heavy jacket and hurried into the corridor. Marek and the inspector were chatting away like old friends. Robak was dressed in a thick jacket and trousers. He was turning the Russian-style hat in his hands, and smiling at something Marek was saying. Seeing Dania, his smile widened. He glanced at her clothes, and nodded his approval.

He held out the hat. 'This is for you, Pani Górska. It'll give you more protection than your woollen one.'

'What about you?' she said.

'Mine's in the car.'

She put on the hat, and pulled down the flaps. 'I'll see you later,' she said to Marek.

She could see he wanted to tell her to be careful but perhaps thought it inappropriate in front of another police officer. 'I'll have hot chocolate waiting when you come back,' he said. 'You too, Maks.'

Robak smiled his thanks, and shook hands with him. He stood back to let Dania pass.

Maks? she thought. But, then, men were like that, quick to form friendships. She wondered what they'd been talking about.

They rode the lift to the ground floor. Outside, an unmarked car was waiting, its engine running. Robak opened the rear door, and she clambered inside, taking a seat beside Dolniak. Robak sat next to the driver, who pulled away. Although it had stopped snowing, the roads were only partly cleared. But the car would have had snow tyres fitted. This was Poland.

'So, Pani Górska,' Dolniak said, 'let me go through what will be happening in Praga. My people are already there. There are plenty of trees and bushes around the beach, but everything's bare, so the team will have to be imaginative in finding hiding places. Do you know the area?'

'Not well.'

'La Playa is what you call a beach club. It's one of the places where the youth of Warsaw come for drinking and dancing,' he said, in a voice tinged with irony. 'There are raves at night and you can often hear the music from the opposite bank. However, at this time of year, and at this time of night, it'll be deserted.' He shifted in his seat. 'There's a pier, although the gates will be locked. Mind you, if you're bringing in a shipment of heroin, that's hardly likely to deter you. But there's also a narrow jetty north of the beach. It's easier to get to if the shipment is coming from that direction, but further away from the zoo where Merkury said he'll park his vehicle. Although it's only a short walk.'

'Presumably you'll be covering both the pier and the jetty,' Dania said.

'Exactly.'

'I've been on that pier. We took the ferry the last time we went to the zoo.'

'It's a convenient way to cross. Especially as the ferry is free. We'll also have people in the park behind the zoo. Again, there's a problem with bare trees.'

Robak turned in his seat. 'We have no idea where Merkury will be when he takes command of the shipment. It's not enough to arrest him leaving the van. We need to catch him with the heroin in his hands. Everyone's been briefed not to make a move until that happens.'

'I understand,' Dania said. She was tempted to add that she'd been on raids before until she realised these men were not being patronising, but were explaining everything because they wanted to give her the best chance of staying safe.

'The three of us will take position near the jetty,' Robak went on, 'and keep a lookout for river traffic. Oskar and I will be in touch with the team by radio.'

'Do you think it's only the two kings who will be there to help?' Dania asked.

'Hard to say,' Dolniak replied. 'It depends on how much heroin is arriving. But three men should be enough to unload.'

'And there'll be the guys on the boat,' Robak added. 'They'll want to be on their way.'

They crossed a wide bridge and, moments later, reached Praga. Dania had lost her bearings. But then she saw the twin spires of the Cathedral of St Michael and St Florian, and knew they were south of the park opposite the zoo. The driver slowed at the crossing and took a left turn, following the deserted road north. He pulled into a large car park, manoeuvring the vehicle to a spot tucked out of the way, and cut the engine. They left the vehicle. The packed clouds were threatening to release another load of snow, but so far they'd behaved themselves.

Robak took Dania's arm and pulled her gently to one side. He brought his face close to hers. 'Remember to stay behind me at all times,' he said. 'Okay?'

'Okay.'

Oskar leading, they set off across the road, and reached the woodland. Dania kept within Robak's shadow, taking long strides to keep up. The driver, a huge bear of a man, had, on Robak's orders, taken up position to guard her back. The traffic had disappeared, and all she could hear was the snow squeaking beneath her boots, and the panting of the driver. To the right loomed the huge two-deck structure known as the Gdański Bridge, its lamps providing the main illumination in the area. Ahead, beyond the ridge of trees, lay the slate-grey Vistula, slowly winding its way north.

Oskar stopped suddenly, and lifted a hand. He wheeled round and put a finger to his lips, then gestured with his head towards the trees. The sounds of laughter and clinking glasses reached Dania's ears. He indicated they should get into a huddle.

'There's a party on the jetty,' he said quietly.

'Do you think the guys have come early?' the driver said.

'I doubt it. But the only way to know for sure is to look. We'll go single file.'

He headed into the trees, the others following. Dania was unprepared for the slope and lost her footing. She'd have fallen and crashed into Robak had the driver not gripped her arms and held her until she regained control. Her mother's footwear, although technically snowboots, was inadequate for this terrain. They pressed on, following Oskar, who skirted the mesh of bushes skilfully, as though he knew the area, which might have been the case if he'd been on drugs raids here before.

They neared the jetty, the voices growing louder. After listening for a few moments, it was clear the two men had nothing to do with the heroin shipment. They sounded the worse for drink, and were arguing over payment. One claimed the other owed him money, since he'd bought the vodka the last time.

'That's all we need,' Oskar murmured. He peered at his watch. 'It's a quarter to ten.'

'We could get them to leave,' the driver said quietly. 'They're breaking the law by drinking in public.'

'Too risky. If they make a fuss, and the delivery guys are on their way, they'll hear the commotion and take fright. And we'll have missed our chance.'

'So, what, we let Merkury and the kings deal with them?'

Oskar seemed undecided.

Dania peered through the branches, seeing the lights of the bridge mirrored in the water. Two men dressed in thick parkas and fur hats were staggering around. The taller approached the brazier, picked up a large petrol can and poured the contents into it. The fire roared into life. He stepped back, nearly falling into the rowing boat moored at the end of the jetty.

'God Almighty,' Oskar muttered. 'He's lost his mind.'

'I doubt he has a mind to lose,' Robak murmured.

'What's that pile of metal beside the brazier?' Dania said quietly.

Robak pulled out a pair of night-vision binoculars. 'I can see a line, and a grappling hook. And a weight on the end of the line.' He lowered the binoculars. 'They're magnet-fishing.'

Oskar snorted. 'And what have they found? A load of junk.'

The men were passing a bottle back and forth.

'Hold on,' Robak said, in an urgent whisper. He thrust the binoculars at the driver, and lifted his handset to his ear. 'The men are on their way. They've passed the tennis courts. Which means they're almost at the jetty.'

'Okay, everyone down,' Oskar murmured. 'And stay quiet.'

They dropped into a crouch. Dania realised she'd been holding her breath. She felt as she always did on a raid: never sure of what would happen and mentally preparing herself for the worst. Minutes passed. Then they heard voices from their left.

Three figures came into view. They stopped a short distance from the jetty. There was the sudden sound of an engine and, a second later, a speedboat cleaving the water appeared from under the bridge. The swell reached the stone, slapping against it.

'Hey!' one of the figures called to the drinkers. 'Get the hell out of here.'

The man at the brazier shouted something that sounded like an obscenity. He picked up the line and, after swinging the magnet round his head like a lasso, hurled it into the river, nearly losing his footing. He managed to grab the end of the line before it, too, disappeared into the water.

The speedboat had passed the jetty and seemed unsure as to how to proceed, moving in circles at some distance from the bank. Dania could hear the muffled grind of the engine as the boat turned. Whoever was piloting must have made up his mind it was either unsafe or undesirable to approach, because he straightened the boat, revved the engine, and sped off towards the bridge. A moment later, the boat disappeared under the pillars.

There was a shout from one of the newcomers, followed by a loud curse. He pulled off his cap and hurled it to the ground. After a heated discussion, the men stalked off the way they'd come. Robak lifted the radio and climbed the incline towards the road, presumably so he could speak loudly enough to be heard. Dania followed, anxious to listen to what he was saying. Because, if one of the three men was Merkury, she wanted to hear Robak tell his people to arrest him.

It was as they reached the pavement that they heard the

explosion. It was so loud it must have carried across the river into the city centre. Robak wheeled round, then grabbed Dania's shoulders and thrust her against a tree. He pressed his body against hers, covering her head with his arms. Seconds later, she heard what might have been huge hailstones. Except that whatever was raining down around them was heavier than hail. Dania had no idea how long it lasted, but eventually the barrage lessened and finally stopped altogether.

Robak stepped back. She couldn't see his expression because the streetlamp was behind him. He lifted her chin so he could see her face. 'Are you all right?' he said, in a hoarse voice.

'Yes, I'm not hurt. Thanks to you.'

He relaxed visibly.

'But are *you* hurt?' she said, realising he'd been more exposed.

'Nothing a shot of vodka won't cure. Can you wait here while I check the others?'

'I'm coming with you.' Without waiting for a response, she ran down the slope, slithering in the muddy snow.

Had she not seen the Gdański Bridge, she'd have concluded she was in an entirely different section of the riverbank. The jetty – and everything and everyone on it – had disappeared. A figure was floating face down in the water, rising and falling with the strong swell. Another was lying curled up on the snow.

Dania rushed to the water's edge and waded in. 'Help me get him out,' she shouted to Robak.

He hurried over, and together they dragged the figure onto the snow and turned him face up. Oskar's eyes were closed and he appeared not to be breathing. Dania pulled off her gloves and gripped him under the chin. There was no pulse.

'Is he dead?' Robak gasped.

She unbuttoned the heavy jacket and pulled it open. Then,

placing her interlocked hands in the centre of his chest, she pressed hard and rhythmically.

'I'll call an ambulance,' Robak said. He walked away, speaking into the handset, his back to her.

She was thinking about asking him to take over when she noticed a slight facial movement. Oskar's eyes were flickering.

'Oskar! Can you hear me?'

He mumbled something she couldn't catch. She crawled round behind him and pushed his shoulders up. 'Breathe deeply,' she urged.

She saw his chest move as he breathed in. Then he retched violently, coughing up water.

The noise made Robak turn. He rushed back and crouched over his colleague. 'Speak to us, Oskar.' There was fear in his voice.

'I'm okay,' Oskar gasped. 'I think.' He was trembling.

Robak took off his jacket and placed it round the other man's shoulders. 'The ambulance is on its way,' he said to Dania.

She got to her feet and hurried towards the curled-up figure. She knelt and turned him over. The driver's sightless eyes and the fact that the top of his head was missing told her what she needed to know.

It was as she was straightening that she noticed the scraps of flesh everywhere and the red tinge to the snow. But it was the object not far from the driver's head that commanded her attention. At first she thought it was his, until she remembered he'd worn a Russian-style hat. She crawled over and put her face close to it.

It was a red baseball cap with the white Polish eagle.

CHAPTER 19

Dania stood watching the medics load Oskar and the driver's body onto stretchers. Robak was speaking with the members of Oskar's team, who'd arrived before the ambulance. The cold air scoured her lungs. Worse was the numbness in her legs: her trousers were soaked from having ploughed into the water. The inspector must have been feeling the same since he, too, had waded in, but although the medics had returned his jacket he was in no hurry to put it on. He'd slung it over his shoulder while talking with the other officers. Dania had no idea if she was to be taken to the police station to give a statement. She was tempted to call Marek, but her hands were shaking so much she doubted she'd be able to operate her mobile.

Robak hurried over. 'I'll take you home, Pani Górska,' he said, slipping on his jacket.

'Don't you need to stay here?'

'This was Oskar's show. His number two has taken charge. He'll call Oskar's wife and let her know which hospital he'll be taken to.' Robak looked at Dania respectfully. 'The medics told me your quick thinking saved his life. He'll recover, although they're keeping him in overnight as a precaution.'

Dania looked around at the threads of blood in the snow.

Robak must have guessed her thoughts because he said, 'This area will be closed off. Forensics are on their way. I don't envy them.' He paused. 'Are you ready to go?'

A thought struck her. 'What about the car keys?'

'I removed them from the driver's pocket.' When she said nothing, he took her arm. 'Come on, I'll help you up to the road. Those boots of yours have lost their tread.'

She was glad of his strong grip on her arm as she slipped and slithered up to the line of trees. 'What's that noise?' she said suddenly.

'It sounds like lions. The big cats' enclosure is behind that wall. They'll be roaring for a while. And I can hear the wolves howling.'

They reached the car park. Robak started the engine, turning the heating up full.

'So, what happened, Inspector? Had someone planted a booby trap?'

He glanced at her. 'It's highly unlikely. My guess is the guy who threw the magnet line into the river set off a bomb, or a mortar shell.'

'From the war?' she said, horrified.

'Unexploded ordnance is so unstable that a scrape from a magnet can set it off.'

'This isn't the first time you've come across something like this,' she said, thinking of his rapid reaction in the trees.

He looked straight ahead. 'As soon as I heard the explosion and understood it came from the direction of the jetty, I knew what would happen next. To be honest, I didn't expect Oskar or his driver to survive.'

They travelled in silence, retracing their route across the bridge and into the city centre.

'I'm assuming Merkury and the two kings weren't arrested,' Dania said.

'As agreed, Oskar's people let them leave. We had no evidence against them.'

She nodded, conceding the point.

'That speedboat was bringing in Merkury's heroin,' Robak went on. 'Oskar had decided that, if anything went wrong, we were to let the courier escape. After all, if the plan failed, he'd try again. Merkury will have seen those drunks and understood why the boat sped off. They'll come up with another date and time. And a different route in.'

'Merkury and the kings will have heard the explosion. I wonder if they saw us.'

Robak sneered. 'They'd have raced out of there. One of Oskar's people told me they saw the three of them running along the path as though the Devil was on their tail.'

'And do you think you have a good chance of discovering their next plan?'

'That depends on Oskar's informant. But we know where the kings live and we'll be keeping an eye on them.' He paused. 'I understand your deep disappointment, Pani Górska. I can only say how truly sorry I am that things turned out the way they did. I'm afraid you've had a wasted journey.'

Dania said nothing. His words had only served to sharpen her sense of frustration.

Robak pulled up outside the apartment block. 'I don't think I'll be seeing you again.' There was regret in his voice. 'What time is your flight tomorrow?'

'Mid-morning. But why don't you come up? Marek will be expecting you,' she added, sensing his hesitation. 'Otherwise he'll fear the worst, and won't believe me when I tell him I'm okay.'

'And *are* you okay?' Robak said gently, switching on the inside light. He studied her.

'I'm fine.'

'Forgive me if I say I don't believe you. You're shaking.'

'That's because I'm cold. I need that hot chocolate Marek said he'd make us.'

Robak laughed softly. He switched off the light, and climbed out of the car.

They took the lift to their floor.

'Danka? Is that you?' Marek called, as they entered.

'Inspector Robak's with me.'

There was the sound of a chair scraping and Marek hurried into the corridor. His frown disappeared, and a look of relief crossed his face. 'I've been worried sick about you.'

'Why?' Dania said, shrugging off her jacket. She glanced at the inspector. 'I've been in good hands.'

'There's been a report about an explosion. I tried to reach you but your phone was switched off.'

'The press have been quick off the mark,' Robak said.

There was a stricken expression in Marek's eyes. 'You mean you were there?'

To Dania's relief, Robak had sized up the situation. 'Pani Górska was not in any danger,' he said reassuringly. 'Apart from a short dip in the river.'

Marek gazed at her clothes, then at Robak's. 'Okay, Maks, Danka will show you where my bedroom is. We're roughly the same size. You can put on my clothes. And you,' he said, turning to Dania, 'need to get out of those wet things. By the time you've changed, I'll have the chocolate ready.'

She was relieved Marek hadn't pressed Robak for details. That would happen later. But the inspector was well able to come up with a suitable narrative. He was a police officer.

She led him along the corridor into Marek's room. The bed was unmade and clothes were strewn around. It was usually Dania who was untidy. Marek only let things get out of control when he was so deep into an investigation that nothing else mattered.

'The wardrobe is in the corner, Inspector. I'm sorry the place is a bit of a mess,' she added, avoiding his gaze.

'I wouldn't call this a mess. My bedroom isn't much tidier.'

She smiled. 'I'll see you in the kitchen, then.'

In her room, she pulled off her clothes, rubbed her body with a warm towel, and changed into jeans and a ribbed navy sweater. A glance in the mirror made her reach for her brush. She dragged it through her hair. It would have to do.

In the kitchen, the men were sitting at the table, frowning at the television screen. A newsreader was describing the events of earlier in the evening. Behind her was a photograph, taken in daylight, of the jetty with the Gdański Bridge behind it.

'Our reporter was not allowed access,' she was saying, 'because the area may still be unsafe. No one knows why the explosion occurred, but a Warsaw expert told us ordnance often gets washed along the riverbed, and it's possible it collided with the jetty and ignited. Fortunately, no one was harmed in the explosion.'

Dania caught Robak's eye. She was about to speak when he shook his head slightly. Marek didn't catch this exchange, as he'd jumped to his feet to deal with the milk boiling over. The newsreader moved on to another piece of news. Dania picked up the handset and switched off the television. She sat down and ran her hands over her face. Marek, as a journalist, was used to hearing distorted facts, and was unlikely to take this at face value.

Robak was watching her in silent concentration. As Marek

brought the mugs to the table, he turned to him and said, in a conversational tone, 'How long have you been a journalist, Marek?'

'All my working life. I never wanted to be anything else.' He removed a plate of cheesecake from the fridge and cut it into slices.

'Did you have to go on a course?'

'It was well worth it.' He placed the plate on the table. 'There are things journalists can and can't do, and it's good to know what they are.' He pushed the plate towards Robak. 'I'm sure it's the same with detectives.' He raised an eyebrow at his sister. 'I know that Danka has occasionally crossed the line.'

'Marek,' Dania said, a note of warning in her voice.

Robak looked at her and smiled. 'So, what's the worst thing you've done, Pani Górska?' When she said nothing, he leant forward, adding, 'You tell me your worst, and I'll tell you mine.'

His expression was too inviting to resist. She laughed, and said, 'I've broken into houses to get information.'

'That's your worst?' he said, in mock surprise.

Marek picked up a piece of cheesecake. 'There was that time you were mistaken for someone else, and you carried on with the pretence to get your intel.'

'These are minor transgressions,' Robak said.

'So, what's your worst, Maks?'

Robak's eyes were gleaming. 'I couldn't possibly tell you in front of a lady. But, perhaps after your sister has gone to bed . . .' He left the sentence unfinished.

Marek winked at him. 'And I'll give Danka a watered-down version.'

Dania sipped her chocolate, listening to the men laughing and joking. Before long, Marek had brought a bottle of Wyborowa and three glasses to the table. Dania was careful to alternate vodka with water, as the men were doing. She drank only a couple of shots as she'd be up early. She'd packed her suitcase that afternoon, and all she needed to do the following morning was call a taxi to the airport.

'What's that on the counter?' Robak said suddenly. 'It looks like a puzzle box.'

'Indeed it is,' Marek said. He brought it to the table. 'Can you figure out how to open it?' he added, his voice a challenge.

Robak ran a finger over the brass inlay. 'It's exquisite,' he murmured.

He played with the edges, then turned his attention to the feet. With a frown of concentration, he grasped each in turn and moved it slightly, first one way, then the next. His expression cleared, and with a glance round the table, he rotated three of the feet one way and the fourth the other. There was a click. He lifted the lid. 'Ah, it's empty. I was expecting to see your jewels there, Pani Górska.'

'There was something better than jewels inside,' Marek said. 'It's where the Chopin letters were hidden. But you did that pretty damn quickly, Maks. I spent an hour and got nowhere.'

Robak shrugged. 'I recently interviewed someone who had a collection of such boxes. He told me I had the gift. Whatever that means.'

There followed a discussion of the best design for a puzzle box, and the best way of setting a booby trap.

Dania could feel her eyelids drooping. 'Gentlemen, I need to go to bed,' she said, getting up.

Robak sprang to his feet. He extended a hand. 'Thank you for everything you did this evening, Pani Górska.'

She put her hand into his, and he shook it firmly. 'It's *I* who should thank *you*,' she said. 'Please do give Inspector Dolniak my best wishes. And will you keep in touch and let me know of developments concerning Merkury?'

'I will.' He seemed reluctant to let her go.

'And let me know how things progress with the Okopowa case?'

'Of course. And I hope you have a safe trip back,' he added, squeezing her hand before releasing it. He turned to Marek. 'Perhaps I should take my leave.'

'Nonsense,' Marek said firmly. 'You have to help me finish the cheesecake.'

Dania smiled as she left the room. What he'd meant, of course, was that Robak had to help him finish the vodka.

Dania woke early. She'd had a shower before she'd gone to bed as she'd doubted there'd be time in the morning. Especially not if Marek was hogging it. He could stand under the jet of water longer than anyone she knew, and that included her women friends. She slipped on her bra and knickers, and padded to the bathroom. As she opened the door, she saw Robak, his hair wet and a towel round his waist. He was standing at the mirror, wiping his face. He caught sight of her reflection, and lowered his arms.

'I'm sorry,' she gasped. 'I didn't know anyone was in here.'

He turned to look at her. 'Your brother kindly offered me a bed for the night.' He smiled, keeping his eyes on her face. 'It was the safest option, given how much we'd had to drink.'

Dania was acutely aware she was in a state of undress. Not wanting to embarrass either of them, she returned the smile and said, 'I'll get the coffee going.'

She left quickly, and slipped into her parents' bedroom to use their en-suite loo and washbasin. Then she hurried back to her room and put on her jeans and sweater.

In the kitchen, she cut bread, and set out plates of cheese and smoked sausage. Robak entered, wearing his own clothes, his damp hair pushed back off his face. He wandered across to the window, and watched her operate the coffee machine. She glanced up, seeing his warm smile, and wondered if he was thinking about the encounter in the bathroom.

It was only twenty minutes by car to Chopin airport, and a lift would mean she needn't worry about calling a taxi, which could sometimes prove problematical. 'Would you have time to drive me to the airport?' she asked cheekily.

'I'd certainly have time, but I think we wouldn't get far.' He glanced out of the window. 'Have you looked outside?'

She joined him, seeing what she hadn't spotted when she'd drawn back her curtains. At this time of morning, the sky was usually a watery blue, but what she saw was an ominous smoky grey. Yet it wasn't the colour that claimed her attention, but the depth of snow on the roof opposite. Those clouds she'd seen the evening before must have shed their load in the night. Even if, by a miracle, she reached the airport, it was unlikely planes would be flying.

Dania powered up Marek's laptop, and connected to the airport's website. It was as she'd feared. All flights that morning were cancelled. She tried their online booking system to see if she could book for later in the day, but the system had crashed.

'It seems you're stranded, Pani Górska.' Something shifted in Robak's expression. 'Perhaps you'll get a chance to bring in Merkury after all,' he added softly.

She looked up. 'How long does it take to clear the runways after snow like this?'

'It's not the runways, it's the roads between here and the airport.'

'I'll have to call Dundee and let them know.' She patted her pockets. 'My phone's in my jacket. Will you excuse me?'

In the hall, Dania retrieved her mobile and called the main West Bell Street number. She explained the situation, and impressed upon the sergeant he was to inform DS Randall and DCI Ireland that she was snowed in, and would keep them in the loop as to when she'd get a flight. She imagined Jackie Ireland's reaction. Then she tried to unimagine it.

She was returning to the kitchen when she bumped into Marek. He was heading for the bathroom.

'I thought you'd be gone by now, Danka,' he said, in surprise.

'We're snowed in.'

'Ah. Is Maks still here?'

'We're about to have breakfast.'

He brightened. 'I'll make the shower quick, then, or there'll be nothing left. He ate most of the cheesecake,' he added, over his shoulder.

Dania entered the kitchen to see places laid for three, and the jug of coffee on the table. Robak was leaning against the counter, his arms crossed. 'That's not true what your brother said, by the way. I only ate half the cheesecake.'

Dania laughed. 'I suggest we don't wait for him. He eats like a pig.'

They took their seats.

'Are you on shift this morning?' she said, reaching for the jug.

Robak took it from her hands and poured coffee into her mug. 'My shift starts in two hours. It'll give me time to get home, change, and walk to the palace.'

'Surely no one will mind how you're dressed.'

He glanced at her. 'I'm hoping to interview a politician today. She's been out of Warsaw, but I heard yesterday she's back.' He poured himself a coffee. 'You may know of her, as she was one of Jakub Frydman's pupils. Lidia Lipska.'

'Lidia Lipska? And she's a politician now?'

'She's in the Civic Platform Party.' He buttered a slice of bread. 'Do you follow Polish politics, Pani Górska?'

'When I have time.'

'You'll know of our ruling Law and Justice Party, I expect.'

'The British press constantly highlight its shortcomings. Although they do that with all political parties.'

Robak added cheese to the bread. 'Political opponents waste no time in pointing out how the party is undermining Poland's democratic principles.'

'Why is it so popular, then?'

'I think it's because it's delivered on its spending pledges for social welfare. Many families on low incomes have been helped financially, for example, and there have been the widely publicised tax cuts.'

Dania sipped her coffee. 'Our press tend not to report those. They're more interested in the government scandals, as though they're something new. I can't think why. Show me a party that doesn't have at least one corrupt politician.'

'Which is where Lidia Lipska comes in. This last year, she's been mounting a crusade to root out corruption in the Law and Justice Party.'

'Not in her Civic Platform Party?'

'Interestingly, that's where she began. She decided to clean the mess in her own house first, as she put it, and exposed two of her own party members. They resigned promptly.'

'And now she's going for members of the government?'

'Exactly.'

'So, how many ministers has she outed?'

'None so far. My people tell me she's still gathering the evidence.'

'It must be making the politicians nervous. I can imagine there'd be a few who'd want to stop her before she outs them. Is that where your department comes in? Are you going to offer her protection?'

'If we did that, we'd have to offer every member of our parliament – both houses – the same. And we haven't the manpower.' He lifted the coffee jug questioningly. When she shook her head, he poured himself another. 'No, I want to find out what she knows. And about whom.'

'Why?'

Robak played with his mug. 'Pani Lipska was invited to Jakub Frydman's funeral, but didn't attend.'

'Everyone knew she was his pupil,' Dania said slowly. 'They'd given well-publicised concerts together.' When he said nothing, she added, 'It would be a natural assumption she'd be a guest at his funeral.'

He kept his gaze steady. 'And if someone wanted to silence her before she exposed them and ruined their careers, setting off an Amatol-packed wreath would have been an ideal way.'

'Is she the only person invited who wasn't there?'

'The only one.' He smiled. 'I remember it was you who alerted me that not all those invited might have attended. I'm grateful to you.'

'Do you know why she didn't make the funeral?'

'It's a question I intend to ask her.'

Dania stared straight ahead. She was back at Okopowa cemetery, listening to Rabin Steinberg reciting in Hebrew.

The door opened and Marek breezed in. 'Ah, you've left me some breakfast, Danka,' he said, taking a seat. 'She eats like a pig, you know, Maks.'

She'd hardly touched the food. It was Robak who'd been doing the eating.

'So, did you sleep well?' Marek said to him.

He smiled. 'Like a baby.' He got to his feet. 'But now, I must be going.' He looked from one to the other. 'Thank you for your kind hospitality.'

'Any time, Maks,' Marek said enthusiastically. 'You'll need to come round again.' He stood up. 'I'll see you to the door.'

They followed Robak into the corridor. His jacket was slung over the chair. Underneath were his holster and pistol. He slipped everything on, then struggled into his snowboots.

'You'll let me know how Pan Dolniak is, won't you?' Dania said.

'Of course.'

And with his usual warm smile, he left.

CHAPTER 20

Pola Lorenc stared out of the living-room window. The new snow looked nearly half a metre deep. She was due at Mostowski, although under the circumstances there'd be no penalty for coming in late. But she intended to make it, as she was anxious to hear the details of what had happened at the Praga jetty. It was as she'd been eating breakfast that she'd heard the news of the explosion. She'd sent Maks an SMS but had had only a quick, reassuring reply in return. No details.

On her phone, she checked the situation regarding public transport because it came to a standstill when there was snow as bad as this. The headlines weren't encouraging. The snowploughs that cleared the tram rails had started work, although they'd only be clearing the major lines. Fortunately, the Marszałkowska was one of them. She'd have to trudge through the streets to get to her stop, but she was well prepared.

She dragged her waterproof trousers over her dungarees, and shook out her thick, fur-trimmed parka. After packing a small rucksack, she took the stairs to the ground floor. With difficulty, she balanced against the wall and fastened on her snowshoes. These weren't the modern-style shoes she'd seen in sports shops, but ancient ones that looked like deformed tennis racquets. Her problem was that each time it snowed she promised herself she'd buy new ones but she never found the time. Tottering alarmingly, she stepped outside. Around her lay a thick white carpet, and it was only the position of the snow-covered cars that gave an indication of where pavement ended and road began. But what held her attention was the colour of the sky. The bloated grey clouds signalled there'd be another snowfall before the day was out.

Pola set off, her breath smoking in the cold air. The street was deserted, and there was an eerie silence, the kind in which anything can happen and frequently does. She trudged towards Marszałkowska, catching sight of the distant Palace of Culture and Science. With snow decorating its layers, it looked like a wedding cake, which, given the post-war forced 'marriage' between the Soviet Union and Poland, was probably uppermost in the Russians' minds when they'd built it.

Neither the street nor the pavements had been cleared, but the plough had been busy on the tramlines, piling the snow up on one side. She didn't bother looking for a pedestrian crossing – what was the point when there wasn't a car in sight? – and waddled over to the tram stop. A solitary figure approached. He was without skis or snowshoes, and was struggling to stay upright. Each time he took a step, he sank knee-deep into the soft, crystal snow. It didn't help that he was taking gulps from a brown paper bag. Drinking in public was strictly forbidden, but Pola decided this wasn't the time for a challenge. With his shabby summer jacket and faded jeans, he wasn't dressed for the weather, and seemed oblivious to the rime gathering on his long grey beard. As he passed her, she heard him singing softly to himself.

She stood waiting for the tram, working on her Plan B in case it didn't arrive. But, minutes later, she saw the vehicle approach, trundling more slowly than usual. The driver was being understandably cautious: in such conditions, it wasn't unheard of for trams to derail. She pulled off her snowshoes and boarded the nearest coach, validating her travel pass.

The few passengers didn't give Pola or her snowshoes a second glance. They were too busy staring into their phones. As she gazed out of the window, she thought through the day's tasks, wondering which would now prove impossible on account of the weather. It bothered her that she hadn't finished her research on Adam Mazur. There was something not right about his records. She'd found his name in the card index, which referred to further documents, although there was no indication as to what these were. But when she'd searched the archive, the documents were missing. The archivist concluded they must have been misfiled. He'd add it to his list of things to check, he'd said, adding ominously, 'Time allowing.' He'd contacted her shortly afterwards to say he'd checked the digital archive, but without success. That meant the documents pertaining to Adam Mazur hadn't yet been digitised. So, his paper files were somewhere in the archival repository. They'd reveal what, if anything, the man had been up to. But there was no easy way of finding them. She'd have to tell Maks. Given they were getting nowhere with the Jakub Frydman case, he wouldn't be too happy. She hated it when she came up against a dead end. Yet maybe Adam Mazur hadn't been the target of the unexpected guest. The conversation Maks had yet to have with Lidia Lipska might lead somewhere. Having read about the woman's mission to oust corrupt politicians, Pola had become a fan. Perhaps she could sweet-talk Maks into letting her interview her, or at least accompany him when he did.

Pola reattached the snowshoes and left the tram. On the other side of the road, Krasiński Garden looked like something out of a fairytale, with its spectral trees and snow-dusted bushes. She clumped the short distance to Mostowski Palace.

Inside the building, she paused to drag off the snowshoes, losing her balance and crashing into the wall. She gathered them up and climbed the stairs to the first floor. The door to Maks's office stood wide, giving her a glimpse of the cross-country skis propped up against the wall. Not for him the ridiculous snowshoes that made one waddle like a duck. She'd seen him on skis. He was fast, and he was elegant.

He glanced up from the computer screen and, seeing her, called out, 'Pola! Come in!'

She shambled across the room in her boots, and flopped onto the chair. 'What happened last night? There wasn't much detail on the news.'

'As far as the mission went, it was an abject failure. There were a couple of guys magnet-fishing on the jetty.'

'That narrow stone thing?'

'The one near the Gdański Bridge. Anyway, a speedboat arrived, which I'm guessing was to deliver the heroin. The pilot must have seen the men because he left immediately.'

'And the kings? And Merkury? Didn't they show up?'

'They showed up, but when they saw the boat depart, they took off.' Maks ran a hand through his hair. He looked tired. 'That was when the explosion occurred. I was some distance away with Danuta Górska. We weren't hurt. But Oskar and his driver were nearer the jetty. Oskar was blown into the water. He'd have died had Danuta not saved him.'

Pola was conscious her jaw was slackening.

'I rang the hospital,' Maks went on. 'His leg's broken. Otherwise, he's fine.'

'I take it the men on the jetty didn't survive?' Pola said. She held up a hand. 'Stupid question. So, was it war-era ordnance?'

'I think the magnet hit something on the riverbed. I saw the length of that line.' He straightened. 'Forensics wasted no time in getting there. I understand every spare man and woman was sent over. They'd seen the weather forecast and knew they had to work before more snow came down.'

'What will they learn? The make of the German bomb?' She gave a dismissive shrug. 'And what will that tell us?'

Maks played with his pen. 'One of the three men who arrived at the jetty left behind a red baseball cap. We've seen him before, Pola. He was at King Cross with the two kings. We think he's Merkury.' He put down the pen. 'So, have you anything to report?'

She shook her head. 'Are you seeing Lidia Lipska?'

'She's at Wiejska Street today. She has a number of meetings.'

'I'm surprised the Sejm's open for business.'

Maks smiled. 'Running a country has to go on in bad weather.' He picked up the pen. 'And so does policing.'

Pola took that as the sign she should leave. She scooped up her snowshoes, relieved he hadn't asked her about Adam Mazur.

'How did your phone call go, Danka?' Marek said, making coffee.

'Better than I expected. Honor says hello, by the way.'

'I take it the airport still isn't up and running?'

'The website was out of action all morning.' Dania ran her hands through her hair. 'I'm setting up video calls with my teams this afternoon. It's the closest to being in the incident room.'

'And what's the weather like there?'

'Blue skies. I suspect Honor will set that as a background,' she added sourly.

Marek carried the mugs to the table. 'Want to hear my big success?'

'Another offer of marriage?'

He rolled his eyes. 'Better than that. Remember I told you about the collector who'd owned the puzzle box?'

'He had a grandson.'

'Well remembered. He was born in 1965. And I've tracked him down.'

'Here in Warsaw?' she said, sipping.

'He's a priest. Father Bielski. I'm going to see him after I've had my coffee.'

Dania studied him. 'Wouldn't it be best to ring him first?'

'Priests tend to live next to their churches. He won't be far away.'

'I meant he might not want to talk to you about his grandfather.'

'Why do you think that?'

'He died in a camp, didn't he?'

'Groß-Rosen.'

'Not everyone wants to be reminded of those times,' she said gently.

'It's a risk I'll have to take. He can only ask me to leave.'

'Which church is it? You may have to use the snowshoes.'

'I'm in luck there. It's round the corner on Nowolipki.'

'St Augustine's? You *are* in luck.'

'You're the lucky one, Danka,' Marek said, after a pause.

'Oh? In what way?'

'I saw a photo of what was left of that jetty. The images are all over the media.'

'I wonder how anyone got near enough to take them. The police have closed off the area.'

'They were captured by a drone.' He gazed at her steadily. 'It's a miracle no one was killed in that explosion.'

Before lunch, Dania had rung Robak to enquire after Oskar, and learnt his leg was broken. Other than that, he was fine. Robak was hoping to visit the hospital, adding jokingly he'd come back with a black eye if Oskar's wife was there. She'd called Robak and given him an earful, blaming him for not looking after her man.

Marek gulped his coffee. 'I'm not sure how long I'll be. Do you know where the snowshoes are?'

'I think they're in the cupboard at the end of the hall.'

'Wish me luck.'

'Good luck,' she said, watching him go.

His old enthusiasm was back. But she doubted the priest could help. And, more to the point, if the man did know anything about the manuscript, would he be prepared to divulge it? He'd been quiet for a long time . . .

CHAPTER 21

Marek entered the courtyard of St Augustine's Church, pausing to catch his breath. Snowshoes were great for this weather, but the extra effort had left him panting. He checked the notices on the railing and saw that Mass wasn't until 6.30 p.m. so, unless Father Bielski was in a meeting, he had a good chance of catching him. To the left was a building that looked like the parish house, but he'd try the church first.

He was leaning against the wall, struggling to pull off the snowshoes, when he became aware of a figure in a cassock standing at the top of the steps, gazing into the sky.

'Father Bielski?' Marek said.

The man only then noticed him. 'Father Bielski is in the parish house, my son,' he said, in a helpful tone. 'Do you wish him to hear your confession?'

'Not just now,' Marek said, smiling self-consciously. 'But there's something I'd like to talk to him about.'

'Then please ring. There's a bell on the wall.' And with a friendly nod, he disappeared into the church.

Marek gauged the distance to the parish house, and decided it wasn't worth the risk. His father's snowshoes were two sizes too small, and it took him a while to get them back on.

Outside the house, he pressed the bell, hearing the echo through the building. A moment later, there was the sound of approaching footsteps. The door opened. A man in a black shirt and trousers stood before him. He was tall with thinning fair hair, and a trim body. As he studied Marek, a fleeting look of what might have been recognition crossed his face.

'Father Bielski?' Marek said. 'I'm Marek Górski. Would you have time for a chat?'

'Of course,' the priest said, throwing open the door.

'Let me take these off.' Marek removed the snowshoes with difficulty. He leant them against the wall, taking a gamble no one would steal from outside a priest's house.

Father Bielski led the way down the short hallway, and opened a door on the left. 'We can speak in the living room,' he said.

It was furnished simply but comfortably with a patterned sofa, two armchairs and an oak chest of drawers. A small table, loaded with books and papers, stood in front of the window. There was a slight smell of incense, which Marek assumed was an occupational hazard for a priest.

He took the armchair nearest the window.

The priest sat on the sofa. 'So, how can I help you, Pan Górski?' he said, leaning back.

'Please call me Marek.' He hesitated, remembering Danka's warning. 'I'm here about your grandfather. I believe he was a collector of rare books.'

'That's correct.'

'I wanted to ask whether your parents ever mentioned a puzzle box.'

'Yes, my father told me about it. He'd been a young boy when my grandfather bought it at a local fair. He quickly discovered how to open it.' The priest smiled. 'Puzzle boxes are a law unto themselves, Pan Górski.'

Marek returned the smile, hoping it would encourage Father Bielski to keep talking.

'From what my father said, there were letters inside,' the priest went on. 'They were in French. My grandfather knew the language. He was a scholar, you see, and spoke several languages, including German. That came in useful later when he joined the Underground.'

'And did he tell your father what was in the letters?' Marek asked cautiously.

'They'd been written by Chopin. But some were written *to* him.' The priest said it as though finding Chopin's letters was a normal occurrence. 'My grandfather was extremely excited by this find. He'd concluded that Chopin's sister, Ludwika, had brought these letters back from Paris. And that puzzle box had been hers. It could have changed hands many times, with none of the new owners knowing how to open it. But it was when I saw the article in the newspaper . . .' He smiled. '. . . after *you*'d found them that I finally read the text of the letters for myself.'

Marek acknowledged the recognition with a tilt of his head.

'May I ask where you found the puzzle box, Pan Górski?'

'In a cellar in an abandoned building in Wola.'

'Yes, my grandparents lived in Wola. And my father. I had no idea there was anything left of their belongings.'

'The cellar was full of furniture.'

'It's possible some pieces belonged to the owners of the other apartments. During the Uprising, residents often moved their belongings to the cellars to escape the conflagration.'

'The box was in a crate with your grandfather's books. Many were first editions. They're now at the National Library.'

'Which is the right place for them.'

'But as your grandfather's only living descendant they belong to you.'

Father Bielski looked at him with amusement. 'Pan Górski, I took a vow of poverty when I was ordained. I own nothing.'

'Of course,' Marek murmured. 'And the manuscript referred to in the letters? Did your father talk to you about it? Did your grandfather try to find it?'

'Apparently he did. He spent much of his free time researching Ludwika and her life. My father remembers this time as one of frenzied activity. He said my grandfather had a constant look of cold determination in his eyes.' Father Bielski nodded at Marek. 'I see something of it in yours.'

'And what did he learn about Ludwika?'

'What everyone knows. That she authorised Julian Fontana to deal with her brother's unpublished works.'

'Nothing more?' Marek said, trying not to sound desperate.

Father Bielski looked thoughtful for a moment. 'There *was* one other thing. About six weeks after Chopin died, she arranged for his estate to be auctioned. She offered some of Chopin's manuscripts to his friends. My grandfather concluded this third concerto must have been among them, and Ludwika gave it away by accident or design.'

Marek stared at the priest. 'Would this have been in Paris?'

'My grandfather was convinced it was after she'd returned to Warsaw. Or after the recipient of the manuscript had. This was the result of years of meticulous research, I should add. But then something happened that brought his research to an end.'

'And what was that?'

'The war began. And life as he knew it ended.'

Marek felt a strange mix of numbness and excitement. Excitement because this could be the lead he was looking for. Numbness because he had no idea how to proceed.

'And do you know what happened to your grandfather's research papers?'

'That's exactly what the other gentleman asked me,' Father Bielski said, smiling.

Marek stiffened. 'The other gentleman?'

'Someone came asking about the manuscript. It was during the afternoon, a couple of days ago.'

'Did he give a name?'

'Actually, no. He had on a thick coat, and a black woollen cap which completely covered his hair. And he wore dark glasses. He apologised for not announcing himself, but said he had good reasons for wanting to remain incognito.'

'Was he tall, short?'

'Neither tall nor short. I couldn't tell his age. The sunglasses covered half his face. There was nothing remarkable about him.'

'And you told him what you've told me?'

The priest lifted his hands. 'Why would I not?'

'So, what did you say when he asked about your grandfather's papers?'

'I told him the truth. I said they must have been burnt or destroyed, which I'm convinced is what happened.' He frowned. 'A few months after my grandfather joined the Underground, he sent his wife and son – my father – out of the city for safety. When they returned after the war, well . . .' He gazed out of the window. 'There was nothing to come back to.'

'That building in Wola wasn't destroyed. Did your father try to find those papers?'

'A question the other gentleman also asked. I told him he didn't. Like many who returned, his focus was on helping to rebuild Warsaw. There was no time for anything else.' The priest sighed. 'The gentleman left in great frustration. He mumbled something about going to the National Library to look for those papers.'

Good luck with that, thought Marek. He'd spent the best part of two hours in the reading room, getting nowhere. He wondered who this person was. Could it have been Baletnica, who'd furnished Marek with the name Bielski? Baletnica might have discovered that the collector had a living grandson in the way Marek had. Something to check.

'Father, did this gentleman leave a phone number? Or an email address?'

'Nothing like that. I had the impression I wouldn't be seeing him again.' Father Bielski leant forward, frowning. 'But it was after he'd gone that I remembered something. Years after my father returned to Warsaw, he began to write an account of his life before and during the war. He had a clear memory, from what I recall. There was so much he wanted to say that he needed several notebooks.' The priest gazed into the distance. 'It was while he was writing that he told me about my grandfather's hunt for the manuscript. I've no doubt that everything my father remembered would be in those notebooks.'

Marek waited, but the man was lost in his thoughts. 'Father?' he said softly.

Father Bielski gave his head a small shake, as though trying to shake off the past with its dark memories. 'He was eventually arrested for anti-Communist activities, and died in prison.' The priest must have seen the shock on Marek's face because he added, 'I was training in the seminary. It was a while before the news of his execution reached me.'

'How did your mother manage?'

'My mother had died giving birth to me. As for the notebooks, although there was nothing there that should have alarmed the authorities, my father was careful to keep his writings secret.' He smiled thinly. 'There's nothing Communists fear more than a writer, Pan Górski.'

'And where are the notebooks now?'

'I've no idea. I can only assume the authorities took them.' A puzzled look crossed his face. 'Perhaps not. When that knock at the door comes in the small hours of the morning, I've heard you're instantly awake and in full command of your senses. However, knowing my father, he wouldn't have taken the risk, and left them lying about. He'd have hidden them each day after he'd finished writing.'

'Hidden them where? In his apartment?'

'Under the floorboards or behind the walls. Who knows? I'm not an expert in secrecy, Pan Górski.' He studied Marek. 'Let me write down his address in Praga. Although, having tracked me down, I'm sure you'd have no difficulty in finding it yourself.' He crossed to the table, where he scribbled on a notepad. He tore off the sheet and handed it to Marek.

Marek got to his feet. He was about to thank the man, when Father Bielski said, 'My father told me it was his wish to have the notebooks published. I ask only that, if you *do* locate them, then once you've found what you're looking for, you'll honour his wish.'

'I give you my word, Father. And I'll translate them, and also have them published in English. I'll make sure the proceeds come to your church, and you can decide what to do with the funds.'

The priest smiled, and laid a hand on Marek's arm. 'I'm most grateful. And for my part, I give you *my* word that, if anyone calls asking about the manuscript, I'll tell them nothing.'

CHAPTER 22

'You're thinking about the chess player, aren't you, Dad?' Konrad said, his voice even. 'It's been – what? – three days, and you still can't get her out of your mind.'

Zygmunt gazed at his son. It was mid-afternoon, and he was drinking as though it were evening.

'So, what happened to your great plan to discover where she lives?' Konrad added.

Zygmunt narrowed his eyes. He hadn't shared his plans. 'How did you know about that?' he said.

'Oh, come on. Nothing happens without my knowing. You used one of my guys, for heaven's sake.'

'Well, your guy made a mess of it. She gave him the slip.'

'Give it up, Dad. Anyway, what will you do when you find where she lives?'

'I'm thinking about it.'

Which was a lie. Zygmunt had already decided. As the head of a construction company, he had access to a number of empty buildings destined for demolishing. He imagined Motylek beating her wings against the walls, trapped in the glass jar he'd created especially for her. He closed his eyes and breathed in and out deeply. When he opened them, Konrad was standing over him, holding out a glass of whisky.

'Better drink this before you pass out,' he said, looking at his father with a disdainful smile.

'Have you been up to see your mother?'

'I thought we could have a chat first.'

Zygmunt took a gulp of whisky. He was glad it was Glenfiddich. At least he'd taught his son something about Scotch. 'What do you want to talk about?' he said.

'Rabin Steinberg.' Konrad stared into his glass. 'I had no idea he'd be at that funeral. You know, the one in Okopowa. The pianist's.'

'All right. So, the police have come calling. That's to be expected. They'll be scrutinising the guests to see who might have been the target. And, of course, with Steinberg having written that article about you, you'll be on their radar, no question. You said it yourself to that policewoman when she was questioning you about the explosion.' Zygmunt waved a dismissive hand. 'I heard everything from the corridor. Talking about explosions, what have you heard about Praga?'

'The papers are saying it could have been a mortar or bomb on the riverbed.'

'So, for once, the police aren't running straight to the construction industry, blaming our men for selling explosive charge.'

'But that could change, Dad. They'll have sent out forensics specialists.'

'You think someone deliberately blew up the jetty?'

Konrad made a gesture to indicate he was no longer interested in the subject.

'Go up and see your mother,' Zygmunt said. 'She's expecting you.'

'And what about you? Are you going to sit and drool over that chess player? You're going to be no good to anyone in your condition.' His expression changed. 'I've an idea. Hold on.'

He left the living room, returning a minute later. He held out a small object. 'These have just come in.'

'What is it?' Zygmunt said, turning it over in his hand. It looked like a round tile.

'It's a location tracker.'

'And what am I supposed to do with it? I don't know anything about these devices.'

'Never mind that. I can set up everything for you. What you need to do is slip this to the chess lady in a way she won't notice.'

'How do I do that?'

Konrad rolled his eyes. 'First thing is to get close to her physically. You can do that, can't you?'

'And then what? Drop it into her handbag? That would be near impossible.'

'You're going to have to work on it. It'll have to be somewhere she won't find it, at least until she gets home. Because by then you'll have her location on your phone.'

Zygmunt felt a tingling in his blood. It sounded too easy.

'One thing, Dad. Avoid trying to slip it into her coat pocket or anything like that. Unless you're an illusionist, someone will see you. And she might put her hand inside the pocket before she leaves, or on her way home. And realise what it is. You have to hide it in something she'll be happy to take away with her.'

Zygmunt stared at his son. And in that instant he knew how he'd do it.

Marek left the parish house, clutching the scrap of paper with the Praga address. His head was swimming. Finally, he was getting somewhere. He stepped onto the snow, forgetting how deep it was, and sank to his knees. Cursing silently as he felt the cold wetness in his trousers, he searched for his snowshoes. They were where he'd left them, for which he sent up a silent prayer. He fastened them on, and headed for the street.

He was in two minds where to go. He could return to the apartment, but Danka would be deep in her video calls and he didn't want to disturb her. A glance at the sky told him the clouds were thinning, but he was too long in the tooth to believe the worst of the weather was over. For one thing, there was that crystal sharpness to the air that told him the temperature was right for snowfall. For another, this was Poland in December. The best thing would be to find a warm, pastry-scented coffee house and work through his plan of attack.

But as he set off along Nowolipki Street towards Krasiński Garden, his high spirits evaporated. Who was the 'other gentleman' who'd paid Father Bielski a visit, asking the same questions? He'd thought it was Baletnica, and it might still prove to have been him, but another possibility was creeping into his consciousness. With a growing feeling of unease, he remembered Baletnica's warning: *Marek, you are not the only person looking for the manuscript. Be aware that you may be in danger. You must constantly be on your guard.*

Whoever this gentleman was, he was on the same trail. And he'd beaten Marek to Father Bielski's, so he'd been at least one step ahead. However, provided the priest was true to his word – and Marek had no reason to believe he wouldn't be – it was Marek who was now in the lead.

He realised he'd been holding his breath, and let it out in a rush, fogging the air. *Be aware that you may be in danger.* He paused in front of a shop window, pretending to study the items on display, but in reality scanning the reflection of the pavement opposite. There were people with snowshoes or on skis, but no one was wearing a black woollen hat and dark glasses. That meant nothing, as Father Bielski's visitor might be dressed differently today. Marek continued along Nowolipki, quickening his pace as far as was possible with snowshoes, and trying to tamp down his deepening anxiety.

His unease diminished as he approached Mostowski Palace. Any danger would surely decrease exponentially as he approached Warsaw Police Headquarters. He glanced through the side entrance, seeing the row of cars beyond the red-and-white barrier. They would likely belong to the officers on the night shift, who'd found themselves trapped by the snow. As he trudged along, he became aware of a figure a short distance in front. Whoever it was was wearing old-fashioned snowshoes that were too big, with the result that the only word to describe their forward motion was 'waddling'. The figure stopped, and bent forward, hands on knees. As Marek caught up, the figure straightened quickly. She was wearing a thick jacket, but was without a hat. Dusk was falling, but the snow reflected the dimming light, so visibility was good.

'Pani Lorenc,' he said, in surprise.

'Pan Górski,' she gasped. She was pink-cheeked, and out of breath.

'Are you going to work?'

'No, I've finished my shift.'

'Excellent. There's something I'd like to ask you, if I may. I think there's a *kawiarnia* across the street. May I offer you coffee and cake?' He felt rather than saw her hesitate. 'Or are you rushing off?' He regretted his choice of words immediately. No one was doing any 'rushing' in this snow.

'Coffee and cake is just what I need, Pan Górski.'

They crossed the empty street and, minutes later, were standing shaking the snow off their snowshoes.

There was only one guest in the café, and he was poring over a book, no doubt enjoying the warmth and making his hot drink last as long as possible.

Marek ordered coffees, and fluffy pancakes dusted with cinnamon. As they waited, he studied Pola, keeping his expression friendly. She looked tired and there were flecks of snow in her dishevelled hair, suggesting she'd fallen over. Perhaps she'd lost her hat and not noticed.

She smiled apologetically. 'Are you wanting to know how the Okopowa explosion case is going, Pan Górski?' Before he could reply, she added, 'I'm afraid no one has come forward claiming to recognise the E-FIT. As it was over a week ago, we'd have expected something by now.'

'Could it have been someone from outside Warsaw, contracted to throw the wreath?'

'It's possible,' she said. But she didn't sound convinced.

'Actually, that's not what I wanted to ask. I'm looking for a collection of notebooks. They belonged to someone arrested for anti-Communist activities.'

The look of tiredness on her face vanished. Her gaze sharpened. 'This is to do with one of your investigations?'

'That's right.'

'And you know this person's name?' She held up a hand. 'You don't have to tell me,' she added quickly.

'I know his name, and his address when he was arrested.'

The coffee and pancakes had arrived. The waitress set everything down, throwing Marek a smile of recognition before returning to the counter.

Pola lowered her voice. 'If he was arrested for anti-Communist activities, all his documents would have been seized by the SB, the Communist secret police. If it was in the early years of the Communist régime, they were known as the UB. But I'm sure you're familiar with this history.'

'And where would the notebooks be now? Could they have been destroyed?'

'Highly unlikely,' she said grimly. 'They'd have been filed away in the archives.'

'At the Institute of National Remembrance?'

'Do you know the building?'

'I've not been there but I know where it is.'

Pola cut up her pancakes. 'The reading room has only a small number of tables, and it's always crowded. Researchers have to book seats several days in advance. Waiting a few days may not be a problem,' she added, looking up, 'but if you request files or documents, you must wait much longer – from several weeks to several months – before you can view them.'

Marek tried not to show his dismay. 'Were *all* the papers from those arrested seized at the time of the arrest? Regardless of what was in them?'

'The police wouldn't have stopped to read them. They'd have taken everything.' She stabbed a piece of pancake with her fork. 'Can you give me an idea of what was in these notebooks?'

'Memoirs of life in Poland, before and during the war. There would have been little to interest the SB.'

Pola paused in the act of lifting the fork to her mouth. She set it down slowly. 'Pan Górski, that's not how the Ministry of Public Security worked. In the early years, their main target was former Underground soldiers of the Home Army. A war memoir? Of course they'd have taken it. They'd have been looking for names.'

Marek's mind was churning. Weeks or months before he could

view the records, assuming they were there? But that was the job. He had a mental image of a stack of well-thumbed notebooks gathering dust in the dark depths of an archive. And his application form being pushed to the bottom of the pile. It had happened before.

Pola was looking at him with sympathy. She glanced around, then pulled out her notebook. 'I'll give you the name of the archivist who helps me with my queries. You can mention my name. It might speed things up for you, but I can't guarantee it.' She wrote quickly. 'He'll be there on Monday.' She pushed the paper across.

Marek gazed at her. 'I can't thank you enough, Pani Lorenc.'

Her expression softened. She hesitated, then said, 'And how are things in general? Is everything all right?'

'How do you mean?'

'Your face is well known in Warsaw.' She glanced towards the counter. 'The lady there recognised you.' She stirred her coffee. 'Celebrities sometimes find themselves the centre of unwanted attention. People stalking them. That sort of thing. Have you noticed anything like that?'

'I can't say I have. I've been tailed before as part of an investigation, and I can usually spot the perpetrators.' He smiled. 'And who's going to follow me in this snow?'

'The snow won't last for ever, Pan Górski.'

He was struck by the concern in her eyes. Without thinking, he reached across and laid a hand on hers. 'Don't worry about me, Pani Lorenc. I can look after myself.'

She made no reply. Nor did she try to move her hand away. She gazed searchingly at him. Slowly, he withdrew his arm, and picked up his fork.

They ate in silence.

'Well, those pancakes were even better than the ones my mother makes,' Marek said, sitting back.

'I've never mastered the art. Mine turn out too thin.'

'Mine too.'

'You're a cook?'

'I have to be. I live on my own, so cooking started as a necessity, but then became a hobby. I'm staying for Wigilia, so I'll be preparing the carp.' He shook his head. 'I've never understood why that particular fish became so popular. All those bones.'

'And do you observe the traditions? Laying an extra place for the unexpected guest, and waiting until the first star appears before sitting down to eat?'

Marek made his eyes wide. 'Of course. How can you even ask?'

She laughed softly.

They finished their coffees, and then she said, 'I'm afraid I need to be going.'

'I'll walk you to your tram stop,' he said, pushing back his chair.

'There's no need, Pan Górski. It's not far.'

They left the *kawiarnia*. The clouds had dispersed, and the first stars were glittering coldly. Maybe by Monday his luck would be in and the snow would have been swept away, because he didn't want to have to traipse down to the Institute of National Remembrance in snowshoes.

'Thank you for the pancakes,' Pola said.

'It was a pleasure.'

'But please do be vigilant,' she added, after a moment's hesitation. 'If you see anything unusual, call me. Any time of day or night. You have my card.'

He was struck by the anxiety in her voice. 'Of course,' he said, in what he hoped was a reassuring tone.

He held out his hand. She put hers into his, and he lifted it to his lips. He had the impression she wanted to ask something, but must have thought better of it.

'Goodbye, and thank you again,' she said. She tottered away, her silhouette fading into the dusk.

CHAPTER 23

'Pan Dolniak is in the room at the end of the corridor,' the nurse said.

'And how is he?' Maks asked.

'In good spirits.'

'And the leg?'

'It was a clean fracture. The doctor thinks he'll be back to normal in two to three months.'

'Thank you.' As Maks turned to go, the nurse said, 'His wife's with him.'

'Ah.'

'Is that a problem?'

'It might be.'

'Well, good luck.'

He watched the woman dash down the corridor. Nurses were always in a hurry, except when they were with patients. Maks assumed this was to keep them calm. As he strolled towards Oskar's room, he wondered how the man would react to his visit. And how Oskar's wife would react to Maks.

The door was ajar. Maks peered round the edge. Oskar was lying in bed, his leg in a hoist. A petite woman with her back to the door was pulling on a padded jacket.

Oskar caught sight of him, and his face broke into a grin. 'Hi, Maks,' he called. 'Come in.'

The woman wheeled round. Her eyes were gleaming with malice. Had she smiled, with her soft green eyes and complexion like milk, she'd have been breathtakingly beautiful. But her expression transformed her into something demonic.

She strode towards Maks and, reaching up, slapped him hard in the face. '*Idiota!* You were supposed to take care of him,' she shouted. 'So, where the hell were you? No, don't speak to me,' she said, as Maks opened his mouth. 'Lucky for you, I have to leave now.' She stormed out.

Maks blew out his cheeks. He glanced at Oskar, whose eyes were twinkling.

'Admit it, Maks, if you're a red-blooded male like me, you must enjoy being hit by women.'

'I see your sense of humour hasn't changed,' Maks said, moving a chair to the side of the bed.

'Don't take it personally. She's annoyed I'll be here over Christmas.'

'And how are you, Oskar? Apart from being pleased to see me.'

'Not bad, not bad. They say that after physiotherapy I'll be back to normal. But, look, how's Karol, my driver? I thought he'd be here in the same hospital, but no one knows anything.'

So, they'd not told him, thought Maks. He played with his fingers, then looked at Oskar. 'I'm afraid he didn't survive the explosion.'

The light faded from Oskar's eyes. He lay back, staring at the ceiling. 'He'd only been married a few months,' he murmured.

'There'll be a ceremony at Mostowski next week.'

'What about his wife? Has she been told?'

'That's been taken care of, Oskar,' Maks said gently. 'Don't trouble yourself over it.'

'Was anyone else hurt? Danuta Górska?'

'She's fine. She saved your life. Did they tell you?'

He sat up slowly. 'They didn't.'

'You were blown into the water. She was quick to pull you out, and gave you CPR.'

'I don't remember a thing.'

'Perhaps it's just as well.'

'Anything from Forensics?' Oskar said, after a while.

'I called in at Ujazdów Avenue this morning.'

'And what did Roman have to say?'

'War-era Amatol.'

'No surprises there. So, what was it?'

'An 8-cm Granatwerfer 34.'

'A German mortar?'

'He'd pieced the fragments together. Actually, he'd scanned them and the software did the rest.'

'We've come across these mortars before. They're the ones with the percussion fuses, right?'

'Right. The crime-scene people think it was lying in the mud, and the magnet caught it and set it off. For once, we won't have to chase up the construction workers.'

Oskar's eyes were fixed on Maks. 'Listen, we need to find this Merkury. He's our Ace of Spades, I'm convinced of it. The chief's going to appoint someone to take over from me temporarily.' He swallowed noisily. 'I want you to persuade him to let you do it. There's no one else experienced enough to take over.' There was a pleading note in his voice. 'Promise me you'll persuade him, Maks. Promise me.'

The chief had already summoned him to his office and given

him Oskar's job, adding, with the clear-eyed gaze police chiefs have, that he was to take this on alongside his other duties, and give particular attention to bringing in the person responsible for the pure-grade heroin appearing on the streets.

'It's okay, Oskar,' he said.

Oskar lay back, a look of relief on his face. Suddenly he said, 'Don't forget our two kings, Clubs and Diamonds.'

Maks made a calming motion with his hands. 'I'll ensure we don't lose them. Do you want me to keep you informed as to progress?'

Oskar shook his head. He gazed through the window. Maks knew he was thinking about the driver.

'Karol told me his wife's expecting their first child.' His eyes filled with tears. 'Make sure you find that bastard.'

'Get some rest, Oskar,' Maks said softly, pushing back the chair.

As he left the room, the sound of gentle sobbing followed him.

Lidia Lipska lived in an ultra-modern curved-glass structure not far from the Uprising Museum. By the time Maks reached it, it was later than he'd intended, as he'd stopped to have a light supper. But he'd checked that morning, and Pani Lipska had informed him she'd be at home all day, the evening too. The inspector could call at his convenience. As he left the tram, he thought about Oskar, and the man's silent grief over Karol's death. When a colleague died, it hit hardest, and Maks had already discussed the details of the commemorative event with the chief.

At this hour, darkness had claimed the city, but the area of Warsaw around the museum was brimming with brightly lit high-rises. The streets had been cleared of the worst of the snow, and he concluded he needn't have brought his skis. He entered the building. The stocky man behind the desk asked for his name, and the name of the person he was visiting, then checked his computer.

'Pani Lipska is expecting you, Inspector,' he said smoothly. 'You're to go straight up. It's the tenth floor.'

'And the number of the apartment?'

'There *is* no number. Pani Lipska has the entire floor. You need a four-figure code, which you enter inside the lift.'

'And that takes me directly to the tenth floor?'

'The door opens automatically.' He studied Maks. 'May I ask if you're carrying a firearm?'

'I'm not, no.'

'Do you mind if I check?'

'Not at all.'

Maks unzipped the snow jacket, and lifted his arms. The receptionist patted him thoroughly. 'You may leave your skis and poles here, if you wish. I'll put them in the store room.'

Maks handed them over.

'The lift's at the end of the corridor, Inspector.'

'Thank you.'

He entered the code, and the door closed smoothly. The mechanism was so quiet that, had he not seen the floor number changing, he'd have assumed the lift was broken.

The door opened into a tiny hallway with an entrance directly opposite. Maks was about to press the buzzer, when he heard a piano. He paused to listen, his hand in mid-air. The piece was not one he recognised. It was brooding and fiery, its relentless darkness punctuated by romantic interludes. He listened, amazed anyone could play like this. As soon as the music had come to an end, he leant against the buzzer.

'It's unlocked, Pan Robak,' he heard a voice say. 'Come in, please.'

He opened the door into a huge room decorated in quiet shades of blue and grey. Curving away to left and right were large picture windows, which gave an unparalleled view of Warsaw. Several expensive-looking sofas and chairs were scattered around in an arrangement suggesting comfort was more important than style. As he removed his shoes and snow jacket, his eye was drawn to the white grand piano, its lid open.

A woman in a red-patterned dress got up from the seat. She had long fair hair scooped up in a messy bun and held in place with a metal pin. She came towards him with a well-groomed smile.

'Pan Robak, it's a pleasure to meet you. I'm Lidia Lipska.'

Maks shook her hand. 'The pleasure's mine, Pani Lipska.' He was conscious he was staring, but it was impossible not to. Her eyes were the exact shape and hazel colour as Danuta Górska's. And their expression, confident but thoughtful, was identical.

He realised he was still holding Lidia's hand. He released her. 'May I ask what you were playing?' he said.

'It was Paderewski's Piano Sonata in E Flat Minor. The first movement. When I heard Rena Adler play it, I decided I wanted to become a pianist. Although I'm a politician now, I try to keep in practice.' She smiled knowingly. 'Careers in politics are often short, Pan Robak.'

'I don't doubt it.'

'May I offer you a drink? Tea? Something stronger?'

'Tea will be fine.'

'I won't be long. Make yourself comfortable.' She looked round the room. 'Anywhere you like.' She disappeared through a door.

Maks wandered around, wondering why there were no pictures

on the walls. It was a complete contrast to Adam Mazur's. It, too, had a grand piano in the centre of the room, but that was where the resemblance ended. Given the choice, Maks would have favoured an arrangement with some colour. But the lack of distraction might be necessary for a concert pianist. There was no point in tackling a piano concerto if your gaze was constantly wandering.

He tested an armchair, remembering how he'd nearly sunk without trace at Mazur's, but the upholstery was strong and springy.

Minutes later, Lidia returned. Maks got to his feet and, taking the tray from her hands, set it down on the low glass table.

'Please help yourself to jam, Pan Robak,' she said, taking the chair closest to his. 'There's gooseberry or plum.'

'After you.'

She added a heaped teaspoon of gooseberry jam to her glass. Maks did the same.

'Now, what do you wish to talk to me about?' she said, looking at him enquiringly.

He decided to try an indirect approach. 'I'm interested in how you're getting on with rooting out corruption in our political system.'

'This is something that concerns the police?' she said, in surprise.

She was so close he had to divert his gaze, or she'd think he was staring. He couldn't get over how much she looked like Danuta.

'It concerns us if it puts you in danger,' he said.

'All politicians face danger. Having an egg thrown at you is a hazard of the job.'

'I meant in government. You must have made enemies among your colleagues.'

'Everyone has, Pan Robak. Surely you've experienced the same.'

'My enemies come from outside the police force, and I can lock them up.'

A smile flickered on her lips. 'You should do the same to mine.'

'Have you received any threats recently?' he said, sipping. 'Two members of the Civic Platform Party have resigned.'

'I received letters from their wives.'

'Do you have them here?'

'I threw them away. There was nothing but expletives.'

'And from the men themselves?'

'Nothing. From what I remember, one has gone into business and is making obscene amounts of money. The other has taken up a lucrative post at the Jagiellonian University in Kraków.'

'I was intrigued you started this anti-corruption drive with your own party.'

'As parties veer towards extremes, Pan Robak, they don't look all that different. I started with mine because I had easy access to information. And I didn't want to be accused of favouring my party over another. I've now moved on to my main target, the Law and Justice Party.'

Maks looked at her for a long moment. 'Can you tell me what you've uncovered about members of that party?'

She hesitated. 'Why are you asking me this?'

'Would you mind answering the question?' he said, softening the remark with a smile.

'I'm afraid I can't. I'm still at the stage of gathering evidence, and I need to corroborate that evidence before making it public.'

'And you're not prepared to tell a police officer?'

'I'm not prepared to tell anyone.'

'Let me put this another way. The politicians you're gathering evidence against, do they know they're being scrutinised?'

'They don't. I'm careful how I conduct my research, Pan Robak.'

Seeing the resolution in her eyes, he knew he had no option but to get to the point.

'Pani Lipska, I'm investigating the explosion at Okopowa cemetery.'

'The explosion?' she responded, with a vague smile.

'It was at Jakub Frydman's grave. We think it was intended to kill one of the mourners.' He paused. 'Who knew you'd been invited to the funeral?'

Fear registered in her eyes as the implication sank in. But she quickly took control of her emotions. 'I don't remember telling anyone.'

'When did you receive the invitation from Pan Mazur?'

She frowned for a moment. Then her expression cleared. 'I remember now it was hand-delivered on the Monday morning.'

She must have been one of the first on Mazur's list, thought Maks.

'Was it delivered here?' he said.

'To my office at the Sejm.'

'Did your secretary open it?'

'She was off that day. I opened the envelope myself.'

'May I ask why you didn't attend the funeral?'

'I meant to, but I fell ill the evening before. It was gastric flu. I was incapable of functioning the following morning. In fact, it was a couple of days before I could crawl out of bed.'

Then no one other than Adam Mazur and Rabin Steinberg had known she'd been invited.

As if reading his mind, Lidia said, 'One second, I *did* tell someone.'

'That you'd be at the funeral?'

'My secretary had made an appointment with Zygmunt

Zelenski for the Wednesday morning, for the time of the funeral, as it happens. I'd received Pan Mazur's invitation and was marking it in the diary when I saw Zelenski's name. I contacted him immediately, and tried to rearrange for the following week.' She frowned. 'He was polite but distant, so I felt the need to explain. I told him Pan Mazur's invitation had just arrived. Jakub Frydman had been my piano teacher, and I wanted to attend his funeral.'

Maks tried not to show his concern. 'And did you meet with Zelenski the following week?'

'He cancelled there and then. He didn't say why he'd changed his mind.'

'Did he say why he'd wanted to see you?'

She tilted her head. 'What do you know about property restitution, Pan Robak?'

'Only what everyone knows. That, thirty years after the fall of Communism, claims are still being made, and few properties are restored to descendants through lack of documents, which is why there are these empty pre-war apartment blocks in Warsaw.'

She looked at him appreciatively. 'An excellent summary. And, as a property developer, Zelenski knows where these empty buildings stand.'

'As does the whole of Warsaw. Walk through districts like Praga, and you see them.'

'So, I'd tabled a paper to be discussed at the Sejm next year. It has to do with the difficulty descendants are experiencing in having property restored. They have to hire lawyers and go through the courts and, as you've mentioned, they have to produce certain documents, and then they discover there are more documents they need to provide, and more after that.' She lifted a hand. 'I won't bore you with the details, but many of the applicants give up through lack of time or money.'

'And where does Zelenski come in?'

'I alluded to his business practices in the paper.'

'I don't understand.'

She lowered her voice, as if the walls could hear. 'I've researched the apartment blocks that *have* been restored, Pan Robak. In almost every case, the new owners then sold the property to Zelenski. My suspicions were raised when I discovered how little he paid them. It was considerably less than they were worth, and a fraction of what they'd ultimately be worth when redeveloped.'

'So, he'll make a fortune when he finally sells them on,' Maks said, frowning.

'I don't know what pressure he put on the descendants to sell. Many of these buildings were crumbling, and it's possible they didn't need much persuading.'

'You didn't spell this out in your paper, did you?'

'I simply stated I'd be looking into his property dealings.'

Maks ran a hand over his face. 'Could Zelenski have found out about your proposal? And that was why he wanted to see you?'

'And it means someone on my team leaked it. For a not inconsiderable sum.' She looked fixedly at Maks. 'You can see now why I'm so keen to expose corruption in our system.'

But Maks was thinking less about corruption and more about the consequences of her actions. Without having to think too hard, he constructed a likely scenario. Zelenski, learning of the contents of Lidia's paper, makes an appointment to see her, either to find out how much she knows or to persuade her against tabling it, or both. Then he discovers she's attending Jakub Frydman's funeral and seizes an opportunity to silence her permanently. Yet Maks could be wrong, and there was an innocent explanation for Zelenski's appointment and its subsequent cancellation. Another politician could have seen the funeral notice in Monday morning's paper, assumed Lidia would be present, and arranged for a wreath packed with explosives to be thrown into the group of mourners. Then, again, the explosion might have had nothing whatsoever to do with Lidia.

She was studying him. 'How long have you been a detective, Pan Robak?'

'Too long.'

'Have you considered becoming a politician?'

'Exchange one filthy job for another, you mean?'

'It's only filthy if you can't make a difference.'

He shrugged. 'I'd like to think I make a difference where I am.'

'From what I've heard, you do.'

He looked into her eyes, suppressing the urge to ask what she knew about him. Perhaps the police were to be her next anti-corruption target, and she was already asking questions.

'Are you on duty?' she said, setting her glass on the tray.

He glanced at his watch. 'Not any longer,' he said, smiling.

'Would you join me in a drink? A real drink?'

'Of course.'

She got to her feet. 'What would you like?'

'Whatever you're having.'

He took the tray and followed her into the kitchen. Much of it was taken up by a long dining table and chairs. Was this where Lidia entertained members of the Civic Platform Party, discussing matters of political importance? Or did she invite her musical friends for supper and an evening of Chopin? He knew which he'd prefer.

He deposited the tray beside the sink – once he'd found it at the other end of the room – and joined Lidia at the table. She was holding a fat bottle. The light caught the red liquid.

'This is Hernö sloe gin,' she said.'It's from Sweden. Are you a gin drinker, Pan Robak?'

'I can't say I am. But there's a first time for everything.'

He watched her pour, only then noticing the two-leaved door behind her. It was standing wide, giving him a view of a double bed and a mirrored dresser, its surface littered with jars and bottles. So, Lidia's bedroom opened into the kitchen? But, then, why not? If she felt hungry in the middle of the night, she didn't have far to go. Perhaps on her days off she made breakfast and took it back to bed. Maybe there was a television. Maks thought of his own bedroom, with so little room to manoeuvre when dressing that he was constantly bumping his arms against the wall.

Lidia handed him a glass. 'Tell me what you think.'

He took a sip, then a gulp. 'I can taste something sweet,' he said, licking his lips.

'That's the honey. But I'm guessing you're a vodka man.'

He tipped his glass in acknowledgement. 'How can you tell?'

'Your physique.'

'My physique?' he said, in surprise.

'I see a powerfully built man with toned muscles.'

'You think that's down to vodka, Pani Lipska?' he said, laughing. 'It's hours in the police gym.'

'Did I not read somewhere that you were a speedway champion?'

'That was years ago,' he said, looking at her with interest. 'I'm afraid I no longer have the time.'

'What do you do when you're not chasing the bad guys?'

'I'm always chasing the bad guys. They multiply by the hour.'

'You must miss speedway, though.'

To win at speedway you had to take risks. Maks thought about the number of times he'd narrowly cheated death. 'I prefer karting now. And in the summer, I take my kayak onto the river.' He lifted the glass to his lips. 'And you? I'm guessing to play the way you do, you need to devote your spare time to the piano.'

'I'm lucky to live in Warsaw. It's the piano capital of the world. There's so much music here it's easy to find opportunities to play.'

Maks cradled the glass. 'What was Jakub Frydman like? As a person, and a teacher?'

A wistful expression crossed Lidia's face. 'Unbelievably kind. Whenever I made mistakes, he didn't so much point them out as suggest ways I could reposition my hands to avoid making them. He was careful in his choice of words, which is important for someone learning the piano. It's easy to criticise, but that's guaranteed to ruin a young player's confidence. It's then difficult to get it back. And he had all sorts of tricks for memorising the notes.'

'Do you need to? Surely you have the sheets in front of you.'

'Ah, that's a common misconception, Pan Robak.' She swirled the gin round her glass. 'The more difficult the piece, the more time you have to spend looking at the keyboard. If you have to keep glancing back and forth at the sheets, you're likely to play a wrong note. What pianists need is an excellent memory.'

'I hadn't thought of it like that.'

'Do you play an instrument?'

'I'm afraid I don't.'

'Did your parents not push you to learn?'

'I was an orphan. The nuns who brought me up didn't have the funds to engage music teachers.' He downed the rest of the gin. 'What I remember is the singing. I was in the choir.'

Lidia was looking at him strangely. 'Was this one of the orphanages run by the Franciscan Sisters of the Family of Mary?' she said, topping up his glass.

'That's right.'

'Were you left outside the building?'

'I was.'

'So was I.'

Maks stared at her. He knew of no one personally who'd had the same experience. He wondered if they'd been placed in the same children's home.

She was smiling. 'Who would have thought we'd had an identical start in life?'

She was so like Danuta, Maks thought. The same expression in her eyes. And a mouth that smiled easily.

They chatted about life in the orphanage. Lidia picked up the bottle. She was about to replenish his glass, when he said, 'I think I need to be going.'

'One more, Pan Robak. We can drink to Jakub Frydman.'

For an instant, he saw the same wounded expression he'd seen in Danuta's eyes. So, who was this man whose death had had such an effect on his pupils? Maks was now wishing he'd known him.

'One more, then,' he said.

She started to pour, but her hand was trembling.

'Here, let me.' He took the bottle and refilled their glasses.

'To Jakub Frydman,' she said.

'Jakub Frydman.'

They drank in silence.

Lidia got to her feet. 'Shall I make more tea? You'll stay for that, won't you?'

Maks stood up. She was so close to him he could see the dark flecks in her irises. He had a strong urge to gather her in his arms, to bring his mouth down on hers, but he always left it to the lady to make the first move.

She stood on tiptoe and turned her face upwards, her lips brushing his. The expression in her eyes was unmistakable. Slowly, she lifted the bottom of his sweater and started to unbuckle his belt. He felt himself grow hard. He slipped an arm round her waist and pulled her towards him. A second later, they were shedding their clothes and stumbling towards the bedroom. His main thought as they collapsed onto the bed was that at least he was no longer on duty.

Chapter 24

Dania was at the kitchen window, peering into the street. The worst of the snow had been cleared, and what was left was melting rapidly. She scanned the sky, seeing the cloud thinning, and the scraps of blue growing by the minute. And it didn't look as though more snow was on the way. As the forecast was promising, she had no excuse to put off arranging a flight back. Hopefully she'd return to a not-too-frosty reception as her video calls had been productive. It was a strange way of working, hearing reports from her officers and issuing instructions from her laptop. She'd even managed to operate the incident board remotely. Better still, she had to look smart only from the waist up; no one had spotted her pyjama bottoms and slippers. She'd estimated at least 80 per cent of her work could be done remotely. On her return she should suggest home working.

Marek was bustling about, clearing away the remains of the late breakfast. They'd attended Mass at St Augustine's but, to her disappointment, Robak had been absent. She'd need to see him before she returned to Dundee, to establish who Oskar's replacement would be, as she intended to keep in touch with Mostowski Palace until they finally apprehended Merkury.

'I'll do the washing-up,' she said.

'Why don't we leave it till we get back?'

Having heard the account of what Marek had learnt from Father Bielski, it had been Dania's suggestion to go to the address in Praga and see what they could uncover. Maybe the current owners could shed light on the notebooks the priest's father had written. Perhaps they'd renovated the place and found them. It was worth a try. And if it turned out to be a dead end, well, Marek could cross it off his list.

'No news from Baletnica?' she said.

'Nothing. I emailed him and told him about Father Bielski.' Marek shrugged. 'I may hear from him later. So, are you ready?'

'Have you worked out our route?'

'We take a tram, then a bus. Our multi-use tickets should suffice but, just in case, I've bought us a couple more.'

Dania smiled to herself. If there was one thing she could rely on her brother for, it was to be well prepared. 'Do you think we'll need snowshoes?' she said.

'I doubt it. I've checked online. They say they've cleared that area of Praga. Let's risk it. If we get stuck, we can go tomorrow.'

'It's possible the owners of the apartment will be at Mass.'

'I've thought of that, too. If there's no reply, we'll go to the zoo. It's open on a Sunday. And then we can return to the apartment.'

'Looks as if you've planned for every eventuality.'

'One of us has to,' he said cheekily.

He was so full of enthusiasm she hadn't the heart to be offended. Her main concern was that the residents wouldn't let them in. Marek could usually charm his way into any situation and might be relying on his new-found celebrity status, but it was possible the owners or tenants hadn't heard of him. And if a woman was living there, it was unlikely she'd let in a stranger, especially a man. Which was why Dania had suggested she accompany her brother.

They put on warm outer clothes and left the building. The dirty snow had been cleared off the road and was banked up on the pavement. It left room for two people to walk side by side, which wasn't a problem until they met someone coming from the other direction. Although there was no wind, the cold settled into Dania's lungs. She wondered what it would be like on the east bank of the river.

They didn't have long to wait at the tram stop. The vehicle travelled over the same bridge Dania had crossed on Thursday when they'd staked out the jetty. As she gazed out of the window, she wondered if the police would ever catch Merkury, and if having abandoned her team in Dundee and followed him to Warsaw had been a colossal waste of time. But it was too easy to let such thoughts overwhelm her, and she forced herself to think about something else.

They passed the zoo, then left the tram to board the bus. The route took them through the streets of pre-war Warsaw, its brick buildings pockmarked with bullet holes. Their parents had avoided the district because of the high crime rate, although Dania and Marek had visited the area on a school trip. Other than the abandoned warehouses, disused factories and grey Communist apartment blocks, what she remembered were the *kapliczki*, or shrines, for which Praga was famous. Some dated from before the war but most had been built in 1943 and 1944. They were shrines to the Virgin Mary, erected in courtyards out of view of the Germans, and serving to replace bombed-out churches. What their teacher had told them was that, during the Uprising, the insurgents had hidden weapons and ammunition inside.

'Do we know on which floor the priest's father lived?' Dania said.

'Given the low number in the address, it would have been the ground floor. Why do you ask?'

'I remember these old brick apartments have no lifts.'

'How high can they be, Danka? Four, five floors? No more than that.'

She gazed out at the buildings, many of which were decorated with multicoloured graffiti. That was something she hadn't seen as a child.

Marek was frowning into his phone. 'Okay, it's the next stop.' He grinned at her. 'Where would we be without Google Maps?'

She had to smile. His enthusiasm was becoming infectious. 'Have you worked through what you're going to say?' she asked.

'That depends on whether it's a man or a woman. Right, it's this stop.' He sprang to his feet.

The street was a mix of old and new, not uncommon for Praga, with abandoned buildings remodelled into bars and restaurants. But as she followed Marek, who was staring fixedly at the phone, what she was starting to see were partly plastered brick buildings with rusting wrought-iron balconies. In many cases, the discoloured plaster was flaking off, and the glass in the windows was cracked or missing. Despite Marek's assurance, no attention had been paid to clearing the pavements, and she found herself slipping and stumbling in the snow.

Marek stopped and held out his arm. 'Hold on to me. We're nearly there. It's the second building on the next street.'

He turned sharp right, stopping so suddenly she lost her footing and fell. Fortunately, the snow was deep enough that she didn't hurt herself.

'I don't believe it,' Marek murmured. He glanced at the phone.

Dania struggled to her feet. And then she saw what had caused him to stop abruptly. 'Are you sure that's it?' she said.

Marek approached the building on the corner and peered at the number on the blue-and-red plaque. 'I'm sure.'

Where the apartment block should have been, there was a pile of rubble. Whoever had demolished it had taken care not to touch the *kapliczka* in what had been the courtyard. It stood proud amid the sea of bricks and concrete, an indisputable testament to the miraculous power of the Virgin.

Maksymilian Robak opened his eyes, seeing the array of ceiling lights that told him he wasn't in his Karmelicka apartment. He raised himself on his elbow, trying to remember whose room this was. He knew only that he'd spent the previous night love-making. The thing with sex was that, because he put his creative imagination into it, it often left him exhausted. And last night's activity had been more imaginative than usual, he remembered then. He could still feel the restraints round his wrists where Lidia had tied him to the bed.

Through the partly open door, he heard the sounds of the kitchen: crockery laid out, a kettle being filled, cupboards opening and closing. He swung his legs out of the bed. His clothes were folded in a neat pile on the chair, and a large fluffy towel hung over the back. He dragged it off and wrapped it round his waist, wondering which of the doors led to the bathroom.

He was considering asking Lidia when she appeared, wearing a blue silk dressing-gown. There was a look of amused complicity on her face. 'If you'd like a shower, Pan Robak, the door to the bathroom is the one next to the dressing-table.'

'Thank you,' he said, smiling.

She disappeared into the kitchen, leaving him intrigued that, after the activities of the previous night, she was still addressing him formally. But it was up to the lady to suggest otherwise. A gentleman never did.

The large bathroom was finished in shades of lemon, and had two washbasins, and a double shower. Maks stood under the hot jet, soaping his body and working shampoo into his hair. The water was exactly the right temperature, and the temptation to keep standing there was irresistible. But it was midday, and he was on shift in the afternoon.

He towelled his hair and used the pearl-handled brush to sweep it back off his face. In the bedroom, he dressed quickly and, after a quick check round the room, headed for the kitchen.

The table was laid with an assortment of cheeses and cold meats. Lidia held out a mug of coffee.

He took it, nodding gratefully.

She angled her head. 'How did you get that huge bruise on your shoulder?'

At first, he couldn't think, but then remembered the explosion, and how he'd tried to protect Danuta. 'In the line of duty,' he said. 'I was hit by a rock.'

'Did someone throw it at you?'

'There was an explosion.'

Her expression changed. She'd have read about the Praga jetty, thought Maks, eyeing her over the rim of the mug.

'By the way, Pan Robak, do you know you talk in your sleep?'

He froze in the act of lowering the mug.

When he said nothing, she added, 'You mentioned someone called Dania.'

'And what did I say about her?'

'Nothing. You muttered her name once or twice.'

He looked away. It was bad form to have sex with one woman while mentally making love to another. Fortunately, Lidia didn't press the issue. He finished the coffee, and set down the mug.

'Would you take breakfast with me?' she said, gesturing to the food.

'I'm greatly tempted, but if I don't leave now, I'll be late for my shift.'

She nodded, her expression suggesting she understood.

Maks rummaged in the pocket of his jeans. 'I'm going to leave you my card, Pani Lipska. If Zygmunt Zelenski or for that matter his son, Konrad, gets in touch, you must let me know immediately.' His eyes locked on hers. 'Do you understand?'

'I do.'

He could see she wanted to ask him something, but thought better of it. She responded with a faint half-smile. 'Goodbye, Pan Robak,' she said, holding out her hand.

He shook it, then squeezed it hard, his gaze sweeping over her face. 'Do I need a code to operate the lift?' he said.

'Press the blue button. It takes you down to the reception.'

'I'll let myself out. Thank you for your hospitality.'

At the door, he slipped on his shoes and snow jacket. He rode the lift to the ground floor.

The same man was on reception. He must have remembered Maks because he disappeared into the store room without a word, and reappeared with the skis and poles.

'I believe these are yours, sir,' he said. A knowing smirk crossed his lips.

'Have you been on duty all night?'

'Yes, sir.'

Maks was tempted to reply, 'So have I.'

The archivist was late. And that was unusual, Pola thought. She was loitering at the steps leading up to the Palace of Culture and

Science. The area had been cleared of snow because Sunday was the day parents took their children to museums and exhibitions. It was lunchtime, and there were fewer visitors than usual, which was perhaps why the archivist had chosen this time and place. No one to spy on them. No one to listen in to what they were saying.

Pola drew her head back as far as it would go, and peered at the tall structure, which looked taller from this angle. She had a fear of heights, and had never been to the viewing terrace on the thirtieth floor. Someone had told her that in Communist times it had been a favourite place for suicides. She could well believe it.

She let her gaze wander over the square and across the multi-lane highway towards the shops. She knew the department stores well, as her street was round the corner. Today, however, it wasn't shopping on her mind but Adam Mazur. And specifically what the archivist at the Institute of National Remembrance had uncovered. That he'd wanted to meet well away from the institute was what had made Pola agree promptly. He wasn't a particularly nervous man, so this unprecedented behaviour was significant. She scanned the square, wondering what was making him late. Perhaps he lived in an area of Warsaw that hadn't yet been cleared of snow.

Pola walked around the square, scrutinising the streets. And then she spotted him ambling along the Marszałkowska. His tall, angular build and thick shock of brown hair were unmistakable. Rather than raise a hand in greeting, she stopped and stared fixedly to attract his attention. As soon as he started to hurry over, she returned to the steps, knowing the archivist would follow.

'Thank you for seeing me, Pani Lorenc,' he said, slightly out of breath. His eyes disappeared when he smiled, which was often. Except today he was frowning, his gaze darting left and right.

She was tempted to put him at his ease with a joke about a spy meeting her contact, but decided it wouldn't go down well. 'So, what can you tell me?' she said.

'Remember we talked about Adam Mazur's documents being misfiled?' Without waiting for a reply, he added, 'I finally located them.'

'You did?' she said, her voice drifting. There were miles of paper documents in the archives and, unless you knew where to look, the chances of stumbling across what you were after were negligible.

His gaze slid away. 'Best if I don't give you the details. At least, not all.' He lowered his voice. 'There's an area of the archives where I once found misfiled documents. It was last year. I was looking for particular papers and found a misplaced folder. It was inside another folder, as though pushed in by someone in a hurry. Archivists aren't normally so careless. But I assumed it was a mistake on the part of one of my colleagues – we'd been particularly busy – and I filed the folder correctly.'

He played with his fingers. Pola didn't rush him. She'd known this man for years, and they had a good working relationship. He'd tell her in his own good time. But his state of anxiety alarmed her.

He looked around furtively, then said, 'Something made me check the card index for the name.'

'The name on the misplaced folder?'

'That's right. Anyway, it was no one of note. At least, I'd never heard of him. But there was something else. Something odd. The card should have made reference to this folder. But it didn't.'

Pola stared straight ahead. 'So, someone deliberately misplaced the folder and then created a new card, removing all reference to it.'

'Spot on, Pani Lorenc. That was my conclusion, too.'

'Why didn't they destroy the folder?'

'Who knows? Maybe they thought it would come in useful.'

'I wonder what was in it.'

He tried a grin but it came out as more of a grimace. 'I wondered that too. I thought about it off and on over the next few days. In the end, I decided to read the contents for myself. So, I went back to where I'd filed it correctly.'

'Let me guess. It was missing.'

'And I went back to where I'd *originally* found it.'

'And it wasn't there either.'

'The conclusion I came to was that someone must have seen me restore the folder to the correct section in the archives.' His gaze rested on hers. 'And this someone must have been the person who'd deliberately misfiled it.'

Pola's mind was racing. The majority of cases under investigation by the Institute of National Remembrance had been Communist-era crimes. She imagined what the folder must have contained.

'Did anyone see you go back to look for the folder?' she asked. 'Either to where you'd refiled it or to its original location?'

'No one. When I saw the index card, I realised one of my colleagues was taking bribes to misfile documents. I became extremely cautious after that.'

'And you've no idea who this colleague is?'

'I don't want to know.'

'And where do Adam Mazur's documents fit into this story? You said you'd found them.'

'The section of the archives where I found that misfiled folder last year is rarely used. The documents there relate to an obscure period of Warsaw's history. So, after making sure no one was around, I crept in and began systematically to search the files.'

'And that's where you found Adam Mazur's?'

'I was lucky there. I stumbled across his documents on the second day.'

'And you're sure no one saw you enter or leave?'

'One hundred per cent.'

Pola stared into the sky, her thoughts in a whirl.

'I made a copy of the documents,' the archivist went on. He reached inside his jacket and pulled out a folder. 'I'd have scanned them, but I didn't want the evidence left behind, so I made paper copies. I returned the originals to where they'd been hidden.' His eyes searched hers. 'I know you'll keep my name out of this if you decide to act.'

Pola nodded firmly. One thing she intended to do above all else was preserve their working relationship. She shrugged off her rucksack and slipped the folder inside. 'There's something else,' she said. 'Nothing to do with Adam Mazur. There's an investigator called Marek Górski. You may have heard of him in connection with this missing Chopin manuscript. He's looking for information on someone arrested by the Communists. I gave him your name and said you were in a position to speed things up. I'd be grateful for any help you can give him.'

'Of course. I'll do what I can.' The archivist took her hand, and brought it to his lips. 'Goodbye, Pani Lorenc.'

She watched him hurry through the car park until he reached Marszałkowska. Then he disappeared.

CHAPTER 25

Maks left Oskar's office and made for the stairs. He'd had a long meeting with the Anti-drugs team, at which he'd reassured them he'd be dividing his time between the two offices. The group had been broadly receptive, and between them they'd drawn up a plan of action. Their fierce loyalty to Oskar was a credit to him, Maks thought, and he was determined not to let down the man and his team, even if it meant working every shift going.

One of the women had taken over liaison with Oskar's informant. So far, the brass were keeping a low profile, and the number of heroin packets the sellers were now receiving had dwindled, indicating stocks were low. When the informant had asked the King of Clubs how soon more heroin would be coming in, the man had shrugged his shoulders. Maks had impressed upon the team it was vital they discover when the next shipment was arriving. There was a lively discussion as to whether the approach would be made by river or overland. Given that roads were being cleared, it could be either.

The kings were being shadowed whenever they left their apartments, and weren't in any hurry to continue trading. But as for Merkury, there had been no sighting of him. And it was Merkury – the Ace of Spades – they were after.

Maks reached his office. He hoped his own team meeting would be over in time for Mass at 6 p.m. He also hoped he'd learn something that would take the Jakub Frydman case forward. Because if any of his investigations had stalled, it was this one.

The buzz from the group reached him as he opened the door. He took it as a good sign.

'Right, let's get down to it,' he said, striding towards the white-board. 'I'll go first. I met with Lidia Lipska yesterday.'

'Did she play the piano for you?' someone asked cheekily.

'As a matter of fact, she did.' Briefly, he filled them in on what he'd learnt. 'The timing is the thing here. On Monday morning, we have Lidia telling Zygmunt Zelenski she can't make their Wednesday-morning meeting because she's attending Jakub Frydman's funeral. He tells her he's changed his mind and there's no need to reschedule. Why?' Without waiting for a reply, he went on, 'Because in that instant he sees a way out of his predica-ment. He plans to kill Lidia, so why bother making another appointment?'

'The wreath was ordered on Monday morning, and picked up later the same day,' Pola said. 'The timing would have been tight, but perfectly doable for a man like Zelenski.'

'And he'd have had no difficulty getting his hands on Amatol.' With a felt tip, Maks drew two circles on the board, a large one at the centre with the word 'Zelenski' inside, and a smaller one above it. In it, he wrote the name 'Lidia Lipska'. 'Now we come to Rabin Steinberg,' he said.

'He's back in Jerusalem,' someone chipped in. 'Taking a sabbat-ical. He'll be there until spring.'

'If he was the target, then it's the safest place for him.'

'You still think that article he wrote would be enough to make him a target?' Pola asked.

'Accusing the Zelenskis of operating fraudulently, resulting in a loss of business, is a strong enough motive.' Maks added a circle with Steinberg's name, and connected it to Zelenski's. 'But we have one more possible victim. And that's Adam Mazur.' He looked at Pola.

She put on her reading glasses and opened her folder. 'These are documents I received this afternoon. They're from the archivist at the Institute of National Remembrance.'

There was a stir in the room. Maks leant against the wall, his arms crossed.

'When Pan Mazur was director of the Chopin University of Music,' she said, 'he collaborated with the authorities, and betrayed several of his colleagues. The file the secret police kept on him lists the sums he received for his cooperation.'

'I can check his bank account,' someone offered.

'No point,' Maks said, remembering the man's living room. 'He received the money too long ago, and used it to buy paintings. He must have concluded that, if anyone were to check in the future, he could say they were gifts, or he'd bought them at knock-down prices.' He nodded at the folder. 'Where's our link with Jakub Frydman?'

'It wasn't only his colleagues at the University of Music he betrayed,' Pola said. 'One of the men he denounced was Leon Zelenski. He was Zygmunt Zelenski's father.'

The officers gaped in astonishment.

'Zygmunt could have been told about this,' Maks said.

'Agreed. Adam Mazur's documents were deliberately misfiled by someone in the institute who's taking bribes. But that's not to say this person couldn't have taken a peek, seen Leon Zelenski had been denounced, and sold that information to Zygmunt. And for a price higher than Adam Mazur had paid him to suppress it.'

'What happened to Leon?'

'He died in prison. Suicide, according to the record. Although . . .'

'So, if Zygmunt *did* learn that Adam had denounced his father, it gives him the strongest possible motive to dispatch him.' Maks frowned. 'Does the archivist know who is misfiling documents?'

'He doesn't,' Pola said emphatically. 'Given the nature of what's in the folder, he doesn't want to know. I promised I'd keep his name out of it.'

Maks looked at her searchingly. This would have to be taken further. And, because the Communist-era secret police were known to have fabricated documents, an investigation would be lengthy. Fortunately, it wouldn't be conducted by him or his team. Being in the Policja Kryminalna had its compensations.

'Okay, so if Adam Mazur was the intended target of the unexpected guest,' someone was saying, 'Zygmunt would have had to know he'd be at Jakub Frydman's funeral.'

'Lidia Lipska told him,' Maks said, 'on the Monday morning when she rang Zelenski to rearrange their meeting. She said Mazur's invitation had arrived. It suggests he'd be present, too. And it puts him in the frame as a target.'

'It's been nearly two weeks since the funeral,' Pola said. 'Why do you think there have been no further attempts?'

'Zelenski will have had his work cut out coming up with a plan that won't lead directly to him,' Maks said. He gestured to the folder. 'Let me have a look at that.'

He leafed through the documents. None of the names of those arrested meant anything to him, but then he knew little of the history of the Chopin University of Music. The archivist had also added a page noting the prison sentences handed down.

Maks closed the folder, dizzying himself as he went round the possibilities. Zygmunt Zelenski had clear motives for killing Rabin Steinberg, Lidia Lipska and Adam Mazur. The problem was that, two weeks on from the explosion, they didn't have a shred of evidence against him.

The sound of sniggering made him turn.

One of the female officers had added a circle with Adam Mazur's name, and connected it to Zygmunt's. Not only that, but she'd drawn a web across the whiteboard, and added legs and a head to Zygmunt's circle, turning it into a spider. The three possible victims were flies with legs and wings.

'All right, so which one is the victim?' Maks said, trying not to laugh. 'Mm?'

The officer smiled. 'It's obvious, isn't it?' she said flirtatiously.

'Not to me.'

'They were *all* meant to be victims. What's that English expression? Killing three birds with one stone?'

Tufts of cloud were drifting across the bleached blue sky, and the roads were clear of snow, thanks to the good work of the council. There was therefore no excuse for Dania not to book a flight. The website was still down, but she'd phoned the airport and discovered there was a flight to Edinburgh the following day. She'd dithered over whether to book, but in the end had decided to take the one on Friday in the hope that Inspector Robak would be in touch. There was still a chance, albeit a dwindling one, that they'd apprehend Merkury, but it depended on whether Oskar's informant delivered the goods. Marek had suggested Dania ring Robak, but she'd concluded that first thing on a

Monday morning wouldn't be the best time. She'd get some fresh air and try him before lunch.

It was a short walk from Dzielna Street to Okopowa cemetery. Forensics would have finished by now, snow or no snow, although what could they have detected other than traces of explosive?

The iron gate to Okopowa was open, and a black van was backing slowly into it, watched by the custodian standing on the pavement with a mug in her hands. She had on the same moth-eaten fur coat she'd worn on the day of the funeral, but was without hat and gloves. Her short dark hair was plastered over her forehead and down the sides of her face. As Dania approached, she turned milky eyes in her direction. Dania didn't think she'd remember her but a fleeting expression of recognition crossed her face, followed strangely by one of guilt. She opened her mouth to speak but a loud, metallic noise caused her attention to return to the van. The driver had scraped the vehicle against the gate. Although the damage was on the van's side, the custodian thrust the mug into Dania's hand and hurried round to the driver's door.

An altercation followed, with much gesturing and swearing. Then the driver trundled forward and inched back through the gate, successfully this time. The custodian scowled at the van, which disappeared into the depths of the cemetery. She glanced in Dania's direction, and rolled her eyes as if to say, 'Men!'

Dania nodded knowingly, although she doubted she'd have made a better fist of it.

'We're having repairs done,' the woman said, taking the mug. 'Many headstones are falling.' She gazed at Dania, her eyes narrowing. 'You were here for the funeral.'

'You helped me and my brother with directions,' Dania said, with a quick smile. 'We'd never have found the grave otherwise.'

'That was a terrible business.' She crossed herself. 'I can't understand it. Why would anyone do such a thing?'

'I presume the police have finished here.'

'Have you come to pay your respects? I can show you how to get there, if you like.'

'I'd be grateful. I'd only get lost.'

'Visitors usually come to see Adam Czerniaków's grave,' the custodian said, making for the gate. 'That's an easy one.' She shuffled towards the booth, drained the contents of the mug and left it on the counter. 'Please follow me.'

She ambled off, stopping now and then to point out a particular headstone and its intricate carvings. Many stones were rimed with hoar-frost, like white mould. On parts of the path, the snow had turned to ice, and thin slivers crackled into powder under their feet. Dania was amazed the woman knew where to go. The track would suddenly disappear, yet she didn't pause to get her bearings but stepped confidently in a particular direction. Her weathered face was stippled with acne scars, and Dania guessed she was well past the age of retirement but worked out of necessity. Given her knowledge of the graveyard and its winding trails, its potholes and tangles of undergrowth, the council would be glad of her services.

A while later, they reached a section of the cemetery cordoned off with red-and-white tape.

'There,' the custodian said, indicating to the right, 'is where Pan Frydman's grave was.'

Dania gazed at the large crater. A spidery web of ice had formed on the surface. She was unable to recognise her surroundings but, then, she'd seen little in the fog.

'Was Pan Frydman a friend?' the custodian said, peering up at her.

'He was my piano teacher.'

She said nothing for a moment. 'I heard him play once,' she blurted. 'A friend had bought a ticket and couldn't go, so, she asked if I wanted it. Of course I said yes.'

'When was this?'

'I can't remember now. It was too long ago.' She looked into the sky. 'But he played so beautifully, it was like listening to God.'

'Was there an orchestra?' Dania asked, thinking Jakub might have played one of Chopin's concertos.

'Just a grand piano. The lid was open.' The woman grasped Dania's sleeve, and gestured to the crater. 'Who would have wanted to do this to such a wonderful man?' she whispered. 'It was a sin. A mortal sin.'

'I think the police are trying to find the person who threw the wreath.'

'I saw the picture in the *Express Wieczorny.* It was an excellent likeness.'

Dania felt her pulse quicken. 'So, you managed to get a good look at him?'

'He asked for directions. He told me he was there for the funeral of the pianist. I saw the scars on his face.' She gripped the collar of her coat. 'He looked like the Devil.'

'Do you remember anything else about him? His voice, perhaps?'

'Nothing unusual. But he was holding the wreath in a strange way. Low down, like this.' She moved her hands to show Dania.

It would have been heavy if it was packed with explosives, Dania thought.

'Shall I take you back to the gate?'

'Yes, please, or I'll never find my way out.'

They picked their way to the entrance. The custodian paused, and laid a hand on Dania's arm. 'It's just as well everyone had left before the bomb went off,' she said, lowering her voice. 'My father fought in the Uprising. He told me many things about that time. For example, towards the end, people erected loudspeakers in the streets and played Chopin. His music had been forbidden during the Occupation. But what I remember most vividly is his account of an incident when a truck carrying many people took a direct hit from German artillery. There was nothing left. No truck, no people.' She dropped her voice further. 'I recall what my father said as if it were yesterday. People rushed away. But they couldn't run quickly enough. A minute later, everything rained down on them, dark red and sticky.' She shook her head, and slowly made her way to the booth.

Dania gazed after her.

Everything rained down on them, dark red and sticky.

The image continued to haunt her as she left the cemetery.

CHAPTER 26

Dania had finished her piano practice, and was leaving the apartment when she caught sight of Inspector Robak. He was brushing snow off the police car. It had been loitering outside the building since they'd returned from the Praga jetty.

'Inspector,' she said, 'will you get a hefty parking fine for leaving your vehicle there so long?'

He turned, and his face broke into a smile. 'Pani Górska.' He was without hat and gloves, and his coat was open, showing his paisley-patterned waistcoat. 'I thought you would have left for Scotland by now.'

'I'm going on Friday.'

'You said that last week.'

She laughed. 'Did I?'

He tapped the brush against his leg, causing crusts of snow to fall off. 'Of course, it could snow again between now and Friday,' he said, his smile widening. 'The Russkis are always threatening to send more.'

'If it does, I may as well stay for Christmas. And if it doesn't, you'll have to find a reason to arrest me.'

'You haven't seen our prisons.' He studied her. 'You want to stay in Warsaw that badly?'

'I want to find Merkury that badly.' She pulled her hat over her ears. 'So, what news of Inspector Dolniak?'

Robak started to brush snow from the windscreen. 'I spoke to him this morning. He's doing as well as can be expected. I've taken over his assignments.'

'On top of your own?'

'That's a detective's life. I'm sure it's happened to you.'

'Once or twice. And any news from Inspector Dolniak's informant?' she said, trying not to sound too eager.

'There's been no movement. The street men are running out of heroin, suggesting there hasn't been another shipment. We're tailing the two kings day and night, but they don't seem to be up to anything.' Robak stopped and looked at her. 'As for Merkury, there's been neither sight nor sound of him.'

'Do you think he'll wait until after Christmas before bringing in another load?'

'I doubt it. He'll want to get the heroin out. Think of all those Christmas raves and parties.' He finished clearing away the snow. 'It's now down to our informant.' He opened the car door and threw the brush inside. 'So, may I give you a lift somewhere?'

'Thank you, but my tram stop's at the end of the road. By the way, Inspector, I was at Okopowa cemetery this morning.'

He looked at her sharply. 'Okopowa is closed. At least, it's closed for burials.'

She felt an explanation was necessary. 'I decided to go for a walk.'

He didn't look convinced.

'I ran into the custodian. She told me she'd seen the unexpected guest on the day of the funeral. He was carrying the wreath. And he asked her for directions.'

'Interesting. She told my officer she'd seen no one.'

'Some people are less prepared to open up to a detective. I didn't tell her who I was, only that Jakub Frydman had been my teacher.' Dania met his gaze. 'It's possible she'll remember more with a bit of prompting.'

'If you keep this up, Pani Górska, we'll have to put you on the payroll.'

She laughed lightly. 'Oh, don't do that. It would make filling out my tax return a nightmare.' She took off her glove and held out her hand. 'Goodbye, Inspector. Now, don't forget to let me know when you plan to pull in Merkury. I want to be there when you do.'

He shook her hand. 'I won't forget,' he said.

'Your hand is warm, Inspector. Yet you've been out in the cold, clearing snow away.'

He smiled. 'I'm sure you know that in Poland those with warm hands also have warm hearts.'

She returned the smile. Then she pulled on the glove, and left.

Dania jumped off the bus, pausing to get her bearings. The journey had been an improvement on the last time, when the bus had struggled in the snow. But the council had started to clear the roads in this area. Although a mist clung to the river, the sky gave no indication that more snow was on the way.

Since her trip to Praga with Marek, Dania had been unable to get the shrine out of her mind. So, before she'd left her parents' apartment, she'd asked her brother for the address. Marek had been reluctant to accompany her: he'd decided to spend the day at the Institute of National Remembrance, following up on Pani Lorenc's advice to work with a particular archivist, and he couldn't see why Dania wanted to return to what was a pile of rubble. But the shrine had been left standing because the workmen would have viewed its demolition as an act of sacrilege. And that could work for her. Or, rather, work for Marek.

Now, as she approached the street, it struck her she didn't need Google Maps: the noise of the bulldozer would guide her. At the corner, she turned right, seeing workmen engaged in the thankless task of clearing the courtyard. The vehicle was some distance away, and she hoped the men wouldn't bother her. To be absolutely sure, she picked her way to the shrine and waited until she'd caught their attention, then crossed herself and bowed her head as if in prayer. It gave her the opportunity to study what was in front of her.

The Virgin, dressed in blue and white, arms extended, palms out, gazed at her from behind a wooden-framed glass case secured with a padlock. Around the statue were dusty plastic flowers, and at the feet was a photograph of the Polish Pope, John Paul II. As a child, Dania had seen shrines that stood on brick structures, but this case had been placed on what looked like a painted box. It was her teacher's comment about weapons and ammunition hidden in shrines that had been uppermost in Dania's thoughts since she and Marek had visited. Could it be that Pan Bielski, having finished writing in his diary of an evening, had slipped out of his ground-floor apartment under cover of darkness and hidden his notebooks inside the shrine? The possibility had been churning in her mind until she knew she'd have no peace unless she returned to investigate.

Now, as she stared at the dark-blue cube, she began to wonder if it wasn't an example of a large puzzle box. If so, she might as well go home, as she had no aptitude in that department. It was Inspector Robak who had the gift. Maybe she should call him.

The area around the shrine was free of rubble, again presumably a deliberate act on the part of the workmen. Dania knelt, and studied the blue cube. It was made of stone, and a careful examination told her there was no way inside, assuming it was hollow. She got to her feet and, after a glance in the men's direction, walked slowly round the shrine.

It was as she was viewing it from the back that she realised the statue was standing on a box. It wasn't visible from the front because of the paraphernalia surrounding it. The box was several centimetres in height, easily enough to accommodate several notebooks. And it had two metal hinges, suggesting all you had to do was lift the lid . . .

Dania returned to the front, and scrutinised the small padlock on the case's frame. As she gazed at it, she became aware that the noise of the bulldozer had stopped. The workmen were gathering up their belongings and making for the road. It was midday, and they were likely heading off for lunch. The sound of their voices faded, then disappeared altogether. Dania glanced around. The place was deserted. She pulled off her gloves and rummaged around in her shoulder bag for her make-up case. One of the items inside was a hair slide. But it was no ordinary hair slide. She'd had it made in London, and always carried it with her.

Carefully, she removed two thin, stainless-steel picks from the slide and, after a final glance around, set about opening the lock. It was a manoeuvre she'd practised many times at the Met. And her discipline had paid off. In a matter of seconds, she felt the mechanism give, allowing her to lift back the U-shaped shackle. She removed the padlock, and opened the door to the case. A pungent, musty smell reached her nostrils. She pushed away the flowers and the photograph, and lifted off the statue, setting it aside.

To her relief, the dark wooden box had no key, just a locking clasp, rusty with age. Her pulse racing, she raised the clasp and lifted back the lid. Inside were several notebooks, their brown paper covers curling at the edges. On the top cover, someone had written '1935–40' in a curling script. She flicked through the pages. There was a strong smell of mildew, and foxing had discoloured the paper, which was neither blank nor lined but the type of checked paper used for graphs. The tiny writing was spidered across the page, but readable if she squinted.

An entry caught her eye: *I remember well that February of 1938. The snow was horrendous. It was impossible to go anywhere except on foot. There were so many storms that the horses pulling carriages couldn't cope. And, of course, the trains could no longer run.*

Nothing new there, Dania thought cynically. She was tempted to read on, but didn't want to press her luck. The remaining notebooks were dated 1941, 1942, 1943–4 and the final one, 1945. Although there was no name on the covers, she imagined the identity of the author would be in there somewhere, and now was not the time to go looking. She lifted the flap of her bag and bundled the notebooks inside, then replaced the items in the shrine and closed the case. She pushed the shackle into its hole, hearing the click as it locked. After pulling on her gloves, she picked her way towards the street. She was tempted to call Marek and give him the news, but she guessed he'd be at the Institute of National Remembrance and would have switched off his phone.

Dania reached the road, and was about to head for the bus stop when she remembered she'd seen a shopping mall, Galeria Wileńska, on Google Maps. As a multi-level shoppers' paradise, it would offer a variety of eating places, even if they only served fast food.

Minutes later, she was climbing the steps to the Galeria's main entrance. The warmth and the buzz of conversation hit her as soon as she was inside. The spirit of Christmas Present had taken over the mall and every pillar and chandelier was decorated with tiny winking white lights. She wandered along the main corridor, gazing into the shops, wondering if this was where she could buy Marek something for Christmas.

After a thorough look around, she doubled back to Starbucks, which was as good a place as any, and ordered a cheese toastie and a flat white. There were more filling items on offer, but she saw no point in pigging out as Marek would be cooking that evening. She carried her tray to the corner table and ate slowly, looking through the window. Interesting how the food at Starbucks tasted the same everywhere. Gradually, her attention shifted to the interior and she began to notice the other diners. Her gaze lingered on a figure at the far end. He had on a black sheepskin, which came down to his knees, and a comical grey fur hat with earflaps.

Dania put down her toastie. Although his back was to her, she had no difficulty in recognising the figure as Tomek. The last time they'd spoken was the previous Thursday when he'd invited her to dinner. He'd told her he was taking the train to Kraków the following morning. It was now Monday, so what was he doing here? A quick check on her phone told her there were no problems with the Kraków trains.

Slowly, not wanting to draw attention to herself, Dania tucked her hair under her woollen hat so no strands were showing. She rummaged inside her bag for her horn-rimmed glasses. These had plain glass instead of lenses. She slipped them on. She was now unrecognisable.

Tomek was reading a newspaper, skimming the pages, and sipping from a large mug. Moments later, he drank what was left, pushed back his chair and got to his feet. He folded the paper and left it on the table. Then he headed for the door without giving the other customers a second glance. Through the window, Dania saw him turn right onto the main road. She hurried out in time to see him cross at the zebra.

Fortunately, there were a large number of pedestrians and shoppers, and it was unlikely she'd be noticed if Tomek decided to turn round. But he was marching purposefully, head down. She pulled out her mobile and rang his number. He paused, and put his phone to his ear. It was the same red-and-white mobile he'd had that day she was attacked by the river.

'Dania? What a pleasant surprise. How are you?'

'I'm fine. Did you have a good trip to Kraków?'

'Yes, the train tracks had been swept, so there was no problem. But it's been snowing here. I'm in the main square and there are Christmas lights everywhere. Even the statue of Adam Mickiewicz is lit up. Anyway, what about you? Did you make your flight?'

'Unfortunately not. But I managed to get one on Sunday.'

'So, you're back in Dundee?'

'I am. Look, the reason I'm ringing is to say that I hope you didn't think I was being standoffish when I didn't accept your dinner invitation.'

'Not at all.'

'It was my last night with my brother, you see, and I wasn't sure if I'd be spending Christmas with him, so we decided to make an evening of it.'

'You don't need to explain, Dania,' Tomek said, in a reassuring tone. 'I understand completely.' A pause. 'And my invitation to visit Kraków still stands.'

'Thanks, Tomek. Well, I'd better leave you to get on.'

'I'm deep in a case at the moment.' A short laugh. 'We detectives never get any rest, do we?'

'We don't,' she said, appreciating the truth of what he'd said. 'Good luck. And have a great Christmas.' She rang off.

She watched him put away his mobile. He strode off, taking the next right. She followed, keeping a reasonable distance, her phone in her hand so she could gaze into it if he turned round. This wasn't a part of Praga she was familiar with, although she had a vague recollection that the Vodka Museum was nearby. The area was being redeveloped, with giant cranes hulking like dinosaurs over the buildings.

Tomek stopped at a finialled iron railing, entered a code and pushed the gate open. Dania crossed the street and loitered at the bus stop, where she could watch without attracting attention. Behind the railing a paved courtyard was strewn with stone pots. At the front entrance, he fished inside his coat pocket, and produced a set of keys. He unlocked the door and disappeared inside. It was then Dania noticed that the two-storey building – the last on that section of street – was detached. So, was it split into apartments? A light came on in the ground-floor windows and, a few seconds later, in the windows on the first floor, suggesting Tomek had the house to himself. Given he'd told her he was visiting friends, perhaps they were renting the entire building.

She made a note of the street name and the location of the house, which was opposite a bank, and left the way she'd arrived. But as she retraced her steps, it dawned on her there was a flaw in her argument. Hadn't Tomek said he was visiting friends in Żoliborz? Żoliborz was on the other side of the river. Wouldn't he have stayed with them? Or rented a place in the city centre? At this time of year, he'd have had little difficulty in finding a suitable let. So, what had made him come to Praga?

More to the point, why had he told her he was in Kraków?

CHAPTER 27

Dania let herself into her parents' apartment, her thoughts spooling round in her mind. The smell of yeast wafted into the corridor. She pulled off her coat and boots and padded into the kitchen.

Marek was wearing an apron, and his hands were covered with flour.

'I thought you'd still be at the institute,' she said.

He wiped his hands on a cloth. 'The archivist wasn't in today. He'd phoned in sick. So, I came home.'

'Wasn't there anyone else who could help?' she said, setting her bag on the table.

'I didn't want to wait weeks. This particular guy was supposed to fast-track me. I'll try again in a day or two.'

'There may be no need. I think I've found your notebooks.'

Marek gazed at her, speechless. She loved the way her remarks could have that effect.

'I went back to Praga and picked the lock on the shrine,' she said, as though it was something she did every day. 'The notebooks were in a box inside.'

He dropped the cloth onto the counter. 'What made you think they'd be there?'

'Where would you hide notebooks you didn't want the authorities to see? The man lived on the ground floor, remember. It would have been easy to slip out under cover of darkness.'

Marek stared at her bag.

'I think you need to get every scrap of flour off your hands first,' she said sternly. 'What are you making?'

'*Pączki*. I'm waiting for the dough to finish rising.'

'And what are you putting into them?'

'Chocolate blancmange.'

Dania felt herself salivate. These doughnuts were difficult to make. At least, she'd never succeeded. But Marek had the knack, and she'd heard people say they were better than the famous *pączki* at Blikle's café. She watched him cover the bowl with plastic film. He washed his hands thoroughly.

'And you need to take the apron off,' she said, opening her bag. She lifted out the notebooks and spread them over the table.

Marek sat next to her. 'Do we know if they're written by the priest's father?' he said.

'I didn't have time to read them. The workmen had left, but someone could have walked past.'

'You said you picked the lock,' Marek said, as if only then appreciating what she'd said.

'I'm relying on you not to tell Inspector Robak.'

His lips curved into a smile, but he said nothing. He picked up the 1943–4 notebook, and opened it at random. The slight smell of damp reached her.

'The writing's tiny,' she said. 'I wonder if notebooks were hard to buy, and people needed to get as much as they could into them.'

Marek was squinting at the text. 'It's not like a diary with daily entries. It's more of a memoir. Listen to this: *The executions continued. They took the prisoners from Pawiak prison to Dzielna Street, and murdered them there.'*

Dania laid a hand on his arm. 'Before you go on, wouldn't it be best to digitise each page?'

'Good thinking. By the way, have you eaten?'

'I had lunch in Praga.' She got to her feet. 'I'll leave you to it. I'll be in the living room setting up a video call. I need to let West Bell Street know when I'm returning. Give me a shout when the *pączki* are ready.' She had a sudden vision of Marek being so wrapped up in his work that he forgot to put the doughnuts into the oven. 'Have you set the timer?'

'Mm?' He glanced up.

'I'll do it,' she said.

As Dania played with the controls, her thoughts slipped back to Tomek and the villa in Praga. She'd need to decide what, if anything, to do about him. Because the more she thought about it, the more she was convinced there was no innocent explanation for his lies.

Dania disconnected from her video call, deeply satisfied with the progress at West Bell Street. Honor had done a first-class job in moving the cases forward. On her return, Dania would suggest she put in for promotion, although she'd then be running her own cases, resulting in the two of them working together less. Dania wouldn't want that, and she suspected neither would Honor.

She checked her phone but there were no messages from Inspector Robak. Why hadn't he been in touch? she thought irritably. He knew she was leaving on Friday. But her irritation evaporated. It was because there'd been no movement. No news of an incoming shipment, no meeting with Merkury, no nothing.

At this rate, she'd be back in Dundee without fulfilling her mission. But, although she was greatly tempted to call Robak, she was a detective, and knew better than to hassle him.

In the kitchen, she found Marek sitting gazing into the laptop. The *pączki* were cooling on a tray.

'So, are you convinced these are the Bielski notebooks the priest told you about?' she said.

'There's no mention of a name, or specific address, but there's no doubt they were written by the priest's father. He talks about his childhood in Wola. And he mentions the puzzle box the collector brought back from the fair. It's this first notebook – 1935 to 1940 – that refers to the hunt for the manuscript.' He looked up. 'By the way, I finally heard from Baletnica. He denied he was the gentleman who'd called on Father Bielski. He repeated his warning that there are others after the manuscript.'

'I wonder how they're getting their information.' And how badly they want to get their hands on the manuscript, she thought. She filled the kettle. 'What have you discovered so far?'

'I got a bit side-tracked reading about pre-war life in Warsaw. Did you know the Sixth Chess Olympiad was held here in 1935?'

'I didn't, no.'

'It was in August, and the weather was unbelievably hot. Apparently, the world champion had brought his Persian cat. It went missing and he couldn't concentrate on the game. The story went on the radio and the cat was eventually found. Anyway, I've got to the part in the memoir where the collector has translated the letters in the puzzle box, and is starting his research. It hinges on the fact that Ludwika gave some of Chopin's manuscripts to his friends.'

'And do we know who these friends were?'

'I'm hoping to find out.'

'Email me a copy, and we'll work on it together. If you're reading from 1935, I can start on 1936.'

'You're not too busy?'

She detected the hope in his voice. 'I've finished my call,' she said. 'I'll make coffee, while you put the filling in the *pączki*. They should be cool by now.'

He grinned. 'It's a deal.'

By the time the coffee was ready, Marek had filled the doughnuts.

'We'll just have one each,' he said. 'I don't want either of us falling asleep.'

'Better give me the biggest one, then.'

They ate in silence, Dania savouring the taste of the blanc-mange, and the consistency of the pastry. Marek ought to give up the day job and open a *kawiarnia*, she thought, wiping her fingers on her handkerchief.

'Right, I've emailed you the 1935 to 1940 file,' he said. 'It contains the digital images stitched together. You'll want to enlarge the writing.'

She downloaded the file and opened it. 'I remember Grand-mother used to write like this.'

'If you see anything of interest, shout. I'll do the same.'

As Dania started to read, she was transported to another world. She could see why Marek had lost himself.

A light snow fell nearly every day in January. The university hadn't yet reopened, so Father divided his time preparing for the new term and doing his research, which always seemed to drive him to distraction. He would smoke frantically, sitting in the study, poring over his books and papers. Mother would have to go out to the kiosk almost every day for more cigarettes. I was glad when school resumed, because I would no longer have to breathe in the strong, bitter-smelling smoke.

There was a painstaking account of what the son was studying, who his friends were, what they did after school, et cetera. Given this was written forty years after the events, Dania was amazed at the attention to detail. But, then, she could remember her childhood years vividly.

She skimmed the following pages, and then sat up suddenly.

'Marek! Listen to this.

'It was before school broke for the summer holidays, and Father rushed home in great excitement. He'd been to a fair in a nearby village and had bought a puzzle box. It hadn't taken him long to open it. Inside were some old letters. He spent the afternoon transcribing them, and we didn't see him until dinner. At the time, I couldn't understand what could be so fascinating about these letters. It was only much later, when I was older, that I asked to see them. I couldn't read them, of course, as they were in French, but Father told me about this third piano concerto, which the world had never heard performed.'

Marek's eyes widened. 'These are the letters between Chopin and Jane Stirling!'

'Okay, here's more.

'With teaching at the University finished, Father spent nearly all his time quarrying at Krasiński Library researching Chopin's sister. There were days he'd come home in such a state of despair that I vowed never to become an academic!'

Dania glanced up. 'Must be Ludwika he's talking about.'

'Don't stop,' Marek urged.

'Each day, Father would discuss with us what he'd found in the Library archives, which seemed to be precious little, other than a bundle of letters sent to Chopin's sister. I have to confess that I paid scant attention to what he said, as I was more interested in listening to the radio, and how Polish athletes were doing at the Berlin Olympics. But once the games were over, I found myself becoming drawn into the discussions. From what I could gather, Father had compiled a list of names, and his research consisted of uncovering whatever he could about them. But then school started, and all my attention was on my studies.'

Dania paused. 'Do you think those letters he found in the Krasiński Library were sent to Ludwika by Chopin's friends? Perhaps thanking her for sending them his manuscripts?'

'I'm certain.' Marek gestured to her laptop. 'You're obviously coping with this handwriting better than I am. Look, why not skip straight to 1939? See if you can find a single name.'

'Right.' She scrolled down.

He sat back. 'Read it all out loud.'

'Term started in the New Year and we learnt about the Spanish Civil War, and the death that had rained down on that unfortunate nation. We all agreed that war is a terrible thing. But our teacher assured us that, thanks to the German-Polish non-aggression pact that was signed in 1934, Poland would be safe from war for the foreseeable future.'

'Oh, boy,' Marek muttered.

'Father had finally eliminated all but two of the names from his list.

He firmly believed that Ludwika had given the third concerto to one or other of these friends of her brother's. Mother was greatly relieved, as it meant that the quest was nearing its end, and the piles of paper that had accumulated in every corner of Father's study would soon be filed away.

'I remember being almost as excited as Father. As I'd grown older, my interest in his research had developed, and I asked him to explain his methods. I had to admit that he had left no stone unturned. My question was: what would he do once he'd found the manuscript? His reply had been unequivocal. He would donate it to the Warsaw Conservatory. Even Mother had grown enthusiastic at the thought of hearing this new concerto.'

Dania glanced up. 'I think Rubinstein was touring America. They were probably wondering if he'd return to Poland to play it.'

'He'd be the obvious choice.'

'There's more about school. Oh, and in April, the Spanish Civil War came to an end. Ha! Listen to this: *There was news of a boat race won by a team from Cambridge. I had never heard of Cambridge, although Father had.*'

Marek grinned. 'No internet in those days.'

'Mother was greatly cheered by the news that Britain and France had pledged to come to Poland's aid in the event of a German attack. We all thought we could sleep easily knowing their tanks and planes would be heading in our direction to stave off those of the Germans. We were such fools.

'With the advent of the Easter holidays, Father returned to the Library to research these two friends of Chopin's, one French, one Polish. The French name had surprised me, but Father had explained that Chopin made many friends in Paris. He hoped to have an answer as to which of these two had received—'

She broke off. 'That's odd.'

'What?'

'I've come to the end.' She looked up. 'The end of the file, I mean. Did you send me all the images from the 1935 to 1940 notebook?'

Marek tapped at his keyboard. 'I'm sure I did.'

'We're still only in the Easter holidays. That's 1939. We haven't even come to 1940. Let me look at the original.'

Dania picked up the 1935 to 1940 notebook, and turned to the back. The words on the last line were: *He hoped to have an answer as to which of these two had received*

She showed it to Marek.

'Has anything been torn out?' he said.

She ran a finger along the spine. The neat stitching suggested no pages had been removed. If they had, it was likely that the same number would have fallen out from the front. She turned to the first page. It was headed 1935.

'The notebooks look identical,' she said. 'I'll count the number of pages in this one, and perhaps you can do the same for one of the others.'

'Good idea.'

A short while later, she said, 'I've counted ninety.'

'Same here. Let me double-check with the last notebook, the 1945.' He turned the pages slowly, Dania counting along with him. 'Ninety,' he said unnecessarily.

They looked at one other.

'You know what this means, Danka.'

She closed her eyes briefly. 'There's a notebook missing.'

And, given what Father Bielski had said about the war putting an end to the research, if this collector from Wola had indeed uncovered the name of Chopin's friend who'd been gifted the manuscript, it could only be in the 1935–40 account. In other words, in the missing notebook.

Dania walked round the kitchen, running her hands through her hair. Had she left a notebook behind in the shrine? She remembered putting her hands into the wooden box and curling her fingers round the notebooks. Was it conceivable she'd missed one? But then another possibility presented itself. Perhaps the missing notebook wasn't inside the box, but somewhere else in the cluttered shrine. Maybe under the box.

She stopped and gazed at Marek. 'There's only one thing for it,' she said.

'And this time I'm coming with you.'

CHAPTER 28

Dania and Marek were preparing to leave the apartment when the bell rang.

Marek opened the door. 'Pan Mazur,' he said, in surprise.

'I see I've come at an inconvenient time,' Adam said, his gaze taking in Marek's thick coat and outdoor boots.

They only had a short window of opportunity before the Praga workmen returned from lunch, and Dania could tell Marek was growing restless. But good manners prevailed. 'Would you like to come in?' she said to Adam.

'I won't stay, Pani Górska. I've come to give you this. It's a bequest from Pan Frydman.'

'But you've given me my bequest,' she said, taking the envelope.

'This was intended for Rena Adler. But I discovered this morning that she's passed away.'

'Oh? When was this?'

'Nearly three weeks ago.' A pained expression crossed his face. 'No one thought to tell me. Mind you, it's possible someone mentioned it, and it slipped my mind. A couple of days later, Pan Frydman died and I had enough to do with arranging his funeral. Anyway, as she had no descendants, it wasn't clear who should receive this. But I'm sure Pan Frydman would have wanted you to have it.'

'I feel greatly honoured,' Dania said, gripping the envelope. Was there more sheet music inside? Perhaps another Rubinstein-annotated manuscript? But from the thickness, it felt like several manuscripts. Or a single large one. 'And how are things going with the estate?' she said. 'Are you close to finishing?'

'Nowhere near it.' Adam pulled out a handkerchief and mopped his brow. 'It'll be spring before it's done, I fear.' He smiled bravely. 'I'd better be going. I'll bid you good day.' Without bothering to shake hands, he hurried out.

Dania was about to open the envelope when Marek said, 'Danka, we need to go.'

He was worried she'd want to stay behind and play the music. She laid the envelope on the hall table, and followed him out.

They arrived at the building site at a good time. The workmen had passed them on their way to lunch, and hadn't given them a second glance. They waited until the men had rounded the corner, then picked their way over the rubble to the shrine.

'Right, Marek,' Dania said. 'Can you keep watch?'

She removed the hair slide from the make-up bag and set about picking the lock. Annoyingly, it took her longer than last time, but she got there eventually. She opened the case, and pushed away the plastic flowers and the photograph of the Pope. Marek was suddenly at her side, peering over her shoulder. So much for keeping watch, she thought.

She lifted down the statue of the Virgin, and removed the wooden box, handing it to Marek. Careful not to catch any splinters, she ran her hands over the floor of the case in the hope that there was a way of lifting it, but the surface was smooth. She rapped it hard with her knuckles. It sounded solid.

'Let me take another look inside the box,' she said. She pushed up the clasp and lifted the lid. The box was empty.

Marek muttered what might have been a swear word.

'Do you think this could be a puzzle box?' Dania said. 'Give it a shake.'

He pushed the lid down and shook the box violently.

'I think if there was anything hidden inside, we'd have heard it,' she said. 'My money's on the notebook having been mislaid. There's an outside chance it's at the Institute of National Remembrance. The man was arrested, remember, and if it was in the house, the secret police would have found it.'

Marek was looking at her doubtfully.

'The notebook covered the start of the war, but also 1940,' she went on. 'From what you've told me, the collector joined the Underground then. There could be names in that notebook that would have interested the Communist authorities.'

'You're right. I'll try this archivist again. At least we now know what we're looking for.'

'You can take one of the other notebooks to show him. And you know the author's name. It should be a straightforward search.'

Marek handed back the box. 'It's so frustrating. The collector was down to two names.'

Dania arranged the objects in the shrine, and locked it. 'You might be one step back, Marek, but you're also two steps forward.'

He smiled. 'Thanks to you.'

'Come on, let's get something to eat.'

'We could go to the Vodka Museum.' He glanced around. 'I think it's not far from here.'

'I'd rather eat than drink.'

But his attention had been taken by something behind her. He was frowning, as though trying to understand what he was seeing. Then his look changed to one of horror. She wheeled round. He was staring at a huge pile of rubble.

'What is it?' she said.

Without replying, he hurried towards it, stopping suddenly. She followed, trying to keep her balance on the bits of broken brick. As she approached, she saw what had caused him to stare.

'Don't go near it, Marek,' she said, gripping his arm. 'I'll call the police.'

Inspector Maksymilian Robak was adjusting his tie. He smoothed down the jacket of his dress uniform, and picked up his officer's cap. He was in plenty of time for the commemorative service in the Sala Biała and, fortunately, it was Oskar's superior officer who'd be delivering the eulogy for the driver. Maks made a mental note to have a copy of the speech sent to Oskar.

He'd left the office, and was heading for the corridor to the Sala when his phone rang. It reminded him he'd need to set it to silent before the ceremony. He was about to switch it off when he realised he still had time. And it could be urgent.

'Maksymilian Robak,' he said.

He listened, his concern growing as the details were relayed to him. When he heard the name Górski, he told the officer he was on his way. He hurried along the corridor, running into Pola, who was also in her dress uniform.

'I won't be able to make the ceremony, Pola. There's been an incident in Praga.'

'Shall I come with you?'

'You need to attend to represent our unit.'

'Of course.'

It didn't take him long to reach Praga, despite the growing early-afternoon traffic. He spotted the red-and-white police tape and crime-scene officers before he'd even pulled up. As he left the car, an officer approached, his eyes widening as he saw the dress uniform. Maks was suddenly conscious his appearance was becoming a distraction. The crime-scene staff had turned to stare at him.

'Who called it in?' he said, although he knew the answer.

'That lady there. Her name's Danuta Górska. The man with her is her brother, Marek.'

'Have you taken their statements?'

'I've got their address. Nothing more yet. I've been too busy organising the crime scene.'

'So, what do we know?'

'The Górskis were looking at the shrine when the brother noticed something.' The officer nodded at the figure lying on the ground beside a pile of bricks. 'Had it not been for the red coat, he wouldn't have seen her. From the condition of the body, she's been dead for several days.'

'Can you tell how she died?'

'The injury suggests she was shot in the head. We'll know more at the autopsy.'

'I wonder why she wasn't discovered before now. You can't miss that red coat.'

'She was dumped under the bricks. Marek Górski saw a dog trying to drag her out by the arm.'

Maks gestured to the crime-scene officers balanced on top of the rubble. 'Why are they still up there?'

'The woman isn't the only victim, Inspector. There's at least one more.'

'And do we know which construction company is doing the demolition?' Maks said, glancing at the crane. 'Is it our friends?'

'The Zeleński̇s?' The officer shook his head. 'It's a small company I've never heard of. I've got their details. The workmen were on their lunch break, but arrived shortly before you did. We took their details and sent them home. We'll get their statements in due course.' He glanced at the Górskis. They were standing well out of the way of the crime-scene officers. 'Shall I send them home, too?' he said.

'Leave them with me. You carry on with the crime scene. And let me know as soon as you've finished here.'

The officer nodded and left.

Maks picked his way across the courtyard.

'Inspector,' Danuta said.

'Pani Górska.'

'Hi, Maks,' Marek said glumly.

Maks studied their faces. Danuta was watching the crime-scene officers in silent concentration. But, then, as a detective, she'd have seen her fair share of corpses. Marek was more anxious.

'Since you were the ones who found the body,' Maks said, 'I'll have to ask you to come to Mostowski with me, and make a formal statement.'

'Of course, Inspector,' Danuta said promptly.

'The car's over there.' He stepped back, letting them pass.

As he followed them to the pavement, he glanced back at the pile of rubble. A second body had been laid out next to the first, a man, judging by the clothes. It suddenly occurred to Maks there might be several more concealed under the bricks. Given everything that was going on at Mostowski, he thought gloomily, Christmas would have to be postponed.

'And can you tell me what you were doing in the courtyard?' Maks said, looking from Danuta to her brother. They were sitting at the table in his office. He'd arranged for coffee to be brought in, which they were gulping gratefully.

'It's a long story, Inspector,' Danuta began.

Maks opened his notebook. 'I'm listening.'

She glanced at her brother, who indicated she should continue. 'It's to do with this Chopin manuscript Marek's looking for. He received a tip-off there might be a lead in some old notebooks. They were written by the son of the man who'd found Chopin's letters.'

'And the son had lived in an apartment in that courtyard,' Marek chipped in.

'We went there on Sunday to see if the current occupant knew anything. But we found the entire building demolished.'

'But not the shrine. So, on a hunch, Danka went back yesterday and found the notebooks hidden inside.'

Maks held up a hand. 'Those shrines are usually locked. Didn't I see a padlock?'

Danuta looked uncomfortable. 'I picked the lock,' she said finally.

He sat back, crossing his arms. 'Can you tell me how?'

She reached into her bag and withdrew a hair slide. She took it apart, and held up two long, metal pins.

He said nothing. He was savouring the expression on her face.

'Danka's pretty good at that sort of thing,' Marek said, in a feeble attempt to come to her defence.

'And apart from the shrine, Pani Górska, have you picked any other locks in the Republic of Poland?'

'Absolutely not!' she said, trying to look affronted. But the smile creeping onto her lips gave her away.

Maks ran a hand over his mouth. He was struggling not to laugh. 'Very well. So, why did you return to the shrine today?'

'We discovered there was a notebook missing,' Marek said. 'And we believe the information we need is in it.'

'And did you find the notebook?'

'Unfortunately not. Danka had just replaced the padlock when I spotted that animal dragging something out of the rubble. The more I think about it, the more I'm convinced it was a wolf. Is that possible?'

'Kampinos National Park is only ten kilometres away. From time to time wolves escape.'

'Would they cross the Vistula?'

'Wolves are excellent swimmers. But I'm more inclined to think it escaped from the zoo. I'll make enquiries.' He put down his pen. 'To get back to this missing notebook, what do you think happened to it?' he asked, addressing Marek.

'The man who wrote it was arrested for anti-Communist activities. The secret police would have searched his apartment, so it's possible they took it. I intend to try at the Institute of National Remembrance tomorrow.'

It was a while before Maks spoke. 'I'll have this typed up. Perhaps one of you could come in tomorrow afternoon and sign it.' He looked at Danuta. 'As your brother will be at the institute, would you do it, Pani Górska?'

'Of course.'

'I don't for one minute believe you're guilty of a crime . . .' he kept his face straight '. . . except perhaps for lock-picking, but protocol requires me to retain your passports until we have a better understanding of the case. I'll have them photocopied, so you have ID to carry around with you.'

'We understand, Maks,' Marek said.

They laid their passports on the table.

'I think that's everything.' Maks got to his feet. 'The officer outside will escort you to the front entrance. If you wait there, someone will bring the photocopies to you.'

They shook hands. As Danuta was leaving, he said, 'A word, Pani Górska?'

Marek smiled and left the room.

'Yes?' she said.

He rested his gaze on hers. 'As a detective, you'll know how long cases like this can take,' he said. 'As we'll have to retain your passports until then, it would be best to cancel your flight on Friday. Which means, of course, if there's movement on apprehending Merkury, we'll be in a position to involve you.'

Something shifted in her expression. At the door, she turned to look at him and a slow smile of understanding crossed her lips.

CHAPTER 29

Maks was in the green-tiled dissection room in the Forensic Medicine Department at Warsaw's Medical University, a department that offered medico-legal autopsies to the police. He was leaning against the wall, as far as possible from the dissection tables, watching the pathologist in the green scrubs. The man was bent over the second of the two corpses excavated the previous day. Maks was relieved there were only two. Any more and he wouldn't be able to bear the sweet, rotten stench. Even from a distance, it seeped through his mask and into his lungs, where it settled like fog.

The pathologist, a professor with a stern manner but a delicate touch with the scalpel, had pronounced cause of death for the first victim, and was now pronouncing the same for the second. In both cases, the 9mm parabellum had entered the back of the head. Death would have been instantaneous, or as instantaneous as death can be. There were no muzzle burns from a contact shot, or powder rings indicating firing at close range. The pathologist had extracted fragments of material from the wounds, suggesting the weapon had been fired through something like a mattress, either in a vain attempt to limit the sound, or a more successful attempt to prevent the killer being covered with blood spatter. The bullets should enable them to identify the weapon, Maks thought, although finding it would be the main challenge.

The victims were lying side by side, their chests open and rib cages removed. The pathologist's assistant, a young woman with huge blue eyes, had carried the organs to a table at the back, where she'd weighed them, and made notes. Maks wondered if she was a final-year student. As far as the pathologist was aware, there was nothing remarkable about the condition of the organs. The victims were estimated to have been in their late thirties and, apart from the bullets lodged in their brains, in good health.

Before the autopsy, Maks had had the opportunity to view the corpses. The man had fair hair but no remarkable features, although it was difficult to tell from the bloated face. He'd been dressed in a shabby suit. The woman's hair was bright red and messy. She'd worn a dark red coat, black woollen trousers and a cream jumper.

The pathologist straightened, and studied Maks over his mask. 'Is there something you'd like to ask?'

'Can you estimate the post-mortem interval, Professor?'

The creasing at the corners of the man's eyes suggested he was smiling. It was evidently a question he'd anticipated. 'I can't state it with a high degree of certainty, as I'm sure you'll appreciate. There's pronounced lividity, and the patterning is consistent with being buried under rubble for several days. There's also the low temperature to take into account.'

From previous experience, Maks knew the professor had arrived at an answer, but he liked to leave his clients dangling. All he could do was glue an expression of anticipation onto his face.

'Between one and two weeks,' the pathologist said finally. 'They died sometime between the first and eighth of December. I can't be more precise.'

'Any evidence of a struggle?'

'None.'

Maks was starting to sweat into his clothes, although the temperature in the room was low.

'Do you know their identities?' the pathologist said.

'We found no ID on either. They're wearing wedding rings, so we're assuming they were married to each other.'

'There's something you need to see. But you'll have to come closer.'

Maks took a few steps forward. The cloying stench grew stronger.

'Look at the man's arm, Inspector.'

Maks had no option but to approach the table. He'd seen corpses up close before, but none that had smelt like these.

On the man's left forearm, faintly visible on the mottled, yellow-grey skin, was a tattoo. It was a series of numbers.

'What do you make of that?' the pathologist said.

'The man's too young to be a Holocaust survivor. And Auschwitz tattoos were smaller, and never as neat. I suspect this was done after the war, in memory of someone.'

'And if it's a grandfather, then . . .'

Maks said it for him. 'We have a chance of establishing the identity of the grandson.'

It was after midday before Maks returned to Mostowski Palace. He'd taken a detour to his apartment so he could shower, wash his hair and change his clothes. As he entered the palace, he alerted the duty officer that Pani Górska would be arriving that afternoon, and she was to be escorted immediately to his office.

On the way to his corridor, he looked in on Pola. She was at her desk, her plaited hair wound round her head. Her elephant slippers were on the floor, and she was massaging her toes.

'Pola, have you got a minute?'

She swivelled the chair to face him. 'What do you need?'

'Can you come to my office?'

She pulled on her slippers, and followed him to his room. On the desk, his secretary had placed the Górskis' statement for signing. Maks pushed it to one side. He indicated to Pola to bring a chair round.

As briefly as he could, he brought her up to speed. 'We'll get the full autopsy report in a matter of days,' he finished, 'but I think the cause of death is clear.'

'There are many types of firearm that take a 9mm parabellum.'

'That'll be our second challenge.'

'And our first?'

He tapped at the keyboard, and pulled up an image. 'I had this sent from the Forensic Medicine Department before I left. It's a photo of the man's arm.'

'I've seen that before. Descendants who get the same tattoo.'

'And what we're going to do now is discover who had this number originally.'

'You know the chances are small, don't you? The Germans destroyed most of the records before they abandoned Auschwitz. We'd do better asking around the tattoo parlours.'

'We'll do that if we get nowhere with the online records.'

'It's worth a try, I suppose.' But she didn't sound convinced, making Maks wonder if she'd had cause to query the database in another – more personal – connection.

He brought up the main website for the Auschwitz Museum, and searched for the online database.

'Here, let me,' she said.

He surrendered the mouse and watched her negotiate the site expertly. 'You've done this before,' he said.

'Okay, here it is.'

The page was headed 'Auschwitz Prisoners'. In the 'Search data' field, she entered the tattooed number.

Only one record was returned: Pomorski, Bogdan. Underneath were the date of birth, and the place: Warsaw. The personal card was listed as the source of information.

'It looks as though he survived,' Pola said, sitting back.

'How can you tell?'

'If he'd been murdered, it would say so, and give the date and the source, which is usually one of the Death Books.'

Maks nodded at the screen. 'And what data is there on the personal card? That would help us?'

'His address in Warsaw, his profession, name and address of his parents.' She paused. 'How many children he had.'

'I think you know what to do.'

She nodded. Her face was expressionless.

'And as soon as you find anything concrete, send it across. Don't wait until you have it all.'

'Right.'

She was at the door when Maks said, 'Are you playing chess tonight?'

'I am. But I can cry off if you want me to stay and work on this.'

'No, I'd like you to go. If you're prepared to.' He returned her gaze. 'Remember to take your firearm.'

After Pola had gone, Maks thought through the implications of what he'd learnt. He had little doubt Pola would deliver the goods. She knew her way round the databases, and had contacts who were more than willing to redirect her when she hit a dead end. Once he had the names of Bogdan Pomorski's descendants, he could establish whether they were linked to the couple found under the rubble. It was the fact they'd been there for some time that had got Maks thinking. The killer had evidently intended to hide them. The Vistula would be the obvious place but it wasn't deep enough, and bodies dumped there were discovered quickly. Perhaps the rubble had been a temporary hiding place, and the killer had intended to bury them in the Kampinos forest. If that were the case, then, unfortunately for him, the snow had arrived, blocking the roads. As for timing, the couple had been shot between 1 and 8 December. Maks had learnt that the buildings overlooking the courtyard had been bulldozed in November, but no further work had been carried out until a couple of days previously. The killer would therefore have had plenty of opportunity to hide the bodies under cover of night.

Maks was toying with the idea of checking how many people with the surname Pomorski were resident in Warsaw when his phone rang.

'Inspector Robak?' came the voice. He recognised the woman from Anti-drugs, who'd taken over liaison with Oskar's informant.

'Speaking,' he said.

'It's not good news, I'm afraid.' There was a slight hesitation in her voice. 'I met with our informant. A new shipment of heroin must have arrived, because the street men are flush with packets. The two kings, Clubs and Diamonds, have been handing them out.'

'*Kurwa!*' Maks exclaimed. He suddenly remembered himself. 'I'm sorry. I didn't mean to swear.'

'It's all right, Inspector. It's exactly what I said when I got the news.'

'Did the informant say anything else? Where the heroin is being stored? Did he mention Merkury?'

'He didn't. And, as you'll know, he can't be seen to be asking too many questions.'

'The kings were supposed to be shadowed,' Maks said, trying to keep the frustration out of his voice. 'Didn't anyone see them leave?'

'We dropped the ball on that one. But they won't be storing the heroin in their apartments. I'll make sure we don't lose them again.'

'Because if you do, we'll lose Merkury. He's Oskar's Ace of Spades, remember.' Maks kept his voice level. 'The instant you have anything concrete, call me.'

'Understood.'

No sooner had she disconnected than the phone rang again. It was the duty sergeant, announcing Danuta Górska.

Maks wiped his face. He'd have to tell her about the shipment, and that they'd screwed up. He felt a plunge in his stomach because he knew he'd let her down.

There was a knock at the door.

'Enter,' he said.

An officer poked his head round but before he could speak, Maks said, 'Show the lady in.' He got to his feet as Danuta breezed through the door.

'I hope this isn't a bad time,' she said prophetically.

He smiled warmly. 'It's never a bad time, Pani Górska.' He gestured to the chair. 'Please take a seat.' He laid the statement in front of her. 'Perhaps you could check this is factually correct to the best of your knowledge, then date and sign it.'

She studied the text. 'Yes, that's fine.'

He handed her a pen, and watched as she scribbled on the sheet.

'So, are you able to tell me anything about the body found under the rubble?' she said.

'There were two bodies, a man and a woman. We're trying to establish their identities.'

'You don't think their deaths are linked to the notebooks in the shrine, do you?'

'I hadn't considered that, but I'll keep it in mind.'

'Talking of notebooks, Marek's at the Institute of National Remembrance today. He didn't come home for lunch, which suggests he's getting somewhere.'

'What will he do if he can't find this manuscript?'

'He'll cry. You know what men are.'

She must have misread his silence because she said quickly, 'I meant that as a joke.'

'No, no, Pani Górska, you're right. When it comes to disappointment, men cope less well than women. Which is why I'm reluctant to relay the report I've had from Anti-drugs. Because I, too, feel like crying.'

'Is it about Merkury?'

'A heroin shipment has come in, and my people failed to discover where and when. The first they knew was when Oskar's informant told them the two kings are handing out packets to the street sellers.'

He'd expected her to be angry, or frustrated. Coldly polite, even. But her response surprised him.

'Then that's good, isn't it?' she said brightly. 'It means things have finally started moving. Okay, so Merkury wasn't apprehended taking in the heroin, but it's not the end of the world. We can still catch him handing it out to the kings.'

Maks crossed his arms, his gaze moving over her face. 'I'm amazed by your positive attitude.'

'The British have a saying: do you view the pint as half full, or half empty?' She smiled. 'I view it as brimming over even when there's only a mouthful left.'

He felt the corners of his mouth lift. 'You should leave Scotland and come and work with us.'

She said nothing and, for one delicious moment, he imagined she was seriously considering it.

She glanced at the computer screen. The Auschwitz Museum page was still up. He could see she was intrigued but was too polite to ask about it.

'The man we pulled out of the rubble had a number tattooed on his arm,' Maks said. 'This Bogdan Pomorski with the same number could be an ancestor. It's the only lead we have as to the couple's identities.'

'Whoever ordered the killing wasn't aware of the tattoo, or he'd have removed it. It suggests he didn't know the couple that well.'

'Excellent point.' He hesitated. 'It would be good to have your help with this case, Pani Górska.'

'I've nothing much else to do. I've cancelled my flight, and informed everyone at West Bell Street I won't be back any time soon.'

'And how does your boss feel about it?'

'Resigned. I've been working remotely, so that's sweetened the pill. And my number two is moving things forward. So, I'd be delighted to help. What have you learnt so far?'

His mood lifting, Maks went through the case, including what he'd heard at the autopsy. 'We'd thought the construction company was Zelenski's but it turns out it's another builder,' he finished.

'Is that *Zygmunt* Zelenski?'

Maks studied her. 'How do you know the name?'

'I had dinner with him a couple of weeks ago. I was given his table by accident. The others were all taken, so I invited him to join me.'

'You're full of surprises, Pani Górska. So, what did you talk about?'

'He was interested in Marek's search for the lost manuscript. He even offered to help him find it. And we talked about Rubinstein, and Chopinists like Rena Adler and Jakub Frydman.'

'Did he tell you what he does for a living?'

'He said he was in business, but didn't elaborate. It was the waiter who mentioned property. And that he's involved in charitable works.'

'Did you tell him you're a detective?'

'I didn't. I find that tends to kill the conversation.'

Although, in this case, it would have fired it, Maks thought. Zelenski would have been interested to know he was having dinner with a detective.

'The waiter gave me his full name,' she went on. 'Zelenski had asked me to call him by his pseudonym, Salamandra.'

'Salamander? *Wąż*, or snake, would have been better.'

'Why do you say that?'

'Zygmunt Zelenski isn't whiter than white. He's involved in a number of shady property deals. The problem is that we lack the hard evidence to prosecute him. It's why, when we found those bodies in the rubble, we were interested to learn which company had bulldozed the place.'

'We have people like that in Dundee. I think wherever there's big money to be made, there'll be corrupt property dealers.' She picked up her bag. 'I have video calls to make tomorrow, but would you like me to come in on Friday? Mid-morning, perhaps?'

'If you would. And as soon as we have a lead on Merkury, I'll be in touch.'

She got to her feet. 'I wanted to ask how Inspector Dolniak is doing.'

'Oskar?' Maks said, standing. 'I haven't spoken to him today.'

'Do please give him my best.'

The officer outside was waiting for her. Before she disappeared, she turned and smiled at Maks.

He remembered then that she hadn't asked him when she'd be getting her passport back. But she'd cancelled her flight. And she'd agreed to help with the Pomorski case. He'd worked with detectives from other countries before, but sharing a case with Danuta Górska would be a singular pleasure.

Pola was late. Not because of her burgeoning workload, but because the diamond-shaped electric rod on the tram had decoupled itself from the power line. The driver claimed he knew how to fix it, but after climbing up in the dark and trying to slot everything back, he eventually gave up. The other passengers resigned themselves to finding another tram, but Pola decided to walk. Consequently, by the time she reached the basement, not only was she half an hour late, her toes were screaming in pain.

'Gentlemen,' she said, looking around the smoke-filled room, 'I do apologise for my late arrival.' She was about to tell them the tram had broken down but, seeing their expectant faces, decided against it. Let them speculate. And, anyway, there was nothing like delayed gratification.

Zygmunt Zelenski approached and offered her a cigarillo, not from the silver case, but from a packet. He lit the cigarillo, then handed her the pack, curling her fingers round it and squeezing.

'I know these are your favourite, so please do keep them,' he murmured. Before she could reply, he called to a man standing with his back to them. 'Let me introduce you to my son, Konrad.'

Pola's throat tightened. It was only a week since she'd questioned him at the Golden Sunrise. She'd been dressed differently and had worn glasses, but some men were more observant than others.

'Konrad, this is our Motylek,' Zygmunt said, beaming.

Konrad took her outstretched hand and bent to kiss it. As he lifted his head and gazed into her eyes, she thought she saw his expression change slightly. But at that moment, the barman came over with her glass of *wiśniówka*. She thanked him, and drank the vodka before opening her bag and thrusting the cigarillo packet inside.

She was now anxious to play the match and get the hell out of there, but the chess table was still being prepared. She exchanged pleasantries with the barman, and did the rounds of the guests, chatting while keeping her ears tuned to the conversations around her. A history professor was holding forth about the missing Chopin manuscript and a priest called Bielski, but there was nothing of relevance to Maks's cases.

They were inviting her to take her seat at the table. It was time. She cleared her mind of everything but the forthcoming match.

An hour later, Pola left the building, clutching her wad of money. But rather than go straight home, she hurried into a nearby late-night café. During the day, it was frequented by readers of crime novels, who'd exchange their books for ones on the shelves, often consuming coffee after coffee in the well-heated room. As someone whose life revolved round crime, Pola had never been tempted.

The owner, an elderly man with wispy white hair, didn't give her a second glance. She took her coffee to the window seat, and gazed into the murky dark. As far as she could tell, no one had followed her. In fact, after the match, the men, including Zygmunt Zelenski, had become embroiled in a heated discussion about Polish politics, and she'd managed to slip away. The only person who'd spotted her leaving was Konrad. He'd flashed her a smile as she passed him. She'd wondered why he'd bothered to attend, as he seemed entirely uninterested in chess, and hadn't even bet on the duration of the match.

As she was the only person in the café, she removed the packet of cigarillos from her bag and held them up to the owner with a question on her face. He smiled and nodded over his half-moon spectacles, then went back to his newspaper. She took out a cigarillo and lit up, inhaling the smoke gratefully. Her thoughts wandered back to Konrad. Had that been an expression of recognition on his face? If so, what would he do about it? Perhaps it was time to draw these matches to a close. She'd discuss it with Maks and decide whether to return in the New Year. How would she end it? Perhaps she'd send the group a card showing a butterfly on the wing . . .

She reached for the coffee mug, knocking the pack of cigarillos onto the floor and sending the contents flying. Swearing silently, she bent to scoop everything up. The packet, one of those with a hard lid that hinged open, had landed under the adjacent table. As she picked it up, the soft lining fell out. Something was wedged underneath. It looked like a large, dark coin. She stared at it for several seconds before realising what it was.

Back at her table, Pola examined the device. She slid the cover back, seeing a tiny battery and SIM card. Her thoughts were tumbling over one another. So, this was Zygmunt Zelenski's plan: to track her movements. But to what end? Her first reaction was to throw the tracker into the river, or slip it under the seat of a tram. But she'd do neither. She removed the SIM and, flicking open her cigarette lighter, ran the flame over the front and back. Then to make absolutely sure, she dropped it onto the floor and ground it under the heel of her stiletto. She looked up to see the owner watching her with a knowing look on his face.

'Your man keeping track of you, is he?' he said, with a soft chuckle.

'Something like that.'

'You could have hidden it on a tram. That way he'd spend the rest of his life following it around Warsaw.'

And he'd know she'd found it. No, what she intended was for Zelenski to think the battery had died, or the device had malfunctioned. Chances were he was still at the club, and wouldn't start monitoring her movements until he left. She knew she'd been lucky. But luck has a habit of running out . . .

She picked up the SIM and replaced it in the tracker. She put everything back into the packet, smiled a quick goodbye to the owner, and left.

CHAPTER 30

It was mid-afternoon when Pola hurried into Maks's office. She was smiling, which he took to be a good sign.

'I take it from the look on your face that there's news,' he said.

'I've established the identity of the couple pulled out of the rubble.'

'Already?' he murmured. 'Take a seat,' he added, pushing out the chair.

She laid a sheet on the desk. 'Here are the details, but the main thing is that Bogdan Pomorski survived the war, married and had two girls and one boy. His son went on to have a son of his own, whom he called Feliks,' she said, in a rush. 'Feliks married, and his wife's name was Katarina. So, we now have the couple's identity: Feliks and Katarina Pomorski.'

'You've done brilliantly to have got this far.'

'It's not difficult when you know how.'

'And Feliks's father? Where is he?'

'Living in the US. In Chicago. I've been on the phone to him. It turns out he has the exact same tattoo as his father, Bogdan. And he told me his son Feliks had decided to have it done, too. There's no doubt as to identity.'

'Did you tell the father what happened to Feliks?'

'He didn't take it well. He's arriving on the next available flight to make the formal identification.'

'I don't envy him. I saw the state of the bodies. So, what else did you uncover?'

Pola consulted her notes. 'According to their tax records, Feliks worked as a private physiotherapist. But the number of clients he had was dwindling. Here's the list, with dates of his sessions.'

Maks scanned the sheets. 'I see what you mean by dwindling. He was down to four.' He glanced up. 'What about his wife?'

'Katarina was a carer. She worked privately, too. According to the invoices supplied with her tax return, her only patient was the pianist Rena Adler.'

'And Rena was also one of Feliks's clients, according to the list.'

'Convenient. They could have visited her together. But Rena passed away recently. Her death must have made a dent in their coffers.'

'We'll need to send people over to the Pomorskis' apartment.'

'Already scheduled. Do you think we'll find the motive for their murders there?'

Maks studied her. 'I'm more inclined to think we'll find it at Rena Adler's.'

Rena Adler's apartment was in the fashionable Żoliborz district, on the top floor of an elegant building overlooking the park. The caretaker, a droopy-eyed man with thinning locks and a sour smile, who'd introduced himself as the concierge, had studied the officers' warrant cards with disdain before sighing and letting them into what he referred to as the pianist's salon. The room was a riot of colour, with Persian rugs on the walls and red-patterned carpets.

'You're not the first people to come here since Madame died,' he said sniffily.

'Oh?' Maks said, in what he hoped was an encouraging tone. He'd already concluded they'd have an uphill struggle with this one.

'Madame had no relatives, so members of the Jewish Community Centre dealt with the funeral arrangements.' He glanced fondly around the room, his gaze resting on the black-lacquered grand piano. 'In the New Year, they'll empty the place and sell her effects. The proceeds to go to the Community Centre, I believe. Although I understand the piano has been gifted to the Chopin University of Music.' There was pride in his voice, something not lost on Maks.

'I heard Pani Adler play when I was younger,' Maks said, smiling. 'They say she was as gifted as Rubinstein.'

'More so. Many have said it.'

Pola pulled out her notebook. 'Perhaps you can help us with our enquiries.'

'If I can,' the concierge said, with a small bow.

'We understand Feliks and Katarina Pomorski often visited Pani Adler.'

'That's correct. They worked here for over a year, although I haven't seen them for a while.'

'Can you remember the last time they came?'

'It was the day Madame died. Pan and Pani Pomorski arrived, and I let them in. A short while later, Pani Pomorska hurried down to my office. They'd found Madame in bed. She'd died in the night.' He lowered his voice. 'She had a rare form of cancer.'

'And can you remember the date?' Maks said, although he could find it easily enough.

'It was a Friday. The last Friday in November.' He lifted his hands. 'It was not unexpected as she had had only a short time left. The Pomorskis contacted the Jewish Community Centre, and they took over.'

'What can you tell us about the Pomorskis?' Maks said gently. 'What sort of people were they?'

'I didn't know them personally. I can only tell you what Madame said. We'd occasionally have a chat when I brought up her mail, you see.'

Maks smiled encouragingly.

'Pan Pomorski was so good to Madame. He did much to ease her pain. And Pani Pomorska acted as a nurse. She did the necessary, such as washing her, making sure she ate properly. Madame's appetite was starting to go, which worried us. And she did the cleaning, although there wasn't much to do. She came daily, whereas Pan Pomorski came once a week.'

'He must have had other clients,' Pola said.

'From something Madame let slip, he had very few. They'd either finished their treatments, or given up. It worried him. And me, as I didn't want him to leave Warsaw and start up elsewhere.'

'And Pani Pomorska?' Maks prompted. 'What was she like?'

'A kind lady. Nothing was too much trouble, according to Madame. She was in tears when she saw Madame had died.' He looked at his feet. 'I suspect, given how much time she spent here, she had no one else to care for.'

'Did Madame say anything else about the Pomorskis? Were they in any trouble?'

The concierge stared at them with a vacant expression. It was clear he was reluctant to say more. Maks couldn't tell whether it was to protect Rena Adler's reputation or that of the Pomorskis.

'We're asking these questions because the Pomorskis' bodies were found two days ago,' he said.

The man closed his eyes, crossing himself. '*Jezus Maria*,' he murmured.

Maks waited until he'd got himself under control. 'Anything you can tell us would be very helpful. I'm sure Pani Adler would want you to assist us in finding their killer.'

The concierge swallowed loudly. 'Madame told me the Pomorskis were in financial difficulties. She added she'd mentioned it to her visitor, hoping he'd be able to find them some clients.'

'Her visitor?' Maks said, exchanging a glance with Pola.

'This man was a great fan. He came often. When she had the strength, she'd play for him. Chopin, of course.' He lowered his voice unnecessarily. 'Her money was tied up in this apartment. She'd emptied her savings account to pay for her treatment. It was this visitor who took on the payment when the money ran out. I think she welcomed his visits, not because of the money but because she was so lonely.'

'What did this visitor look like?'

'Nothing remarkable about him. Well turned out. His hair was grey and neatly cut.' The concierge grew animated. 'Madame told me he was greatly interested in the missing Chopin manuscript, and asked her where she thought it might be.'

'And what did she say?' Pola said.

'I'm afraid she didn't know any more than the rest of us.'

'Do you know the visitor's name?' Maks said.

'He never supplied it. And Madame referred to him only by his pseudonym.'

'And that was?' Pola said, when nothing further was forthcoming.

The concierge frowned, trying to remember. Then his expression cleared. 'It was Salamandra,' he said triumphantly. 'That's it. Salamandra.'

* * *

'What do you think?' Maks said to Pola, when they were back in his office.

'We've learnt the Pomorskis had money worries. And the last sighting of the couple was the last Friday in November. That's November the twenty-sixth.'

'But this visitor intrigues me. Someone prepared to pay for the treatment.'

'And also interested in the missing manuscript.'

Maks threw her a grin. 'So is most of Warsaw.'

'I wonder if that was behind his visits. Trying to tease out what she knew before she died. So, who is he?'

'I believe we know him. Danuta Górska told me she had dinner with someone who used the pseudonym Salamandra. It was the waiter who revealed his identity: Zygmunt Zelenski.'

Pola's eyes grew wide.

'It's possible there's more than one Salamandra in Warsaw,' Maks said. 'We need to check a few bank accounts.'

There was a ping from the computer.

'Right, here's the first report from the crime-scene officers.' He ran a hand through his hair. 'No cartridge cases. I'd hoped we'd be lucky there.'

'My bet is the Pomorskis were killed elsewhere,' Pola said. 'They died sometime between the first and the eighth. The killer would have had time to transport them by car before the snow arrived on the ninth.'

'My bet is he didn't drive far.'

'What makes you say that?'

'It's how I'd have done it. Most killers go well out of their way to dump bodies, so I'd find a place nearby to throw the police off the scent.' He shrugged. 'He'd have had plenty of opportunity to chat to the workmen and see what was going on. I think we're dealing with a smart individual.' He smiled. 'Talking of smart individuals, how did you get on at the chess club?' He widened his smile. 'By that, I mean how long did it take you to win?'

'Not long.'

'And did you hear anything useful?'

'The talk was about a priest called Bielski. One of the professors thought he'd know something about the Chopin manuscript. But there was nothing of interest to our cases.'

She was fidgeting, and running her hands down her skirt. Maks recognised this behaviour. There was something she both wanted and didn't want to tell him.

'Is there anything else?' he asked softly.

'Zygmunt Zelenski was there. And his son, Konrad.'

Maks looked hard at her.

'I don't think Konrad recognised me. But Zygmunt gave me this.' She fished inside her bag and pulled out a packet of expensive cigarillos.

'That's nice.'

'He usually offers me cigarillos from his own case. After the match, I went somewhere for coffee. And I found this.' She opened the packet and teased out the lining. Underneath was a dark object.

Maks's eyes narrowed. 'A tracker.'

'It was pure chance I found it. Anyway, I've destroyed the SIM. With luck, the Zelenskis will put it down to a malfunction.'

Maks felt his anger swell. 'Right, that's it. You're not going back.'

'I had my firearm with me.'

'You're not going back. It's not up for discussion.' When she opened her mouth to speak, he added, 'That's an order.'

She stood up slowly. Before leaving, she paused, and looked at him.

Maks waited until the door had closed, then threw down his pen in frustration. He hated giving orders. Fortunately, he rarely had to pull rank. He'd worked with Pola long enough to know what she was thinking. But this time was different. The look she'd given him was either one of resignation, or of relief. His problem was that he didn't know which.

CHAPTER 31

Dania had finished her video call, and was practising Chopin's Ballade, replaying the more difficult phrases, when she heard the front door open.

'You're back early,' she called through.

Marek sauntered into the living room. 'The archivist and I decided to give it one final go, but we couldn't find this notebook.' He flopped onto the sofa. 'You know, Danka, it's situations like this that swearing was invented for.'

She joined him on the sofa. 'All right, so it's not at the Institute of National Remembrance. What are the other possibilities? It became separated from the other notebooks, and was left in the apartment?'

'The Communists would have searched the place.'

'But it's not impossible they overlooked it. Maybe the next person who lived there found it.'

'And threw it out.'

Dania chose her words. 'Marek, have you considered the collector might have been wrong in his assumption that Ludwika gave the concerto to one of Chopin's friends? I mean, although he believed it, it doesn't make it true.'

Marek stared at her balefully.

'Even if you find this notebook, it may lead nowhere.'

'You think I should give up?'

She held his gaze. 'The hardest decision you make when climbing a mountain is when to turn back.'

'I've never known you do that.'

'I don't tell you everything.'

He looked away. 'Well, I've decided it's time to call time. I'll devote what's left of my energy to translating the notebooks. I promised Father Bielski I'd have them published.'

After a silence, she said, 'We need to think about getting in food for Wigilia. I'd go myself, but I'm due at Mostowski Palace.'

'I put in the order yesterday. Although there'll be more than we can eat. Pity our parents didn't tell us sooner that they'd decided to stay in the US for Christmas.'

The phone call had come in the day before. Their parents had made so many new friends at the Polish-American genealogy convention that they'd accepted an invitation to celebrate Wigilia in Florida. And who could resist the sunshine?

'What about the *opłatki*?' Dania said. These thin wafers made of flour and water were shared at the Christmas Eve meal.

'I'll get them from St Augustine's.' His expression brightened. 'Father Bielski might be there. I can show him the notebooks.' He sprang to his feet.

As the front door closed, Dania considered her brother's decision to abandon his quest. Yet she was unconvinced he'd give up. It was more likely he'd have the notebooks published, and return to looking for the manuscript. It was his tenacity that had made him such an excellent investigative journalist, she thought, as she slipped on her coat.

* * *

'The Pomorskis' house was ransacked?' Maks said, gazing at the officer.

'The place had been thoroughly turned over. Forensics are there now.'

'Did you find anything useful? Mobiles? Laptops?'

The man shook his head. 'And they didn't have a landline.'

'Papers?'

'Gone. Whoever killed them went to great lengths to hide their identities. Eventually, someone would have noticed they were missing, although the neighbours were remarkably unforthcoming. We checked the Pomorskis' online presence, but there was just a website advertising their services. We could dig deeper.'

'CCTV?'

'In that part of Praga?' the officer said, in a tone suggesting Maks must be losing it.

'The absence of anything that could identify them means we're dealing with a pro. Okay, let me know what Forensics find.' Maks put down his pen. 'What was the place like?'

'A small, crumbling house.' The man nodded and left.

Maks sat back, stretching his arms above his head.

There was a knock at the door.

'Enter,' he said.

Danuta Górska was ushered in by a uniformed officer.

Maks got to his feet. 'Pani Górska, thank you for coming.'

'I hope I'm not too early?'

'Not at all.' He pulled out a chair.

Briefly, he brought her up to speed on what they knew about Feliks and Katarina Pomorski. Danuta's interest rose further at the mention of Salamandra.

'So, this Zygmunt Zelenski knew Rena Adler?' she said.

'Interesting he kept that quiet when I had dinner with him. And he said nothing about her having died.'

There was another knock, and Pola popped her head round.

'Come and join us,' Maks said. 'Have you met Danuta Górska?'

'I haven't had the pleasure.'

He made the introductions. 'I've already briefed Pani Górska.'

'Excellent.' Pola sat down, and opened her folder. 'I've just finished going through the Pomorskis' bank account. Regular weekly sums were paid in by Zygmunt Zelenski. Always the same amount, and enough to cover the services they provided.'

'How far back did this go?' Maks asked.

'About nine months. Before that, payments came to them from Rena Adler.'

'What the concierge told us checks out, then.'

'But there's something else. Roughly three months ago, a large sum of money was transferred into the Pomorskis' bank account from an unknown source.'

'How large?' Danuta said.

'Twenty thousand euros.'

'*Twenty thousand?*' Maks said.

Danuta frowned. 'Can this source be tracked?'

'We're doing our best, but we've got nowhere. It's a numbered account in Switzerland.'

'Good luck with tracing that. We had a similar case in Dundee. We never found the source. I think it's time banks gave up that practice.'

'So, let's talk about why,' Maks said.

'The Pomorskis knew something, and the money was to hush them up,' Pola ventured. 'They decided to spill the beans, and so were murdered.'

'Then why not murder them at the outset and be done with

it?' Danuta said. 'And save yourself the money,' she added, smiling. 'There's also the time difference. They received the money three months ago. But they were murdered recently. Why wait that long to threaten to spill the beans?'

'Excellent points,' Pola said, leaning forward eagerly.

Maks listened to the women batting theories back and forth. For the sake of his manhood, he felt he should interject. 'Why didn't they give up working once they had the money? Okay, it wouldn't have lasted for ever, but it could have meant a new start somewhere else, or a way into more lucrative careers.'

The women stared at him. Then Danuta said, 'Perhaps because they couldn't give up. Or leave Warsaw. They were waiting for something.' She pushed her hands through her hair. 'The money wasn't for what they knew, but for what they'd agreed to do. Something that would take time.'

'What would take three months?'

'Anything involving bureaucracy, Inspector.'

He laughed. 'That's something we learnt from the Communists.'

'Believe me, it's the same in the UK.'

'But who would want anything from them?' Pola said.

Danuta shrugged. 'Who knew they were strapped for cash?'

'Zygmunt Zelenski knew,' Maks said. 'Rena Adler told him.'

'Zygmunt Zelenski. A property dealer. Then we have a possible motive.'

'How do you mean?'

'It must involve his construction business. Where did the Pomorskis live?'

'In Praga, east of the zoo.'

'In a run-down building?'

'So I understand.'

'Did they own it, or were they renting?'

Maks glanced at Pola. She lifted her hands to signal she didn't know.

'If they owned it, maybe they'd agreed to sell it to Zelenski, and this cash was a down-payment. And perhaps they changed their minds, and refused to refund him. Although it doesn't explain why he used a numbered bank account.' Danuta looked from one to the other. 'I don't know much about the tax situation here, but could he avoid paying tax on the purchase that way?'

'And if they rented the place?' Pola said.

'Then the theory doesn't hold up. But I have a feeling that property is the key to their murder.'

Maks thought back to his conversation with Lidia Lipska. She'd researched property restitution, and Zelenski's part in subsequently buying up the buildings. He turned to Pola. 'Can you find out everything about the Pomorskis' house? Not just whether they owned it, but who owned it before them. Go back as far as possible.'

'Right.' With a smile at Danuta, she hurried out of the room.

'You said their place had been ransacked, Inspector. Could it have been Zelenski? Who wanted to remove evidence of his transactions by taking their computer? Just a thought.'

'And a valid one. If we can find a motive for Zelenski to murder the Pomorskis, we may have enough for a warrant to search his premises.'

The phone rang. He excused himself and picked up the handset. As he listened, he felt a rush of blood to his head. 'I'm on my way.' He got to his feet. 'We've had a report of the two kings. They've left the city centre, and my people think they're planning to pick up a consignment from Merkury.' He inclined his head. 'So, Pani Górska, are you ready to accompany me?'

* * *

Dania and Robak scrambled into the unmarked police car.

'Thanks for taking me, Inspector,' she said, as he pulled away.

He threw her a glance. 'I'm as anxious to find Merkury as you are.' The radio clipped to his jacket suddenly crackled.

'Inspector?' came the woman's voice.

Robak pressed a button. 'Speaking. Where are you?'

'We're approaching the Śląsko-Dąbrowski Bridge. They're heading to Praga.'

'Stay on the line and update me as you go.'

'Is this one of your Romeo pairs?' Dania said.

'One of my best.'

Dania listened as the female officer gave a running commentary. The directions meant little to her.

'They've turned into a side street,' the woman said. 'Now they're leaving the car.'

'Pull up somewhere, and follow them.'

'Okay, they're heading west along the main street. They've got rucksacks, although they don't look particularly heavy.'

Robak was now on the bridge, behind a lorry carrying crates of bottles. They passed a tram trundling along on the left, making Dania wonder how many accidents were caused by cars straying onto the tramlines. But Robak was a good driver and not prepared to risk overtaking.

'Boss! They've gone into a house. I'll send the location to your phone. We'll hole up in the coffee shop where we can keep an eye on the front door.'

'Good work. We'll be there in a matter of minutes.'

But as they were leaving the bridge, one of the lorry's back tyres blew spectacularly, causing that side of the vehicle to drop. A number of crates tumbled out of the back, and the bottles smashed, streaming liquid across the road. Robak hit the brakes but there was no way of avoiding the broken glass. The tram caught up with them, and he had no option but to swerve on to the wide pavement. He might have avoided disaster had it not been for the lamppost. There was a loud crash and a judder that shook every bone in Dania's body. The airbags inflated, leaving the sharp smell of gunpowder hanging in the air.

'*Kurwa!*' Robak exclaimed. He pushed away the airbags. 'Are you hurt?'

'I'm fine.'

'I've got the location. Let's go.'

'What about the car?'

'We'll worry about that later.'

Dania struggled out of the vehicle, and they hurried along the pavement. As they reached the now stationary lorry, they saw the driver clambering out. He looked as shaken as she felt.

Robak gripped his shoulder. 'You okay?'

The man nodded. He was pulling out his phone with a trembling hand.

Robak glanced at Dania. 'Come on,' he said.

They'd reached the busy intersection when they heard the female officer's voice. 'Boss, where are you? They're leaving!'

'We had an accident. We're on foot.'

'They must have picked up a load, because their rucksacks look heavy. They're on the street now. Shall we pull them in?'

'Follow them to their apartments and arrest them once they're inside with the heroin. You've got photos of them entering and leaving the house?'

'We've got it all.'

'Did you see who came to the door?'

'No. It was open. And there's a security gate where you enter an access code, and it was left open, too. It's as if they were expected. One of them was speaking into a phone as he left the car. I guess they must have rung ahead.'

'Send me a photo of the house.'

'Hold on! There's someone else leaving. He's closed the front door and locked it with a key. Now he's going through the gate. And he's pulled it shut.'

'Is he following the men?'

'He's walking in the other direction. And he's getting into a car. We can't follow him *and* the kings. What shall we do?'

'Stick with the plan. What's the house like round the back?'

'We didn't have time to investigate. But it's the last one on that section of the street. You can't miss it.'

'Okay. Good luck.'

'You too, boss.'

Minutes later, Robak stopped and studied his phone. 'We're going to approach the house from the back, Pani Górska. It's that one there, behind the brick wall,' he added, gazing along the deserted street. 'I'll climb up first and check out the place, and then I'll pull you up.'

'What's the plan?'

'I think the man who lives here is Merkury. I don't intend to waste time applying for a warrant, so we're going to break in and look around. If we can uncover his identity, and find proof that he's running a heroin ring, we'll have everything we need to arrest him.'

'Is breaking into a house legal in the Republic of Poland?'

He threw her a smile. 'No, but you can visit me in prison.'

The wall had been roughly constructed. Robak jumped, grabbed the top and hoisted himself up. He held the position and gazed about. Then he dropped back to the ground.

'There's a small yard. But no German Shepherd.'

Dania felt a tingle of excitement. 'I'm ready.'

He pulled himself up again. Sitting astride the wall, he bent and reached down. She climbed, placing her feet on the misplaced bricks, until she was within reach of his outstretched arm. He hauled her onto the top.

A two-storey house faced her, giving her the feeling it was staring at her out of all its windows. Below was an area laid with flagstones. Whoever lived there wasn't much of a gardener – they'd let weeds grow between the stones. A garden shed with a dilapidated door stood in one corner.

She swung her leg over, and jumped down, landing on all fours. A second later, Robak joined her.

'I'm assuming the back door's locked, Inspector,' she said, getting to her feet.

'I was hoping you could pick it. It's a skill I've never mastered.'

'Ah, so *I'm* the one breaking in.'

'Rest assured, Pani Górska, I'll visit you in prison.' He pulled out two sets of white latex gloves. She drew on a pair, studying the lock. It was the type that should pose no problems.

She rooted about in her bag for the hair slide, and set to work. A few seconds later, she felt a slight give in the locking mechanism, followed by a loud click.

'Impressive,' Robak said, throwing her an appreciative look. He gripped the handle, opening the door a few inches. 'No burglar alarm. Now, remember. Stay behind me at all times.'

Dania stepped back, letting him in first. The door opened into a small, functional kitchen, its walls lined with old-fashioned flower tiles. Unwashed dishes were piled in the sink, and there was a smell of burnt toast.

Robak slid open the drawer under the counter. 'I'm looking

for something like utility bills, something with a name. But there's only cutlery here.'

The partly open door led into a long corridor with a wooden banister. He peered into the under-stairs cupboard. Several coats hung on pegs. He searched the pockets, but they were empty. The only other item was the vacuum cleaner.

The front door, painted white with a decorative glass inlay, was at the far end. To the left was a sitting room, comfortably furnished with deep sofas and armchairs, and a wall-mounted television. The room on the right contained an oval dining table and six chairs. On the floor were two large cardboard boxes, which had been sealed with shiny brown tape. Someone had cut through the tape, probably with the steak knife lying on the table. Robak pulled back the flaps.

'They're empty,' he said. 'I wonder if this was how the heroin came in.'

'It says "Children's Toys" on the sides.' Dania glanced around. 'So far, we've found nothing to indicate who lives here.'

'It's possible he uses this place only when deliveries come in, which means he may not return for some time. Shall we try upstairs?'

'You think there are love letters?'

'Do women still send those?' Robak said wryly.

There were two long rooms on the upper floor. In one, a pair of single beds stood side by side. The en-suite bathroom consisted of a toilet, washbasin and shower, but the absence of towels and soap suggested the bedroom was rarely used. Dania opened the door in the narrow wardrobe. It was empty.

Robak motioned towards the other room.

'Now, this looks more promising,' he said, gazing around.

The double bed was a mess, with the duvet half on the floor. Robak opened the drawer in the bedside cabinet.

'Several packets of condoms, and nothing else. Looks as if this is where he entertains his ladies.'

The en-suite bathroom was identical to the other, but towels hung from the rail and men's toiletries lay scattered over the shelf. The scent of peppery aftershave lingered in the air.

Dania's attention had turned to the huge mahogany wardrobe with inlaid mirrors. She gazed at it for several seconds. 'Inspector, something's not right.'

'How do you mean?'

'I need to see the other room.'

He followed her back in.

'Look at the dimensions, and the position of the windows,' she said.

'Okay,' he said slowly. 'There are windows on the back and side walls. And a window in the bathroom.'

'Now, let's look again at the main bedroom.'

Robak gazed at the wardrobe, seeing it immediately. 'This room's shorter.'

'Yet that's not the impression from outside. And where's the back window?'

He strode across and examined the wardrobe. 'There's a false wall behind this.' He flung open the doors. Inside there were mostly jeans and sweatshirts, with a few smart suits. 'Help me with these, Pani Górska.'

They unhooked the hangers and dumped the clothes on the bed.

The wardrobe was tall enough that Robak could comfortably stand in it. He studied the panels and shelves, running his fingers along them, then turned his attention to the wardrobe's exterior.

'Can we move it?' Dania said. 'I'll help you.'

'I'm afraid it's fixed to the wall.'

'Shall we look for an axe? There might be one in the shed.'

He held up a hand, frowning. 'We may not need to.'

Slowly, he ran his fingers down one side of the wardrobe, then the other. He closed the double doors, and backed away, gazing at his reflection for several seconds. Then he stepped inside, and moved his hands over the inside panels. Dania couldn't see what he was doing, but she heard a sudden loud click and the back of the wardrobe swung away. Light streamed into the room.

She stared at Robak in amazement. 'How on earth . . . ?'

'It's nothing more than a giant puzzle box.' He smiled. 'So, Pani Górska. Shall we?'

CHAPTER 32

Dania followed Robak into a small room. Two cardboard boxes marked 'Children's Toys' stood under the window. They'd been cut open.

'This must be the next batch to go out,' she said, staring at the packets of white powder.

'I suspect he opened the boxes to check everything was there. We should get his fingerprints.'

The only other items were a desk and chair.

'Stage make-up,' Robak said, lifting a thick tube. He examined the selection of bottles. 'And here we have various shades of hair dye.'

But Dania's attention had been taken by a framed black-and-white photograph on the wall. It showed two insurgents from the Uprising, smiling into the camera, their arms round each other's shoulders. They were wearing German helmets with the red-and-white headbands identifying them as Poles. Submachine guns hung from their necks.

'Inspector, look at this.'

Under the photo was the name of a battalion. And the pseudonyms of the insurgents. One was Diament, or Diamond. But it was the other that caused Robak to draw in his breath.

'So, Merkury was a Home Army pseudonym,' he said.

'Do you think this insurgent is related to our Merkury?'

'Or our Merkury is related to Diament, but preferred the pseudonym of his companion. Either way, it's a lead.'

They gazed at each other. Robak was smiling, his eyes glowing.

There was a sudden noise from downstairs. The front door had opened and closed.

In an instant, Robak drew out his weapon. He lifted a finger to his lips, suggesting they might get away with hiding in the room. Then he closed his eyes briefly, and whispered, 'The clothes.'

They crept into the bedroom. Dania hurried to the other side of the bed to scoop up the clothes on the floor. But the sound of someone climbing the stairs told her they were out of time. Robak was waving frantically at her to move away from the door when it opened and a man walked in. He stopped short when he saw the officers.

He was wearing a padded jacket, thick jeans and heavy boots. His hair was tucked under the peaked woollen hat, but it didn't stop Dania recognising him, even with his slack-jawed gaze.

'Tomek,' she said vaguely, as if she couldn't believe what she was seeing.

'Police! Hands in the air!' Robak shouted, levelling his pistol. 'Now!'

Tomek grabbed her and pulled her towards him, holding her tightly with one arm round her waist and the other round her neck. They were roughly the same height so, even if Robak was an excellent shot, he wouldn't risk aiming at Tomek's head.

Tomek inched into the corridor. He must have realised he couldn't walk backwards down the stairs because he paused, and pushed her so violently that Robak had to lower his pistol as she crashed into him. Footsteps pounded down the stairs.

Robak released her, and headed for the corridor. Dania heard the front door open and close, and Robak running down the stairs. The sudden fear that Tomek would escape gripped her. She hurried after them.

She ran out in time to see Tomek exit via the iron gate. His mistake was that he didn't shut it behind him. Robak reached the pavement, shouting to him to stop, then lifted his pistol and fired into the air. This had the desired effect. Tomek came to an immediate halt, and raised his hands.

Robak sprinted towards him, pulling a pair of handcuffs out of his pocket. He holstered his pistol, then yanked Tomek's hands behind his back and cuffed him while speaking the words of arrest. He was wheeling him round when Dania caught up with them.

'You bastard, Tomek!' she shouted, slapping his face hard. It was the expression of insolence in his eyes that made her follow it up with a knee in the groin. He bent over, howling.

'Enough, Pani Górska,' Robak said, gripping her arms and dragging her away. 'Why are you calling him Tomek?'

'Because that's his name.'

He was looking at her strangely. 'His name is Konrad Zelenski.'

Maks watched as the police van taking Konrad Zelenski to Mostowski Palace sped off in the direction of the bridge. He'd asked for a car for himself and the lady as they still had business here. Oh, and could the sergeant see to the vehicle abandoned on the Praga side of the bridge?

Danuta Górska had pulled off her hat and was tapping it against her thigh as she walked back and forth. She stopped and stared at the villa, then across the street at the bank. The fire was back in her eyes. The speed and accuracy with which she'd kneed Konrad in the groin made Maks glad she was on his side.

'Pani Górska, shall we go back inside and see what else we can find in that room? Before Forensics arrive? Mm?'

'All right,' she said, calming visibly.

'The front door's open, so you won't have to pick the lock,' he said, trying a joke.

Her lips twitched. 'Well, you did say you'd visit me in prison.'

As they re-entered the house, he said, 'You know Konrad Zelenski. Tell me how you met.'

'Remember I told you about my bag being snatched? And that someone came to my rescue? Well, that was Tomek. He said he was with the Kraków police. I saw his warrant.'

'It's too much of a coincidence. I suspect he staged the whole thing. The question is: why? I'll add it to the list of things I intend to ask him.'

They'd reached the bedroom. Now that Maks knew whose this was, he recognised some suits as belonging to Konrad. The man had a preference for checked jackets.

He followed Danuta into the room behind the wardrobe. 'So, what have we here?' he said, lifting a stack of passports out of the desk drawer. Some were from Poland, the rest from other European countries. He handed them to her. 'Do you recognise any of these names?'

She flicked through them. 'Tomek Hodak,' she said, holding up a passport.

'Here's the warrant card with his photograph,' Maks said, pulling it out of the drawer. 'We'll add impersonating a police officer to the charge sheet.'

'That's his mobile. There, at the back.'

Maks lifted out the red-and-white phone. 'I wonder what we'll get from this.'

Danuta was studying the passports. 'In some of these, he has blonde hair.'

'A master of disguise. I wonder what the make-up was for.' His radio crackled. 'Robak speaking,' he said into the device.

'Boss, we've arrested the two kings in their apartments. It's taken this long because they stopped off for something to eat.'

'And the rucksacks?'

'More heroin than we've seen for a long time.'

'You've done well,' he said warmly.

'We'll hold off the celebrations until you get here.' The female officer disconnected.

Maks gazed at Danuta. 'I wouldn't have found this hidden room without your help.'

'But it was you who discovered the way in, Inspector.'

They heard the doorbell.

'Forensics,' Maks said. 'We'd better let them in.'

The officers were assembled at the front entrance. Maks briefed them. They gowned up and traipsed inside.

'I suggest we leave them to it,' he said. 'I've asked them to keep me updated.'

When they were in the car, Danuta said, 'This Konrad Zelenski, is he related to Zygmunt Zelenski?'

'He's his son.'

'If Konrad Zelenski is indeed Merkury, do you think his father knows about the heroin ring?'

'Not only knows about it, but condones it.'

They were approaching the bridge. The smashed police car was still in front of the lamppost.

'I'd offer to take you to lunch, Pani Górska, but I need to get the paperwork started.'

'No, that's fine. Please drop me off here,' she said, as they neared General Anders Road.

'Can you be at Mostowski Palace early tomorrow? We may be in a position to start first questioning.'

'As soon as that?'

'And I'd like to be able to brief you on what Forensics find.'

'I'll be there.'

Maks pulled up at the traffic lights. 'Until tomorrow, Pani Górska,' he said, reaching across to open the passenger door.

'Until tomorrow, Inspector.'

He watched her hurry round to the zebra crossing, then pulled away. His Romeo pair would have started the paperwork on the two kings. With luck, they could put enough pressure on the men to give up the details of Konrad Zelenski's operation, because if anyone would put up a fight, it would be Merkury. Maks felt his spirits rise. The first thing he'd do on reaching his office would be to put in a call to his good friend, Oskar.

CHAPTER 33

It was 8 a.m. when Dania was shown into Robak's office. He was standing speaking to two of his team, a man and a woman. They smiled at Dania as they left.

'That was the Romeo pair who arrested the kings, Pani Górska,' Robak said, without preamble. 'Let me update you on where we are,' he added, indicating the chairs. 'First of all, the white powder in the boxes marked "Children's Toys" is indeed heroin. And Konrad Zelenski's fingerprints are all over the packets. That's enough for us to detain him.'

'And is he Merkury?'

'Pola discovered that Merkury is the Home Army pseudonym of a Leon Zelenski. He happens to have been Konrad's grandfather. We have his records from the Institute of National Remembrance, and can confirm he's one of the men in the photograph.'

'Konrad would use his grandfather's pseudonym.'

'We need him to confirm it.'

'What about the kings? Could they confirm it?'

'So far, they're saying nothing. But the quantity of heroin we found in their rucksacks means we're in a good position to put pressure on them.' He searched his papers. 'You gave Oskar the names of Poles who'd flown from Edinburgh to Warsaw on November the nineteenth. One of those names appears on a passport with Konrad's photograph. So that puts him in Edinburgh at that time.' He gazed at her. 'But we still have to prove he's your man.'

'Does his father know he's been arrested?'

'People detained have the right to have a close relative informed, but, strangely, he's asked us not to send word to anyone, especially his father. And he doesn't want a lawyer. Not yet, anyway.'

'He surely doesn't think he'll be released, and his father won't find out about his arrest?'

Robak rubbed his neck. 'I suspect he has something up his sleeve. But if his father doesn't know he's here, it could work for us. Anyway, as soon as the interview room is ready, we can start the questioning.'

'Suppose he denies everything, despite the evidence. We've had cases like that in Dundee.'

'I find the best tactic is to lay out the worst that could happen if he doesn't cooperate.'

'Here's a suggestion, Inspector. Threaten him with extradition to Scotland. He knows who I am and that I'm here because my informant was murdered.' Dania picked up the pen and scribbled on the sheet. 'That's her name.'

'You think this will frighten him enough?'

'In Scotland we have something called an indeterminate sentence. It doesn't have a set end point.' She shrugged. 'Okay, there's a minimum time served before consideration for parole but, in this case, the victim was working for the police. The judge will take that into consideration.'

Robak narrowed his eyes. 'It could work.'

There was a knock at the door, and an officer poked his head round. 'Maks, he's ready.'

'We're on our way.'

Robak smiled apologetically at Dania. 'I can't invite you to the interview, but you'll be able to observe everything from the next room.'

'That's fine. I won't be able to knee him in the groin if I'm not with him.'

'Pani Górska . . .'

Dania held up her hand. 'I know. Violence towards a prisoner is against the law in the Republic of Poland.'

The interview room was on the ground floor. As far as Dania could tell, the set-up was the same as in Scotland. There was a recording device on the table, and a uniformed officer guarding the door.

Konrad had been given a change of clothes. He was looking distinctly jittery. Every so often, he ran a hand over his blonde-streaked hair.

Robak entered the room and took the seat opposite. He switched on the recording device, and spoke into it. Preliminaries over, he addressed Konrad. 'Last name, first name, father's first name.'

'Zelenski, Konrad, Zygmunt,' came the sullen reply.

'Pan Zelenski, I want to ask you about the incident in Praga yesterday.' Robak opened his file. 'The interim Forensics report states that the packets found in two boxes in the room behind the wardrobe contained pure-grade heroin. Traces of the same-grade heroin were found in identical boxes in the dining room.'

He laid a series of photographs on the table. 'Do you recognise these boxes?'

'I've never seen them before.'

'That's interesting, because your fingerprints are all over them. And over the heroin packets. Oh, and over the packets of heroin we found in the rucksacks of the two men who visited you yesterday.' He laid more photographs on the table.

'I've no idea how my prints got there,' Konrad said insolently. 'With tech these days, it's possible to reproduce someone's fingerprints and use them to frame him,' he added smugly.

'And we found heroin traces on your clothes.'

'There's so much heroin in the air in Warsaw, you'll find traces on everyone's clothes.' He sneered. 'You've got the wrong man, Inspector. I'm innocent.'

'If you're innocent, why did you run when you saw us? Why did you grab Danuta Górska and use her as a shield?' When nothing was forthcoming, Robak went on, 'You staged an attempted robbery so you had an excuse to talk to her. Why was that? We found the police warrant you used, incidentally. Impersonating a police officer is an offence. And this one is hard to deny, given your photograph is on the warrant.'

Robak had hit a nerve. Anger flared in Konrad's eyes. He turned his head and scowled at the two-way mirror. Dania realised that he'd guessed she was watching.

'Let me show you what we have,' Robak said, reaching into his waistcoat pocket. He laid out the cards, face up. 'These are the men we arrested yesterday,' he said, tapping the kings, Clubs and Diamonds. He pushed the Ace of Spades with the question mark towards Konrad. 'And now we know the identity of the main man. Not only do you control the heroin import into Warsaw, but you set up a ring in Dundee. Do you deny that?' He removed a passport from the folder and laid it open at the back page. 'This passport was used on November the nineteenth by someone flying from Edinburgh to Warsaw. Do you deny this is you?'

Konrad looked away. He was distinctly rattled. Now was the time, thought Dania.

As if hearing her thoughts, Robak said, 'Does the name Magda Sadalska mean anything to you?'

To say he'd hit another nerve was a gross understatement. Konrad turned his head so sharply that Dania imagined she heard his neck crack. He stared at Robak with stinging hatred in his eyes.

'Magda was a police informant, who worked for Danuta Górska,' Robak went on. He sat back and crossed his arms. 'Inspector Górska will be starting extradition proceedings. You'll be tried for murder in Scotland where, I understand, the sentence is served without an end date. Murdering a police informant will result in a long sentence, much, much longer than you'd get here for running a heroin operation.' He gathered up the photos. 'I'm not familiar with the process of extradition but I doubt we'll be putting obstacles in Inspector Górska's way.' He closed the folder and got to his feet. 'It will get you out of our country, and save us the bother of prosecuting you ourselves.' He made for the door.

'Wait!' Konrad said.

As Robak turned, he looked directly at the mirror. Although he couldn't see Dania, a small smile crossed his lips.

He resumed his seat. 'Is there something you'd like to say, Pan Zelenski?'

Konrad was staring at the table. 'If I help you, will you block the extradition? And make sure I get a lenient sentence here in Warsaw?'

'I can certainly push for a lenient sentence, and the courts do look more favourably on those who help the police, but the extradition is out of my hands.'

Konrad gazed at the mirror. 'Bring her in here,' he said, using the familiar form of the verb.

'Excuse me? Did you give me an order?'

Konrad took a deep breath. 'I'm sorry, Inspector. Please will you ask Pani Górska to come in?'

Robak nodded at the mirror. It was the signal to the uniformed officer.

'Will you come with me, please?' the man said to Dania.

He opened the door to the interview room. As she entered, Robak got to his feet. Konrad made to do the same, but the uniform behind him put a hand on his shoulder and pushed him down.

Dania took the chair beside Robak, her gaze drifting to the Syrenka Warszawska round Konrad's neck.

'If I talk, will you promise not to start extradition proceedings?' he said, looking at her.

'It depends on what you tell Inspector Robak.' She saw him frown, and added, 'Until we know the value of your intelligence, I'm promising nothing.'

It rested on his believing she had the evidence to put him away for Magda's murder. Which she hadn't. But she had to act as though she had. She gazed directly at him, a serene expression on her face.

Konrad stared at the ceiling. Then he brought his head down and said to Robak, 'Show me those playing cards again.'

Robak laid them out.

'I can supply you with evidence against them all,' Konrad said. 'And the names of the street men. Most of them work for the Zelenski construction company, and peddle drugs on the side.' He held up the Ace of Spades. 'But you're wrong about this one. Much as I'd like it to be me, it isn't. It's my father.' He sneered. 'He controls the entire heroin operation. I'm his errand boy. That house where you caught me? He owns it.'

'How does the heroin come in?' Robak said, after a silence.

'In those boxes marked "Children's Toys". The shipments arrive by river.'

'Including the one on December the ninth?'

'You know about that?' he said slowly.

'We were there, watching you. Why did the pilot go for that narrow jetty and not the pier at La Playa? You were parked near the zoo, which wasn't far away.'

'That was the plan, for him to land at the pier. But literally at the last minute, he phoned to say he'd deliver at the jetty, as the pier would be too public. We got there just in time.'

'But you didn't get the drugs.'

'The pilot saw those idiots, and that fire, and left. My father decided against trying the river again. Then the snow came. When the roads were cleared, he arranged for the boxes to come in by land.'

Robak moved the cards around. 'Where's the evidence your father's behind this ring?'

'It's on the phone, the one in the hidden room. With the red-and-white case.'

'But I saw *you* use that,' Dania chipped in.

Konrad smiled, but it was without humour. 'Anything to do with heroin, he makes the calls on that phone. And I use it for calls to my men.' He clasped his hands behind his neck, and looked from one to the other. 'A while ago, I installed an app that records conversations. I activate it when I know he's going to use the phone,' he said unashamedly. 'My father has no idea how to use technology.'

'And what was the purpose of these recordings?' Robak said. 'An insurance policy?'

'And I'm cashing in now.'

'You're prepared to give up your father?' Dania said, not bothering to keep the disgust from her voice.

'Why wouldn't I?' he said, with venom. 'He's held me back my whole life. Everything I've tried to start for myself he takes control over. Or cuts himself a piece of it.' He tapped the table. 'When I went to Dundee with my guys and started up a new enterprise, I'd hoped to make it mine. But no, my father had to step in and grab the reins.'

'And presumably seize most of the profits,' she said. 'Is that why you shut down Dundee?'

'It was over when I discovered Magda was your informant.'

'And what was your father's reaction?'

Konrad ruffled his hair. 'He blamed me for being careless. He said I'd let him down. Dundee was a lucrative assignment.'

'And then what?' Robak said. 'You started up in Warsaw?'

'I rejoined the Praga operation.'

'What made you take the pseudonym Merkury?' Dania said, challenging him.

'It was my grandfather's. He fought in the Uprising.'

'I wonder what he'd think if he knew you'd used it for your illegal operations.'

Konrad said nothing, but the way he avoided her gaze made her conclude that the comment had hit home.

'Tell me about the attack on Inspector Górska,' Robak said, after a pause. 'What was behind that?'

'My father had run into her at his restaurant. When he told me her name, I realised she'd come to Warsaw to find me. I had to get her to tell me what she knew. She was Magda's handler.'

'And you knew that because you'd beaten it out of her, hadn't you?' Dania said softly.

He said nothing, giving her her answer.

'It wasn't difficult to find out where Pani Górska was staying,' Konrad went on. 'So, I and one of my guys decided to stage an attempted robbery. When we saw she was heading to the riverbank, it was easy to set it up there. Many people go jogging along those paths.'

'And by making sure I saw your forged warrant card, I'd assume you were a detective and open up to you,' Dania said. 'It was a good plan.'

He looked directly at her. 'The day the shipment was coming in, I rang you. Do you remember?'

'You asked me out to dinner. Why?'

'I wasn't convinced you weren't working with Dolniak. I thought that, if you knew about the shipment, you'd tell me.'

Dania felt a sudden knot in her stomach as she remembered how close she'd come to revealing details of the stake-out.

After a pause, Robak said, 'I think that's it for now. But we'll have further questions.'

Konrad ran a hand over his face. 'I don't doubt it.'

'In the meantime, you can stave off boredom by writing down everything about these guys,' Robak said, tapping the playing cards. 'I want the names and modus operandi of the street men. And when you've finished that, you can give us the details of the Dundee operation, including how you murdered Magda Sadalska.' He paused. 'And I want the name of the man who attacked Inspector Górska.'

He signalled to the uniformed officer to take Konrad away, and switched off the recorder.

'So, Pani Górska, we've gone further than I expected. I think it was your suggestion of threatening extradition that did it.'

He was looking at her in a strange way. It was on the tip of her tongue to ask what his views were about having Konrad extradited. She wondered what his reaction would be.

'What now, Inspector?'

'Zygmunt Zelenski will have the best lawyer money can buy. We need hard evidence before we can arrest him. Shall we see what the Central Forensic Laboratory has found on that red-and-white phone?'

CHAPTER 34

The report from the Central Forensic Laboratory arrived later the same morning.

'Pani Górska,' Maks said, glancing up from the screen. 'We have something.'

She hurried across from the table, where she'd been poring over the preliminary report on the Pomorski case.

'It's not the red-and-white phone,' Maks said. 'This is Konrad's personal mobile.'

'That's better, isn't it? He can't deny the evidence.'

Maks smiled. 'Ah, yes, the pint brimming over. Right, so what has Zelenski Junior been doing lately?' With each click of the mouse, the map changed showing Konrad's location. 'He's in Praga much of the time.'

'Inspector,' Danuta said.

'Mm?'

'Can we go back two or three weeks? I've been thinking about the make-up we found in the hidden room.'

'Yes, Konrad must use it for his various disguises.'

'But this is no ordinary make-up, according to Forensics. It's a thick, malleable foundation, which can alter the shape of your face. It means it can be used to create burn scars.'

Maks stared at her. 'Jakub Frydman's funeral was Wednesday, December the first.' He brought up that day's map.

'Ah, he wasn't anywhere near Okopowa,' Danuta said, disappointment in her voice.

'There's something else we can try. Pola tracked down the florist who'd sold the wreath.' A few seconds later, her report appeared. 'It was ordered not long after ten o'clock on Monday, November the twenty-ninth, and picked up in the late afternoon the same day.' He returned to the map and scrolled to the Monday. 'And there we have it. He was at the florist's twice. The times fit.' His pulse was racing. 'Konrad is our unexpected guest. And, according to the phone-mast data, he switched off the mobile before he went to the cemetery. But not before he visited the florist.' Maks gazed at Danuta. 'The idiot.'

She smiled, making his pulse race faster. 'And I'm guessing, Inspector, that in the Republic of Poland attempted murder is more serious than drug-dealing.'

Dania was watching proceedings through the two-way mirror. Konrad had been brought in, and was complaining vociferously that they hadn't given him enough time to finish his statement.

Robak was sitting astride a chair, his folded arms resting on the back. 'It's not the heroin we're going to talk about now. It's what we found on your phone. Your personal phone,' he added.

As he went through the details, Konrad's expression changed, suggesting he was lining up his defence.

'So, how do you account for that, Pan Zelenski?'

Konrad chewed his thumb, saying nothing.

'We talked about a lenient sentence,' Robak said. 'I'm afraid attempted murder will seriously add to it.'

'It wasn't attempted murder,' Konrad blurted. 'It was an anti-Semitic attack.'

'On Rabin Steinberg?'

'On Jakub Frydman.'

'Who was being interred.'

Konrad shrugged.

'Then you don't deny buying the wreath and throwing it into the grave?' Robak pressed.

'There's no point, is there?'

'Where did you get the Amatol?'

'My father's construction workers dig it up and sell it.'

'How did you set off the detonator?'

'With a burner phone. That's how it's done, these days. And before you ask, I've destroyed it.'

Robak ran a hand through his hair. 'You realise all the guests at Pan Frydman's funeral could have been killed.'

A slow smile crossed Konrad's face. 'I made sure to detonate *after* the mourners had left. You can't get me on attempted murder,' he said, with contempt. 'Anyway, I was following my father's instructions. Can I go back to my cell now? I'm in the middle of writing.'

Dania wondered how Robak could stop himself from punching him, but he was an experienced detective. He stood up and nodded to the uniform to take him away.

'At least he didn't deny it,' Dania said, after Robak had joined her in the observation room. 'Although I don't believe it was an anti-Semitic attack on a dead person.'

'Neither do I. The target was one of the guests.'

'Interesting he tried to pin it on his father again.'

'We need the evidence. What I'd like more is evidence to connect the Zelenskis to the murder of the Pomorskis.' He glanced at his watch. 'You'll have to excuse me, Pani Górska. I have a meeting with the state prosecutor.'

She watched him stride away, then nodded at the uniformed officer. He escorted her from the building.

She considered going home, as she needed to touch base at West Bell Street, but found herself strolling in the opposite direction. Although her quest to bring down Merkury had come to an end, something niggled.

She strolled through Krasiński Garden, savouring the silver morning. As she was leaving, she remembered the Chopin bench in front of the Uprising Monument. These granite benches were found across the city in places associated with the composer's life and music. In this case, Chopin had given a performance in front of Krasiński Palace.

Dania reached the square, and sat on the bench. She tapped the button, and the Mazurka in A minor, Opus 68 Number 2 tinkled out. She'd played this as a child, as it was one of Jakub Frydman's favourites. He would constantly stress the need to complete the trills evenly and softly. Although the bench supplied only half a minute of music, she knew the piece well enough to hear the rest in her head. She closed her eyes and thought of nothing else, seeing the notes dancing in front of her.

It was as the Mazurka was coming to an end that something drifted into her mind. Adam Mazur had visited the previous week and handed her Rena Adler's bequest. But what had he said about Rena?

I discovered this morning that she's passed away. A couple of days later, Pan Frydman died and I had enough to do with arranging his funeral.

And then Dania remembered the custodian's words. She was speaking about the scarred man with the wreath.

He asked for directions. He told me he was there for the funeral of the pianist.

And in that moment, everything fell into place. Dania sprang to her feet, colliding with a young man pushing a pram.

'I'm so sorry,' she gasped. She peered into the pram, hoping she hadn't disturbed the baby, but it was full of shopping.

The man smiled. 'No harm done.'

She hurried through the park, stopping briefly at the apartment to pick up the *makowiec* before continuing along Dzielna.

The wrought-iron gate of Okopowa cemetery stood open. Dania slipped inside and made for the custodian's booth. The woman was sitting reading a newspaper, holding a chipped yellow mug against her chest. She wore a blue bobble hat, and her moth-eaten fur coat. Dania wondered what it must be like to work in the open air in all weathers. The woman glanced up and peered at her over tortoiseshell glasses.

Dania made her voice friendly. 'I hope I'm not disturbing you.'

'No, not at all.'

'I've got some *makowiec* here,' she said, glad she'd taken the time to slice it.

The woman's expression changed. She licked her lips. 'It's my favourite.' She set down the mug. 'I can't offer you coffee, I'm afraid. I've drunk it all.'

'That doesn't matter.'

'Come in out of the cold.'

The booth was hardly any warmer. Dania perched on a stool, and lifted the *makowiec* out of her bag. She pulled back the wrapping paper, releasing the scent of poppy seeds. It was so strong it almost masked the smell of wood preserver.

'Please help yourself,' Dania said, thinking that *kanapki* might have been better. But the woman pounced, taking the biggest piece.

'I was wondering if I'd see you again,' she said, her mouth full.

'Oh?'

'I thought you would want to pay your respects at Pan Frydman's grave.'

'Actually, that's not why I'm here. Can you remember back to the day Pan Frydman was being buried?'

'How could I forget?'

'Was anyone else being buried the same day?'

The woman paused in the act of bringing the *makowiec* to her lips. Her eyes widened. 'Are you police?'

'I'm working with them.'

'I've done nothing wrong,' she said, with a catch in her voice.

Dania laid a hand on her arm. 'Of course you haven't. But you might know something that'll help us.'

The woman gazed at her, saying nothing. But the wild expression in her eyes had gone.

'You keep a register of which funerals take place,' Dania said.

She studied Dania's face closely for a long moment, then reached down and pulled a dusty, blue-backed book from under the counter. She laid it next to the *makowiec*. 'What is it you want to know?'

'Can we look at entries for December the first?'

She opened the book with slightly shaking hands. After leafing through the pages, she turned the book round. Some writing was in Hebrew. But the names of those interred were written in Polish, as were the times at which their funerals had taken place.

'Would you mind if I took a photograph of this page?' Dania said, her heart thudding.

'If you wish.'

'Do you remember we talked about the man with the scarred face?' she said, positioning her phone. 'The one carrying the wreath? He asked for directions. He told you he was there for the funeral of the pianist.'

The custodian's voice softened to a whisper. 'He didn't give me a name. How was I to know which funeral it was? I'd been thinking the whole time about poor Pan Frydman, so I assumed that was the pianist he was referring to. It never crossed my mind to ask him.' She gripped Dania's sleeve. 'Did I do wrong? Will I go to prison?'

'You've done nothing wrong. In fact, you've saved people's lives. Had you sent that man to Rena Adler's funeral, many would have died.'

The woman's eyes widened. 'Rena Adler's service was in another part of the cemetery. The guests had arrived, but it hadn't started. I realised only later that they'd all left through another gate. Even where they were, they'd have heard that huge explosion.'

'There's one final thing. Can you remember if this couple attended Rena Adler's?' Dania swiped through the images on the phone until she found the one from the Pomorskis' website. 'Do you recognise these people?'

The woman screwed up her face. Then her expression shifted. 'Oh, yes, I remember that orange hair. She had on a red coat. I thought at the time that the colours clashed.'

Dania closed her eyes briefly. 'Thank you,' she said. She was about to add that the woman would be called to make a statement, but decided to leave it to Robak. With his good looks and melting smile, he'd charm her without even trying.

'I need to be going,' she said, getting to her feet.

'What about the *makowiec*?'

'Why don't you have the rest? I've got plenty more at home.'

The woman smiled for the first time.

At the gate, Dania glanced back. The custodian was gazing at the *makowiec* as though she couldn't make up her mind which piece to eat next.

CHAPTER 35

Robak and Pola were deep in conversation when Dania was shown in. They stared in surprise, making her wonder if she had poppy seeds round her mouth. Robak got to his feet and pulled out a chair.

'I'm just back from Okopowa cemetery,' Dania said. She gazed at him. 'Inspector, you told me you needed evidence to connect the Zelenskis to the murder of the Pomorskis. Well, I think I've found it.' She pulled out her phone. 'Can we get these images on to that screen on the wall?'

'Let me, Pani Górska,' Pola said.

'Right, these register entries show that Jakub Frydman and Rena Adler were to be interred on December the first. Rena's funeral was to start half an hour later, in a different part of the cemetery. When Konrad arrived with the wreath, he asked for directions, saying he was there for the funeral of the pianist. The custodian thought he meant Jakub Frydman, but I think he meant Rena Adler.'

'And the custodian unwittingly gave the wrong directions,' Robak said, sitting back.

'When Konrad arrived at Jakub's grave, it was too foggy to see anyone's face, except perhaps Marek's. He threw the wreath into the air and left. Fortunately for us, the explosive didn't go off immediately.'

Robak wiped his mouth. 'It was detonated by a signal from a mobile phone. And we thought he'd simply got his timing badly wrong.' He studied the screen. 'Zygmunt would have assumed the Pomorskis had been invited to Rena's funeral, given how close they were to her. But did they attend?'

'I recorded our conversation. As you'll hear, I myself made no mention of the red coat.'

Dania played the clip. She guessed Robak wanted to know if she'd obtained permission from the custodian, because clandestine recordings were frowned upon in the Republic of Poland. But he said nothing. If anything, he looked amused.

'Konrad would have wanted to distance himself from the Pomorskis,' Pola said, 'so he came up with Jakub Frydman and anti-Semitism.'

Suddenly Robak started to laugh.

'Something funny?' Pola said.

'We've been chasing our tails trying to establish which guest at Jakub Frydman's interment was the target, when it was a simple case of mixing up two funerals.'

'Okopowa has between twenty and thirty burials a year,' Pola said. 'It's unusual, although not impossible, to have two in one day.'

'What we need to do,' Dania said, 'is confirm that Zygmunt Zelenski didn't attend Rena Adler's funeral. Because if he did, we'll have to ditch this theory.'

'I'll check with the Jewish Community Centre.'

Robak was gazing at her. 'What are you thinking, Pani Górska? I've seen that look on your face before.'

'I'm wondering what I'd do if I discovered that my attempt at killing the Pomorskis had failed.' She turned to Pola. 'Can we put up Google Maps on the wall?'

At the screen, Dania moved the image until she found the area of Praga where they'd apprehended Konrad. 'Okay, so this is the villa where we found the heroin. And *this*,' she said, moving her finger, 'is where the Pomorskis' bodies were hidden. It's within walking distance.'

'We noticed that, too,' Robak said.

'Do you think the Pomorskis were murdered in the villa and their bodies taken to the courtyard?'

'It's possible. It's a pity there are no cameras in that street.'

'No CCTV, perhaps. But there's a bank directly opposite. Don't banks have their own cameras? Shall we try Street View?'

Moments later, an image of the bank filled the screen. Robak and Pola were on their feet now, standing next to Dania.

'No camera,' Pola said.

Robak brought his face close to the screen. 'Banks sometimes mount their cameras higher to make it difficult for robbers to spray them with shaving foam.' He adjusted the image. 'Could that be a camera?' he said doubtfully.

Dania peered. 'I'd say so. What do you think, Pani Lorenc?'

'I'm thinking it's a pity it's Saturday. We won't be able to check the footage until Monday.'

'*Kurwa!*' Robak muttered.

The women looked at him.

It was Monday mid-morning before Maks returned with the camera footage. The bank manager, a man with little respect for the police, had taken his time copying the film to Maks's device. But Maks had learnt one useful tip as a rookie detective, and that was never to lose it when someone was putting obstacles in your way.

'Is Pani Górska not here?' he asked, as Pola arrived.

'She rang to say she's had to make a video call. Something's come up in Dundee. The woman is doing two jobs.' Pola gazed into his eyes. 'Do you think we could persuade her to come and work with us?'

'I've dropped enough hints,' he said, fiddling with the USB. 'Right, it's running. Now, according to the pathologist, the Pomorskis were shot between the first and eighth of December. That narrows it down.'

They ran the footage, which covered the area around the bank, but didn't reach as far as the villa. But Maks was betting that a car arriving from the Pomorskis' house would pull up at or near the bank. That was the beauty of driving on the right.

They'd reached the evening of Sunday, the fifth of December, when Pola said, 'There! Look!'

A black car drew up outside the bank, and three people climbed out. From the camera's angle, it was impossible to make out the faces. Two were men, both wearing hats, but the woman was bare-headed.

'She's got red hair,' Pola murmured.

'And she's wearing a red coat.'

'They look as though they're about to cross the street.'

Maks slowed the film. 'We need to check the timing, because if this is what I think it is, one of the men will reappear shortly. It doesn't take that long to shoot two people.'

Less than a quarter of an hour later, a single figure returned, got into the car and drove off.

'It fits, Pola.'

'What about the Pomorskis' bodies? When do you think they were taken to the courtyard?'

'Later the same night. A van would have arrived on the other side of the street, out of range of the camera.' Maks glanced at her. 'We've taken a step further.'

'Not far enough to pull in Zygmunt Zelenski.'

'I'm not so sure. He owns the villa. And the description of Katarina Pomorska matches. By the way, did you get anything on the Pomorskis' house?'

'They were renting it. Had been for a number of years. The man who rented before them has passed away. Oh, and I checked with the Jewish Community Centre. Zygmunt was invited to Rena Adler's funeral but declined, citing pressure of other things.'

'What about the recordings on the red-and-white phone? The Central Forensic Laboratory should have been back by now.'

'I'll call them.'

Maks heard only Pola's side of the conversation, but whoever she was speaking with seemed to be apologising for not getting in touch sooner.

She disconnected. 'He's just sent them over,' she said eagerly.

Maks connected to the shared drive. 'I'll set them to play automatically.'

His excitement mounted as he listened to Zygmunt Zelenski arranging for batches of heroin to come into Warsaw, sometimes by river, sometimes by land. He gave dates and times, and detailed how payment would be made. Although he never used his name, and neither did the people he spoke to, his voice was unmistakable. To be certain, the laboratory would have to match these to a known recording of his voice. They'd not been granted permission to search his house as part of the inquiry into Konrad's heroin dealings, because Konrad's registered address was the villa in Praga.

But Maks didn't have to listen long before realising that, not only could they now pull in Zygmunt for questioning, they could obtain the relevant authority to seize his assets and search his mansion. Because it was only by digging deep that they would find the evidence to convict him of murder.

As the recordings came to an end, Maks turned to Pola. She was smiling knowingly.

'We've got him,' he said softly.

CHAPTER 36

Maks and Pola were studying Zygmunt Zelenski. The man was the epitome of style in his navy coat and tailored light-grey suit. Surprisingly, he'd refused a lawyer, but then he had no idea what Maks had up his sleeve. He'd conducted himself with dignity, politely batting away accusations that he was involved in drug-dealing; yes, he knew one or two of his construction workers peddled drugs on the side and the finger was occasionally pointed at himself, but surely the inspector knew he was an honest businessman, and wouldn't police time be better spent chasing the *real* drug barons? What was clear from the exchange was that Zelenski had been here before, which was why he'd not bothered contacting his lawyer. What was also clear was that he had no idea heroin had been found in the Praga villa, and that Konrad had been arrested. Maks, who'd learnt it would be a while before authority came through to search Zygmunt's house, had decided on a gamble and pulled him in anyway. But he had a trump card, and he was about to play it.

'Pan Zelenski,' he said, referring to his file, 'how well did you know Katarina and Feliks Pomorski?'

Zelenski's expression didn't change, but Maks noticed a slight tremor in the fingers of his left hand.

'I met them at Rena Adler's,' he said, with a strained smile. 'Pani Adler and I would chat about this missing Chopin manuscript. Like many in Warsaw, I'm actively looking for it.'

It was an elegant way of deflecting the question. Maks decided to let it go. But he'd noticed Zelenski hadn't asked what the Pomorskis had to do with anything. An innocent man surely would have.

'I understand you own a property in Praga,' Maks said.

Zelenski laughed lightly. 'I own many properties, Inspector.'

Maks pushed across a photograph. 'Including this one?'

Zelenski looked at it for longer than was necessary. He lifted his gaze. 'Including that one.'

'And who lives there?'

'It's empty at the moment.'

Maks feigned surprise. 'That's interesting, because it's your son's registered address.'

'He used to live there, but he lives with me now.'

'We found his clothes in the wardrobe.'

The quiver in the left hand again. 'He must have forgotten to bring them.'

Maks tapped the photograph. 'Pan Zelenski, are you aware there's a bank directly opposite this property?' When there was no reply, he added, 'This morning, we examined what was on the security camera. On the evening of Sunday the fifth of December, a car drew up outside the bank and two men and a woman got out. The woman had red hair, and wore a red coat. They headed towards this villa. Less than a quarter of an hour later, one of the men returned, and drove off.'

Zelenski was staring at him with a stony expression.

'It's my belief the woman was Katarina Pomorska and one of the men was her husband, Feliks. That's the last time they were seen. Until last Tuesday when their bodies were found not far from this property.' Maks smiled. 'You may be wondering how we established their identities. Feliks had his grandfather's Auschwitz number tattooed on his arm.'

For the first time, something registered in Zelenski's eyes: a fleeting expression of fear.

Maks kept his voice brisk. 'Since the villa is your son's registered address, Pan Zelenski, we will be charging him with the murders of Katarina and Feliks Pomorski. Konrad drove them there, murdered them, and left. Sometime later, he returned and transported their bodies to a nearby courtyard where he buried them under rubble.'

The gamble had paid off. Zelenski's left hand was trembling visibly, and his breathing was becoming shallow. 'My son is innocent, Inspector.'

Maks returned the photograph to the folder. 'A jury may come to a different conclusion.' He nodded at Pola, who started to gather up her papers.

'You cannot pin this on my son. I'm the one who owns that villa.'

'That's immaterial.'

'Why would my son shoot those people?'

Maks paused in the act of getting to his feet. He sat down slowly. 'I didn't say the Pomorskis had been shot, Pan Zelenski. I said they'd been murdered. We kept the details of how they were killed from the press.'

Zelenski's face sagged. He lowered his head and grasped his shaking left hand in his right. He looked up, his eyes empty. For a second, Maks almost felt sorry for him.

'If I tell you what happened, will you give me your word you won't arrest Konrad for these murders?'

'If he didn't kill them, he won't be charged with murder.' Maks indicated the machine. 'You have that on record. But you need to provide me with evidence to the contrary.'

Zelenski straightened his shoulders. 'It was I who murdered them, Inspector. I drove the Pomorskis to the villa, and shot them in the back of the head. I fired through a pillow to prevent blood contaminating my clothes. An old trick from Communist times.'

'Can you remember what you wore? That coat, perhaps?'

'My black coat. But you won't find blood on it.'

They'd find gunshot residue, though, Maks thought.

'I disposed of the pillow and cartridges, and everything that would identify the Pomorskis.'

'And the weapon?'

'A wartime Radom Vis 35. It belonged to my father. It's in my desk drawer at home.'

The Toolmark and Ballistics Unit hadn't found a match for the bullets in their database, but a test fire with the Vis would do it.

'After I killed them, I hid their bodies. I thought the rubble would be there for weeks, by which time they'd be unrecognisable.'

Maks crossed his arms. 'Why did you kill them, Pan Zelenski?' Seeing the man's hesitation, he added, 'Whatever you tell us can't make the situation worse.'

Zelenski gazed at the table, then looked Maks straight in the eye. 'I've been forging documents that specify rightful ownership of an empty property, then bribing court officials to expedite the claim by the new owners.'

'And once the claim has gone through?'

'I buy the property from the owners at a fraction of its value.'

Maks felt his heart accelerate. This tied in with what Lidia Lipska had told him. 'And where do you find these "owners"?'

'There are many people in need of money.'

'Like the Pomorskis?'

'I paid them twenty thousand euros to make the claim. But, instead of selling me the property for the price we'd agreed, they held out for more. They threatened to expose my . . .' He struggled for the word.

'Scam?' Maks suggested.

'I decided to cut my losses with the building. But I had to ensure they were silenced. And in such a way that their demise couldn't be traced to me.'

'Which was why you arranged for a wreath packed with Amatol to be thrown into Rena Adler's grave. You knew the Pomorskis would attend and, with so many dead, the police would struggle to identify the intended victims.'

Zelenski drew his brows together. 'How did you discover the wreath was intended for Rena's funeral?'

'And what happened then? You learnt the Pomorskis were still alive?'

'They contacted me, demanding to know why I hadn't replied to their phone call. I knew immediately that something had gone badly wrong. I told them the money was at my villa. I'd pick them up.' He lifted a hand to indicate that the officers knew the rest. 'I took their keys and returned to their house, where I removed their laptop and their papers, so nothing could be traced to me.'

The men gazed at each other. Then Maks said, 'It's a pity your son happened upon the wrong grave. Had he found Rena Adler's and not Jakub Frydman's, I doubt we'd be having this conversation.'

'My son?' Zelenski said, letting the words drift. 'He didn't throw the wreath. It was someone I hired.'

'Konrad has admitted it, *and* his part in the heroin trade.'

The colour drained from Zelenski's face. 'But he has nothing to do with the heroin. And neither have I.'

Maks removed the red-and-white phone from under the folder. 'It was the clandestine recordings Konrad made of you arranging the heroin shipments that gave us what we needed to pull you in. I'll play you one or two clips. You'll find them interesting.'

He watched the expressions come and go on Zelenski's face. 'We'll match the voice with what we're recording in this interview,' he said, stopping the playback. 'It was your son who betrayed you, Pan Zelenski. And to think you damned yourself confessing to murder, believing you were saving him.' He leant forward. 'Was it worth it?'

Anger radiated off Zelenski. But was it towards his son, or towards Maks?

Maks spoke into the recorder, terminating the interview, and switched it off.

Pola, who was wearing tinted spectacles, took them off. The action caught Zelenski's attention. He glanced at her, then gazed deep into her eyes.

She reached into her jacket pocket and drew out a packet of cigarillos. Zelenski's expression turned to disbelief as she lifted out the destroyed tracker and placed it on the table. His lips mouthed the word, Motylek.

'Checkmate,' she said, with a soft smile.

Maks nodded to the uniform to take Zelenski away.

CHAPTER 37

It was mid-morning, and Marek was being escorted to Pola Lorenc's room. The uniformed officer kept glancing at the bouquet of red chrysanthemums in Marek's arms. He knocked at Pola's door and ushered Marek in, throwing him a wink as he left.

Pola got to her feet, peering at Marek over her spectacles. She was wearing a white shirt, blue dungarees and her elephant slippers.

'These are for you, Pani Lorenc,' he said, handing her the bouquet.

'Flowers?' There was surprise in her voice. 'They're beautiful. But why?'

'To thank you for having a word with the archivist at the institute. He went above and beyond the call of duty.'

'And did you find what you were looking for?' she said, setting the flowers on the table.

'Unfortunately not. Remember we talked about those notebooks? My sister found them. But one was missing. If we'd located it, I'm convinced it would have led me to Chopin's manuscript.'

She threw him a look of commiseration. After a pause, she said, 'I don't know how much you know, but we've now arrested the unexpected guest who threw the wreath in Okopowa cemetery.'

'Danka told me. Who would have thought it was the very man she'd come to Warsaw to find?'

Pola sat down and pulled off one of the slippers. She massaged her toes, screwing up her face in pain.

'Is something wrong?' he said, taking the chair next to hers.

'I'm prone to ingrowing toenails. It's something I've struggled with since childhood.'

'I'm sorry to hear that.'

'It's why I wear these fur-lined slippers.'

He raised an eyebrow. 'I did wonder.'

'I've had to abandon my childhood dream.' She said nothing for several seconds. Then, keeping her gaze on his face, she said softly, 'I've always wanted to be a ballerina.'

'A ballerina?' he said, smiling. The smile faded. 'A ballerina. *Baletnica!* It's *you*!' he gasped.

She slid her foot back into the slipper. 'When I read your article about that Polish minister making secret deals with the Russians, I knew you'd do the right thing if you found Chopin's concerto.'

Marek shook his head. 'And all this time I thought you were a man.'

'That's the beauty of the Polish language. You can disguise your gender.'

'Then it was you who tipped me off about the basement in Wola.'

'When you told me you'd be on the next flight, I checked the manifest. I followed you from the airport. I wanted to be sure no one was on your tail. When you went into that building, I went in after you.'

So, it had been Pola he'd heard on the floor above. 'Tell me something, Pani Lorenc.'

'Please call me Pola.'

He smiled. 'Pola. How did you come by your information?'

'I play chess. The guests at the matches range from businessmen to academics.' She stroked the petals of one of the chrysanthemums. 'Before the game, when we'd be having drinks, I'd listen to snippets of conversation. That's where I learnt things about the manuscript. More than one man was actively searching for it. Depending on what I'd hear, I'd do some research of my own, but I lacked the time to do any serious hunting. So, I contacted you again.'

'And that message you sent me, telling me to be on my guard?'

'The men who attend the matches will stop at nothing to get their hands on the concerto. But there was another reason. The unexpected guest at Jakub Frydman's funeral had seen your face, and would have guessed it was you who'd helped us with the E-FIT. He might have taken it into his head to do something about that. You're well known in Warsaw.'

'I hadn't thought of that. But why didn't you tell me who you were?'

'I attended the chess club undercover to spy on people. Dangerous people. I had to keep my identity secret from everyone.' She looked at him for a long moment. 'And what will you do now? Keep searching for this last notebook?'

'It's tempting. No one else knows about them. That was clear from my last meeting with Father Bielski. A few people visited him recently, but they talked only about the manuscript.' Marek smiled sadly. 'I'm ahead of the game. But to be frank, I think I've already lost.'

'And I'm no longer in a position to help you. The chess matches have come to an end. At least, they have for me.'

'I'll spend the next few weeks translating the notebooks, and then have them published. So, it's not been a totally wasted journey.' He got to his feet. 'But now I need to start preparing for Wigilia.'

She looked as though she wanted to say something, making him wonder what she'd be doing on Christmas Eve.

Marek took her hand and kissed it lightly. At the door, he paused and said, with a question in his voice, 'Perhaps, before I return to Scotland, we can meet for pancakes again?'

'Of course. And thank you for the flowers.'

With a final smile, he left the room.

'And you have Zygmunt's written confession?' Dania said.

'It was easier than I'd thought,' Robak admitted. 'I did wonder if he was lying to save his son, but we found gunshot residue on his black coat. And none on Konrad's clothes. But I'm not convinced Konrad wasn't an accessory. Carrying two bodies into a van isn't easy for someone of Zygmunt's age. As for the property scam, we have the evidence that it's been going on for years. Zygmunt kept everything in the safe at his nightclub.'

Dania twirled a lock of hair round her finger. 'And the heroin shipments?'

'He knew it was impossible to wriggle out of that. Thanks to Konrad's recordings.' After a pause, Robak said, 'So, Pani Górska, shall we talk about the elephant in the room? Are you going to start extradition proceedings?'

'I'll talk to my DCI. I think she'd be prepared to leave it if she thought Konrad would be convicted for murder in Warsaw.'

'We've no evidence he murdered the Pomorskis. Although we might get him to admit he killed that construction worker a year ago, the one whose throat was cut.'

'That would satisfy my boss.'

'And would it satisfy *you*?'

Dania rubbed her face. 'I think so. At least I won't be able to knee him in the groin if he's in Warsaw.'

'Thinking back to how we got here, we couldn't have done it without your help. There's a place for you at Mostowski should you decide to return to Poland.'

'I think my DCI would have something to say about that. We're short-staffed in Dundee.' She paused. 'Now that the case is closed, Inspector, perhaps I could pick up our passports. Unless, of course, you wish to detain us in the Republic of Poland a little longer.'

Robak straightened his green waistcoat. 'You're surely not thinking of booking a flight before Christmas. I doubt there'll be seats free.'

'I'm not returning to Scotland until the New Year.' She smiled. 'But I've no reason to come to Mostowski Palace again.'

He opened the desk drawer, and handed her the passports.

After a brief silence, she said, 'Well, I'd better leave you to get on with catching the bad guys. They seem to be multiplying.'

'Faster than we can snare them, I'm afraid.' He paused. 'I'll accompany you to the entrance.'

They were passing the Sala Biała when Robak said, 'One moment, Pani Górska. I was wondering if I could ask a favour.' He gestured to the open door. 'Would you play something? I know the piano's not exactly in tune, but having heard you, I think it won't matter.'

'Now, that's what I call a compliment. Is there anything in particular you'd like to hear?'

He closed the door behind them. 'I'll leave that up to you.' He unclipped the corded barrier, and took a seat in the front row.

Dania was tempted to play something light and cheerful, but in the end went for Chopin's Ballade Number 4 Opus 52. She'd been practising it long enough to have memorised Rubinstein's annotations. As the piece came to an end, she hoped Robak hadn't noticed the mistakes.

He was looking at her thoughtfully. Perhaps he knew this piece well enough to have heard the slip-ups, she thought, getting to her feet.

He stood up. 'Thank you, Pani Górska,' he murmured. He extended his hand.

Thinking about their shared experiences, she saw no reason to continue with formality. She slipped her hand into his. 'Please call me Dania,' she said, using the familiar form.

'And I'm Maks.' He kept his gaze on her face as he brought her hand slowly to his lips.

CHAPTER 38

'So, what else do we need to do?' Dania called from the dining room. Marek was in the kitchen, cutting up the vegetable salad and keeping one eye on the beetroot soup. He'd already laid out the other dishes: pickled cucumber with sour cream, sauerkraut, buckwheat and herrings in oil. Pride of place was reserved for the carp in aspic.

Dania's task had been to clean the apartment. It hadn't taken her long as she and Marek kept the place in reasonable condition. Every so often, she'd slip into her parents' room and peer through the large window to see if the first star had appeared. Until it did, they couldn't sit down to eat.

'Can you check the sky again?' Marek called back.

Perhaps she should climb onto the roof, where she'd get a better view. Because she was starting to salivate at the thought of the food. And there was *makowiec* for dessert. Marek had hidden it somewhere in the kitchen.

Dania pulled on her coat, and was picking up her gloves when she noticed the envelope on the hall table. At first, she couldn't think why it was there. And then she remembered Adam Mazur's visit. With everything that had happened since, the envelope had slipped her mind, not helped because she and Marek dumped their hats and gloves on it. But curiosity got the better of her and she carried the envelope into the kitchen.

Marek was standing at the window, gazing out.

'Did that come in the post?' he said, glancing at her.

'Adam Mazur brought it, remember?'

'Vaguely.'

'It was intended for Rena Adler.'

She slit open the envelope, and removed the contents. Her heart jumped when she saw it.

'Marek,' she murmured, 'look at this.'

Together, they gazed at the handwritten manuscript.

'I had no idea,' Dania said, turning the pages.

'Do you think you could play this?'

'With practice.' She stared at Marek in bewilderment. 'Jakub Frydman never told me he'd composed these sonatas.'

'How many are there?'

She leafed through the pages. 'Five.'

'You're probably the first person to hear them. That's an honour. We could have a concert after Wigilia.'

She returned the sheets to the envelope. 'I have to check the sky.'

'No need, Danka.' He gestured to the window. 'I've seen the first star.'

She shrugged off her coat. 'Right, let's eat.'

'The *barszcz* needs a few more minutes. We can make a start on the carp, I suppose.'

They were about to take their seat when Marek said, 'Hold on, you've laid only two places. We need one for the unexpected guest.'

'Do you think anyone will arrive?' Dania said, fetching cutlery and another plate from the kitchen.

Before he could reply, they heard the doorbell.

EPILOGUE

Adam Mazur gazed out of the window. Spring had arrived, and Warsaw was awakening from its winter slumber. What he could see of the sky was tinged with grey but, at this early hour, that was to be expected. As he sipped his tea, he thought of the long furrow he'd ploughed to get to where he was: living in a comfortable apartment, with no financial worries. Whenever the ghosts of those he'd betrayed rose accusingly, he stamped them down, telling himself he wasn't the only Communist-era collaborator, and it would have been a matter of time before someone else did what he'd done. He'd had a brief wobble when investigation into so-called crimes against the Polish nation began in the early 1990s, but the money he'd received from the SB was put to good use in ensuring that his records at the Institute of National Remembrance were destroyed.

His role as executor of Jakub Frydman's estate was at an end. And with it, his search for Chopin's missing manuscript. Part of him was sad to see that door close, as he'd relished trying to outfox those on the same quest, Marek Górski in particular. But another part of him was relieved that he could now move on. No more long sessions at the National Library, or following leads that led nowhere. Visiting Father Bielski incognito had proved to be a complete waste of time.

It was as he'd been clearing the last of Jakub Frydman's effects that he'd come across the box with its ancient Sellotape intact. The attached note indicated that Frydman had bought it at auction decades before. The contents were described as 'miscellaneous manuscripts'. Being a busy man and someone who regularly bought at auction, Frydman had evidently forgotten about the box, which had been pushed into a corner of the study and covered with books. Adam, having spent months dealing with bequests, had been strongly tempted to throw it out. But curiosity had prevailed, so he'd peeled back the Sellotape and lifted out the dusty manuscripts. He'd nearly fainted when he'd discovered what was among them.

Being familiar with Chopin's script, he'd had no difficulty in deciphering the note on the cover. The composer's sister, Ludwika, was to keep the original manuscript, although he asked her to have it performed once everything was settled. What Chopin couldn't have foreseen was that, a short time later, she would die of the plague sweeping through Warsaw. How the manuscript had come to be buried with a pile of works by lesser composers, Adam would never know, but he guessed that Ludwika's husband, who never hid his animosity towards Chopin, would have had a hand in it.

What Adam kept coming back to, however, was that the third piano concerto had lain in the box for years without Jakub Frydman ever knowing. And tucked inside the manuscript was a notebook with a brown-paper cover. Adam had leafed through the pages at random, but it appeared to be yet another war memoir. He'd thrown it out with the other manuscripts. Jakub's estate disposed of, he'd begun to study the concerto, particularly the orchestral section, until he could hear the accompanying music without playing a note.

He finished the tea, pulled back the seat and settled himself at the grand piano. Then, after letting the music flow through him, he brought his hands down onto the keys.

ACKNOWLEDGEMENTS

I owe a huge debt of gratitude to Jenny Brown and Krystyna Green, both for their support, and for reading this novel and suggesting ways in which it could be improved. I am also deeply grateful to Hazel Orme for doing such a magnificent job of editing. My heartfelt thanks go also to Amanda Keats and her team at Little, Brown for all their hard work in getting this novel to publication.